THE DEVIL AND HIS SPARROW

Cover Design: Ludwig Designs
Book Design and Typesetting: Enchanted Ink Publishing

The text type was set in Garamond Premier Pro

ISBN: 9798990890503 (Paperback)
ISBN: 9798990890510 (Hardcover)

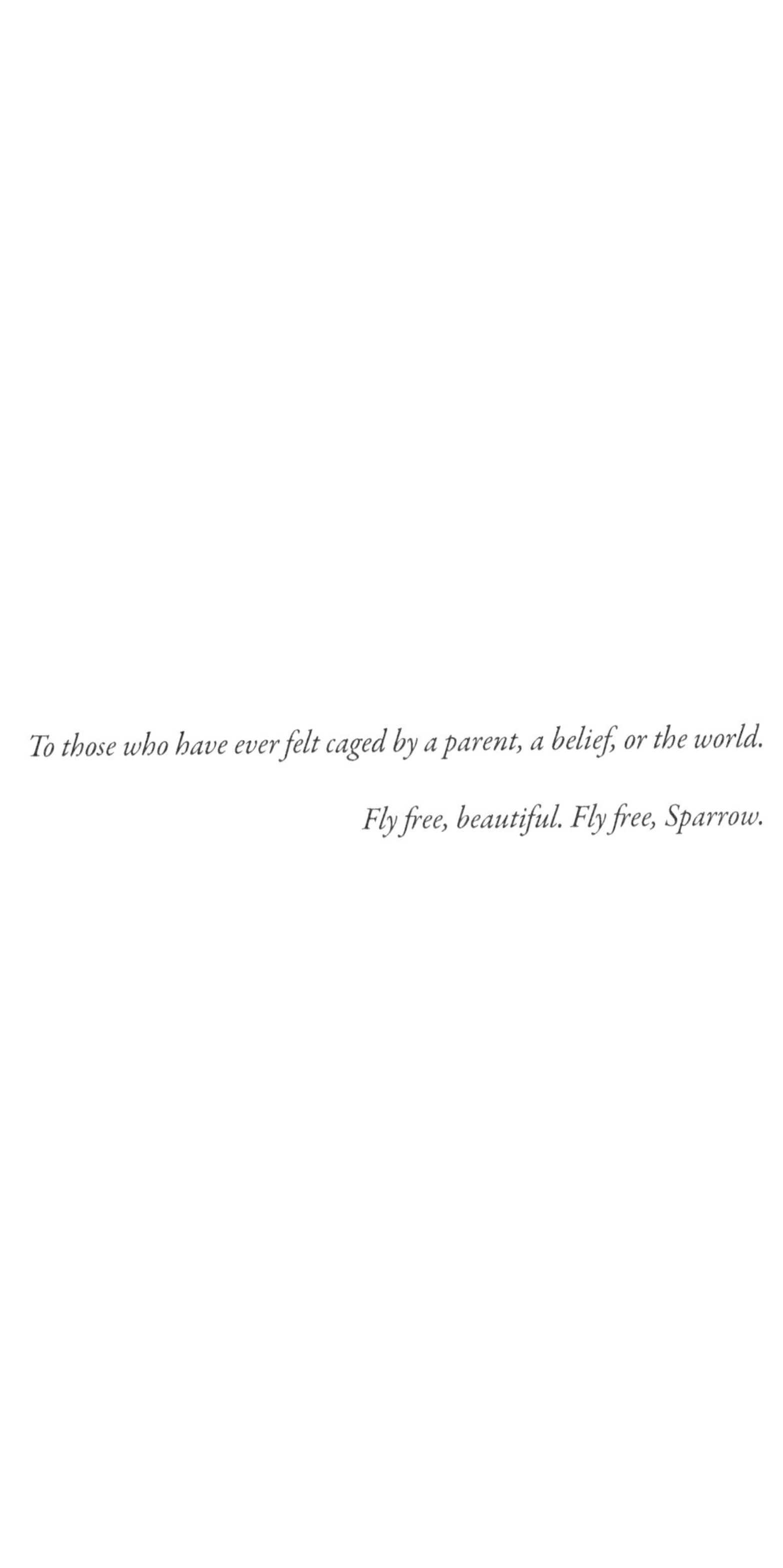

To those who have ever felt caged by a parent, a belief, or the world.

Fly free, beautiful. Fly free, Sparrow.

TRIGGER WARNINGS

This book contains the following:

Mental Triggers:

Mental/emotional/physical abuse from a parent

Negative view of oneself/sex taught by a parent

Ill minors in a medical setting

Demons (literally)

Spicy Triggers:

Orgy (witnessed, not a part of)

Shadow-play

Brief bondage

Praise/ "Good girl"

Exhibitionism

Threesome (Sort of? You'll have to read to see what I mean hehe)

PLAYLIST

"SACRILEGIOUS" - PLVTINUM, Tokyo's Revenge

"My Oh My" - Camila Cabello, DaBaby

"Duality" - Set It Off

"Body Language" - WE ARE FURY

"Gemini" - NiGHTS

"Mind Games" - Sickick

"Desert Rose" - Lola Zouaï

"Rain" - Sleep Token

"Beast" - Mia Martina, Waka Flocka Flame

"This Mountain" - Faouzia

"Night Drive" - hxnry

"We Go Down" - Dove Cameron, Khalid

"Wicked Game" - Ursine Vulpine, Annaca

"Heaven" - Julia Michaels

"Church" - Chase Atlantic

For the full playlist, please scan the QR Code!

THE DEVIL AND HIS SPARROW

Sinners Do It Better

SYLVER MICHAELA

CHAPTER 1

Tyla

THE TEST RESULTS ARE STILL INCONCLUSIVE. I WAS hoping I'd have an answer for you by now, but unfortunately, we still don't have one."

My heart clenched painfully, and I bunched the fabric of my shirt in my hands in an effort to do *something*. All the hope I'd had when walking into this room vanished as easily as it had come.

"So what now?" Mom questioned, her voice taking on that all-too-familiar edge.

Dr. Seward folded his hands on top of the desk and handled my mother's clear disappointment—if not contempt—with ease, no doubt used to her by now. "We keep testing and monitoring her. There's an answer out there somewhere. We just haven't found it, yet."

My mother's lips curled in disapproval, and her huff was overly loud, as if she wanted to take extra care to make her annoyance known. "How is it that in this day and age, a little girl can be sick, and you doctors don't know what's wrong?"

"It's frustrating," Dr. Seward admitted with a nod. "But I assure you, we are remaining diligent and hopeful. I really think we're getting closer to an answer, and until then, we'll continue to treat her symptoms as we determine the accurate diagnosis."

I understood Mom's exasperation. I wanted a solution for Gemma just as badly, but I also tried to remind myself that Dr. Seward was doing all he could. Taking her anger out on him wouldn't get us anywhere.

I scooted to the edge of the leather seat and leaned toward Dr. Seward. "How is she doing?"

Dr. Seward's blue eyes softened as they met mine, and he offered me a small smile. "She actually had a pretty good day yesterday. She managed to eat all her meals and keep the food down. A nurse even reported that Gemma played all afternoon with the other kids. Dolls. Board games. She didn't have any fainting spells."

It was a small victory, but it was great news all the same. The mental image of Gemma smiling and having a day of fun with the other kids here made the rock in my gut easier to stomach. One day, we'd find out what illness she had, and we'd be able to get her the cure she needed.

It was just going to take a little longer.

"Can we see her before we go?" I asked a bit too eagerly, which earned me a biting sideways look from my mother.

Dr. Seward hesitated, but with some reluctance, he said, "If you make it quick. She's been on the lethargic side today, so I want her to rest."

Desperate for even a moment with her, I nodded quickly. "I'll make it fast."

I pushed back my chair and immediately turned down the hallway that led to my little sister's room. I smiled and waved at the nurses as I walked past, telling them good morning. All the nurses here were kind and friendly, and we'd grown even closer as my mother and I visited regularly. Though, even as I developed friendships with the staff, it was never them I was here to see.

I swallowed hard, a *real* smile climbing my face when I rounded the corner to stand in the doorway. Gemma sat up in her bed with a coloring book and pencils spread out on her tray table. Her shoulder-length brown hair, once shiny like mine but now dull and thin, was pulled back in a loose ponytail, and today's gown—a dusty pink with white clouds—hung off her thin form.

Whatever she was coloring had her full attention. She didn't notice me leaning on the doorframe, and I didn't mind. It gave me time to just watch her little hands switch between pencils before going back to work on her design. I needed this second of invisibility to gather myself and to train my face not to let on how broken and helpless I felt over her situation.

Steeling myself, I walked into the room. Gemma finally noticed me, and when her hazel eyes found me, her face instantly brightened.

"Iyla!" she squealed.

I darted to her bedside and wrapped my arms around her. Lead filled my gut when I felt how small she'd gotten, but I kept the worry off my face as I leaned back to look down at her. "Surprise!"

"I'm so glad you're here," she chirped.

"Always, Gem," I said, running a hand over the top of her head.

She glanced over my shoulder, and without even looking, I knew what figure waltzed in behind me. There was no missing the distinct click of her heels or the scent of her expensive floral perfume flooding the room.

Understanding crossed Gemma's face. "Oh. You were meeting with Dr. Seward."

Not wanting her to worry, I tucked a loose strand of hair behind her ear and said, "He was just giving us an update on how you were feeling. Nothing bad. Right, Mom?"

Mom ignored me. She stood beside the bed and ran her hand over the top of Gemma's head. "How are you feeling today?"

Gemma took on a forlorn expression. "Tired. I've been coloring to help. Noya said it helps with fatigue and keeping my brain engaged. Reduces stress."

"You're stressed?" Mom asked sharply, her slender brows plunging down. "Are they not helping you? Making you feel at ease?"

"Mom," I whispered, noticing the alarm in Gemma's eyes.

"They do," Gemma quickly reassured. "I really like all of them. They're nice and helpful."

"Clearly not enough," Mom grumbled. "I'll speak to the nursing supervisor as we leave to make sure your schedule and health plan are good enough."

Guilt seeped into the lines of Gemma's face. Mom was going to make a big deal out of nothing like always, no doubt griping at and belittling the people taking care of Gemma. Now Gemma was going to carry that with her, thinking it was her fault that Noya and the others got in trouble.

The only one causing her stress is you, I thought to myself as I stared at Mom. I wouldn't dare say that aloud, though.

Seeking to distract Gemma from our mom's continuous glowering, I pointed at the drawing on the table that sat across her lap. "What are you coloring?"

Her weary eyes brightened a fraction as she looked down at the half-colored picture. "It's a butterfly. Sienna's dad just brought her a coloring book, and she gave me this page."

A knock came at the door before I could respond, and my mom and I turned to find a smiling Noya standing there. She wore black scrubs with smiling moons on them, and her black hijab wrapped around her head.

Her warm brown eyes passed between us. "Sorry to interrupt," Noya apologized. "I'm here to give little Gemma her medication."

"Just who I wanted to see," Mom hissed, narrowing her eyes on Noya. "Give Gemma what she needs. Then I need to speak to you and the nursing supervisor."

My mother didn't wait to hear Noya's reply. She turned to place a kiss on Gemma's head and said, "I'll visit soon. Keep doing what the doctors tell you, and don't worry about *anything*." Her eyes met mine and immediately lost the softness that had just been there. "Say goodbye so we can get out of Noya's way."

My chest constricted. This was never easy, and I hated that I'd just gotten here, just gotten to see and talk to Gemma. Saying bye was always difficult, especially since the scared little voice in the back of my head always wondered, *will this be the last time I see her?*

I leaned down to wrap her in my arms, forcing myself to hold back. I wanted to squeeze her tightly to me, hugging her with all I had in me, but I knew her fragile body couldn't take that. So I held her with the barest of touches and pulled back to grin at her. "I love you, Gem."

Her chapped lips widened into a smile. "I love you, too."

Mom and I left the room, and I flashed Noya an apologetic look as I passed her. My mom was about to unleash her terror on the nurses and team taking care of Gemma, and Noya knew that. They *all* knew what to expect by now.

That Mrs. Winters. She's a real bitch.

God, Mrs. Winters is the worst. She acts like we sit back and do nothing. Can't she see we're doing everything we can for her daughter?

Watch out for Mrs. Winters. She has a fiery temper and all the money to back her nasty attitude.

I'd heard all the whisperings about my mom over the eight months since she'd brought Gemma to this residential treatment facility. It was great, because it gave Gemma the twenty-four-seven surveillance and care she needed with doctors and nurses *really* focused on her and the other patients staying here, but despite the tremendous care they gave her, it was never good enough for my mom.

Things rarely were.

"I'm gonna go wait in the car," I said to my mom, who hovered by the nurses station to wait on Noya. I never liked being around when she threw one of her fits.

She waved her hand, effectively dismissing me, so I spun on my heel and retreated. I waited in the silent car for nearly fifteen minutes before my mom finally came out. I winced at the lengthy reprimand, knowing that today's outburst must've been a bad one. But my mom had gotten what she wanted—as she always did. That much was clear from the calm poise of her eyebrows and mouth.

Silence filled the car as she drove me back to my apartment near campus. No music. No chit-chat. Nothing. But that wasn't anything unusual. We'd always been that way.

When we made it to my apartment, she followed me up. As soon as we crossed the threshold, she rummaged in her purse then produced a small box. "Here. Go take this while I do my sweep."

Heat flooded my cheeks while bitter annoyance filled my gut like a swarm of bees. I took the box and stiffly walked into my bathroom to take the pregnancy test. It seemed like she was making me do this more and more frequently, and it pissed me off for a handful of reasons, the biggest one being that I wasn't even sexually active. But, of course, she'd never believe that.

No. Her word was law, and she was *always* right, even when she wasn't.

So if she thought I was having sex, then I was having sex. If she thought I was neglecting my studies to party, I was neglecting my studies to party. If she thought I was being a bad daughter, I was a bad daughter.

I didn't even bother looking at the result of the test as I left the bathroom to wait in my kitchen. She was still in the middle of her routine walk-through, snooping to make sure I wasn't hiding anything like music or erotic books.

Fresh pain lanced my heart.

Music.

I shook the thought away and dug out a bottled water from my fridge in an effort to keep myself from even thinking about my dead dream.

"Where did you get these pants from?" Mom demanded when she returned to the living room. She held up a pair of jeans that Nahla had forced me to buy, and despite my many layers of built-up armor, dread filled my body like cement.

"I got them at the mall," I answered calmly.

She held them up to show me the rip right above the right knee and snapped, "I don't give you money so you can spend it on tattered clothing. You aren't homeless. You aren't a slob. You are a *Winters*, and you will *not* walk around, giving people this impression. Showing skin. Looking like some cheap hooker." She stormed over to where I stood and threw the pants into the trash.

I stared at the discarded clothes, letting the numbness take hold and allowing it to dull the ache trying to form. I'd told Nahla that my mother would never let me have something like that, but Nahla, being the daring and encouraging soul she was, convinced me to get the pants. After all, everyone wore jeans like this these days. Hell, people showed far more than just a bit of skin where some strategic holes and frays were in the pants. So in the heat of Nahla's reassurances and high energy, I said to hell with Mom's silly rules. I'd get myself a little something crazy and bold, just this once.

But of course, I had been right. My mother would never allow that kind of self-expression.

Control was her drug of choice. It always had been. This very apartment we were in wasn't truly mine. It was purchased, furnished, and managed by her, despite me being the only one here. I didn't get to choose what food came in and out of the house, nor did I get a say in how my life ran.

I glanced nervously at her while I fiddled with the test she'd given me, and I decided to breach the topic that I'd been weighing for awhile. "Mom. Um … I was thinking. There's this café down the street that's hiring. I thought I might apply there."

She stopped her look-through of my pantry and turned to lock her sharp eyes on mine. "Why on earth would you do that?"

The ice I stood on was starting to melt and crack under her hot annoyance. I knew I had to tread carefully if I wanted to see this conversation play out the way I wanted—with me gaining even a sliver of freedom.

"Well, you just always have to give me money for everything," I hurried to explain. "I thought I should contribute and start—"

"Iyla," Mom snapped. She let the silence hang between us for a moment before she continued, "Do you not appreciate all I've done for you? I've given you everything, haven't I?"

I'd definitely touched a nerve, and I was about to unleash a monster best kept hidden. Quickly trying to calm her down, I held a hand up. "Yes, of course. I was just—"

"I work very hard to take care of you. This apartment. Your phone. Your groceries. Utilities. Anything you could possibly want, I've worked tirelessly to get you. And now you want to wash your hands of my generosity? Are you really that ungrateful for all you've been given? Most girls your age would kill to have their parents give them all I've given you."

My stomach soured, and my head sank in shame. All thoughts of my own washed away like sand on the tide, because she was right. My life had mostly been worry-free, and I definitely hadn't struggled financially, all thanks to her. Grateful didn't even come close to how I felt toward her generosity. I was being egotistical in trying to throw that kindness away, all so I could have a life of my own.

With a deep sigh, she pulled the negative pregnancy test over to her, briefly looked at it to confirm the results, dropped it in the trash can, then dug her black planner out of her bag and flipped through it. "Glad to see you aren't pregnant. Have you been interacting with boys?"

I shook my head. "No, ma'am."

She rolled her eyes. "A lie if I've ever heard one, but since your test is negative, I'll let it slide. Keep it that way, and you won't have anything to worry about. Now, according to my notes, you have an exam in Political Theory on Monday, correct?"

I nodded robotically. "Yes, ma'am."

"Are you ready?"

Another bob of my head. "Yes, ma'am."

She narrowed her eyes and stared at me like she was trying to see inside my head. I didn't know what she was looking for, but finally, she said, "Even if you think you're ready, you can't be stagnant. You need to spend this weekend really studying. I won't tolerate another B minus on an exam, Iyla."

My eye twitched in an effort not to roll. That B minus was from *middle school*. She never forgot mistakes, though.

"This apartment, your phone, your bills, all the things I've provided for you can be taken away," she continued, a clear warning laced in her tone. "Do you understand me?"

How could I forget? You certainly never let me.

I swallowed the grit filling my mouth. "Yes, ma'am."

She accepted my answer with a firm nod and stuffed her planner back into her bag. She took a deep breath and ran a hand over her perfectly pinned auburn hair. "There's a reason you were born, Iyla. You don't have that brain for nothing. It's your job to take over my firm one day, especially with Gemma as sick as she is. You need to be able to afford her care. You need to be able to fight for her since only you and I care about her. Prove your worth, yes?"

I twirled my water bottle in my hands and focused on the liquid sloshing around inside. "I know, Mom. I'll do my best."

The pressure always swirling around my gut tightened with the reminder of what was expected of me. My sole purpose, the reason I worked so hard in school, was all for the sake of becoming a lead prosecutor and taking over my mom's firm one day. I had a name to carry on, a duty to uphold, and a sick sister to care for. Nothing else mattered.

I listened to my mom walk back to the door, never looking away from the chaotic churning of the water in the plastic bottle. She made her exit without another word. I let out the breath I always seemed to hold when she was around and slumped forward to rest my head on the island. The tension in my shoulders didn't leave, nor did the tightness in my throat.

No matter how used to Valerie Winters I was, it was still so exhausting to deal with her.

I moved away from the counter and pulled out my phone to dial my one reprieve from the stress.

"What's up, sexy bitch?"

I immediately snickered. "My mom just left. We went and saw Gemma."

"Shit." Nahla's tone immediately softened as she asked, "How was she today?"

"I didn't get to see her long. It wasn't one of those kinds of visits. The doctor said she had some good days this week, but he still doesn't know exactly what's wrong with her. Just that her own body is trying to kill itself from the inside."

"Iyla, I'm so sorry. I know you must be ready to fall apart. Why don't you hang with me tonight? You could really use a night out."

I shook my head, even though she couldn't see me. "Can't. I have homework."

"Homework?" Nahla asked with a disbelieving laugh. "You don't have homework. You already did it."

I weaved around the end table in the living room to sit on the black suede couch. My backpack was still at the foot of it with my textbooks and notes spread out on the coffee table. "I have that exam on Monday, remember?"

She sighed deeply from the other end of the phone. "And I bet you've already studied for it. To the point where you know the material better than the Professor."

I absently flipped through my notes but stayed quiet, because ... I couldn't argue with that.

"There *is* such a thing as *too much* studying," Nahla continued. "And you're basically there. Your brain is literally going to fall out if you try to force anymore info into it without taking a break. Especially with everything else you have going on with Gemma and your mom."

"I took a break," I argued, raking a hand through my long, brown hair. "I visited Gemma."

She scoffed. "That's not the kind of break I'm talking about." She paused then declared, "You know what, you don't get a choice. I've decided. You're going out with me tonight."

Nahla *always* had something cooked up for Friday nights. Parties. A hot date. Mini vacation to some resort or casino. There was absolutely no telling what she had planned for tonight, but whatever it was, I knew I couldn't get involved. Not only would it probably be completely outside of my comfort zone, but my mom would kill me if she found out I'd done whatever Nahla had planned, no matter how innocent it was.

"You know I can't go out," I said. "My—"

"Your mom isn't there. What she won't know won't hurt her. Plus, you're twenty, babe. You can do whatever the hell you want."

Not when Valerie Winters is your mom. Not when your life doesn't belong to you.

I didn't bother saying that to Nahla. It never did any good, but what did I expect? Trying to explain why I followed Mom's demands so faithfully to someone whose parents encouraged her to live her life to the fullest was like talking to a brick wall. I couldn't explain my mom's ability to control so easily or my swift compliance, not when that reality was as normal as breathing for me.

It wasn't until I saw Nahla with her family that I realized how different other people's relationships were with their parents.

Where my mother demanded obedience and perfection, Nahla's mom and dad smiled at her differences and embraced both of their daughters—Nahla, who was spunky and determined to carve her own path in the world, and Noya, who was reserved and chose to embrace her family's traditions. The Turkish sisters couldn't have been more different in attitude and goals, yet the Bayrak's loved them fiercely and equally.

Could I say the same of my own mom? Maybe. Maybe she loved me in her own way. It wasn't something I had truly questioned until Nahla.

"I'm going to be there in forty-five minutes," Nahla barreled on, stopping my wandering thoughts in their tracks. "I'm taking you with me, forcibly or not. Either way, you are coming with me tonight."

Knowing Nahla meant every word—she would absolutely kidnap me, if necessary—I rubbed a hand over my forehead. "No need to resort to violence. I *might* come willingly. Just depends. What exactly would we be doing, may I ask?"

I could hear the smile in her voice as she answered, "We're going to a concert."

I raised my eyebrows, because that wasn't what I'd expected. That sounded too contained for the boisterous Nahla, and I actually found myself considering letting her whisk me away. A concert? It didn't sound too crazy, dangerous, or like something my mother would disembowel me for joining in on.

But then I remembered that this was Nahla.

"And ..." I drew the word out, already dreading whatever answer I was about to get. "Who would we be seeing?"

"The best, obviously," she answered excitedly. "Sinners Do It Better."

CHAPTER 2

Zagan

I DOUBLE-CHECKED MY REFLECTION TO MAKE SURE EVERY-thing was still in place. Black hair tousled with a section in the front pushed back, long-sleeved shirt pushed up to the elbows with the top three buttons undone, demon eyes and horns on full display.

"Tonight's going to be a good night," I said, smiling at my own reflection, my fang-like canines glistening.

"Damn right it is," Dante agreed.

His tall and wide build filled the doorway of my dressing room. He was in his show clothes, too—black leather pants, no shirt, and silver bands wrapped around his dark flame-tattooed biceps. His black eyes with their red vertical slit for a pupil met my matching ones in the mirror, taking stock of my appearance. His black horns, only slightly larger than my own, pointed straight into the air on either side of his head.

Dante tossed me a bottled water and waved for me to follow. "Get your slutty ass out here. There's a large crowd outside. I'm ready to find tonight's meal."

I caught the water with one black-clawed hand and smiled at his mischievous tone. Of course, I shared his eagerness. It had been three days since the last time I fucked, and now I was *famished*. My dick twitched in my pants at the thought of sinking into soft, wet folds later tonight.

"I still think you're an idiot for going so long without fucking," Dante scoffed.

I chuckled. "Makes it even better when I finally get a taste."

Despite my nature, I loved abstaining from any sort of sexual release for a couple days before each of our concerts. I felt it added a certain sensual, angry edge to my voice while I performed, and the fans went wild over it. According to the tabloids, when I sang with my deep, rich, smooth voice, it felt like I was teasing and making love to the listener without even touching them.

It was a laughable statement considering what I was. The irony of it always gave me and the other guys of Sinners Do It Better a good laugh, because while we wore our demonic forms on stage, humans thought it was a mere costume. Little did they know, we were the real fucking deal.

Dante and I waltzed into the backstage lounge where Perseus, Xander, and Coldin waited.

"Ready to scope out our options?" I asked, licking my lips and the piercings there in anticipation.

"Hell, yes!" Xander hollered. His ribbed horns jutted out of his head, which had been freshly shaved on one side with the rest of his black hair flopping over the other half. His black septum piercing glinted in the light against his pale skin, which would be ghostly if not for all the ink covering it, and his gold eyes glinted with a certain glee.

The five of us made our way to a section that had been blocked off for us along a set of windows that overlooked the gates of the stadium we were playing at this weekend. Sure enough, hundreds of fans were already piling up outside, waiting to be let in. Excited screams filled the air, and my body vibrated with the energy of it all. I couldn't wait to get on stage and have all that intensity directed right at me.

"Shit," Perseus said, raking a hand through his golden curls, careful to pass through his pointed black horns. The shoulder-length strands flopped back into his red-slitted eyes, which tracked our dark-cladded fans outside. "So many gorgeous souls out there."

"I bet they're delicious," Xander said with a salacious smirk, draping his arm over Coldin's shoulder.

The stoic demon made no response to Xander's remark and continued to stare blankly at the unsuspecting humans below with his nearly solid black eyes. Orange flames flickered in the depths of those voids. Since his demonic eyes couldn't be explained as contacts like the rest of ours, our drummer wore a black and white skull mask during our performances, hiding his eyes behind the empty black eye sockets of the mask. Slits had been cut in the top of the mask for his large, ram-like horns.

I leaned a shoulder against the window pane and scanned the sea of people. I couldn't see everyone from here, and this wasn't even a *dent* in the number of people set to arrive, considering we'd sold out the entire place. Still, we only had so much time to pick our snacks before we had to get backstage for final preps. So with limited time, we looked over who was already here, and the choices were plenty.

Beautiful men and women dolled up in blacks, purples, deep reds, greens, and blues stood around outside. People of all shapes, sizes, colors, and backgrounds were here, offering a variety of flavors for later. Just looking at all of them made my fists clench and my mouth dry with hunger.

But also with desperation.

With centuries of seduction and sex under my belt, it was getting slightly harder to feel the thrill of it. I *loved* having a new body to try every night, and the excitement of each fuck was everything an Incubus like me could want. But every so often, there was another feeling that followed each high of a successful seduction. Almost like something was missing. It left me wanting something new—which was weird, considering each person and scenario I took to bed was *always* different from the last.

"Found my pick," Xander announced with his gold gaze locked on someone out there. He patted Coldin's chest where his hand rested, still draped around the demon's shoulder. "Want the one with pigtails next to mine?"

Coldin shrugged and ran a finger along the black ring of his labret piercing, uncaring about his partner nor the unruly brown hair falling into his eyes. "Whatever."

Perseus chuckled and shook his head. "You never care, do you? Not unless it's your next *victim*." Perseus turned back to the humans and announced, "I'll take that other one that seems to be hanging out with pigtails and goth boy."

Our manager, Leo, came over and jotted down their picks to take with him to the gates. He'd wait there with special VIP tickets to give our meals and anyone they came with—tickets that would get them access to the Airbnb we were staying at.

When Leo died and got sentenced in the afterlife, he'd fallen under my command. He now worked for our band, and I made sure to run the little bastard ragged. In his human life, he'd decided to be a piece of shit who raped women, so as penance, he was stuck serving us and watching us get to fuck every sort of beauty out there but never being able to do so himself. For all eternity.

Having finished what they came to do, Xander, Coldin, and Perseus left. Dante stayed next to me, taking his time to choose, as per usual. I'd been taking just as long as he did these days, trying to find that taste of something extra exciting.

"See anyone that piques your interest yet?" Dante asked.

I made a non-committal sound and downed some water while I continued to look. There was a whole lot of skin to see with how our fans—the Sinners, as they liked to call themselves—dressed. I loved it. Humans were so beautiful and delicious to look at, and the more I could see of their bodies, the better.

But it wasn't catching my eye tonight.

No. Tonight, I wanted a challenge. Someone who didn't see me, the guy flooding their minds as they fucked themselves senseless while alone at night. I wanted the *chase*. I wanted to put real effort in convincing someone to spread their legs and let me in. I wanted—

My breath caught. I straightened a hair and leaned closer to the window.

Two girls hovered to the side of the crowd. While both were beautiful, my attention zeroed in on the shorter, thicker of the two. Fishnet tights covered her legs, which disappeared into a black, pleated skirt, and hanging around her torso was one of our band t-shirts. Her long brown hair was curled, and half of it was pulled back and secured with a big black bow. She fidgeted with the shirt she wore while her big brown eyes looked nervously around her. Her friend was tugging on her with a wide grin as she bounced on her feet. The brunette offered a smile that, even from this distance, seemed cautious.

Timid.

Unsure.

Like a bird that wanted to fly but was too scared to take that first leap.

I'd bet when she *did* leap off the branch, though, she was hot, eager, and a great fuck.

The shy ones usually were.

She glanced up at the building, most likely just to take in the magnitude of the scene, and somehow, her eyes locked on mine. I raised a brow at her in silent question. What would the little birdy do? Scream and pant from having *the* Zagan make eye contact with her? Flash me her tits? Yell for everyone else to look up here to see me, too?

Her eyes widened, and a blush swept over her cheeks. She quickly averted her gaze and ducked her head.

My lip curled up. "Perfect."

"Find one?" Dante and my manager asked at the same time.

"Yeah." I pointed her out and described her for Leo to jot down.

Dante gave a low whistle and said, "Jot me down for the friend she's with." He nudged me and added, "Maybe we can have a foursome."

I looked back out the window at the girl I'd picked. She didn't glance back up here to sneak another peek of me. Instead, she kept her back to the window like she was too afraid to catch my eye again. My groin ached anew as I pictured fisting my hand into the hair around her bow, shoving her forward so she had to expose that ass beneath the skirt, and plowing into it until tears covered those rosy cheeks.

"Nahh," I finally replied. "My little bird is probably the type to only want one partner at a time. If I'm wrong, though, maybe we will."

Dante scoffed. "Fucking lame."

I slapped a hand on his shoulder. "Not necessarily. It just means I get her all to myself, and I'm willing to bet, she's a freak when she's like that." My dick twitched in my pants again, and I smiled, thinking about what was to come. "*Definitely* gonna be a good dinner tonight."

CHAPTER 3

Tyla

THERE'S NO WAY HE LOOKED AT ME. I'M IMAGINING THINGS.

I kept chanting it to myself as I shuffled alongside Nahla and the rest of the crowd. I wasn't familiar with the band, Sinners Do It Better, but the guy I'd seen in the window definitely looked like the guy on Nahla's shirt, which she'd forced me to wear along with the rest of my outfit. I was just glad she'd let me wear the t-shirt. She'd initially tried putting me in a *bra.*

I glanced at the crowd of people around us, noticing that I would've blended right in if I'd worn such a thing. Some women literally had no tops on. Just stickers of a demon head taped over their nipples.

What kind of concert is this?

"I'm so glad you're here!" Nahla cheered for the third time as we neared the entrance. She'd opted to wear the bra I'd rejected with a lace mesh shirt over it and tucked into her black skinny jeans. Her dark hair cascaded down her back like a silky curtain, and she brushed some behind her heavily studded ear as she looked down at me. "When I won the two tickets at work, I was so bummed thinking the second one would go to waste. I'm glad I convinced you to come with me."

"*Forced*," I corrected with a teasing laugh. "You forced me."

That earned me a glare. "Did I stick a gun to your head? I think not."

"I mean, you came to my apartment, stole my phone and textbooks, and wouldn't let me leave the living room until I agreed."

She smiled wide as though I'd complimented her. "You'll thank me later. This band is the best! Everyone in it is hot as fuck, and their music is unreal. It always feels like the songs are reaching *inside* of you, encouraging you to unleash all your inner desires. Something you could definitely give a try, Miss Always-Thinking-Of-Others-First."

Nahla stood on her tiptoes to peer over the heads of the people in front of us, trying to see how close we were to the entrance. I was glad she was momentarily distracted, because her words struck something deep inside me. I swallowed hard and looked down at the ridiculous outfit that I wore to this ridiculous concert. A tightness wound through my stomach and up my throat.

Inner desires.

Things I wanted.

I closed my eyes, and despite the thunder of voices and sound all around me, all I could hear was my mother's voice.

You want to play piano again? How could you even ask that of me? Do you not understand what hearing or seeing that would mean for me? The memories it would bring up? Do you think of no one but yourself, Iyla?

I looked down at my band t-shirt, and the unease that had already crept inside me pressed in harder. Unleashing my inner desires was ... dangerous.

So I stomped on any semblance of those wishes just as Nahla and I finally made it to the gate to have our tickets checked.

A bald man dressed in a crisp button-up shirt and dress slacks took ours. When he scanned them, his eyebrows shot up, and he smiled at Nahla. "Wow! Looks like you are the 100th patron to be scanned in." He passed a finger between her and I. "Is it just you two in your party?"

Nahla and I nodded. The man was clearly excited about scanning our tickets, which made me wonder if we'd just won something. I'd never been to a concert before, but I figured we were about to get a free t-shirt or something.

He clapped his hands and cheered, "Amazing! As a prize for being the 100th ticket scanned, you two get VIP passes to meet the band and hang out after the show. Come around to the rear entrance after it's over, okay?"

I slowly took the pass, glancing between my ecstatic friend and the shiny black card. On one side of the card, rose stencils surrounded a deep red snake curled around the "I" in "VIP," and the other side had a red devil head with horns. The wariness brewing inside me grew as Nahla continued her happy dance. She was clearly over the moon, and she'd brought me out here for a night of fun as any friend would do with my situation. I was apprehensive about all of this, especially given the name of the group and the look of their fans, but Nahla ... She wanted this.

I glanced at the rectangle in my hand again. The little red head on the card taunted me.

Are you going to ruin your friend's fun like a selfish brat?

Or are you going to put on a smile and pretend to have a blast for her sake?

With a resolved nod, I plastered on a grin and held my pass up to smack it against hers in cheers. "Look at us! You'll get to meet your favorite band tonight."

She screamed a joyous cry and kissed the card. "This is the greatest day of my life!"

I hooked my arm with hers and listened to her rave about the band and their lore with so much enthusiasm that my own nerves began to melt away. This may not have been my scene, I may have been hella uncomfortable showing off this much of my body, and I might've feared my mom somehow finding out I was here. But this was Nahla's night. She'd gone out of her way to include me and cheer me up after a hard day. So I wouldn't take this away from her.

Plus, it might be kind of fun going to a concert and meeting a *real* band.

"So they're supposed to be demons?" I asked as we finally made it to the floor.

We had front row floor tickets. Nahla had initially wanted to try to touch one of the band members from here, but now that we had VIP passes, she wanted to do *much* more than just brush hands.

She nodded. "Their costumes are top-notch. They seriously look like real demons. Or at least, what I think they'd look like if demons were real. Anyway, all their songs are about sex, letting your desires win, not being held down by the world, and badass shit like that."

"That's definitely ... something," I said with a laugh.

The sky overhead grew navy as the sun set, and the cheering in the open stadium made the ground beneath my feet shake. I looked around at everyone, watching their faces light up with excitement as they stared at the stage, waiting for their idols to appear.

Even though I wasn't familiar with the group or all that comfortable, the energy in the air was infectious. I found myself grinning, chanting the band's name with everyone else, and laughing with Nahla as the crowd jostled us around a bit.

The lights in the stadium suddenly went out, and it momentarily took the noise of the crowd with it.

Until everyone realized what the loss of lighting meant.

A dull, thrumming of guitar strings and a beat of drums shook the stadium, and a flash of red lights briefly lit up the silhouettes of five people on stage.

Screams and chants of different names flooded the air, and my heart thundered with another string of beats from guitars, pounding of drums, and a flash of red lights. Then it went quiet again.

The music stopped.

The crowd hushed.

And the most intoxicating, deep, sensual voice began to sing.

Fire lit my skin and swept through my entire body as lights lit up the stage, and the man singing swept his red-slitted eyes over the crowd.

My mouth dried at the sight of him.

He was everything parents warned you about. Tall and broad, he had to be well over six feet tall. He wore a long-sleeved button up, but half the buttons were undone, exposing a sculpted chest covered in tattoos. Ink covered his hands, which gripped the mic, and the dark images trailed up his arms. His ears, lip, and eyebrow were pierced, and a voice in the back of my head wondered if that was *all* he had pierced.

Then there were the demonic horns and eyes that he wore as part of his costume.

Every part of him dripped sex, sin, and seduction.

Something between my legs throbbed as he continued to sing softly into the crowd about silk sheets, ripped clothes, and sleepless nights. My breath hitched as images flooded my mind with the lyrics, and I clenched my thighs in an effort to expel the thoughts and feelings coursing through me.

It was then that his gaze moved over the crowd, and like before, it seemed to find me. His lips lifted ever so slightly. It was such a fleeting look that by the time I blinked and found him looking elsewhere, I wondered if he'd been looking this way at all. Though it *had* to be real, because my entire body felt that gaze as though it were a physical caress.

I bit my lip and groaned inwardly. This was going to be a long night.

MY LIMBS TINGLED WITH THE LINGERING EFFECTS of the heavy, loud music. People shuffled out of the stadium while still singing, gyrating, and screaming their approval of tonight's performance. Even I found myself having a really good time watching the members of the band lose themselves to their songs. I couldn't sing along, but that didn't stop me from holding onto Nahla and jumping up and down with her while she sang.

"What a phenomenal night," Nahla said with a content laugh. "And it's just getting started." She held up her black-and-red VIP pass. "Now we get to *meet* them."

Still feeling the high of the excitement from during the concert, I followed after her with a pep in my step. We weaved through people and stopped near the rear of the stadium where a crowd had formed. Barricades were set up with very large men stationed around it. That didn't stop people from milling about, trying to steal a glimpse of the members of Sinners Do It Better.

A trio of people—two girls and one boy—approached one of the guys standing guard. They flashed him what looked like the passes Nahla and I had. The man moved part of the barricade to let them through, making sure to keep others back as he did.

"Guess that's how we get in," I said to Nahla.

We pushed our way to the front of the crowd and showed our own passes to the same man. He wordlessly let us in, and we moved to where the trio who'd just gotten in stood, talking to the bald man who'd given us the passes.

The bald man noticed us approaching and smiled. "Hello again. I was just telling these three that the band is on their way to the meeting place now. The limo that's picking you guys up should be here momentarily. The security team will help you get in and keep the crowd back."

My eyebrows shot up in alarm. The others didn't seem surprised by the news, instead giggling and bouncing on their feet.

The manager stepped away to speak to a guard.

I dropped my voice and leaned into Nahla. "Limo? We're not meeting them here?"

"You don't know?" one of the girls from the trio asked. Her blonde and pink hair sat high on her head in two pigtails, and her makeup was dark and elaborate. She wore a black bralet, leather shorts, and a choker with a pendant that read, "BITE ME," which rested against her cleavage.

"Know what?" I questioned.

She smiled wide. "Sinners Do It Better doesn't do backstage meet-and-greets like other artists." She held up her VIP pass. "This gets you *so* much more. We're about to go spend the *whole* night with them at some hotel or something."

The guy of the group, who was shirtless with only black cargo pants on, held his hands together as if in prayer and pleaded, "I really hope I get to suck one of their dicks. I've heard they're *so* big."

Pigtails laughed. "I'm sure that will be allowed, considering what the rumors say."

My breath got shallower, and my heart picked up tempo. "Rumors? What rumors?"

Before she could answer, a limo rolled up to the barricade. The bald man came back over with a throng of people wearing shirts labeled, "Security." They ushered the five of us to the waiting limo.

"Nahla, do you know what's happening?" I hurriedly whispered to her.

Her eyes shined with excitement. "I know what I *hope* is happening. Holy shit, I can't believe my luck. I hope I get to see Dante naked."

My stomach was in knots as I walked alongside Nahla and processed what little info I'd been given so far. We were being taken to some place to hang out with the band, and rumors suggested that … *sexual acts* … were done during that time? I mean, their music had definitely been suggestive and encouraging, but was I about to waltz into an orgy or something?

I bit my lip, unsure of what to do. If I followed along with the group and got into that limo, I might see, hear, or become involved in things that were completely outside my realm of comfort. I was a homebody, an introvert who stayed in the lines. This seemed *very* beyond my lines.

I glanced at Nahla, who still wore the largest grin I'd ever seen on her. She wanted to go. She'd probably even love whatever *activities* the band had planned. This was a once-in-a-lifetime opportunity.

I wouldn't take that from her.

I couldn't.

I'd just say no if I was asked to participate in anything I didn't want to.

With my mind made up to go along with this for her, I slid into the limo. With all five of us piled in, the car took off toward our destination.

"I'm Nahla, by the way," Nahla introduced, reaching her hand out to shake Pigtails, who she'd just been chatting with.

"Addie," the girl replied. "This is Parker." She gestured to the shirtless guy in the trio then pointed at the girl with a tapered black bob. "And that's Iseul."

Parker and Iseul waved.

Smiling, I leaned forward in my seat. "I'm Iyla." I'd already come this far and decided to be here for Nahla, but I still had questions. I wanted to prepare myself for what I was about to walk into. Licking my lips, I asked, "So what were the rumors you were talking about before? You know, the ones about the band."

Addie's eyes widened. "How do you not know the rumors?"

Nahla wrapped her arm around my shoulders and pulled me in to squeeze me. "She's not actually a fan. That's me. I'm pretty sure she'd never even heard of the group until tonight when I convinced her to come with me."

"Holy shit!" Parker laughed and shook his head in awe. "What luck. Not even a Sinner, and you got a VIP pass."

I gave a nervous chuckle and straightened my bow that had gone askew when Nahla pulled me in for a hug. "Might be luck. Depends on what these rumors are."

The trio and Nahla shared a knowing smirk and let the silence hang in the air for a moment.

Finally, Parker leaned toward me and whispered, "Wild, filthy sex."

"W-What?" I asked, recoiling in my seat.

"That's the rumor," Parker explained. "People with VIP passes get to indulge in wild, filthy sex with the band all night long, and it's the best sex you'll ever have."

"Parker is right," Addie said. "And if the rumors are true, we're all in for a stellar night. Hope everyone wore sexy underwear!"

Nahla laughed and flipped her dark hair over her shoulder. "*Please*. I'm not even wearing any."

Everyone cheered and whistled at the news, but I was too stunned to even breathe.

Sex? With a stranger?

Make sure you save yourself for marriage, Iyla. Don't be one of those dirty girls. You know what happens to girls like that. The consequences *that come with having sex.*

My mother's voice was like a brand in my mind, and I worried I'd turn my head to find her sitting right next to me in the car, whispering her warnings in my ear. The hair on my neck prickled as if she were watching me, waiting to see if I gave into temptation and broke her rules.

Be a good girl. Good girls listen to their parents and become successful. Good girls win in life. Make sure you're a good girl, Iyla.

I swallowed my mounting nerves as the limo pulled up to a large mansion on a lone farm road. It slowed, and as I stared up at the house that music poured out of, I knew I was about to stare temptation directly in the eyes.

"Be a good girl," I whispered to myself.

CHAPTER 4

Zagan

M Y PREY WAS SLOW TO GET OUT OF THE LIMO. SHE hung close to her friend and stared up at the house as if it might bite her.

Of course, her fear was misplaced. It wasn't the house, but the demons lurking within that would do that.

"Dinner is here," I called to my bandmates, who were queuing up music for the night.

I ran a hand through my tousled hair, making sure my horns were firmly hidden away. Since we were supposed to be humans who wore demonic costumes, we'd made quick work of putting on our human forms the moment we got offstage. No horns or slitted red eyes for me. Just a head of dark waves and cerulean blue eyes.

I made my way down the stairs just as the door opened. A trio of friends were the first to walk in, and as soon as they spotted me, I could practically smell their arousal permeating the air of the entryway.

"Oh my God!" the one in the middle squealed. She covered her black painted lips and shook her head, making her pigtails sway. "Zagan! You were amazing tonight!"

"So good!" the shirtless guy beside her cried, and even through the black pants he wore, I could see his dick twitching as his eyes raked over me.

"It was legendary," the Korean girl exclaimed.

Flashing my charismatic smile that had gotten me more than one meal in the past, I said, "Thank you. I appreciate that."

Their eyes looked past me as the rest of the band appeared, and more chatter than I cared to listen to erupted as the trio drifted further inside. I leaned against the landing post of the staircase with my arms crossed and waited for my prey of the night to walk in.

The first one I saw was the friend who seemed to be pulling my bird behind her. She immediately saw the rest of the members who were doing introductions in front of me. I peered in between them all as my target appeared, and as if she could feel me watching, her big brown eyes found mine. As soon as our gazes met, I lifted the corner of my mouth a fraction, just to let her know the eye contact wasn't simply a random gesture.

You're mine.

She quickly turned to Dante as he approached the two girls, and I let her look away. For now. Because later, I'd have her so focused on me and all the things I was doing to her that she wouldn't be able to look anywhere *except* at me.

"Let's head in," Dante called to everyone. "We have loads of drinks, food, pills, whatever you guys might want, in the back sunroom."

Excitement flooded the space as the guests trailed after my bandmates with mine and Dante's picks following in the back. I didn't move from the post I leaned on, but instead, I let my eyes track my bird as she walked past. My dick throbbed when I saw her glance my way and swallow.

Oh yeah. She knew. She knew she was going to be mine.

Smiling to myself, I finally turned and followed the group, keeping a couple feet between my prey and I. Her back straightened, and she glanced over her shoulder to see me following. Her eyes widened, and she quickly turned back to face the way we were heading.

A dizzying sense of thrill fired inside me. This. This was what I'd been missing.

Chasing.

Stalking.

Seeing a pretty human that didn't go out of their way to try to seduce *me*.

That was my job, one that I'd missed. Now I'd get to test those skills out again, seeing how long it took to break my little bird's will. Because she *would* break. She'd give in.

They all did.

Everyone filed into the sunroom where the back bar stood with plenty of alcohol and a bowl full of colorful pills that some were already popping with no encouragement necessary.

The two girls stopped just inside the doorway of the room as Dante came over to start his flirting with the tall beauty. I stopped right behind my own snack. The sweet and subtle scent of lavender and vanilla wrapped around me.

She smells fucking divine.

Her shoulders pulled back, and she slowly turned to look at me. She sucked in a breath, which seemed to catch the attention of her friend, who'd been caught up with speaking to our lead guitarist.

"Holy shit," the friend hissed, her cheeks darkening. She didn't hide her appraisal of me, looking at me from head to toe. "Z-Za-gan."

"In the flesh," I said with a smirk. I looked between the two girls. "I'm afraid I wasn't paying much attention in the hall. I was a bit … distracted." My eyes briefly met with the shorter of the two, and my smile widened as the color rose to her cheeks, glad she caught my meaning. "What were your names?"

"I'm Nahla," the tall one said, pressing a hand to her chest.

I grinned just so she felt like I cared then turned my gaze on the only one I truly had an interest in right now.

She peered up at me through thick lashes and tucked a strand of hair behind her ear. "I'm Iyla."

Dante slung an arm around Nahla's shoulder and said, "Why don't we get you two girls some drinks?"

"I'd love one!" Nahla waved for Iyla to follow as Dante guided her away.

Iyla nibbled on her lip as she watched her friend go before glancing my way again. The blood rushing in my body heated instantly. I couldn't wait to claim that mouth and make it spew profanities.

I nodded in the direction of her friend. "After you."

She quickly followed behind them, and I walked beside her as we made it to the bar. Dante and Nahla were quick to fix their drinks and move on, seemingly already knowing what they wanted, and they shuffled away so that Iyla and I stood there alone. Already, people were dispersing to mingle, get their fan questions and comments out of the way, and eventually, get what we all really wanted.

"What will it be?" I asked, waving my hand at the wide array of drinks.

Her doe eyes scanned the various bottles of liquor. Something wild briefly flashed in her eyes, and if I'd been paying more attention to reading her instead of thinking about what I wanted to do to her later, I might've been able to pick up on whatever it was. Seeing as how I wasn't though, the look was expelled before I figured it out.

She stood on her tiptoes to try to peer over the other edge of the bar. "Is there any water back there?"

I snickered. "Water? Why not have something a bit better than that? There's no need to hold back since no one has to worry about driving. That's what the limo is for."

Her brow furrowed. "First of all, I'm only twenty. I can't drink. Secondly, I don't know anyone here, except Nahla. I'm not impairing my judgment in a house full of strangers."

The sudden push back from her sent a sharp dart of electricity straight down my spine and right to my groin. She was fighting me, and I fucking loved it. I *wanted* it. I wanted her to push back. I wanted her to keep telling me no. I wanted her to make me work for my dinner, because it was going to make it a thousand times better when she finally said yes.

Offering an understanding nod, I said, "Smart." I reached my hand over the bar where bottles of water were stashed. I offered one to her and poured myself a glass of whiskey. "I guess that means you have no interest in the ecstasy, then?"

Her eyes doubled in size. "Absolutely not!"

I laughed under my breath. She shifted on her feet and drank some water. I followed her lead and downed some of my whiskey. Her nervous hesitation was a refreshing change from the normal reaction I typically received, and I waited to see what else she'd do.

Her eyes found mine. "So ..." She paused, then said, "You sing."

The statement caught me off guard, considering it was both random and obvious. A short laugh broke past my lips before I could stop it. "Yeah," I replied, clearing the mirth from my throat. "Yeah. I sing."

She fiddled with the cap on the bottle, and a pink hue dusted her cheeks. "You have a really beautiful voice. I'm sure you hear that a lot, though."

A smile tugged my lips higher, and I shrugged. "I get compliments on it, though *beautiful* isn't typically how it's described."

"It should be. Your voice is ..." She hesitated and seemed to search my face for an answer. "It's deep yet has this sort of soft and haunting sound to it. It's nice."

The compliment threw me. My fans definitely loved my singing, but that was never what they wanted to talk about when they had the chance to be around me in this setting. And when they did compliment me, it was typically on how hot I was, how good I was in bed, or how *sexy* I sounded. Never *beautiful*. Never *nice*.

She's an odd one.

"Thank you," I finally said. "I appreciate it."

She took another nervous sip of water before saying, "The concert was really fun, too."

"Yeah. You looked like you were having a good time."

Her lips parted in surprise, and I had to *really* focus on her words and not on how fucking hot she looked with her mouth like that. "Y-You saw me?"

I rested my elbow on the bar and leaned in closer to her. "Of course I did. How could I not notice someone as gorgeous as you?"

She stared at me in bewilderment before ducking her head to stare at her feet. The compliment seemed foreign to her, which was a shame. A human as lovely as her should be showered in praise, but I had to admit that her sheepishness made the beast inside me pace, eager to claim and ruin her with my filth. It made the fire in my veins burn hotter with the need to seduce and feed off this little bird.

"Yo, Zagan."

I had to force my eyes away from her to look over my shoulder at Perseus, who stood in the center of all our guests with his arm slung around the shoulders of the girl with the bob. "Would you two like to join us for the tour?"

My gaze found Iyla's again. I raised a brow to let her know it was her choice. She looked all too eager to join her friend's side. Nahla pulled her in for a quick peck on the cheek before focusing on Dante and the story he was telling. Everyone began filing through the hallway to check out the different rooms—or more likely, noting the ones that offered the best scene for tonight. Nahla leaned into Iyla's side to whisper something in her ear, and after a moment, Iyla slowly fell into step beside me.

"Did you get sentenced to walk with me?" I teased.

She stared at the back of Nahla's head and murmured, "She's

just giving me some advice that I don't know what to do with. If anything, *my* presence is *your* sentence."

I pressed my wrists together in mock-cuffs and held them out to her. "Then consider me your pleased prisoner."

Iyla laughed softly and shook her head at my gesture. The momentary ease vanished as quickly as it came. Her body tensed again as the large group shuffled in and out of rooms. She walked around on eggshells, and I figured she was probably the type to get more comfortable as she got to know someone.

Excited that my meal tonight required some coaxing, I queried, "What do you like to do for fun, Iyla?"

Her brown eyes found mine. "I study a lot."

I quirked my pierced brow at her. "Study?" I chuckled and rolled my eyes. "I said *fun*."

She frowned. "Yeah, I guess studying isn't necessarily *fun*." She thought about my question some more. "I hang out with Nahla in my free time. We go shopping, watch movies, things like that."

"What kind of movies do you like?"

"Horror movies," she answered absently, looking into another room we passed. Her body was still rigid, and for someone who supposedly liked scary shit, she resembled a rabbit cowering in the shadows as if she were being stalked by a snake.

Little did she know that was exactly what was happening.

I leaned closer to her and whispered, "So are you always this tense, or is it because of me?"

She quickly whipped her head around to look up at me as her cheeks turned pink. I watched her throat bob on a swallow as her eyes briefly flicked to my lips, which still hovered close, before meeting my gaze again. "Maybe a little of both."

I titled my head slightly. "Do I make you uncomfortable?"

She considered the question with another fleeting glance at my pierced lips, but instead of answering, she asked, "What kind of movies do you like?"

The dodging of my question was a clear indication. She was definitely interested in me, and she was attempting to ignore it by changing the subject. The truth was obvious, though. It was in the rough tone of her voice, the heat smoldering in her gaze, and in the scent of her arousal. The smell was fucking divine, and my stomach clenched as I pictured sinking my face into it later.

I straightened, giving her distance to catch her breath.

For now.

"I don't really watch movies," I answered.

Her eyes widened. "What? What do you do for fun then?"

We reached the room my bandmates had been leading everyone to. The music was loudest here, and prior to the humans' arrival, we'd turned the lights off with only red LED strips lining the edge of the open room. The couches that had been set up by the home-owners were now pushed against the wall to create an open space for what we were currently here for.

Looking at Iyla as I walked backward into the room, I winked and purred, "It's a secret."

Everyone immediately gathered in the center of the space to dance in small groups or solo. Nahla grabbed Iyla and held her hands as she lost herself in the song. I stood with Dante and Coldin, watching the two girls laugh and sway with the other humans and my bandmates.

"We've got a good feast tonight," Dante said with a salacious grin plastered on. His hungry eyes watched the bodies moving around us. "You boys ready to eat?"

Coldin grunted in response as he crossed his arms and watched the human girl with pigtails.

My tongue traced the piercing on my lip as I finally replied, "Not quite. My little bird needs a bit more convincing."

He laughed and clapped my shoulder. "Good luck. If you get tired of trying to convince her, we can share mine. No need to chase these days."

Yeah, no kidding. But that was exactly what I wanted right now. The chase. The fight. The *sin*.

He left to join Iyla and Nahla where they danced. Nahla backed it up on him, and he moved along with her. Iyla watched the two for a moment before she realized she was now the third wheel. Her gaze flicked to me where I stood on the outskirts, and I could see her weighing whether or not to join me now that she was the odd one out. And that was exactly how I wanted it. The more Dante swept Nahla up in the dance and music, the closer Iyla shuffled toward me, seeking someone to be with.

The crowd slowly thinned as demon and prey left the room to get busy. Eventually, a tipsy, giggly Nahla whispered some stuff to Iyla before slipping her hand into Dante's and leaving the room. Iyla smiled at her friend and gave her two thumbs up as Nahla happily followed the crowd, leaving just the two of us in the room.

Music thrummed in the dim space. Iyla and I stood opposite each other, our gazes locked in a silent challenge of what to do now that we were alone.

I sat my whiskey on the floor where she had placed her water earlier and pushed off the wall. "Wanna dance with me?"

She quickly held up her hands and shook her head. "Oh. Oh, no. You don't want to dance with me. I don't get out much, so I'm not very good at it."

"There's no one here but you and me. No one to judge you or to critique your dancing. I know *I* certainly won't."

"Wicked Games" by The Weeknd flared to life over the speakers as I stalked closer to where she stood in place. I slowly walked around her, passing her side and coming around to her back, making sure to keep only a centimeter of space between her skin and mine. I wanted to get close, making her body painfully aware of me, but not giving it the satisfaction of touching.

Not yet.

I stopped behind her, and even over the music, I heard her quick intake of breath as I leaned forward to whisper in her ear, "Just let the music guide you. Let it make your hesitation disappear. Let *me* make it disappear. Dance with me, Iyla."

The song pulsed around us, and I eagerly waited to see if I'd gotten her yet. Had I convinced her to take this one little step that would lead to many more? A small dance that would lead to my cock filling her up later? My entire body practically buzzed with the need to feel her skin, but I was a patient Incubus. I'd wait until she gave in and made the step herself.

Her response was nearly drowned out in the beat of the song, but I heard it with my entire being. "Okay."

I smiled.

Good fucking girl.

CHAPTER 5

Iyla

I DIDN'T KNOW WHAT COMPELLED ME TO SAY YES. MAYBE it was because I was alone in this dark room with a sensual song playing and a hot guy giving me attention that I'd never had before. Maybe it was because I was bored and looking for something to do while I waited on Nahla to have her fun. Maybe it was because Nahla kept encouraging me through happy whispers to let loose this one night, doing whatever I wanted. Maybe it was because in this little room with just Zagan and I, a little secret dance couldn't hurt anything.

Or maybe it was because I desperately wanted to feel his hands on me. Just for a second. I wanted to take this fleeting chance to simply see for myself what it felt like to be touched and held by someone. And I wanted to see if it was as wrong as my mom always made it out to be.

Now was my chance to do that.

Besides, ever since I'd walked into this house, I could practically feel his attention as though he were actually brushing up against me. It had me restless, nervous, and excited. I wanted to know if his actual touch felt as good as his gaze alone.

And it wasn't like I was having sex with him.

It was just a harmless dance.

He stepped into me, and my skin electrified with the weight of his torso pressing into my back. My breath hitched with an onslaught of nerves and something sharper. Brighter. Hotter. My eyes fluttered shut as he placed his hands on my hips and slowly started to sway to the beat of the song. I felt his head dip closer to mine, his warm breath on the shell of my ear making goosebumps break out over my skin.

The beat of the music thrummed beneath my feet, and it shot through me as Zagan pressed closer. His hands felt good on my hips—warm, strong, and steady. I found myself secretly wondering what they'd feel like if they moved a bit higher or lower. If having them firmly in place on my waist made me feel this hot, this light, this *good*, what else could they make me feel?

My body moved against Zagan's broad form, almost as if I were on autopilot and just letting the hedonic song and druglike-inducing effects of his touch guide me. His hips rocked, and I pushed back into him, moving with his guidance. His hands coasted up my sides, making my stomach tighten with a fresh wave of sickly sweet heat. They glided up my curves, his fingertips nearly brushing the edges of my breasts, before trailing down my arms. He grabbed my hand, and with ease, he stepped back and twirled me around to bring me face to face with him.

My breath got lost in my chest as my eyes locked onto his. A wide grin spread over his lips, and I couldn't fight the urge to glance at them, imagining how they'd feel pressed on mine. Wondering what those two silver rings on his bottom lip would feel and taste like.

Seeking a distraction from my dangerous thoughts, I met his gaze again and asked, "Do you dance a lot?"

"All the time," he answered, draping my arms around his shoulders. "Do you?"

I shook my head, continuing to move with the beat. "No. I've always admired people who could dance, but I haven't had many opportunities to try it myself."

"Well, we can't have that," he drawled, amusement lacing his words. "Let me teach you some stuff."

He pulled me flush against him and placed one hand on my lower back. My entire being sparked as his other hand gripped the back of my thigh, right beneath the hem of my skirt. The warmth of his palm against my bare flesh made my heart thunder harder than the music and sent a dizzying sensation sweeping through my body.

"Lean back," he whispered against my ear.

At the same time that he gave me directions, he hooked my leg over his hip and dipped me low before slowly circling me around and back up against him.

"Oh my God!" I gave a breathless laugh as we came face to face again. "That was fun."

"Yeah? We can do more."

His body moved against mine, his hands pushing and pulling me along with the slow beat of the song. I wasn't sure if he meant to, but as the seconds ticked by where the two of us continued to rock and sway, I could hear him softly singing along with The Weeknd. His enchanting voice, nearly hidden over the actual track, made a prickle of desire wash over me like a bucket of water being dropped over my head. I swallowed hard and strained to hear him as he grabbed my hand and flung me wide to twirl me in his grasp.

When he spun me back into his arms, I blurted breathlessly, "Sing louder, please."

He quirked a pierced brow at me and smiled. Pulling me in again, he placed my arms around his shoulders and did as told, singing louder so that I could easily hear him. I pressed further into his hold, my gaze transfixed on his lips as he sang in that deep yet soft tone. My heart thundered. He dipped me low again before curling me back up. This time, my body came to a stop right in front of him. Our noses brushed with the faintest of touches, and mere inches separated our lips as he sang low about dancing with the devil.

I knew I should pull back, but something hungry kept me in place, breathing hard and dancing against him as he sang sweet sins in the miniscule space between us. For the first time in my life, I stopped worrying about everything. Nothing existed outside of this secret moment for just us two. My own little moment of freedom, fun, and fire in my blood.

The song came to an end with another quickly taking its place. I realized then that we'd stopped moving at some point and now stood, locked onto each other, his head leaned down toward mine so that our noses grazed fully and our breath danced across the others lips.

"Thank you for the dance," he whispered roughly.

I couldn't seem to find my voice amid the riot of emotions and sensations darting inside of me, so I gave a single soft nod.

His blue eyes looked at my parted lips, and he seemed to tilt closer. "Want to go upstairs?"

My chin dipped in the start of a nod when the warm fog blanketing my mind suddenly cleared.

Upstairs.

Bedrooms.

Sex.

The rumors were true. Zagan was clearly offering to hook up. I'd been having a genuinely good time dancing with and touching a guy that practically stepped out of my ideal romantic fantasy. In doing so, I'd completely forgotten to keep my guard up. I'd stopped hearing my mother's voice.

But now it was back, pounding into my head like a jackhammer with warnings about what happened to girls who gave into their desires.

I swallowed hard and reluctantly stepped away. He watched me but made no move to reach for me and pull me back, for which I was glad. I'd nearly lost my head with him, and I couldn't risk getting swept up in his voice and hands again.

I tucked some loose hair behind my ear and cleared my throat. "I-I think I should find Nahla."

I didn't wait to hear his response. I spun on my heel and fled the room in search of my friend and my sanity. I mean, what was I thinking, letting myself get swept up in the music and gaze of some hot guy? I knew better than to give into desire.

I peeked into rooms on the first floor, but there was no sign of Nahla or anyone else. The deafening music followed me as I climbed the stairs and checked more rooms to no avail.

"Where is everyone?" I mumbled to myself.

I drew closer to another door when muffled sounds filtered through the barrier amid the pounding tempo of some song. I slowly opened it, and my eyes went wide at the onslaught of sounds and images before me.

Moans and cries of pleasure filled the lounge room.

Nahla leaned over a table, licking at Iseul's spread pussy as Dante fisted Nahla's hair and pounded into her from behind. Iseul gripped the edge of the table above her head, gasping around a mouthful of Perseus's cock while he threw his head back in a rough groan, his hands palming her bare breasts beneath him. Addie was on a couch next to the four of them, watching the display while she bounced on Coldin's dick, his large hands helping her to keep pace on his lap.

That was all I saw before I quickly pulled the door shut again. I stared at the closed door like a deer in headlights. I'd never seen so much *nakedness* or heard sounds like that. And the expressions on their faces like they were in pure bliss ...

I worked to catch my breath and quickly turned to walk away, only to come face to face with a grinning man. It took me a moment to realize it was Xander, the bass guitarist, and he had a drunk looking Parker tucked under his arm.

Xander tipped his head at the door behind me. "Would you like to join?"

I held up my hands and shook my head. "N-No. No, I'm—"

"No need to be so nervous," Xander cooed with a chuckle. His grin stretched as he nodded at a giggling Parker beside him. "You can join us. We'd love to include you."

He stepped closer, and I tried to step back only to hit the door behind me. I kept my hands in front of me as my stomach bottomed out.

"No, thank you," I gritted out.

"Come on," Xander sang, leaning close. "We—"

"Xander."

The three of us whipped our heads to find Zagan walking toward us. The lead singer gave his bandmate a stiff smile. "I believe Iyla said no."

Xander pulled back and stepped aside. I quickly moved past him and closer to Zagan.

The guitarist laughed and said, "All yours. I get it. I'll take mine and leave then." He opened the door to the room everyone else was in, disappearing with Parker.

I stood frozen to the spot with only the muffled moans and pop music filling my ears. My heart was still in my throat from everything that I'd just witnessed, plus Xander's uncomfortable presence, and it rendered me a statue.

"Want some air?"

I looked up at Zagan and found his eyes locked on me. With a sigh of relief, I nodded. "Air sounds great."

I followed him through an expansive bedroom and out onto a balcony that overlooked the trees lining the house. The cool air kissed my cheeks, and I inhaled the fresh scent, already feeling less tense.

Zagan leaned against the railing, and I leaned against the side of the house across from him. Despite the reprieve that the fresh air had just brought me, I found myself slipping into the moments before I came up here. The moments with Zagan and all the forbidden desires he aroused inside of me. He was quite literally the spitting image of what I'd always been secretly attracted to, and having his attention fixed right on me made me painfully aware of how much I wanted to give into temptation.

"Better?" he asked.

I cleared my throat and tried to stamp down my attraction to this stranger. "Yes. Thank you." I gestured behind us. "I don't mean to be a party pooper. That's just not my thing."

He raised that pierced brow of his. "Orgies?"

I felt color rise up my cheeks with the mere word alone. None of it was my thing. Parties. Orgies. Sex in general. Hell, even being *alone* with a guy wasn't something I did. But if I said that, I'd probably sound like a child to someone as experienced as him, and since Zagan was the only one here to talk to right now, I didn't want him brushing me off for being lame. So instead of clarifying, I just nodded.

He shrugged. "Group activities aren't for everyone. Especially with those guys." He laughed and leaned back on his tattooed hands, which rested on the railing behind him.

"So you guys really do this after all your concerts?" I asked, more than a little curious about their rumored habits. It boggled my sheltered virgin mind—the idea of hooking up that often with complete strangers.

"More or less," he answered.

"But you're famous," I said slowly.

His shoulders shook as he dipped his head in a laugh. "Yeah. I suppose we are. What's your point?"

I twirled a strand of hair around my finger. "I don't know. If I was famous, I'd be worried that one of my hook-ups would be crazy or something and go to the tabloids with some story or rumor just to get their ten seconds of fame."

He bounced his head side to side like he was weighing my words. "I guess one could. I don't really worry about it, though."

What confidence he had. That seemed like such a risk, and I was baffled that he—or any of them—would take that chance, all to get their dicks wet for a bit.

Wanting to understand, I asked disbelievingly, "Do you really think sex is *that* good? Enough to risk your livelihood for it?"

The smirk that tugged the corner of his pierced lip up was downright sinful, especially when he wore it while letting his eyes rake over me. "Oh, Little Sparrow," he purred, his voice turning into a sensual chuckle. "If you don't think sex is that good, your partner hasn't been doing it right."

If only you knew.

I bit my lip to hide my smile and shrugged. "I guess he hasn't."

Zagan pushed off the railing of the balcony and approached like a predator zeroing in on their prey. Each step that brought him closer made my heart beat faster and my toes curl in my shoes. He stopped right in front of me, placing his hands on the wall on either side of my head. I held my breath as he leaned in close with those blue eyes locked right on mine.

"Why don't we rectify that?" he asked huskily.

The embers that had been swirling around inside me all night flared with an all new warmth. My skin prickled with the need to have his hands on me. Never had I felt so hungry for someone. The throbbing between my legs made my breath catch in my throat, and I just knew he could do something to help that.

But did I dare?

If my mom knew I was even considering doing anything with Zagan, I'd be severely reprimanded and punished, which was why I'd always stayed within the lines. Being taught my whole life that sex and desires were wrong kept me exactly in the tight, cramped box my mom wanted me in, always watching everyone else experience love and life from within it. I lived my life by her rules, and everything I did was for someone else's sake. My schooling, my actions, my wants. Even tonight had been for Nahla's sake, not my own.

But I wanted things, too.

Despite my mother's efforts, deep down, I wanted to live. I wanted to kiss and touch. I wanted romance. I wanted to experience what that kind of intimacy had to offer.

I'd always obeyed.

I'd always lived my life for other people and what they wanted.

But right now, with this deliciously attractive guy staring at me, making me feel beautiful with his gaze alone, I wanted to choose *me* and *my* wants.

Just this once.

I licked my lips, my cheeks warming as I finally whispered, "Okay."

That one word was all it took.

His lips crushed mine, and my entire body shivered with a rush of euphoria. I thought his two lip piercings would make kissing hard, but the cold metal mixed with his soft lips made me feel even hotter. His large hands moved from the wall to my hips, keeping me pinned in place as he stepped into me. His body pressing into mine made me gasp against his mouth, and he took the chance to sweep his tongue along mine.

I'd stolen a peck kiss here and there senior year of high school and when I first started university. But none of them ever made me feel like *this*—burning with a sweet heat from the inside out, twitchy in the legs, aching between my thighs, and light like a feather caught in a breeze. His kiss was all-consuming, and I tilted my head in an effort to feel even more.

The hands on my hips moved to slip beneath the hem of my shirt, and with the ease of a pro, he pulled the garment off. Instinctively, I went to cover my bare skin, but when I saw the heat, the awe, and the desire burning in his gaze as he traced the flesh that wasn't hidden by my black bra, I found myself enraptured. I wanted to see how much he liked what I always kept hidden, and with that sudden rush of longing, I reached behind me to unclasp the bra. His lustful eyes tracked my unhurried movements, following the article of clothing as it slid down my arms then dropped to the ground between us.

"Goddamn, you're fucking beautiful," he said in a rush before bending down to kiss me again.

His lips traveled from my mouth, over my chin, and down my throat. I leaned my head back against the side of the house with heavy breaths as he palmed one of my bare breasts and pulled the nipple of the other into his mouth.

A gasp burst from my lips at the onslaught of emotions that engulfed my insides. I was feeling so much right now—*too* much. I couldn't even be damned about the fact that I was topless outside or the chill in the air. Everywhere he kissed and touched felt branded in the best way possible, and my head spun from the mix of lustful pleasure and excited nerves firing off inside me.

While his tongue flicked the beaded nipple on my breast, his hand left the other to coast down my stomach and into the band of my skirt. My breath hitched as his fingers slipped into my underwear and down the seam of my aching middle. An exquisite burst of pleasure swept through me as his finger curled and rubbed against my clit.

"Z-Zagan!" I gasped, unable to help myself. I'd never, ever felt something so good.

He made an approving sound in the back of his throat as his mouth once again hovered over mine. "So fucking wet. You like it when I touch you here?"

I nodded, my lips brushing against his as I did. My fingers dug into the house behind me, needing something to squeeze and hold onto as more waves of electric bliss shot through me.

He grinned. Suddenly, he dropped to his knees. He pulled his hand out from my underwear so that he could grip my skirt, tights, and panties all at once, and slowly, he pulled them down to my ankles. I quickly stepped out of the material, needing his touch back on me.

Zagan stayed on his knees as he looked up at me with hooded eyes. "Spread those legs for me, Sparrow."

My body trembled, though whether it was from the chill of the night, nerves, or anticipation, I wasn't sure. Regardless, I did as I was told, opening my legs wider. The cool air hit my middle, making me realize just how wet I was. The chill made everything feel overly sensitive and needy as his blue eyes locked onto my exposed pussy. He groaned at the sight before grabbing my right ankle. He hiked it up and draped my leg over his broad shoulder before leaning in.

The first touch was like a match being struck. The tip of his tongue started at the bottom of my seam then slowly drug up. My eyes immediately fell closed, and my fingers curled to dig into the wall at my back. I gasped out a flurry of sounds, shaking as his tongue flicked and rubbed at the bundle of nerves that felt starved, having gone twenty years without ever getting attention. I was hot, wet, and panting with each pass of his tongue.

"You taste so good," he growled in a quick breath before showering my middle with more attention.

I couldn't even make an attempt at a response. My mind was mush. My tongue was a cinder block. Every bit of my body was locked onto Zagan's mouth, tongue, and hands as he licked and sucked on my clit or squeezed and slapped the curves of my ass. The pulsing of pleasure built deep inside of me as his tongue continued its relentless motion. The pounding euphoria between my thighs grew hotter and coiled tighter until I feared the very world around me would explode. With a guttural groan, I threw my head back and went jelly-like in the legs as I spilled myself onto his mouth.

"Fuck," he said, licking his lips with a smile. "The sounds you make are too good. I can't wait to hear more."

He stood and reached behind him to yank his shirt off. My mouth watered when I saw all the tattoos decorating his chiseled body. The snake head that I'd seen on the top of his left hand with the tongue out on his middle finger went up the entire length of his arm, the tail draping over his shoulder and somewhere onto his back. His right arm had a blooming flower on the top of his hand and a network of vines and spider webs running up the length of it. The hilt of a dagger started at the base of his throat, and the blade fell between his toned pecs, impaling a flower in the center of his torso. A moth adorned one pec, and a detailed spider decorated the other. A silver bar pierced each nipple, and I found myself wondering what it would feel like if I flicked my tongue over one.

My hands itched to touch him and pull him against me again. Now that I'd experienced a taste of what pleasure was, I had to have more. I was sure that was only the tip of the iceberg as far as pleasure went, and if I was ever going to experience such a thing, I knew *he'd* be the master I'd want to teach me.

"I don't want to stop," I announced with my heart in my throat.

His blue eyes held mine, and his mouth curved into a salacious grin. "Oh, don't you worry, baby. We're just getting started."

CHAPTER 6

Zagan

THE TASTE OF HER SWEET RELEASE WAS STILL ON MY tongue, making my insides warm and my appetite peak. Pleasure from oral was always like the basket of bread you get at a restaurant—appeases your hunger but doesn't nearly come close to filling you up. I needed more from this quivering, breathless human.

Much more.

I grabbed the underside of her thighs and hoisted her into my arms. She wrapped her legs around my waist and held onto me as I gripped her ass cheeks tightly and pressed my mouth into the hollow of her throat. I scraped my teeth over her skin, wishing it could be my fangs dragging across her flesh. But I knew better than to bring those out. She shivered against me and made a soft sound in the back of her throat as I kissed and nipped at her neck.

We finally reached the bed, and I quickly tossed her back onto it. A grin pulled my lips up as her eyes widened in surprise. Her breasts bounced as she landed, and she squeezed her pretty thighs together while staring up at me with those innocent brown eyes.

I bit my lip and sucked one of my piercings into my mouth as I unbuttoned my pants. My eyes trailed over her exposed body, and my cock ached to sink into her.

Releasing my lip, I ordered, "Open up. Let me see that pretty pussy."

She sucked in a sharp breath, and her face and chest flushed a nice pink color. Slowly, she spread her legs so that she rested on her elbows and stared at me from between her parted knees. Moisture dripped in the folds of her center, and it had me *famished*.

I shoved my pants and boxers down, letting my dick bounce free. Her attention zeroed in on it, and if I thought they were large before, they were fucking saucers now.

"Oh my God," she gasped on a breathy exhale.

I chuckled and grabbed her ankles, yanking her to the edge of the bed. "Not quite, baby. He doesn't come into my room."

I gripped my cock and pumped it once as I lined up at her entrance. My entire body thrummed with heat as my head brushed against her opening. Her eyes rounded, and her hands latched onto my biceps.

"W-Wait—"

It was too late. The sound of her voice came right as I thrust, shoving in hard and fast.

It was that exact moment that everything went to shit, and even though it happened in a matter of seconds, it seemed to play out in slow motion.

I was met with brief resistance that suddenly eased—a sensation I hadn't felt in a long ass time—just as she threw her head back on a scream. And it wasn't a scream I usually got, one full of blissful rapture. No, this was the sound people made when they *hurt*. In the same moment, a black mark that was only two fingers thick appeared and wrapped around her slender throat like a collar stitching itself together.

I gasped and leapt back. My dick left her body with a wet pop, and I couldn't even be bothered with the blood now mixing with her damp arousal. I clawed at my neck as I felt the familiar burn of a new bond, and if Iyla looked at me instead of rolling onto her side with tear-filled eyes, she'd see the same black band forming around my throat that now wrapped hers.

The physical manifestation that happened when a new bond formed.

An Incubus demonic bond.

One with a clear master and an obvious subordinate.

She finally looked at me, and betrayal burned through my insides like a wildfire eating through a field of flowers. Tricked yet again by another human seeking a demon to control.

Hatred flooded my veins, and suddenly, I was seeing *red*. My human guise dropped. My horns appeared between the waves of my hair, my black-and-red eyes ate away the blue, my fingernails turned black and sharpened, and my canines lengthened into fangs.

Her face paled as she watched me transform, and she quickly crawled away, falling off the other side of the bed, taking the blanket with her.

"W-What are you?" she cried.

Ignoring her question, I roared, "You were a virgin?"

Her head appeared over the edge of the bed, and even without seeing her body, I could tell she was trembling.

Good, I thought with a bitter snarl. *I'm going to make you regret lying to me.*

"Fucking virgin," I hissed and shoved the lamp off the night-stand. The loud crash of the glass vase exploding against the floor made Iyla jump, but not even that appeased the outrage coursing inside me.

"I never said I wasn't a virgin," she whimpered. She scooted back away from me, holding the gray comforter to her chest. "What's going on? What are you?"

"I'm fucking irritated, is what I am." I swiped a clawed hand down my face.

Somewhere in the back of mind, I knew she'd technically never confirmed that she'd slept with someone. But she also never denied it when I implied her sexual experiences. She misled me, which led us here.

It had been so long since I'd gotten bound to a virgin. Well over a century, at least. Those stupid ass stories about demons leering over virgin women and pining after their "innocence?" *Bullshit*. Virgins were the bane of my existence for this exact reason. Contracts. Forced loyalty. No control over my life and my food.

It was a lot more common to get bound back in the day when people were stricter about sex. One could easily fuck a virgin by mistake, and, consequently, get bound to them in servitude. That feature was an unfortunate part of being an Incubus or Succubus—the balance system put in place so that we couldn't run amok, seducing every person we saw. There had to be ancient demonic rules to keep us careful.

So back then, we'd double, even triple check, that our partners weren't virgins. Still, there would be times when they'd deceive us, just to get a demon under their control. The last time I was bound to a human, it was due to a trick that some cult organized so that I'd belong to them.

Over time, that worry of getting bound had dwindled. These days, people were much more open about sex and having those experiences. Not so anal about "saving yourself" or being shamed for enjoying something that was literally meant to be pleasurable. Coming across someone in their twenties who hadn't indulged in sex—*especially* among our fanbase—was rare. So rare, in fact, that it had *never* happened.

Until fucking now.

Turning my fuming attention back on Iyla, I yanked my pants off the floor and pulled them back on.

"What are you?" she asked again. There was no missing the fear coating her words, and that, at least, gave me a little satisfaction.

"Gee, I don't know. What do I look like?" I snapped, not bothering to disguise the acrimony in my voice.

She looked over my true form, the one I only let out in the demonic realm, in my alone time, or when I was on stage since our personas were demons.

She licked her lips and whispered, "A demon."

I clapped my clawed hands. "Bra-fucking-vo." I dropped my hands back to my sides and narrowed my eyes. "You humans never change. So you were playing tricks tonight, hmm? You were really just in it to form a contract with me, is that it?"

"Contract?" She shook her head, her brow scrunched up in confusion. "I don't know what you're talking about. I didn't—I wasn't—"

I swiped a mirror off an end table that I *hadn't* destroyed and tossed it to her. Pointing at my own neck, I explained, "Contract." I gestured to myself. "Incubus." I pointed a finger at her. "Human virgin. When one of my kind screws a virgin, we get bound to them."

She looked at her reflection, and her fingertips came up to brush along the black mark curling around her throat. Her lip trembled like she wanted to cry more. "Bound?"

"Bound," I repeated as my insides burned with renewed anger.

"I didn't mean to," she pleaded, still staring at her reflection and the inky mark decorating it. "I don't even know what the hell is going on. Did you slip me drugs or something? Am I dreaming?"

"That would certainly make my life easier if you were. Regrettably, you are very much sober, and I am very much attached to you."

Panic clouded her eyes. She tried wiping the black around her neck away, but it was no use. That was a magical demonic seal. It wasn't going anywhere. For *either* of us. "Can't you just undo it?"

I gave a humorless laugh. "If I could do that, demons wouldn't have to serve humans who trap us into being their little pets."

She shook her head, like the mere gesture alone could somehow wipe away the last five minutes. "Can't *I* undo it?"

"Sure. Go jump off the fucking balcony for me, because the only way you can undo it is to die." My breath was coming out hard and fast as the acrimony ate away my cool. "We both know you're not really interested in breaking the bond, though, you goddamn liar. So what did you trap me for, hmm? You want endless wealth? Immortality? Fame? World domination?"

"No, no." She held up her hands and shook them as if to dismiss the ideas, but in doing so, the blanket slid down her naked body. She fumbled to grab it and hold it against herself once more. "I don't want anything. I didn't know what you were. I-I didn't even plan on sleeping with you until literally right before it happened." She swallowed. "I don't want anything, so let's just pretend we're not bound or whatever. We'll go our separate ways and pretend this nightmare didn't happen."

Growling, I stalked around the bed toward her, watching as she tried backing away to no avail. "I wish it was that easy. Unfortunately, when an Incubus gets bound, they can only sleep with that one person. And that's how we feed. Sex. Orgasms. Pleasure. Which I can only get from you now."

Stupid motherfucking bond.

They were such an inconvenience. Controlling our food was a huge leverage to have over us, and bonds made that all too easy since we had to rely on them for our meals. To make matters worse, the bond protected the human—for the most part. We couldn't force ourselves on them and simply take our meal. We couldn't feed unless it was consensual on their end. Not that rape was my personal preference, anyway.

Her eyes narrowed, and for the first time, she seemed just as mad as me. "That sounds like a you problem. Why should I care?"

Venom dripped from my lips as I hissed, "Because we'll both die if I don't eat."

Her momentary anger slipped away, replaced by a heavy dose of alarm. "What?" she asked. She inched back more. "Is that a threat? Are—Are you going to kill me?"

I sneered. "I'd love to. Nothing would give me greater joy than seeing the life leave your pretty little eyes right now, but the bond prevents us from killing the human we're bound to. Otherwise, it would be too fucking easy to get out of it. All about balance, ya see? That being said, if I don't eat, I die. And if I die, the bond kills you along with me."

I glanced at a large ceramic statue in the corner, close to where she was crouched on the ground. A new idea popped into my head, and I smirked. "However, if *you* die, *I* don't. One of the only good features of the contract, in my personal opinion."

"But you just said you can't kill me," she said quickly as her hand tightened on the blanket around her.

"I can't, no." My smile widened. "Doesn't mean an accident can't happen."

I zeroed in on the statue, and with a quick jerk of my chin and summoning of my powers, it tipped sideways, heading right for Iyla. She gasped and quickly scrambled out of the way, barely missing being crushed. The stone shattered in a cloud of white dust and debris. Iyla shot to her feet and inched away as I stalked toward her with evil intentions radiating off me.

She must've finally realized the predicament she was in— standing face to face with a murderous demon. She looked over her shoulders as she backed up, almost like she was looking for something to save her. Too little, too late, she realized that she'd backed herself right into the balcony doorway.

Perfect.

A fall from over the ledge onto the cement below should do the trick and handle this new little inconvenience for me.

Though, dealing with the potential aftermath of a human dying while partying with us would be a huge ordeal to clean up. Sinners

Do It Better was my fucking career and life in the human world. I didn't want to ruin the life I'd built just because I got tied to a human again. Thinking about that now had me slowing my steps. Just a hair.

"Wait," she pleaded as she glanced over her shoulder again.

I didn't stop moving forward, corralling her backward.

"Wait, wait!" She dropped to her knees right on the threshold of the door. Her teary eyes met mine as she held a hand up. As if that feeble gesture could keep me back. "What if I give you what you want? If I let you eat, you'll spare me, right?"

I stopped and stared down at her. As much as I hated being bonded, now that it was done, it *would* be easier to fuck her until she either died of natural causes or until a legitamate and less sketchy "accident" occurred. Because that was the only time the contract was broken—when she died or the both of us did.

Her death was the only way to get my freedom back.

Sensing my hesitation, she scooted forward on the wings of hope to see another day. "We can sleep together. I'll feed you all you want without issue." She paused and seemed to be thinking hard before something akin to resolve flashed across her eyes. "But I want something in exchange."

I blew out a sarcastic laugh. "Oh? Ready to make a deal with the devil now?"

She swallowed hard and wrung her hands in the blanket. "Can … Can you heal people?"

I tilted my head and looked her over with a bland stare. "You sick or something?"

Maybe I won't be stuck with her for too long, afterall.

She shook her head. "Not me. It's my sister. She's eleven, and she's been sick for a while now. Nothing the doctors do has helped."

Damn. So close, I thought with a sigh.

My openness to a potential truce between us cracked. I furrowed my brow and held up two black-clawed fingers. "Two problems with that. One, I can only do a major change that affects someone's life like that when I'm in a contract with them. For an Incubus, we form contracts by sleeping with people. Therein lies problem two. I can only have sex with you now, and even if that wasn't the case, minors aren't my thing. I may be a demon, but I have standards."

Her face looked crestfallen. "So you can't heal her? There's no way you can do *something*?"

I sighed and looked up at the ceiling. I was humoring her idea of going along with this accidental bond because it seemed easier than constantly trying to cause accidents that would kill her, but this was already becoming a headache. Still, I considered her question.

"There might be something, but I can't promise it will heal her," I finally answered.

The hint of hope lit up her face, and she scooted even closer. "What is it?"

"My blood," I answered, swiping my hand over my forehead. This was so fucking annoying. "I don't have to be under contract for her to take my blood. If she drinks small portions of it, it should slowly heal her. Too much at once would probably kill her, but giving her a little at a time should infuse my demonic essence into her, allowing her to heal." I paused then shrugged. "Or it could kill her faster. Not sure. I've never personally done it. Only heard of others doing it."

She pressed her lips together and stared at the space between us. I could practically feel her mind trying to decide what to do.

From the sound of it, her sister was bad off. Human life was such a fickle, fleeting thing. Here one minute and gone the next. Her sister would die eventually anyway, but if I knew anything about humans after centuries of living amongst them, I knew they were greedy for life. Giving it and taking it. So if there was a chance to keep a loved one alive, they'd usually always take it. Even if it was risky.

Iyla finally raised her eyes back to mine. "If there's a chance I can save her, I have to try."

Fucking knew it.

I closed the distance between us and dropped to my knees in front of her. "So then, do we have a deal? You let me eat when I want, and I'll try to heal your sister?"

I watched her throat bob on a swallow, and despite the lingering swarm of frustration, I wanted to run my tongue over that neck. Afterall, I was still hungry.

Finally, she nodded. Her voice came out as barely a whisper. "Deal."

CHAPTER 7

Iyla

SPEECHLESS DIDN'T DO WHAT I WAS FEELING JUSTICE. My brain and all its sense of reality had basically been shoved into a meat grinder and shredded to bits.

Demons.

They were very much real.

And I was now stuck with one.

For *life*.

I was sure when I woke up this morning that Nahla would tell me it was all a bad dream. We never went to the concert. Never hung out with Sinners Do It Better. All of it was some weird fantasy I'd built up in my head. I mean, when I woke up that morning, there was no weird black ink around my throat like the night before.

But when Nahla stumbled out of my bedroom where I'd dumped both of us after booking it out of the party, I knew it had all been very real. I guessed that meant the black ring on my throat turned invisible. Thank God. I didn't know how I would've explained that to anyone.

"Please tell me there's coffee," Nahla groaned, rubbing her hand over her face.

Forcing a smile, I pointed to the kitchen over my shoulder. "In the pot. I already have some ibuprofen next to it for you, too."

"Ugh. You're a saint." She kissed the top of my head on her way by the couch where I sat and eagerly poured the hot brew into a mug while popping the pills. "Last night was easily the greatest night of my life."

My cheeks warmed, and I tried to hide the flaming of them behind a hearty sip of my own coffee. Last night was a rollercoaster of emotions. I had a lot of fun dancing once I'd warmed up to letting a little loose, and when Zagan ate me out ... that was like *heaven*. But what happened right after was a shit show of the greatest magnitude.

I let a demon screw me.

And that shit *hurt*.

I stood behind my initial opinion—sex wasn't any good.

Nahla plopped down beside me on the couch. She propped her elbow on the back and leaned her head against her palm while she sipped her coffee. I fought a chuckle at the crazy state of her post-party hair.

"I love what you're doing with your hair," I teased. "Absolutely gorgeous. Are you going for a just-struck-by-lighting look or a birds-welcome-to-this-nest look?"

"Shut up," she grumbled with a laugh, shoving me in the shoulder. "My scalp is sensitive right now from Dante pulling on it. But damn, it was worth it. That man gave me more orgasms than I have shoes." Her eyes took on a dreamy look. "I've never had such wild, amazing sex. And *that's* saying something."

I shook my head, but there was no hiding the smile in my voice. "I'm glad you finally scored your celebrity crush."

"What about you?" She nudged me. "What did you do all night while the rest of us were busy?" She paused, and her eyes took on a conspiratorial gleam. "Now that I think about it, Zagan was missing from the group festivities, too. Were you two hanging out?"

I chewed on my lip, trying to gather my words. My hesitation was all she needed as confirmation.

Her eyes widened, and she sat her coffee aside before practically climbing on top of me. "Oh, hell yes. *Spill*! You better tell me everything? Did you fool around? Did you *finally* have sex?"

I should've known she'd have questions and thought about my answers in advance. Under normal circumstances, I would've immediately poured my secrets out for Nahla to listen to and dissect. But what happened with Zagan was *not* normal. The experience of losing my virginity was a mess with details I wasn't sure how to divulge without sounding certifiable. So I decided to give her *part* of the story.

"We may have kissed," I said slowly. I grabbed a strand of my dark hair and twirled it around my finger. "And he might've, you know ... gone down on me."

"Oh my God!" Nahla squealed, bouncing on her knees. "How was it? Did you love it? My baby had her first orgasm!" Her features suddenly turned serious, and she grabbed my shoulders. "You *did* orgasm. Right?"

Heat swept up my face and burned my ears. I placed my hands on top of Nahla's and huffed a small laugh. "Yes, Nahla. I orgasmed."

Her excitement reappeared in full force, and she shook me in her celebration. "So it was good? Zagan was as deliciously talented as the rumors say?"

I wanted to roll my eyes, because while what he'd done with his tongue had most definitely been wonderful, the sex was *awful*. But I couldn't say that.

"Yeah," I answered. "He was very good at it."

We continued reminiscing about last night and nursing the rest of the coffee before Nahla had to head out. She was meeting her parents for brunch, and even though the Bayraks offered for me to join them, I declined. I was still pretty wiped out from the night before and needed some alone time to process it all.

As soon as I shut the door behind Nahla, I slumped against it. All of my insides were wound tight with apprehension. I'd finally lived a little, let myself step just a hair outside of the box I'd always stayed in. And what did that get me?

A freaking *demon*.

But also a chance to save my sister. That alone kept me from regretting what I did.

I pushed away from the door and gathered Nahla's empty mug to put in the dishwasher. The quiet sounds of me tidying about the kitchen were all that filled the vast room, and the near quiet was starting to drive me a little crazy. It gave my mind room to wander, and that meant acknowledging the heavy weight of dread.

It felt like at any moment, my mom was going to burst through my front door, screaming that she'd caught me. She'd somehow known I'd gone out and, worse, had premarital sex. I'd lose what little freedom I had. She'd take away my food, leaving only bread and water. Or she'd have the water to my apartment cut off so I'd have to stay as dirty and filthy as she thought I was for opening my legs for a man.

"Get out of your head," I mumbled to myself.

I finished wiping down the non-existent dirt on the kitchen counters and looked at my closed laptop on the counter. My fingers itched to get on YouTube and play one—just *one*—song. Like Saint-Saëns, "The Carnival of the Animals" or Debussy's, "Suite Bergamasque."

It was moments like this when I was alone with nothing but silence and my spiraling thoughts that the armor I'd built up against my desires really fractured. Temptation called louder, and I had to squeeze the edge of the counter to keep my feet from carrying me to the laptop.

To music.

I'd always had a love for music. One could say I was bred for it. My dad was a music teacher, and he'd taught me everything I knew about piano. He'd always encouraged me in my pursuit of becoming a professional pianist. When he died, my dream and freedom went with him. I was left with a grieving heart and a mother who despised my love for all things music and piano.

She sold my piano and used the money to get Gemma swim lessons. She burned my music sheets and had me kneel in front of the fireplace to watch. She took all of mine and Dad's records—Beethoven, Chopin, Liszt, all of the great classical composers—and made me snap each and every one in half while she towered over me with crossed arms and sharp eyes.

There was no room for music in my life, she'd said.

I never touched a piano after that. I hadn't listened to music, either.

Sure, I'd heard music out and about or when I was around Nahla. But I never truly listened. Even when I was alone and could sneak a listen to a few pieces, I held firm in my resistance, the loud crack of the records snapping in half and the crackling of fire eating away at paper filling my head and keeping me from daring.

I took a deep breath and bent over to press my head onto the marble of the island top. I let the cold seep into my skin, hoping it would numb the dull ache of longing that had sprouted inside me.

"Fuck. I like this view."

I gasped and whipped around to find Zagan standing in my living room, smirking as his eyes remained where I'd just been bent over the island. He didn't look like he did the last time I saw him. His true form was hidden once more, masked by his blue eyes, normal looking teeth, and human features. He sported a form fitting black t-shirt and black pants, all of which made my mouth water against my will. Even knowing what I knew, he was still the picture of everything I secretly wanted.

"What are you doing here?" I demanded in a startled breath. "How did you get in here?"

"Demon, remember?" he deadpanned. "I can find you through our connection and *poof*." He made an explosion gesture with his hands. "I'm there."

I stared at him, dumfounded. "What if I wasn't alone? What if people were here? Do you not care about exposing yourself?"

"I hid in the shadows to make sure you were alone before appearing. If someone was here, they wouldn't have seen anything but normal shadows until I stepped out of them." His gaze left me and slowly took in the kitchen and living room. "Speaking of here … Is this your place?"

I inched into the living room but kept a good distance away from him. I didn't really know him, but he was a demon, for crying out loud. Who knew how dangerous he was.

"Yes," I finally answered as I put the couch between us. "Now, can you leave? I'm not allowed to have guys here."

That got his attention. He met my eyes with a puzzled frown. "You're an adult. What do you mean you can't have guys here?"

A rush of embarrassment flooded me like hot magma. I looked away from him and tucked some hair behind my ear. "You don't understand. My mom pays for this apartment. So even though I live here, it's technically hers. Her apartment, her rules."

He scoffed and went back to snooping around the living room. "Sounds controlling to me, but whatever." He approached the bare wall and ran his tattooed hand along it as he walked around the living room and started down the hall. Even though he was mumbling to himself, I still heard him say, "Is this your place or the fucking model unit the building uses for showings?"

"It's mine!" I yelled, even though he didn't actually ask me the question. "Can you—Hey!"

I started after him as he unabashedly swept into my bedroom. When I rounded the corner, he was already sitting on the edge of my unmade bed—thank you, Nahla—leaned back on his hands and looking around.

"What the hell do you think you're doing?" I fumed.

"I'm no interior designer or anything, but your place feels cold." He waved his hand around my mostly bare room. "Where's all your photos of you and your girlfriends or your pile of messy clothes? Where's the *life* in your room? Or are you just that boring?"

Another wave of self-consciousness hit me. It was true my place didn't really feel … lived in. But that was how my mom liked things. No clutter. Neutral color palette. No distractions from my schooling.

"This doesn't feel like the room of a college girl," Zagan added on with another glance around the room.

Meeting my breaking point with this judgmental asshat, I snapped, "Yeah well, not everyone can do as they please. Would I love a purple comforter or shelves lined with nothing but romance books or a whole freaking record player to play as loud as I want to? Abso-freaking-lutely, but that's just not a reality for me. It has nothing to do with me being boring or whatever else you might think about me. You don't know my situation, so why don't you keep your opinions to yourself?"

Instead of trying to placate me or get snappy right back over my sudden outburst, Zagan grinned and cocked his head. "Not an opinion, Sparrow. I was merely making an observation. Stating a fact. I see we don't like being confronted with truths, though. Noted."

"I'm sorry. Aren't *you* the one living a literal lie?" I fired back while crossing my arms. "A demon posing as a human?"

"We weren't talking about me."

That smirk was still on his stupid face. Seeing it made my blood boil and made me want to feel those lips on me again, all at once.

Which only pissed me off more.

"Forget it," I huffed. I ran a hand through my long hair and leaned against my door frame. I was still nervous about getting too close to him. "What did you come here for?"

He flashed me a look like I should've known why he was here. "Our deal. I'm hungry. In case you've forgotten, I never got to eat last night after days of already abstaining from sex. I need fuel."

He was here to finish what we'd barely even started. The reminder of the previous evening sent a flush up my cheeks. I cleared my throat and glanced away from him. I wasn't ready to repeat that horrible experience.

"Not until you do your part," I said.

He sighed. "I figured you'd say that. That's why I'm also here to do just that. Let's go see your sister so I can give her some blood."

The change in subject to Gemma and the idea of potentially saving her life put some civility back into my voice. "You said she needs to drink a little at a time, right?"

He nodded, and the muscles in his torso pulled at his shirt as he shifted on the bed. It took a lot more willpower than I cared to admit to focus on his words as he explained, "We can mix a couple drops into a drink of hers or something. Giving her that every week should do something. Hopefully."

I swallowed hard. There was a risk this wasn't going to work. There was a risk that it might make her sicker. But my heart had heard there was a chance of healing her, of *saving* her, and it had latched onto that bit of hope like a leech. I couldn't sit back and watch my sister suffer anymore. If I could do something to help her, I *had* to try.

"Okay," I said. "Let's—"

My phone started going off. I dug it out of my jeans, and my heart fell through me like a cinder block in water when I saw the name on the screen.

"Frick," I hissed. I glanced warily at Zagan, who stared at the phone in my hands with far too much curiosity. I ignored his interest and returned to the living room. My heart raced as I answered and tried to keep the dread out of my voice. "Hi, Mom."

"What are you doing?" she asked, her tone all business.

Shit. Did she know? Did she know I'd gone out last night? Did she know there was a guy inside my house at this very moment?

"Just finished cleaning up the kitchen," I answered calmly.

I leaned my back against the counter, and when I looked up at the living room, my eyes widened. Zagan had moved back out here, and he was now rummaging around inside my backpack, which had been propped by the couch.

"What are your plans for today?" she questioned.

I waved a hand at Zagan to get his attention. When he looked up at me, I motioned for him to get back. He ignored me with a roll of his eyes, going back to his search of my textbooks. He pulled out my Urban Policy and Economic Development book. With the look that crossed his face as he flipped through it, you'd think he'd just stumbled upon some foul smelling garbage or something.

That was secretly how I felt when reading that one, too.

"Iyla?"

The impatient snap of my name had me refocusing on Mom. "Sorry. I-I thought I saw a spider." I paused, mentally slapping myself at the stupid lie.

"Great save," Zagan whispered from the living room. He tossed the textbook onto the couch. He must've decided he was bored with my school material.

"Anyway," I said to Mom, watching Zagan zero in on me with his vivid blue eyes. Too late, I realized that his boredom of looking through my shit meant there was only one thing left for him to mess with.

The light in his eyes turned … smoky as he appraised me where I leaned against the island. I felt the heat in his gaze all the way to my core, and somehow, it froze me in place. All I could do was stand there as the demon stalked toward me while I continued talking.

"I'm planning on getting ahead on some assignments today. Study some more. Like you always say, you can't ever be too prepared."

Zagan was on me then, putting his hands on the counter on either side of me, caging me in with his body. His eyes traced my face, falling to my lips.

"Good," Mom said. "I'm meeting with a client now, so I probably won't be paying much attention to my phone in case you try to get in touch with me."

"Okay. Thanks for letting me know."

My eyes were locked on Zagan's, and even when the call ended, I remained immobile, holding the silent phone to my ear. I was like a deer staring down the barrel of a hunter's gun. I knew I needed to move, flee, escape, because danger was right there, directed right at me. But I couldn't move. He'd ensnared me with the closeness of his broad frame and the hungry gleam in his eye.

"I want to taste you again," he whispered, leaning in close. "I want to bend you over this counter and fuck you so hard, you can't even walk straight."

My words lodged in my throat. I squeezed my thighs together, because that voice uttering such filthy words did something to me. But his wanting to have sex was also a reminder that we had something to do before he got what he wanted.

Swallowing hard, I placed a hand on his chest and gently pushed him back to give myself space to breathe. "After we go see Gemma."

The lines around his mouth tightened in annoyance. That was my only warning before I heard the metallic drag of a knife come from my right. A knife flew toward me, and I ducked with a gasp just as it reached where my head had been. Quick, erratic pants left my lips. I bunched Zagan's shirt in my hands where they still rested against his chest. My frantic eyes bounced from the knife now embedded in my wall to Zagan.

"Damn," Zagan grumbled as he stared at the blade. "If you'd been just a bit slower, I could've been done with this."

I shoved at his chest as fear and anger warred like a storm cloud inside me, but the demon didn't even flinch at my furious shoves. "What the hell? I-I thought we had a deal."

He met my gaze again. "We do. Doesn't mean I won't take a chance when I see an opportunity. Don't forget what I am, *human*."

My heart continued to pound, and my knees wobbled with the lingering effects of terror. He was right. I couldn't forget what he'd shared. While *his* death would result in both of ours, *my* death would result in his ticket to freedom. That knife had been too close, and while it hadn't done the job Zagan had intended, it succeeded in being a reminder.

We may have had a deal to save my sister, but I was far from safe with this demon.

CHAPTER 8

Zagan

BLOOMINGS WAS A SERIES OF CONNECTED BRICK BUILD-ings set on a sprawling field. Wild flowers grew along the outskirts of the parking lot and around the buildings. A playground of sorts sat out back, and there were different posters of kids with varying medical conditions hanging in the windows along the front of the place.

"So this is where your sister stays?" I asked as we approached the building after Iyla scanned us in through the front security gate. The guard gave me a skeptical look through the window of the car, but with Iyla signing me in as a visitor accompanying her, I was allowed clearance.

The entire car ride, Iyla had leaned as far away from me as possible, probably terrified I'd try to create another "accident." The thought had definitely crossed my mind, but as my annoyance faded, so did that need. The moment my irritation returned, however, that might change once again.

Iyla nodded at my question, and there was no missing the touch of sadness that crept into the corners of her brown eyes as they traced the structure. "Yep. She needed constant supervision and medical professionals to monitor her, so she stays here in this long-term care facility."

I frowned. From all Iyla had told me—which was very little but enough—her little sister didn't seem to be doing well. I didn't specialize in healing or restoring life. I was a *sex* demon for fucks sake. But I'd heard of other demons healing people with their blood, despite not being in a contract. It was worth a shot, and if the girl died, oh well. Wouldn't be the first time a human died, nor would it be the last. As long as I got my meals without issue, I'd go along with this. But as soon as the sister died or Iyla made a fuss over the deal, I'd go back to my original plan—looking for a way to make sure Iyla wound up dead.

Just the thought made me grin.

The hallways weren't that shitty, sterile white you'd find in most medical facilities. Nope. It was *worse*. Murals covered the walls, depicting kids and animals running through fields, rainbows and butterflies soaring through the air, or kids riding dinosaurs as if they were horses.

The bright colors and overly cheerful faces in the pictures had my skin crawling and my morning coffee wanting to come back up. How could anyone stand to look at this overly happy shit? It was an *eyesore*.

"Whoever did the decorating for this place needs to be fired," I grumbled to Iyla.

She looked at the walls and actually made a soft sound that could almost be called a laugh. She glanced up at me and tucked some dark hair behind her ear. "It is a bit much, isn't it? I think it's meant to provide some semblance of positivity to the people that come here. The kids and their families."

"Yeah, cause if I'm sick and dying, seeing a kid riding a dinosaur will remind me to keep pushing on," I quipped.

Before she could respond, we rounded the corner into a much larger area. A circular desk stood in the center of the room, and branches of hallways fed off from the vast space. Nurses and staff bustled around the desk and swept down the different paths.

A nurse wearing teal scrubs and a sandy color hijab spotted us. Her face instantly broke into a smile as we approached. "Iyla! So good to see you."

"Hey, Noya," Iyla greeted, returning the warm welcome.

Noya's attention found me, and I immediately knew what her wide eyes and slack jaw meant. Recognition.

Plastering on a charming smirk of my own, I waved. "Hey there."

"You're—You're—" Her voice got higher and higher as she stammered her words.

"Holy cheese balls!" a sudden shrill voice squealed.

The three of us turned to find a group of teenage girls staring at us—or rather, *me*—like their savior had just appeared before them.

"You're Zagan!" one cried. She wore a long blue flannel dress that practically swallowed her frame where she sat in her wheelchair.

Another, who clutched a walker with an IV bag holder, smiled so wide, I worried her chapped lips would split. "I can't believe this. Is this really happening? *The* Zagan. We're—We're all huge fans."

"Fans?" the older nurse standing with the group asked. Her wrinkly face gained a few more creases as she openly scrutinized me, and I knew all she saw was a man with tattoos and piercings. "What have you girls been doing when we haven't been around?"

"Just listening to music, Mrs. Patrice," one of the teens said. "He's the lead singer in our favorite band!"

"Yes, he's amazing!" came a decree.

"The absolute best!" another compliment came.

The five teens, all of whom were patients, nodded their heads furiously, in agreement with all the assessments thrown my way. The nurse didn't look amused at all. Old, judgmental bat.

More times than not, I was a cold bastard. There wasn't much I cared about, and even then, I wasn't sure if *cared* was the right word. Rather, there were only a few things that made me truly happy. Well, as happy as a demon from Hell could be.

One of those things was music. Dancing to music, playing music, writing music. Writing songs was what I lived for these days. Taking absolutely nothing and turning it into this exciting, thought-provoking, heart-pounding string of sounds and words that reached deep inside people, calling to their inner selves. The things they cared about. The things they feared. The things they desired. It was what made this long existence of mine bearable.

Going hand-in-hand with that drive was meeting my fans and seeing those that my songs had touched and inspired. It was something that made my dark soul pulse with just a bit of something more. Something … lighter.

Walking over to them, I made sure to give the skeptical nurse a shit-eating grin before looking at the girls. I scanned their faces—some gaunt and pale, others red and splotchy, one girl even had thick scars from what looked like burns marring her face, though she tried to hide behind her hair while throwing quick glances at me.

"Wow," I said, turning on the brightness in my voice that I reserved for fan interactions. "I've never had such beautiful girls praise me so much."

That earned me a chorus of giggles from all of them. Except the girl with the burns. She tucked her head down even more.

"Thank you all," I continued. "Really. I appreciate your support. What are your names?"

They went down the line, introducing themselves. We'd gathered some more people around us—a couple nurses who looked like they were about to cum just from looking at me, some more patients who lingered in doorways to watch, and some older staff who didn't seem to get what all the fuss was about like Madam-Resting-Bitch-Face who still lingered protectively around the girls like she thought I might eat them.

When they were done introducing themselves, one of the girls—Arianna, the one in the wheelchair—asked, "What brings you here? Do you have a relative here or something?"

I nodded at Iyla, who had drifted over to stare at me at some point. She seemed ... surprised by my attention to my fans. Like she thought I might've just ignored them and moved on instead of hanging around to talk to them. My chest tightened with a wave of satisfaction. I liked proving her assumptions about me wrong, because just as she'd snapped at me earlier about not knowing her, *she* didn't know *me*.

"I'm actually a friend of hers," I said, gesturing to Iyla. "We're here to see her sister."

"Ahh," Noya said, her eyes still starstruck as she fought to look away from me and toward Iyla. "Gemma's in the sunroom with the other kids."

Kalypto, the girl with the walker and IV pole, gasped and exclaimed, "That's where we're headed. We can take you guys."

I nodded happily. "Lead the way."

Iyla and I trailed along with the group of boisterous girls. At one point, Nurse Patrice pulled Noya in close, and she threw me a cautious glance as she not-so-subtly questioned Noya about whether the kids were safe around me or not. It made me chuckle under my breath.

Humans never stopped judging. I'd gathered by this point in life that it was just part of their nature. They see someone and decide they know everything about that person just by their appearance. Full sleeve tattoos of vines, webs, and snakes or lip and brow piercings like mine gave people like Patrice a lot of ammunition to fuel their misguided musings. In the past, those kinds of people were my favorite to fuck with. To torment. To seduce to the dark side.

"You were really nice to all those girls," Iyla observed. There was no missing the edge of bewilderment in her voice, which only confirmed my previous idea that she'd expected me to dismiss them.

"You sound surprised," I noted.

She shrugged. "I guess I am. I've not met many demons, but I thought you'd all be, you know—"

"Evil," I finished with a knowing nod. "Don't get it twisted, Sparrow. Just because I indulge my fans here and there doesn't change that I am, in fact, *evil*."

She inhaled sharply, like the reminder scared her, and she turned away from me.

For some reason, this whole exchange annoyed me. I couldn't decide if it was because of Iyla's assumptions about me or if it was the building itself. I stared ahead, fighting the urge to burn the obnoxiously bright paint off the walls on our way by, when I noticed one of the girls continuously looking over at me.

Marla, the girl with the burns, had been quiet this whole time. She didn't share the same glee as the others. She'd barely managed to tell me her name, but her fumbling hands and tightening of her mouth told me she desperately wanted to say more.

I had a hunch what her timid silence and distance stemmed from, and I couldn't let that slide. When I saw a tortured soul in need of attention, I was compelled to offer my sway. Sprinkle in a bit of self-thought, self-expression, self-empowerment, and eventually, it would bloom into what people liked to call defiance, the work of the devil, and sin. Because being bold and having your own thoughts meant you weren't "drinking the kool-aid" that the world wanted you to. It meant you couldn't be controlled, and *that*, for those who needed to control you, got labeled as sin.

Drawing closer to Marla, I met her fleeting, startled glance before she ducked her head again. There was no missing the look that crossed her face before she looked away, though.

Shame.

"You seem a bit down, Marla," I said softly.

She shook her head hard, and she sniffled beneath her curtain of hair.

"It's okay," I soothed, ensuring my tone came off as gentle as possible.

Her burn-covered hands came up to gingerly touch her face. "I never, ever dreamed I'd get to meet you in person. You're so famous and wonderful and handsome. How am I supposed to face you looking like—like—"

Her steps slowed before finally stopping all together. I stayed right beside her, and the others turned back to look at us. Out of the corner of my eye, I saw Patrice inch her way toward us like she thought I was about to abduct Marla right on the spot.

I ignored our audience as I bent down just enough so that the teen had to look at me. "Do you not like your scars?"

Tears filled her eyes, and she shook her head.

"Why not?"

Nurse Patrice scoffed, and I looked sideways at the old woman as she said, "What an absurd question! She's covered in scars. Do you not understand that? Please consider what you're saying before you speak to my girls."

Marla's eyes pinched in anguish, and she tried to hide even more behind her hair. "My scars are ugly. I'm ugly. I know I am."

"Ugly?" I repeated in disbelief. "They aren't ugly, Marla. You know what they look like to me?"

She shook her head.

"Like a cluster of shining stars." I looked over the shining, raised red and pink skin. "They're like your very own galaxy of stars, creating a constellation that is so unique and so *you*. The rest of us?" I said, gesturing at myself and the lingering party. "We're just like plain, boring rocks. All the same. All lack-luster." I placed a finger under her chin to tilt it up so her hair had to fall back and she had to hold her head high. "Don't hide that pretty face from the world. It would be a shame for us rocks to never get to see such a beautiful star."

Her lip trembled as she seemed to soak in my words. "I'm a star?"

I grinned. "A whole entire glittering constellation." I leaned closer to whisper conspiratorially, "And between you and me, that nurse over there really needs to see some stars because she's the *roughest* and *plainest* rock of us all."

She laughed quietly, and her lips lifted into a smile. She nodded once and squared her shoulders to stand taller. We rejoined the group, and Marla kept her head raised so her burns were on full display. Patrice seemed annoyed by my encouraging Marla to embrace her body, and part of me was glad to see that irritation. I hoped Marla took my words and used them to build up the courage she needed to face assholes like Patrice.

It was a pity the world told people like her, people who were different in one way or another, that they were somehow less than. Unless you looked a certain way or believed a certain thing, humans were quick to slap labels on you that they had no business handing out. And people wore those labels, because others gave them no choice but to do so.

Sometimes I wondered who the truly evil ones were—demons like me who embraced acting out and sinning, or the humans who told girls like Marla that they weren't worthy of acceptance.

Iyla cleared her throat when I reached her side and leaned in close to whisper, "That was really nice what you said to her. I think she needed to hear that."

I glanced at Iyla then at Marla. "I shouldn't have had to say it. She shouldn't have been made to feel less beautiful because of some stupid burns. But humans are quick to judge and reject."

She was quiet for a minute. Finally, she whispered, "I guess we are."

The group made it to the sunroom, which was easily the size of a standard gymnasium. Ceiling high windows spanned every wall, looking onto the lush grass and playground outside. Tables littered with puzzles or activities were spread throughout the room. There was a large TV in one corner with some animated movie playing, and most of the kids were gathered over there. In the back of the room stood an old piano.

"There she is," Iyla whispered.

A sudden sound of elation flooded her voice, which drew my gaze to her like a moth to a flame. I hadn't known Iyla for long, but this was the first time I'd heard that melodic chime of true happiness leave her lips or seen that euphoric sparkle fill her eyes.

I followed her line of sight to see what brought out this rush of emotion and saw two girls sitting at a table, working on a puzzle. A dark-skinned little girl wearing a green pajama set with a matching toboggan chatted away with the other one, who's attention bounced between the puzzle pieces and her friend.

I knew right away that the quieter girl was Iyla's sister. They shared the same nose, jawline, and even the furrow in the little girl's brow looked identical to the one Iyla had when she was working through something in her head.

Iyla started toward her sister, and I followed close behind. Both girls looked up at our approach.

"Iyla!" Gemma squealed in delight.

She went to get out of her chair, but Iyla beat her there, wrapping her arms around the younger girl's shoulders—albeit, gently—and kissing her on top of the head.

"I've missed you," Iyla said with a breathy laugh. She looked at the other girl. "Hi, Sienna. I love your green outfit."

Sienna gave a toothy grin. "Thank you! My daddy just brought it for me."

Iyla turned back to Gemma to clasp her little hands and squatted next to her chair. "How are you today?"

Gemma suddenly turned sheepish. "Okay. I only got sick once so far this morning."

This seemed to make the bracket around Iyla's mouth tighter, but it was so miniscule, I wasn't sure if someone who didn't know how to read human reactions would notice.

Gemma and Sienna seemed to finally notice me hovering close by. When they looked up at me, they gasped.

Iyla followed their line of sight to me, and her smile quickly turned into a frown. "Oh, please don't tell me—"

"Zagan?" Sienna asked in astonishment. "From the band?"

"In the flesh," I said, holding my hands out at my sides.

Iyla had said Gemma was eleven, which definitely wasn't the target audience for our songs. Even the teen girls we ran into were pushing it. Though, were you ever too young for freedom, learning to love and accept yourself, embracing who you were and what you want from this life? I'd say not. And that was really what our songs were about.

"You know his band?" Iyla asked her sister warily.

"That's our fault," Arianna quickly explained with an apologetic smile as she wheeled over. Her friends were right behind her. "We like to listen to their music out in the open, and the band became a huge favorite for everyone here. Don't worry, though. We don't play the—" Her cheeks pinkened, and she glanced at me then back at Iyla. "The super explicit ones."

I smirked. In other words, the ones about sex.

Sienna leaned close to Gemma. "What does explicit mean?"

Gemma shrugged. "Beats me."

A tug came on my shirt. I looked down to find Marla beaming at me. "Do you think you could sing something for us since you're here?"

A whole lot of eyes from kids, teens, and even the adults that had trickled in watched me with bright, eager eyes. It wasn't even a question. How could I deny my fans a little private concert?

Without a word, I walked over to the piano. The crowd followed, gathering around on the floor and in chairs around the older instrument. Iyla stood further back, and I met her eyes between the wall of bodies around me. She looked skeptical. Whether she doubted my ability to play or my motive for giving these people what they wanted, I wasn't sure. All I knew was seeing that look of doubt on her face lit a fire inside of me. I wanted her to see why she should never, ever doubt me.

I fingered a couple keys. The piano needed some tuning, but it would suffice for this little performance. I moved my fingers over the keys. Someone must've paused the movie that had been playing, because all you could hear was the slow and dramatic melody filling the otherwise silent room.

This was one of my favorite songs I'd ever written, one of our earliest songs, when it was still easy to find inspiration. The words and notes and chords came easier back then. These days, I *struggled* to write a solid song, and even when I managed to get a good one out, they never felt as powerful, raw, and real as my earlier ones.

Something I was reminded of only this morning when my manager and bandmates asked for an update on the latest song. An update I couldn't give them, because I still hadn't written one.

It was that desperate need to feel my music like I used to that guided the strong, almost pleading edge to my voice as I sang about finding yourself, about not apologizing for who that was, about not letting the world tell you that you shouldn't want what you do or be who you were. It was about embracing everything you were and standing up for it.

By the time the rock ballad ended, my voice fading into a memory and the chords dying off, everyone had somehow moved closer like moths drawn to a flame. The applause was instant, and everyone, even the stick in the mud, Patrice, looked impressed. It wasn't their reaction I wanted to see, though.

I looked between the bodies and found Iyla. Shock. Longing. Hopelessness. Awe. It was such a dizzying mix of emotions causing her brow to furrow and her lips to part, and it made my heart pound harder.

This. This was why I sang. *This* was what I wanted my songs to do.

While my hands, tongue, and cock could claim her body and fill her up, my songs touched her in a totally different way. One could say, a *deeper* way.

"That was wonderful!"

"So cool!"

"Zagan, you're the best!"

I smiled at all the compliments. There was a rush of people wanting photos or wanting me to sign something, and after the madness of all that, the crowd finally dispersed enough for me, Iyla, and Gemma to settle at our own table.

"That was busy," Iyla said, looking around the mostly appeased room of people. She turned back to me with a curious purse to her lips. "Do you get bombarded like that a lot?"

I shrugged. "Comes with being in a popular band."

"How do you know him?" Gemma asked her sister. She giggled and whispered, "Is he your boyfriend?"

Iyla's face turned an alarming shade of red, and her eyes widened as they bounced between me and her sister. "Absolutely not. He—He's my ..." She paused to look over at me. We'd never really discussed what our story would be, but after only a moment of searching for an answer, she turned back to Gemma and said, "He's my friend."

Friend.

The word made me shift uncomfortably in my seat. I didn't do *friends*. I only cared about myself and my own interests. "Friends" implied there was some sort of care involved between the two parties. Still, it was the only answer that made sense in this situation.

Gemma's smile stayed in place as she stared at her sister. "I didn't know you had such cool friends, Iyla."

Iyla stared at me from across the table and offered an unimpressed shrug. "Meh. He's okay, I guess."

I narrowed my eyes and curled my lip at her, which made a faint smile appear on her face. Seeing the gesture on those plump lips made my stomach bottom out with a fresh pang of hunger. I *needed* to fucking eat. My dick and body were going crazy with the need to fuck her senseless.

Ready to get this show on the road, I announced, "I'm pretty thirsty after all that singing." I made sure to catch Iyla's eye so she understood my meaning. "Would you two like a water or anything?"

"I'd love some," Iyla said, giving me a knowing nod. "Gemma?"

She bobbed her head. "Yes, please."

I pushed my chair back and approached one of the nurses who was tidying up some toy blocks on the floor. After requesting some cups of water, I waited in the hallway for her. She brought me a tray with three cups of water. When she swept back into the room, I hung back just long enough to let my human guise disappear from only my thumb so that my long, black claw came out. With a quick press of the tip into my pointer finger, I let a few drops fall into one of the cups. My wound closed in the same time it took for the black blood to disappear within the drink so that it looked like ordinary water.

"Here we go," I said when I got back to the table. I placed the cups in front of everyone, making sure Gemma got the one with my blood.

"Thank you," Gemma said, pulling her cup closer.

I tried not to watch while she drank some so it didn't seem like anything was amiss. Iyla was less subtle, throwing almost desperate glances at Gemma and fidgeting in her seat like fucking fireants were crawling all over her skin.

Still, as the three of us sat there, talking and working on the puzzle, we eventually finished our drinks. Gemma seemed to be fine after finishing hers. No fits over the taste. No flailing about in pain. No dropping dead. I took that as a good sign that this was going to work.

Which now meant, it was time for me to get what I was owed.

"It was good to meet you," I said to Gemma as Iyla and I stood to leave.

"Will you come see me again?" she asked with hope climbing her face.

I smiled. "I think I can make that happen."

Iyla hugged her sister, and I noticed that she held on a little longer than others might've. Gemma was important to her, that much was obvious. I mean, she could've asked me for anything when our bond formed—still could—but all she wanted was to save her sister.

"I think that went well," I said to Iyla as we climbed into her car. "Gemma didn't seem to have any poor side effects to the blood."

"I just hope it makes her better." Iyla stared at the brick building like a part of her was still in there instead of here in this car.

"Are you ready?" I asked.

Her head slowly turned my way, like she'd just remembered I was here. "Ready for what?"

I cocked a brow at her. "To go have sex."

That amusing red flooded her face once more, and her hands clenched tightly in her lap. "I-I—Um—"

Silence filled the space between us. I knew that she was probably wracked with nerves since she was new to sex. So I gave her a second to gather herself. I didn't know what was going through her head, but, even so, I *never* expected her to say, "I don't like it."

The sudden rush of her voice amid the quiet made my ears ring, and maybe that contributed to my confusion when I asked, "Don't like what?"

She chewed on her lip and looked away from me. "Sex. It ... It wasn't good. No offense, but it was awful."

I nearly fell over. My mind stalled out, and I stared at her, frozen in my seat. "Excuse me?"

"I mean, don't get me wrong. What happened before was great. But when you—" she made a jab gesture with her fingers. "That was horrible. I thought you were supposed to be a sex professional or something."

You have got to be shitting me.

My brain couldn't seem to compute what she was saying. I'd never been so offended in my life. And I'd been here for a *millennium.* Awful, sex, and me didn't belong in the same sentence.

"That doesn't count," I argued quickly, trying to defend my Incubus honor. "I was working with false information. I didn't know the full story of what I was dealing with."

She scoffed and buckled her seatbelt. "Sounds like an excuse to me."

I narrowed my eyes. "You know what. Fine. I'll make you eat those words."

She wanted to taunt me and my skill? Challenge fucking accepted.

CHAPTER 9

Iyla

WE PULLED INTO A LONG DRIVEWAY THAT WAS lined with pine trees, which offered a sense of seclusion for the home Zagan was directing me to. Zagan suggested we go back to my apartment, but I quickly dismissed the idea. My mom was known for making unexpected house calls, and it would be just my luck for her to show up while Zagan was in my apartment. Or worse, while he and I were in the middle of having sex. So we came to his place.

"I didn't know you lived in Tennessee," I said as my car crawled along the driveway.

"I didn't before this morning," he replied, the perfect picture of ease—tattooed arms draped over the console and door arm rest, head leaned back on the seat, and his mouth relaxed.

Meanwhile, it felt like a swarm of bees were buzzing around my insides.

"I bought this place before popping into your apartment," he explained. "I was living in New York like the rest of the band, but seeing as how I can only get what I need from you now, I'll be in Tennessee often. So I pulled a couple strings to get this place purchased and ready today."

I glanced at him with both a sense of amazement and envy. It must be nice to have powers or whatever it was that let him make things happen for himself. If I could do that ...

I shook my head to dismiss the thought since there was no point dwelling on something that obviously wasn't going to happen.

We finally emerged from the overhanging trees and into a vast opening. My jaw nearly hit the floor. The house—or rather, the *mansion*—was like something right out of a gothic fantasy.

Black stone and glass made up the towering house. Everything was tall with sharp edges and beautifully dark. Stone steps led to an intricate front door, which had vines carved into the paneling. The right side of the house featured some sort of room that seemed to have walls made of glass, but I drove past it before I could really look to see what was in there.

"This place is amazing," I mused breathlessly. I didn't hesitate to jump out and follow him up the steps. I wanted to see more of what this gorgeous dark home had to offer. "I can't believe you bought this."

Zagan smirked, seemingly pleased with my awe, as he unlocked the door. "Impressed?"

Not wanting to give him the satisfaction of seeing the full extent of my amazement, I tried to school my features and gave a one-shoulder shrug. "Only a little."

He rolled his eyes, but the smirk was still there. He knew I was full of shit.

The door opened, stealing my breath in the same instant. Black floors with dark gray walls, black sconces on the walls, a sweeping chandelier in the entryway, monochrome furnishings. It could've been plucked right from a gothic home magazine, and I marveled at the stunning beauty of it all.

The living room, which could easily fit five of my own, was immediately to my left. Two sets of staircases—one leading down and one going up—separated the living room from a sleek, clean kitchen. Beyond that were sliding glass doors that looked out onto a large body of water with a dock.

Since Zagan had made himself at home in my place earlier, I decided it was my turn. I crept to my right where an arched doorway led into the room made of glass. Seeing the room in all its glory made my heart stop.

I might as well have walked into a grand gothic ballroom. Black and white marble flooring covered the space, and a black fireplace that was taller than me sat against the interior wall. Two black chandeliers dangled from both ends of the room, which was easily the length of a basketball court. The walls were, in fact, made of windows, except for the interior wall that was connected to the main house. The large room was empty, save for one thing that stood in the far corner by the windows, closest to the water out back.

A glossy, black Steinway grand piano.

I swallowed hard, my feet suddenly stuck in place as I stared at my dream instrument. I wanted to run toward it and away from it all at once. It was everything I wanted.

But also everything I knew I couldn't have.

Zagan came around me and looked between me and the piano. "Do you play?"

The sound of his voice lured me out of my own head, and I forced myself to look away from the instrument so that I could find the ability to speak. "No," I answered softly. I gave a final glance at the piano and turned away. "Not anymore."

"Sounds like there's a story there," Zagan murmured as he followed me from the room.

There was a note of curiosity in his voice, one I knew I had to stomp out. I looked over my shoulder with a quirked brow. "Do you want me to tell you a story, or do you want to have sex?"

The moment the question left my lips, I knew my mistake. I was trying to keep him from prying into me and my life, but in doing so, I'd sped up the timeline for what we were actually here for—what I was an anxious ball of emotions over.

His eyes lost their curiosity, taking on a sensual gleam as they raked over me. He pointed ahead of me and ordered in his deep, velvety voice, "Upstairs. Door at the end of the hall."

I swallowed. For some odd reason, having him order me around in that tone made liquid fire spread through my gut and settle between my thighs. It was such a swift and delirious feeling that I wasn't used to, and maybe that's why I obeyed without complaint.

I turned and made my way up the dark steps. The hallways were just as lovely as the floor we left behind with the same black floors, trim, and doors. When I stepped into the room Zagan had directed me to, my insides fluttered. It was a bedroom, most likely his.

It was pretty bare with only a dresser, black chair in the corner by the balcony doors, and the overly large bed. It was kinda criminal how big the bed was. It could easily fit five people.

I'd stopped just beyond the threshold. Zagan's front pressed into my back, and my breath hitched when his hands landed on my hips then slowly traveled across my stomach and up, making my shirt rise with his warm hands.

"We're gonna make up for what happened last time," he vowed against my ear. "This is the first and only time I'll be overly gentle. Understand?"

I tried to keep my breathing under control, but having him this close with his hands gliding up my torso to cup my breasts over my bra was too much.

Yet also, not enough.

My chest rose and fell hard when he pinched my nipples over the fabric of my bra. A groan slipped past my lips, and the sound made him step closer so that I could feel the hard ridge of his cock pressed into my back.

"You know," he said as he grabbed my shoulder, forcing me to turn and face him. He bit the corner of his lip near one of his piercings as he looked me over, still fully clothed. "This situation of ours could actually be fun. You get to learn what you like, and I get to be the one to teach you."

The idea was both nerve-wracking and exhilarating.

It made me feel guilty for being even a little excited, but it also made me feel … free.

He glanced at my chest. "Do you like that shirt?"

I looked down at the blue button-up. "Yeah. It's—"

"Too bad." He reached forward to grip the material, and with a quick yank, he ripped the buttons right out of the holes, sending the small disks scattering across the floor.

I gasped in surprise from both the act and the sudden chill against my bare torso.

He smirked, pulling the ruined material off my arms to discard. "Better."

I opened my mouth to protest his destruction of my clothes, but before I could, his mouth was on mine. Goosebumps broke out along my back as his tongue swept inside, moving with mine. His large hands made quick work of ridding me of my bra—thankfully, without any more ripping.

Though seeing him do that to my shirt had been hotter than I cared to admit.

His hands coasted up either side of my neck, forcing my head to angle just the way he wanted it to deepen the kiss. He walked me backward until the back of my legs hit the bed.

"Lay your pretty ass back on that bed," Zagan ordered against my mouth, nipping my lip once.

I sucked in a sharp breath. I wasn't sure if he meant what he said—calling me pretty—or if it was just for the sake of the mood, but it made a flutter break free deep inside me. I eagerly sat on the edge, looking up at him.

"Pants," he said, pointing at my legs. "Take them off."

I slipped my fingers into my jeans and underwear. As I removed mine, I watched him yank his shirt off. His muscles flexed, and his tattoos stood out against his cream-colored skin. They were just as mesmerizing as the last time I saw them.

When I was naked, I leaned back but kept my legs firmly closed. I was pulsing between my thighs with a hunger unlike any other kind, but that didn't mean I wasn't still a nervous wreck for what was to come.

Zagan smirked. He rested his palms on my ankles and slowly trailed them up my legs. Delicious goosebumps broke out on my skin, and my eyes fluttered at the intoxicating feel of his hands on my bare skin.

"Feeling shy now? We can't have that." His hands traveled over my knees and along my inner thighs, spreading my legs apart as they went. The heat swirling in his gaze intensified, and he licked his pierced lips. "So beautiful. So wet. Does your pussy like being told what to do?"

My mouth dried, and I squirmed under the lure of his gaze. I was so needy between my legs, and just having his eyes on me felt like the slightest brush against my core. My hips shifted on their own accord, restless and greedy. I needed more.

I needed him.

"Answer me," he hissed, his voice turning firm.

My pussy throbbed with the order, and my nipples hardened. Judging by the enjoyment creeping into the corners of his eyes, he seemed to notice the effect of his demands for himself, so there was no point in denying it.

"Yes," I answered breathlessly. "I like it."

"Are you excited to find out what else you like?" he asked, undoing his jeans and shucking them and his briefs.

My eyes were transfixed on his hard length. I didn't have any previous experience to compare him to, but even without that, I just knew Zagan was well-endowed. Sand weighed down my tongue, and the breath I'd been taking froze in my chest.

Finally, I managed to sputter, "I—I'm excited."

"I bet you are," he said with a lustful look at my bare center. "Now be a good girl and hold those lips open for me while I eat your cunt."

The husky order had me complying without a moment's hesitation. I reached my hands down my stomach and to my middle where I spread my folds open so that I bore even more of myself to him.

He groaned and immediately knelt over me and got to work. His tongue coasted up from my entrance to my clit, and my heels dug into the mattress with the immediate rush of pleasure. My head fell back as I gasped, but as soon as I did, he stopped.

I was on fire and aching for his touch, so with the sudden loss of it, I lifted my head again to look at him.

"Eyes on me, Sparrow. I want you to watch as I devour every last drop of the orgasm you're about to have."

I kept my head raised, straining to keep it upright as he'd demanded. His face hovered above my fingers, which still held myself open. He smirked and blew out a chuckle. The warmth of his breath hitting my wet, sensitive clit made my legs shake with a fierce need to *feel* something.

"Please," I begged, unable to keep the plea from my voice.

The whimper seemed to light a fire inside him. He started placing soft kisses on my fingers and licking off the moisture that had gathered on them from how turned on I was. "Say my name."

I tried to control my already ragged breathing. "Zagan."

His tongue swirled over my pounding clit, and electrifying heat coursed through my entire being. "Again," he hissed with another flick of his tongue.

"Zagan!" I gasped. Sweat already beaded the back of my neck, both from my muscles straining to hold my position and from aching for his touch.

"Say my name when you cum," he commanded.

I watched from hooded eyes as Zagan's mouth and tongue worked on my clit. My legs shook on either side of his head as sparks ricocheted between my thighs, swirling all throughout me. My moans came out breathy and hungry, and they only got louder when two fingers plunged inside me.

His name left my lips on a groan, and I tried to keep my head up and eyes open to watch like he'd told me to.

Even with my limited view, I could see the satisfied smile on his face as his tongue and digits coaxed me closer and closer to that sweet, blissful place. His blue eyes held mine over the hood of my pussy while his tongue flicked and swirled in just the right spot, and his fingers curled to rub inside me. The mixture was too great, and with his eyes firmly fixed on my face, I detonated.

"Zagan!" I practically screamed as my entire body shook with the release. I finally collapsed onto my back and let my hands fall to my sides.

"Goddamn, you taste good," he growled, getting to his knees between my legs and resting back on his heels.

He slid his hands under my thighs and gripped them, yanking me forward. I gasped, and as I watched him line up with my entrance, trepidation tried to replace the high of the orgasm. He didn't give it time to take over, though. With an ease unlike last time, he rubbed the head of his cock through the wetness in my folds and used that to help himself push inside me.

I fisted the sheets beneath me at the burn that came with the stretch, and I gritted my teeth as he pushed deeper. The sting wasn't as bad as the pain from before, and after a few more seconds of him slowly sliding in, he finally grinned down at me and praised, "Good girl. You took me all in. Now I'm gonna reward you."

He kept his firm hold on my thighs with my legs draped over his arms, and he sat up higher as he withdrew to just the tip before plunging back in. My back bowed with the spine-tingling sensation. The burn of fullness had basically subsided, and now all I felt was breathless, warm, and electrified. Each hard thrust of his hips sent my mind scattering.

I couldn't believe I ever thought he was bad at this.

I moaned and curled my toes as the pleasure spiraling in my center built up all over again.

"Oh, Zagan," I cried. "Zagan, I'm—I'm—"

I couldn't find words. I couldn't even think past how amazing I felt with his large, hard dick plunging in and out of me, reaching spots I'd never even known were there.

"That's it," Zagan sang. "Lose yourself to it, baby. Lose yourself to pleasure and sin with me."

This orgasm hit me hard, traveling over my entire body. I threw my head back and screamed with the intensity of it. Stars burst behind my closed eyelids, and if he didn't still have my legs hooked around his arms, they would've fallen like limp, useless noodles.

My brain was fried, but through the haze of it all, I was amazed. Who knew there was something that felt this good out there? To think I'd been missing these experiences all this time.

Zagan's hips didn't stop as he worked for his own release now. He inhaled deeply as he stared down at me, and when he smirked, his eyes seemed to briefly change to their black with red slits. It was there and gone so quickly, I wasn't sure if it was just my post-orgasm imagination or not.

"The way your pleasure tastes ..." Zagan growled, watching me like he was mesmerized. "It's been awhile since I've tasted sex this good."

The grip of ecstasy still had me firmly in its hold with his cock continuing to drive into me. Maybe it was because I was under its spell that I asked breathlessly, "What does it taste like?"

His hips drove in harder, and he angled himself so that he seemed to hit me even deeper. My mouth fell open with another slew of moans, and the pulsing ache between my thighs was nearing a crescendo once more.

"Your pleasure tastes …" He seemed to consider it while his eyes traced over my naked flesh. "Like sunshine on a hillside. Warm. Sweet. Refreshing. Freeing. You taste as close to heaven as a demon like me will ever get."

His words brought me to that peak all over again, and this time, he fell with me. He grunted as he slammed into me once then twice, spilling himself inside me as he did.

He pulled out with a wet pop, and he released my legs to fall back onto the mattress. He sat next to me as he caught his breath while I was basically an empty husk lying there. It felt like my very soul had left my body behind with the dizzying rush of sexual bliss.

He leaned back on his hands and stared down at me with a satisfied grin. "Still think I'm bad at it?"

I fought to regain control of my own breathing and tried to think of something witty to say back. I was too jumbled in the head right now, so instead, I went for honesty. "No. You proved me wrong."

My head fell to the side, allowing me to look my fill of Zagan. The muscles on his tattooed arms stood out as he leaned back on them, and I found myself tracing the beautiful snake up his arm. My eyes moved to the ink on his defined chest and down his chiseled abdomen until my gaze rested on his glistening, still hard cock.

Which I realized with a cold dose of reality was bare.

No condom.

"No, no, no," I said with a sudden rush of alarm. I started to sit up, my eyes locked on his shaft. "You didn't wear a condom."

"Woah," he said, placing a hand on my shoulder to keep me from sitting up. He looked at me like I'd just sprouted a second head. "We don't need a condom. Incubi can't reproduce. I can't get you pregnant. We also can't get or pass STDs." His shit-eating grin came back. "We come with all the perks of sex and none of the consequences."

His smile slipped, and he pursed his lips. "Well, clearly there are *some* consequences." He gave me a pointed look. "Seeing as how *we're* stuck with each other. That little inconvenience and broken hearts are the only consequences. We leave a lot of those in our wake."

The news made me fall onto my back again. I stared up at the ceiling, overcome with a sense of reassurance. It was fine. I was fine. He didn't and *couldn't* get me pregnant. My eyes closed in relief as I let the news settle my worries. The warmth from the handful of orgasms I'd just had found me again, and I held onto that in an effort to not think about all the rules I'd broken in the past two days.

I was still a good girl.

Dirty, my mother's voice hissed in the back of my mind.

I was still a good daughter.

Disobedient, my mother's voice snapped.

I was … I was …

A mistake.

CHAPTER 10

Zagan

THE MUSIC GUIDED EVERY QUICK STEP OF MY FEET, every movement of my body, and every motion of my arms. It was K-Pop month at the dance studio I volunteered at in New York, so I was down in the dance studio of my new house, putting on the last minute touches to the choreography for the song we were working on—"Cake" by KARD. The teachers and I always put together choreography that used moves from the actual group's routines but had our own touches thrown in.

After only one round earlier, Iyla seemed pensive, and before I could even make a move to start round two, she'd fallen asleep. I let it slide, because the one round managed to refuel me more than it typically would've. Her pleasure was so profound that it managed to get rid of any hunger that had been lingering in my gut. And the taste? Fuck. I really couldn't remember having someone who's essence tasted as amazing as hers. It was still kinda blowing my mind that I'd managed to stumble upon her *and* get bound. She was basically like a delicacy to an Incubus like me.

This might not be so bad, I thought with a smirk as I finished up the dance, facing my reflection in the wall of mirrors. That's when I noticed Iyla in the reflection, lingering in the doorway.

Catching my breath after running through the dance a few times, I turned to face her. "Look who finally woke up. You exploring?"

Her eyes were slightly wide, and she gestured behind her. "You have a recording studio in your house."

I raised a brow and rested my hands on my hips as my heart rate started to come back down. "Uh-huh."

She waved her hand at the room we were in now. "And a dance studio."

I shrugged like it was no big deal, and really, for me, it wasn't. The house didn't come with either studio, but that meant nothing for a demon who could have a lot of things at the snap of their fingers.

"I teach a lot of hip-hop classes," I explained, looking around the newly made room. "I also like to dance for stress relief, so having my own studio is convenient."

I glanced down the hallway where my new recording studio was—the studio I hadn't even stepped foot in yet. Because while dance was a way for me to relieve stress, it was also my method of escape from my problems. Right now, that studio—or rather, what I needed to do *in* the studio—was my problem.

I grabbed my water and downed half of it, still looking past her head at the dark room at the other end of the hall. "I'm supposed to be in the music room writing our new song, but ..."

But everything I write these days is garbage.

"You guys write your own music?" she asked with the hint of interest that she typically tried to hide when talking to me.

I drew closer to her and leaned my shoulder against the wall. "You didn't know that? That's pretty common knowledge among our fans. And there's no 'we.' *I* write the music."

Iyla tilted her chin up higher, making her dark hair slip over her shoulder. She took on a defiant, almost cocky purse of her lips.

"I'm not a fan." She winced in a fleeting apology and added, "No offense." She cleared her throat, looking confident once more. "I didn't know who you guys were until last night. Nahla's the fan. I was just along for the ride."

I ran my tongue over one of my lips rings in annoyance and shook my head, mumbling, "Well, that explains a lot. You were very ... *different* from our fan base."

I'd thought her hesitant, almost timid nature was a sort of act. A charade of sorts to come off mysterious or something. Now, like a fucking moron, I realized she genuinely was those things. Unsure. Inexperienced. Stiff.

But also hungry for life.

Iyla's brow plunged in defiance, and she crossed her arms defensively. "Why? Because I don't sleep around? Because I don't party?"

"Because you're afraid to be who you want," I answered calmly, simply stating the facts as I'd observed them. I'd been around plenty long enough to know a lost soul when I saw one. "It's obvious you're letting the world or someone in it dictate your life and what you do with it. Maybe a parent. A religion. An ideal you were brought up with. Whichever the case may be, our fans are typically free, for lack of a better word. Those things don't hold them back from living life anymore."

The indignation had slipped from her face. Now, her pinched brown eyes held mine, and she looked as if I'd just reached across the space between us and punched her in the gut. She swallowed and whispered, "I'm free."

"Not from where I'm standing. You may be bound to me, Sparrow, but that doesn't compare to the chains something else has wrapped around you. You're ruled by another's standards and desires, not your own. Hell, I doubt you truly know who you are, because you're too busy living life for someone else to even find out."

Her mouth tightened, and she shook her head. "You're wrong."

She spun on her heel and left the way she came, and we both knew what her retreat meant.

I was right.

I LET OUT AN ANGRY ROAR AND LIT THE SHEET MUSIC IN my hands on fire. I didn't even bat an eye when the black ash hit the carpet of my brand new studio.

Everything was shit.

The notes? Shit.

The lyrics? Shit.

It was all the same damn thing I always sang about these days, and we were all getting tired of it. I had to come up with something new and fresh to give our fans a reason to keep listening to what we had to say.

"Damn, I like what you've done with the place."

I looked up at the sound of Dante's voice. He, Perseus, Xander, and Coldin filed into the lounge part of the studio where I was currently sitting on the edge of the red U-shaped couch, elbows on my knees, glowering at the ash at my feet.

"What are you guys doing here?" I asked with a heavy sigh.

"We came to see what your new place was like," Xander answered, scanning the room. Just having him here added to the churning sea of rage inside me.

He wore an annoying bright green shirt that made me think of toxic waste from some bad sci-fi film and checkerboard pants. He had Coldin's drum sticks resting between his ears and skull for some damn reason, as if they were an accessory and nothing more.

Xander flashed me a teasing grin after his perusal and added, "Since, you know, our lead heart-breaker got himself tied down here. Nice going, by the way."

"Shut up," I gritted out, trying to ignore the urge to set him on fire where he stood.

"Yeah," Perseus said, dropping onto one end of the couch and making himself right at home. His golden hair fell across his forehead, and he brushed it back into place with his heavily ringed fingers. He pinned Xander in place with his jade-green eyes. "It could've happened to any Incubus. We've been careless these days, not ensuring our partners aren't virgins. Let's take what happened to Zagan as a sign that we can't let our guards down."

Xander didn't take being bonded seriously since he didn't understand what it meant to be bound. To him, it was a joke. But then again, everything was a joke to him. That was the reality for most Mischiefs, demons who existed solely for the antics and fun of chaos. They thrived on pulling jokes, causing a commotion, and being careless. Some of them were alright to be around because they *did* know how to have fun, but the majority of them were just headaches.

Xander was in the latter of the two.

He was also the only one here who didn't have to worry about getting chained to someone from a bond like an Incubi or Succubi did. He didn't have to worry about living his life in the dark pits of Hell, only coming out into the light of day when on a job like Coldin did.

I glanced at our ever quiet drummer, taking note of his closed eyes, crossed tattooed arms, his forever straight mouth with a labret lip ring, and wavy brown hair tousled on top of his head. Coldin leaned against the wall closest to the doorway like he was ready to leave even though they'd just gotten here.

Out of all demons, his kind was the worst of us all. He was a Letum, and just the title alone made my blood run cold. They were a dangerous breed, even among other demons, and because of their drive to kill anything and everything, they were kept under constant lock and key in Hell, only being brought out when they were assigned to a task.

Humans believed the thick black bands of ink on his wrists were simple tattoos, but they were a sign of why he was here, why he was allowed to roam freely right now. Unlike my black collar that faded into my skin, his mark was always visible. It served as a warning and sign for any who found themselves face to face with him.

Run.

Coldin had always been pleasant enough to us when we passed him in his cell in Hell—never yelling profanities at us or making threats to disembowel us like the other Letums—and I'd heard him drumming listlessly on the stone walls of his prison. So when we formed a band, we took pity on the quiet demon.

We struck a contract—a job—with him, allowing him to run around the human world with us as our drummer, but he had to act as humanly as possible. The contract kept him in check, which meant he couldn't go around killing people at the drop of a hat. Still, we let him have his fun every so often since his contract only permitted him to kill once a month and when we gave him permission. The guy was only demon. We didn't feel right, not allowing him his monthly kill, and it was only when his hands and teeth were smeared in blood that he ever smiled.

But that was to be expected of a Letum. They were killers.

"Yes, yes, keep your guards up," Xander chuckled, and I turned to look at him again. "Wouldn't want to have only one partner for the next 70 years or however long the bitch lives." Xander met my gaze with a smirk. "I hope you like the taste of her pleasure since she's all you get for the foreseeable future."

Coldin's eyes opened then, and the human green that he usually wore as a disguise burned away into an endless black with vivid orange flames roaring in the void. "I can kill her for you."

I held my hand up, my stomach bottoming out with those eyes

focused on me. "No need, Coldin. She and I have an arrangement that's working for now. Plus, we don't want another suspicious disappearance associated with us. We all know how much riskier it is to kill off humans these days with cameras everywhere and shit. If things change, though, I'll let you know."

Coldin sneered, and slowly, the black and orange flames in his eyes swirled and changed back to green.

I rubbed my forehead, getting more annoyed with everything. My lack of inspiration. My new bond. Xander's forever irritating personality. I was over it all. "If you guys have seen the house, you can leave the same way you came."

"Zagan," Dante said, sitting next to me on the couch. He clapped a dark hand on my shoulder. "That's not all we're here for, man."

I glared at him. "I know what you're really here for. The song isn't ready."

"Clearly," Coldin said, staring blandly at the ash on the ground.

"Leo wanted us to talk to you as your fellow bandmates," Dante said.

Bandmates. Because none of us were actually friends. Demons didn't have those, or rather, we didn't really understand them. Still, out of everyone here, I was admittedly closest with Dante and Perseus. Maybe that was because we were the only Incubi in the group, so we understood each other. Xander and Coldin joined us in our sexual exploits, because what idiot wouldn't, but they didn't *need* sex like the three of us did. It was that sort of understanding that let the three of us get as close as non-friends could be. It was also the only thing that kept me from ripping Dante's arm out of its socket for touching my damn shoulder.

"We're not trying to rush you," Dante continued, "but we need at least one new song. It's been six months since we've put out anything new. We can't keep performing the same shit. Our fans are loyal as fuck, but we can't gain *more* fans or hold onto the hype without something new."

"You think I don't know that?" I growled before heaving a defeated sigh. "I've been trying, but nothing I write is good these days."

"Says who?" Perseus asked. "You haven't even played anything for us."

"Nothing's been *good enough* to even bother showing you."

"Zagan," Dante said, squeezing my shoulder. His dark eyes stared right into mine like he was imploring me to listen. "It doesn't need to be ground breaking. It doesn't need to be anything but a song that people can enjoy listening to. Stop overthinking and write something."

Yeah, cause it was that easy to just "write something." I didn't half-ass shit. If I was writing a song, I wanted every single one to be my new best. Expectations for myself were already high, and they just seemed to get harder and harder to meet. How could I continue to outdo myself? At some point, there had to be a cap. At least, that's what everyone else here seemed to believe. They thought we'd given our best songs and now just needed to put out stuff that entertained. Not touched minds. Not spoke to the inner human soul. Just *entertained*.

That wasn't good enough for me. Not when music was every-thing to me. Not when my songs were my mark on this world. Incubi were low ranking demons, and the odds of us having any profound impact on lives was wishful thinking.

I was made to seduce. To fuck. To corrupt people into sinning and doing wicked deeds, all in an effort to lure them to "the dark side."

At least, that's what people liked to think of demons. In reality, we were just here for the balance system, to give the impression of right versus wrong, good versus evil, light versus dark. We were the ones who got slapped with the label of "evil" in the coin toss between the higher ups, so that's what we embraced.

Debauchery.

Chaos.

Living.

I personally didn't care much about the whole saints and sinners bullshit. It wasn't important to Incubi and Succubi. We were just tools, kind of like a gateway demon, to aid Hell in meeting their souls quota. Once a human got involved with us, other demons followed, swooping in and drawing them into our darkness. And humans *loved* it.

After all, people had more fun in the dark.

"Babette's been asking about you," Perseus hedged slowly, breaking the tense silence and flicking at the upholstery of the couch. His eyes refused to meet mine, and for good reason. He knew he'd find me glaring at him just for mentioning the Bargainer demon's name.

"If you're about to suggest I make a deal with that Bargainer demon, you're fucking insane," I bit out through clenched teeth.

Babette. She was a Bargainer demon, and I didn't fuck with Bargainer demons. They were sly, deceiving little shits, and that particular one had been breathing down my neck about showing her a good time for centuries. I didn't refuse many partners—especially ones that were as gorgeous as that curvy red-head—but I always refused her. Nothing good could come from getting involved with the likes of her, and Perseus knew this.

His green eyes met mine again, and he shrugged. "She could help with whatever is going on with you. You've been off for a while as far as our music goes. Just make a little bargain with her. She can fix whatever the issue is, and we know all she'll want in return is *you*."

Perseus's suggestion just made the coiled ball of frustration grow inside me. Not only could I not be with Babette the way *she'd* want due to my being bound to Iyla now, but more than that, I just didn't want to make a deal with her. I wanted to fix my issues *my* way. Music was my world. I wasn't about to take some goddamn shortcut to deal with it.

Dante grabbed some blank music sheets and handed them to me. He jabbed his finger at them and ordered, "Forget what Perseus said. Getting back in your zone isn't worth becoming a sex slave to that woman. Just write something, and don't fucking burn it this time. Let us see it first. We'll go from there. Okay?"

I stared at the empty page as they finally left, and I waited to feel the spark of excitement that used to fill me when faced with the chance to make something new, to litter a blank page with notes and lyrics. But that rush never came. I stayed as empty inside as the page in my hands.

CHAPTER 11

Iyla

ASSHAT," I MUTTERED, GRIPPING THE STEERING WHEEL tightly. "I know who I am."

Liar, my inner voice whispered.

I ignored that voice. I *did* know who I was. Or rather, I knew who I *wanted* to be. I knew ... who I *couldn't* be.

The thought only served to spike my annoyance, because I didn't want Zagan to be right. I didn't want this stranger knowing how to read me so easily. He didn't know me. He didn't know anything.

Except how to use his body and yours.

My cheeks heated, and I squeezed my legs together. This was the longest drive home ever. I couldn't stop thinking about the demon, his last words to me before I left, or the amazing sex we had. The silence in the car didn't typically bother me since I was used to it, but the silence tonight only made my thoughts *louder*. I'd never been so happy to pull into my apartment parking lot as I was right then.

Until I saw the white BMW waiting next to where I always parked.

My stomach sank, and a fine layer of sweat immediately broke out on my neck. The pink sky gave way into night. I didn't know how long my mom had been here, but I knew I was going to be interrogated about why I was out so late. I quickly looked at my reflection, praying I didn't look like someone who'd just been thoroughly fucked and satiated.

As soon as I got out of my car, Mom got out of hers. I held my breath and rounded the front of my car, meeting Mom on the sidewalk.

"I thought you were at home studying," she hissed immediately.

"I was," I lied, hoisting my bag higher onto my shoulder. "I mean, I *am*. I just went to the campus library for a bit. A study group was meeting, so I thought I'd go and join. You know, bounce points around with other students and discuss the upcoming exam."

Mom narrowed her eyes. "I see. How did it go? Was it helpful?"

I nodded, hoping my voice didn't give away my nerves. "I think so, yes." I glanced at her car then her. "What brings you here?"

"Not that it's any of your business, but I was grabbing coffee with a colleague. When I drove by, I saw your car was gone, and when I tried tracking your phone, it didn't pull anything up. So I decided to wait here."

I was so glad I'd had the foresight to turn my phone off out of fear that she'd do exactly what she'd done—track it. I would've had no idea how to explain why I was at a random mansion in the middle of the woods.

"Oh, sorry," I said. "My phone died, and I forgot my charger here."

Mom huffed and rubbed her forehead. "You're an adult now, Iyla. Please be more responsible, and keep your phone charged, especially if you're leaving home."

My mouth dried at the sound of her disappointment. It was a tone I'd gotten used to over the years, but that didn't make hearing it now any easier. Part of me wanted to ask her if her demand was because she truly cared for my safety or if it was because she wanted access to me and what I was doing at all times—to see if she had more reasons to be disappointed in me.

"Yes, ma'am," I said quietly. "I'm sorry."

Her hazel eyes met mine, and for a moment, we just stared at each other. I wondered what she saw when she looked at me. Did she see a daughter who tried her hardest from her waking moment to her last, or a daughter that constantly failed her wishes? All I'd ever wanted was to be someone she was proud of, someone she could love. The more I chased her acceptance though, the more I wondered if I'd ever be good enough for Valerie Winters.

How much longer did I have to breathe for her? How much longer did I have to carry the weight of her demands? How much longer did I have to kill off pieces of myself to have her finally look at me and smile?

"I know midterms are coming up for you," Mom started cautiously, like she already regretted saying whatever was about to come. "If you do well on them, I'll take you out to celebrate."

My heart lurched in my chest, and it took every ounce of strength inside of me not to squeal and bounce up and down right there on the spot. I had to be dreaming. "Really?"

She nodded and opened her phone. "I'll add it to my schedule, so you better do well. You know how I hate for appointments to be canceled after I've made the time for them."

I bit my lip to fight my smile. "Yes, ma'am. Thank you. I won't let you down."

Her sharp eyes raked over me, her nose ever so slightly scrunched in annoyance. The sight didn't even bother me for once. I was far too excited at the prospect of sharing a celebratory moment with my mom.

She gestured her manicured hand at the apartment building, which we still stood in front of. "Get inside and get to work."

I didn't hesitate. I made my way inside while she went to her car. There was a pep in my step that hadn't been there before, and a new fire burned to life inside me. I had to do well on these exams, not that I ever doubted that I would've, even without this extra dose of encouragement. I just couldn't believe it. Mom actually wanted to take me out. I couldn't remember the last time she and I spent time together like that.

It gave me hope that things were changing for us. All the chasing I'd done had paid off. She was finally seeing me as a valuable person in her life that she wanted to have around. It sent my heart sailing high over the stars and the moon.

As soon as I got into my apartment, I got to work. I sat at the kitchen island with my notes and textbooks in front of me, reading the material, re-watching lectures, and making myself practice exams. It didn't take long for the embers of determination to slowly die out, because there wasn't anything more for me to study or work on.

As much as Nahla made fun of me for it, my time truly was spent doing nothing but school stuff. I went to class, reviewed lectures between classes, ate, did homework, studied, slept, and repeated. That was my life, seven days a week. So as I stared at all the papers spread out on my island, I realized there was nothing for me to actually do. I knew the material already. I was just re-reading and re-listening to stuff I'd already mastered, and because of that, my attention drifted to the one place it shouldn't.

Zagan.

It still baffled me that I'd gotten myself mixed up with him for two glaring reasons: he was a literal spawn of Hell, and he was a famous singer.

I should've had a greater chance of being struck by lightning while inside a rubber ball than I did of getting demonically bound to him.

Yet here I was.

I thought back to last night's concert, which was, admittedly, a blast. The entire energy of the place was like nothing I'd ever experienced, and their music had been catchy and sexy. Before I knew what I was doing, I had opened a new window on my laptop and googled Sinners Do It Better.

The first thing I watched was a live performance of one of their songs. It was just as amazing to watch on video as it had been to see in person. Their stage presence, the way they commanded their instruments, the way they drew the audience in so you couldn't look away even after the song had ended. It was everything, and I was suddenly invested.

Another video of a different song played after the one ended, and after that was over, I binged a thirteen minute interview of them talking about their newest album. There were Q&A videos, compilations fans had made of sexy moments for each band member, and videos from late night talk show hosts. I watched them all.

Eventually, I even stumbled upon videos of Zagan dancing with a New York Dance Studio, and *those* did something wickedly hot to my insides. The way he moved and danced was mouth-watering. My heart started pounding, my lips dried, and my pussy began to throb. That was my sign that I'd seen enough.

I closed the videos and shut my laptop, glancing at the time. I nearly fell out of my seat. I'd been watching videos of Zagan and Sinners Do It Better for *three hours*.

I'd never wasted time like that, and I mentally slapped myself for letting myself get distracted. It was so unlike me, and that knowledge made a brick form in my gut. If I wasn't careful, Zagan could distract me from my goals—healing Gemma, getting into law school, and working at my mom's law firm.

Because they were *my* goals. All of them, even the law school and future career as an attorney. I wanted those things, regardless of the reasoning behind them. It didn't matter if it was just to make Mom proud of me. My path had been decided, and I couldn't be shaken from it.

Especially not by some hot sex demon.

Friday rolled around, and I'd almost managed to push Zagan out of my mind. The demon hadn't shown up at my apartment the entire week—I guessed demons didn't eat multiple times a day like humans—and not having to see him made things feel almost normal again. My days consisted of school, and after my only Friday morning class, I returned home, ready for the weekend, but even more ready for my weekly visit with Gemma.

Plopping down onto a kitchen stool, I went to call Mom when I got a text from an unknown number.

?: Let's fuck.

I reread the text in shock and finally scoffed, ignoring the message. I dialed Mom and waited until her business-like voice picked up.

"Hey, Mom," I said. "I'm home from class. Are you on your way to get me?"

Her sigh pierced my ear. "We aren't going today. I've got far too much work to do."

My lips opened, but no sound came out. The excitement in my chest slowly dissipated like smoke on a passing breeze. "But Gemma—"

"Understands how hard her mother works," Mom snapped. "Do not try to make me feel bad about this. She knows I'd be there if I could. I have to go."

The call ended.

I wanted to scream, cry, and throw my phone. Gemma was *sick*. She already didn't get to live with us. Seeing us and us seeing her was so important for all of us. My blood boiled with rage as the need to shake my mom and tell her that her work could be ignored for an hour every week took over. I knew she loved Gemma, but part of me worried that she loved her career more.

My phone pinged with another text from the unknown number.

> ?: So is she the one who dictates what happens with your life? She sounded intense.

"What the—" I mumbled before another text immediately followed it.

The air in my lungs stilled. It was a photo of me talking on the phone while sitting on the barstool.

From *right now*.

From the direction of *my* couch.

I whipped around and found Zagan leaned back on my couch, one arm draped over the back, his legs spread in a picture of ease, and his thumb hovering over an open message thread on his phone.

His blue eyes found mine. "You didn't respond to my text, so I decided to pop in."

I clutched my chest where my heart tried to regain a normal rhythm. "Are you crazy? How long have you been here?"

"Since the moment you got here."

My jaw fell open. "W-What? So you were here even when you texted me?"

He nodded shamelessly. "I was waiting in the shadows. I gave you a chance to text back, and if you did, I was going to knock on the door like a normal person. But you ignored my text, so here we are."

My mind sputtered to keep up with his nonsense. "How did you even get my number?"

He snorted and stood. My eyes tracked his every movement as he walked toward me. "Have you forgotten who, or rather, *what*, you're dealing with?"

I guessed it was a stupid question. He could get to my apartment with a simple *poof*. Finding my phone number was probably nothing. Still, seeing him here after nearly a week of silence startled me. I wasn't used to all this magic or whatever it was.

I realized then what his last text said, the one before the photo, and embarrassment coated my insides. I tucked some hair behind my ear and avoided looking at him as I asked, "Did you hear my phone call?"

"I did," he answered without hesitation. "Your mom sounds like a real peach."

Heat swept up my cheeks, and shame filled me to the brim. I felt like a little elementary school girl getting scolded by her Mom in front of a friend. It was mortifying, especially since she and I already had such a tedious relationship. He'd just gotten a small peek at a private conversation that I didn't want *anyone* hearing, especially a stranger like him.

"Don't pop in unannounced anymore," I said finally, gathering the courage to meet his gaze once more. "*Or* hide in the shadows of my home like they're your own personal viewing station."

He shrugged. "Won't make any promises."

Of course he wouldn't.

Even though I was irritated with his sudden presence, it came at a good time. I didn't care if Mom wasn't coming. I could still go see Gemma, and Zagan could tag along to give her another dose of his blood.

"Gemma is probably expecting me and Mom," I said, looking over his black pants and button-up shirt. Desire suddenly swirled deep inside me, because he looked *good* in a button-up. I stomped that feeling down as I finished, "I'm sure she won't mind if it's you that shows up with me instead."

He frowned. "Can I eat first?"

I held my head higher with my hands on my hips. "You've had all week to do that. If you were hungry, you should've come sooner. I'm not making Gemma wait just because you like starving yourself."

His eyes widened at my defiance. "I've been in New York this week doing interviews and dance classes and *work*. I just got back."

"Still your fault."

He stared at me for a solid minute like I'd lost my mind before a smirk slowly formed on his pierced lips. "If I didn't know better, I'd say someone sounds a bit upset that I didn't come to eat. Feeling a wee bit neglected, Iyla? You miss having me between your legs already?"

It was my turn to look at him like he'd lost *his* mind. I was *not* bothered by his silence this past week, nor did I miss what we'd done.

At least, not too much.

But I'd never admit that to him.

Instead, I brushed past him and said, "Let's go before your ego gets too big to fit inside my apartment."

He chuckled but followed obediently. The fifteen-minute drive to Bloomings went by surprisingly fast with Zagan's control of the radio. I typically drove in silence, but Zagan was insistent upon having music. At some point, one of *his* songs came on, and it was one I recognized from the rabbit hole I'd gone down that night I'd wasted three hours of my life. The moment it started playing, he switched to a different channel.

"Why'd you change it?" I asked, glancing sideways at him.

He stared out his window with his cheek pressed into his fist. "No reason."

I bounced my eyes between the road and him, and I noticed he seemed a bit more tense than when I'd last seen him. Like he was stressed or something. I considered prying, but I thought better of it. It wasn't like we were friends.

We pulled into Bloomings and made our way inside. My legs

carried me a bit faster than usual, but I couldn't seem to stop myself. My heart pounded as I thought about what improvement I might see in Gemma after her first taste of Zagan's blood. I knew I was probably getting my hopes up, but logic didn't exist when hope burned brightly.

I reached Gemma's room and stopped outside. Looking over my shoulder at Zagan, I whispered, "Wait here for a second."

Gemma sat cozied up in her bed, flipping through a book. Just the sight of her made all the edginess seep out of my shoulders and made the air come easier in my lungs.

"Whatcha got there?" I asked from the doorway.

She looked up then, and her face brightened like this room's very own sun. "Iyla! You're here!"

"Of course I am," I said, going to sit on the edge of her bed. I took her small—and noticeably cold—hands in mine. "I wouldn't miss our visits for the world."

She glanced behind me, and her smile cracked some. "Where's Mom?"

I dropped my eyes, and my stomach soured. I hated having to tell her that her own mother was too busy to come see her. "She couldn't make it today." I met her sad eyes and forced enthusiasm back into my voice. "But I brought someone else with me."

I held up a finger for her to wait a second and went back out into the hall where Zagan was being ambushed for autographs by patients and staff, including the group of girls who'd spotted us the last time. I fought off a sigh. I was clearly going to have to start making him wear a disguise when we came.

He noticed me peering out and excused himself. When he reached me, he whispered, "Who knew I had so many fans here?"

"I think it's gotten worse since your visit last week," I hissed. "Next thing you know, they'll have posters of your face hanging over all the murals."

He smirked. "That would definitely be an upgrade."

I rolled my eyes and pulled him with me into Gemma's room. I'd thought she'd been happy to see me, but that had nothing on her reaction to Zagan. It made me want to rip all of his beautiful black hair out just from spite.

"Zagan! Oh my gosh! You really came back to see me!" Gemma squealed.

Zagan's mouth tipped up in a warm smile, and he crossed the room to sit in the chair next to her bed. "Good morning, beautiful. You having a good day so far?"

She giggled and looked up at me to whisper, "He thinks I'm beautiful."

I couldn't fight my grin, my previous annoyance with the super-star now gone. "That's because you *are*." I swiped the tip of her nose with my finger.

The two of them started talking about the book she was read-ing—a middle grade fantasy about dragons. It was almost like the two forgot I was there, but that was fine. It gave me a chance to look Gemma over without her noticing my worried gaze.

Her hair was just as dull and thin as it had been the last time I saw her. There was no new shine to it, nor any sign of restored health. Her complexion remained pale, and her little lips were chapped with a fresh split on the corner of her bottom lip. Instead of being up and full of energy, she was lying in bed, piled with two blankets, a flannel dress, and a robe.

I bit the inside of my lip to keep from crying in defeat. I knew it was going to take time for her to get better. Zagan had said it would take multiple doses. Still, not seeing any evidence of progress, even of the slightest kind, broke me a little inside.

"I'll be right back," I said to Gemma, interrupting their discus-sion of what their dream dragons would look like. "I'm gonna go talk to Dr. Seward real quick."

"Hurry back," Gemma chirped.

"Yeah, you still haven't given your input on your dream dragon," Zagan complained, and I could see how hard he fought his teasing smirk.

I ignored him and left in search of Dr. Seward. He was in his office, looking at some papers. When I knocked on the doorframe, he looked up at me. "Ahh, Iyla. Hello."

"I'm sorry to bother you," I said, fidgeting in the doorway. "I don't want to take up your time. I was just popping in to see if there were any updates from this past week."

He gave me an understanding smile, one he'd no doubt practiced over his many years of dealing with families of sick patients. "Her condition has been more or less the same. I know it's frustrating not to have definitive answers. Illnesses that you can't see with the naked eye and work directly on can be especially hard. But Gemma's strong. She's a fighter. I promise to let you and your mother know anytime we get new results or her condition changes in either direction."

His words were meant to comfort, but they were just a reminder that we were still in limbo.

We were still in this place of waiting to see why Gemma's own body was poisoning her.

We were still waiting to see if she'd decline or improve.

We were still waiting on Mom to make time for us.

Always waiting.

CHAPTER 12

Iyla

I HATE THAT SHE'S NOT ANY BETTER," I SAID AS ZAGAN and I climbed into my car.

Gemma got tired after about two hours of visiting, so Zagan and I left to let her rest, but not before he slipped a drop of blood in her drink while I distracted her.

"It's not even been a full week since she's had my blood," Zagan offered. "It's going to take time. You knew that."

He was right. I knew that, but the bite of disappointment remained strong. I just wanted my sister to get better.

"I know you're bummed," Zagan started slowly. "But it's Friday, the day of the week where you're supposed to forget your worries and enjoy yourself. So tell me, dear Iyla. What will you be doing this fine evening?"

I started my car and shrugged. "Same thing as always. Studying. Homework. When that runs out, I'll find more school work to busy myself with."

The car fell eerily quiet, and I looked over at the demon to see why he'd suddenly stopped talking. He stared at me like I'd lost my mind.

"What?" I asked warily.

"Why is it that every time we talk about fun, your mind always goes to school?"

"Because that's what my life consists of. I eat and breathe school. That and worrying about Gemma. It's basically all I have time for."

"Good for you," he said sarcastically. "But let's say, hypothetically, you had no school work. You have the rest of this Friday to do *whatever* you want. Anything. Would you *really* spend it studying?"

I ran a hand through my hair and thought about his question. If I could do anything? I thought about all the events Nahla attended on Fridays. I thought about the college parties I'd always seen other people my age getting excited for that I only fantasized about going to. If I could do anything on my very own Friday night, I'd want to live a little. I'd want to be like an average girl, getting a taste for freedom and thrills.

But for some reason, I didn't want to admit that to him. I didn't want to admit my own wants out loud, because doing so felt like it would open a floodgate that I wouldn't be able to close. It would feel like a betrayal to my mom who'd always kept me away from situations exactly like what I occasionally dreamed about.

So I lied. "Nothing."

Before he could respond, Zagan's phone rang. He dug it out of his pocket as I finally started driving toward his place.

"Yeah?" he answered.

There was a beat of silence as he listened to whatever the person on the other end said.

"Right now?" Zagan glanced at me. "Fine. Give me a bit to get ready." He hung up and faced me. "School's canceled. We're going out."

I whipped my head around to look at him. "Excuse me?"

"We're going to a club with my band. I'm going to show you a little taste of the world outside of your textbooks and harsh expectations of yourself."

I'd never been clubbing. I'd never gone out for a night like that. Did it always sound fun? Sure. But that was outside the box I stayed in. Was I really going to live beyond that line two Fridays in a row? After what happened *last* Friday? The consequence from my last moment of fleeting freedom was currently sitting in my car, trying to convince me that I didn't know what fun was.

"Don't bother arguing," Zagan said. "You don't get a choice. I gave your sister her weekly dose. Now it's time for my payback."

"I thought your payment was sex, not my presence while you partied."

He smirked and looked at me out of the corner of his eye. "Don't worry. That's part of the evening." His eyes raked over me, and his mouth tipped down. "You're not wearing that, though. Do you own any, you know, sexy outfits?"

I looked down at my shirt, cardigan, and jeans. These were some of the cuter clothes I owned, but they definitely weren't "Friday-Night-Out" clothes.

He must've seen the hesitant look on my face, because he sighed and slumped down in his seat. "Of course you don't. It's fine. I'll phone a friend when we get there." He looked at me and said excitedly, "Get ready, Iyla. You're about to see what a real Friday night looks like."

W E STOOD IN THE FOYER OF ZAGAN'S HOME. HIS SHOUL-ders bunched before relaxing once more, and when they did, his features changed. His demon horns appeared amid his black locks, his fingernails sharpened and turned black, his two canines became fangs, and his eyes turned inky black with a red vertical slit. He raised one clawed finger and drew the shape of a door in the open air. The imaginary line he drew glowed red before a solid black door suddenly appeared in the air.

He looked at me with a smirk. "I forgot to mention. The club we're going to is a demonic one called Hell's Gate. Nice, right?"

There was no time to respond or even think about the information he'd just thrown at me. He grabbed my hand and pulled me through the door. One minute we stood in his living room, and the next we were in a spacious hallway of red carpet and ornate black and silver wallpaper. When I looked behind me for the door to potentially jump back through, I found it gone. Only a solid wall stood behind me.

"Nice try," Zagan chuckled, tugging on my hand. "You're stuck here with me, Sparrow."

I wanted to ask him why he kept calling me that, but before I could, he was pulling us down the hallway toward a black curtain, closer to the sound of pounding music. When we finally emerged through the hanging fabric, my jaw dropped, and my question left me.

Flashing and strobing lights illuminated the dark room, and a backlit bar stood off to one side. Loud pop music with a heavy bass played on speakers throughout the room. A dance floor took up residence in the center of the stadium-size space, and it was occupied by a mass of bodies, gyrating and moving to the song.

That all seemed normal from what I knew in my limited club experience. What stood out were the people in cages that hung from the ceiling. Some of them screamed and waved their hands through the bars at the uncaring people below them. Some, naked and slick with sweat, danced seductively for anyone who might be looking. Others had more than one person squeezed inside the black cages, which shook as the parties inside fought and roared.

Artwork depicting roaring flames eating agonized people or hooded figures ripping hearts out of unsuspecting people from behind adorned the walls around the club. Even more horrifying were the glass cases that seemed to have faces frozen in horror displayed around the bar, and they looked ... real. Like real people forever suspended in pain or terror.

Zagan grinned at me, looking much too pleased with my petrified reaction. He nodded toward the cages suspended from the ceiling. "Humans who lost games or owed their soul to the owner of this club. The owner is a Bargainer demon, and a sneaky one at that. People who make contracts with her but don't read the fine print. People who lost in some twisted game with her. They end up here. Displayed as her trophies."

Souls? Did he just say those were ... souls? I couldn't speak. My tongue had been weighed down by horror and rendered useless.

His hand found the small of my back, and he leaned down so his lips brushed the shell of my ear. "Don't be scared. Your soul is safe inside you ... For now." He chuckled darkly and pushed me along. "This way."

My body prickled, first with the cold chills of fear, but the chills slowly morphed into heat and awareness. His strong hand stayed on the small of my back, and no matter how hard I tried to ignore it, I couldn't. Every time he touched me, he was all I could focus on. His touch. His scent. His power. He was intoxicating to be around, and for once, I was thankful for that, given my frightening surroundings.

We reached a large table that had a prime view of the dance floor. I immediately recognized the group of guys sitting there as the rest of Sinners Do It Better, and my nerves skyrocketed when all of their demonic eyes zeroed in on me. It didn't help when I noticed the chairs around the table looked like bodies that had been contorted and rearranged to make seats.

"There he is," Perseus called out to Zagan with an excited grin. His black-and-red slitted eyes swiveled back to me, and he added, "I see you brought a snack."

My cheeks flamed.

Xander laughed and raked his golden eyes over me from beyond the rim of his drink. "Snack? You mean breakfast, lunch, and dinner. That's the only *meal* he'll be getting. Doesn't look like a very good one, either."

The heat in my cheeks burned hotter. I fought not to dwell on my plain looks or casual clothes. I knew I stood out like a sore thumb, and among all these beautiful people, I was nothing.

"Shut up, prick," Zagan snapped, his face darkening and mouth curling up in a snarl.

My heart fluttered with the irritation in Zagan's voice. I wasn't dumb enough to believe that he lost his cool momentarily to defend *me*. He was obviously annoyed with Xander's poking fun at our situation. Still, the idea that Zagan might've wanted to stand up for me was nice. It did something to my insides that I didn't want to acknowledge.

I reluctantly sat in a seat beside Dante, trying not to dwell on what I was sitting on. I just kept chanting to myself that the legs weren't really *legs* and the arms weren't really *arms*. It was all fake. I swallowed hard and glanced at the gray material of the chair, forcing myself to see metal and not flesh frozen in some petrified state.

Fake, fake, fake, fake.

I bit the inside of my cheek and faced the dance floor. Zagan took the chair to my right, and he went around the table, reminding me who each guy was. I forced a smile for them, still reeling from the environment of the club.

"So," Perseus began slowly, pouring himself a refill of whatever drink filled the pitcher on the table. His black-and-red demonic eyes flicked from his glass back to me as he finished, "You're our lead's new bond, huh?"

I nodded stiffly, probably looking rather awkward. "I am."

"How unfortunate," Perseus sighed, running a hand between his black horns and over his blond waves of hair. His eyes raked over my seated figure. "You'll only ever get a taste of Zagan and what he has to offer as a partner. You're really missing out." He winked and downed some of his drink, his arm muscles straining his shirt as he did.

Dante turned toward me, placing one arm on the table and the other on the back of my chair. The anxiety already thrumming inside me doubled as the large demon practically caged me in and pinned me in place with his suspicious eyes. "What did you want out of a bond with a demon, hmm? Riches? Fame?"

"Dante," Zagan warned, his gaze zeroing in on his bandmate. "Knock it off. It wasn't like that."

"I'm just talking, Z," Dante appeased, and even though he was smiling, there was something else, something darker, hiding in his grin, especially when it found me again. "So?"

My mouth dried, but I forced out, "I wasn't looking for anything. It was an accident."

He leaned closer so that we were nearly nose to nose and growled, "Nothing in this world truly happens by accident, *human*."

He pulled back and turned away from me. My heart beat so hard that I feared it would leap right out of my chest. The tension in the air disappeared as quick as it came, and the demons started talking amongst themselves, like Dante hadn't just made me nearly piss myself. He'd been much more charming in the interviews I'd watched.

Zagan grabbed the pitcher in the center to pour himself a drink, also seeming unfazed by the interaction. He raised a pierced brow at me and queried, "I'm assuming you want water, right?"

Eager to down my nerves with something cold and refreshing, I nodded. "Yes, please."

"Okay. I'll—"

"Eeeep!"

My eyes widened at the sudden squeal, and I watched dumb-founded as a curvy, topless strawberry-blonde bounced over and fell into Zagan's lap, nearly whacking him in the face with her tall and thin, pointy black horns. She wrapped her arms around his neck and straddled him in his chair, her round, perky, perfect breasts *right there*.

"Zagan, Zagan, Zagan. You busy-body. I can't believe you actually came tonight!"

Zagan's blank face stayed level with hers, and his hands rested on the table top next to the pitcher and glass he'd been in the middle of pouring. "Yeah, I'm here. Deaf now after your yelling but here. Did you bring what I texted you?"

"Sure did! Where is—" She turned to look around the table, and her golden eyes—the same as Xander's—found mine. Her face instantly brightened, and she released Zagan to face me and leaned across the table. "Oh my gosh, is this her? She's so beautiful!" She grabbed my hands and squeezed them. "Hi! I'm Eden! Are you Zagan's new bond?"

It took me a few tries to get words out of my gaping mouth. "Y-Yes. I'm Iyla."

"Iyla! Such a gorgeous name." She stood and grabbed a shopping bag from under the table. "Come with me, Iyla. I've got you something absolutely stunning to wear."

The energy of this girl had my head spinning. If a golden retriever transformed into a person, it would be her. I was sure if I looked over her shoulder, I'd even see a fluffy tail wagging furiously.

"You're fine with her," Zagan said to me. "Eden is a whirlwind, but she's harmless."

Eden wiggled her waiting fingers at me. She didn't seem to care at all about her bare boobs hanging out. Maybe that was a normal occurrence for a demon club. Who freaking knew? So with my mind still reeling from her seemingly boundless energy, I took her hand and let her pull me after her.

"I suggested you change back there, but Zagan said you were modest," Eden explained as she pulled me down a hall and into a spacious bathroom. "So you can get ready here."

The moment the door closed, she sat the shopping bag down and rummaged inside. She pulled out a strapless red dress and heels, holding them out for me. I stopped breathing. Even without putting the thing on, I knew it would leave nothing to the imagination. I might as well be naked like her.

"Um—" I reached out to take the clothes, trying to form a polite reply.

Before I could, she cheerfully announced, "I'll wait for you in the hall." The bubbly demon left me alone as quickly as she talked.

I held up the dress at eye level, and my stomach fluttered with fresh nerves. I'd never worn anything like it ... but I kinda wanted to. I wanted to see what I looked and felt like in a dress like this.

So with a momentary sense of curiosity and excitement, I shed my clothes, leaving on just my panties. I pulled the soft dress on. The hem barely reached midthigh, and the neckline sat low, exposing the tops of my breasts. My nipples poked through the fabric, and no matter how I adjusted it, that didn't change.

I was so focused on smoothing out the dress that I didn't notice the person slipping into the bathroom until hands landed on my bare legs below the hem of the dress. I gasped, but before I could turn, the warm body pressed into my back.

"You can't wear underwear with this kind of dress, Sparrow," Zagan's rough voice whispered against the side of my neck.

I let out a shaky breath as his hands glided up the swells of my hips, reaching under the dress to hook around my panties. My core throbbed when his body slid down my back, following the tug of my underwear down my legs. I stepped out of them and turned to face him just as he stood and tucked my panties into his pocket.

"Those are mine," I protested, but even I heard the lack of fight in my voice.

He smirked. "Not anymore." His red-slitted eyes slowly traced over my body, starting at my head and working their way to my feet then back up again. "You looking fucking exquisite."

I averted my eyes as a fierce heat swept over my face. My hands fumbled to smooth down the dress, which had risen up around my thighs. "Thank you."

He gestured to the door behind him. "Eden is getting impatient, wanting to dance with you. I made her put a top on since I figured you'd be more comfortable with that."

My heart did a funny little flip. It was strange having Zagan do something to help me feel more at ease. He certainly didn't have to do that, and I was pretty sure he was the type who didn't go out of his way for others. So I appreciated the gesture since it did, in fact, make me more comfortable.

"I better not keep her waiting then," I said, taking a deep breath. "She seems nice. Energetic but nice. I hope I can keep up with her."

He snorted. "Yeah. Good luck with that."

He followed me out into the hallway where Eden waited, now wearing a bright pink sequin top with her black shorts. Her eyes lit up when she saw me come out. "Yes, ma'am! Look how sexy you are!"

I smiled, and despite my earlier hesitation, my nerves slowly washed away. It was impossible to stay on edge with such a friendly soul. "Thanks, Eden. You look great, too."

"Thank you! Now come dance and tell me all about yourself." She grabbed my hand and practically skipped back to the main room with me in tow behind her.

I glanced over my shoulder, catching one last look at Zagan. There was no missing the way his eyes continued to trace over my every curve. His attention made my blood burn with a desire so strong that my knees went weak and my chest tightened. It made me want to pull his body against mine and to dance just like we did last Friday. But I ignored that urge, because it was ridiculous. I couldn't dance with him like that in front of all these people.

The people on the dance floor made room for Eden and I. The music boomed louder here, and each beat shook the ground under my feet. The moment we found our place in the throng of demons, Eden started swaying her hips and moving like a beautiful goddess. Dancing so close to someone who knew how to command their body as well as she did was intimidating, so I kept my own movements slow and small.

"I'm so glad Zagan brought you here. A real human girl!" Eden beamed, leaning in close to be heard over the music. I narrowly avoided losing an eye when one of her gazelle-looking demon horns came extra close. "Don't get me wrong. Demons are great, but they can be such a *bore*. All dark and brooding and black all the time. Like livin' up, you know? Wear some *color*!"

I laughed, noticing that the majority of people around us were indeed dark, brooding, and wearing black. "Do humans not get brought here often?"

She shook her head. "Hardly ever, and when they do, everyone fights over them wanting to either fuck their brains out or consume their soul."

My eyes widened with the mental image of fangy beasts frothing at the mouth as they tore into human flesh, but she didn't seem to notice, talking as if we were discussing the weather.

"Thankfully, everyone can smell the bond on you, so they know not to bother trying."

Alarmed, I bent my head to sniff myself. "I smell?"

She giggled and grabbed my arm to stop my sniff-check. "It's not a bad smell. You just smell like Zagan."

My cheeks burned, and I looked sideways at Zagan. He was back at the table, sitting in my seat so that he faced the dance floor. Perseus and Xander had disappeared, so it was just the three remaining members left. Zagan and Dante were talking while Coldin stared blankly at seemingly nothing.

It was like Zagan could *feel* me the moment I looked over there, because while he continued speaking to Dante, his black-and-red eyes flicked in my direction. His hungry gaze trailed over me as I barely swayed to the music. I sucked in a sharp breath and quickly turned away. I wasn't sure why I was embarrassed. Maybe because he caught me looking at him, or maybe because I worried he'd somehow sense the throbbing between my legs that he'd conjured with his heated gaze.

Maybe it was both.

Something was probably wrong with me. I was in a room full of demons—one of whom wasn't opposed to my dying—yet I couldn't seem to focus on that right now. Not when I could still feel Zagan's lustful eyes tracking my body as I danced with Eden. Worried goosebumps didn't paint my flesh, but rather, pinpricks of desire. He didn't want to kill me in this moment. No, he wanted to fuck me, and having that sort of power over him was a drug I hadn't realized I liked being addicted to.

Eden kept me moving for multiple songs, spinning me and gyrating on me. It was surprisingly a blast, losing myself in the music and just letting instinct take over. It helped that Eden cheered me on and hyped me up while I moved. My heart hammered, and my feet grew tired in these foreign heels. After four songs, a new thrumming, sensual beat took over the speakers, and I perked up in recognition.

"This is ..." I started slowly, turning on autopilot to seek out Zagan. His attention was already locked right on me as I finished, "One of his songs."

Zagan propped an arm on the table and beckoned me to him with a crook of his clawed finger.

"Oh, you better go," Eden said with a conspiratorial gleam in her eye. "He looks serious."

My mouth dried while my mind raced to think of why he needed me. I nodded to Eden and excused myself, walking toward where he now sat alone at the table.

"Do you need something?" I asked when I reached him.

His eyes changed then, morphing from black-and-red to blue, and his horns, fangs, and claws faded until he appeared human once more. He held his hand out for me, and I looked at it as though it may bite me. I wasn't sure what he was up to—there was no telling with him—and it was making a fresh wave of nerves stampede in my gut.

Were we leaving? Getting a drink? Going someplace private so he could "eat?" I wasn't sure which one I was hoping for, even as I placed my hand in his.

The moment our palms connected, he yanked me toward him. I gasped and fell into his arms. His pierced lips spread into a grin as he placed me in his lap so that my back was to his torso, and we faced the bustling crowd while the first lyrics of his song wrapped around us.

"What are you doing?" I asked skeptically, looking over my shoulder at him.

He licked his lips, and his hand moved from my waist to rest on the tops of my thighs. I held my breath, and my eyes fluttered as he grazed his nose along my throat like a predator searching for the best spot to sink their teeth into their prey. I made a soft noise at the onslaught of electrifying desire that zipped around inside me, and I zeroed in on the feel of his strong hands as the sound of his recorded voice taunted me over the speakers about sex and sin.

His hands trailed over my skin, stopping where they met in the crease of my legs. His fingers grabbed my thick thighs, just below the hem of my dress, and he slowly opened them and used his own legs to help keep them parted.

My heart stilled as alarm suddenly mingled with the arousal coursing through me. My eyes darted around the packed club, and

I grabbed his wrists in an effort to stop them from opening my legs any wider.

"Zagan!" I hissed, but it was like he didn't hear me.

My thighs were spread wide, and my dress had ridden up so that the fabric nearly bunched around my waist. The cool air kissed my bare and wet middle, which now ached with a need to be touched, despite the panic clouding my mind.

"Za—" My breath hitched as his finger swiped through my folds and rubbed teasingly over my clit. I bit my lip as my back arched, and I ducked my head, too afraid to look out at the crowd.

My naked pussy was in full view beneath the table. If someone glanced this way, it wouldn't be hard to guess what we were doing based on our position and my inability to keep my reactions off my face. Even more than that, if they looked under the table, they'd be able to see everything happening—Zagan's fingers massaging my pulsing bundle of nerves, my legs subconsciously opening wider in an effort to get more, my ass grinding into Zagan's groin. It was beyond embarrassing.

So why did it only turn me on more?

I let out a shaky gasp as his fingers rubbed and flicked my clit. I dared another anxious glance around the room. No one seemed to be paying us any mind. At least, not that I could see before I was forced to duck my head once again as a tremor of pleasure shook my body.

"You like me playing with this pussy in a room full of people?" Zagan rumbled against my ear.

I pressed my lips together, refusing to answer. That was a mistake.

He slapped my parted folds, eliciting a biting sting of pain amid the swirling pleasure. "Answer me."

"Yes!" I gasped, trying to ignore the burn from his smack and how it made me even wetter. How was that possible?

He pressed two fingers to my clit this time, and my eyes rolled back into my head. My hips bucked on their own accord, and I gripped the table's edge tightly.

"Do you like my fingers touching you here?"

"Yes," I responded immediately. I had learned my lesson to answer when he asked me a question.

"Do you want more?"

I nodded hard, my legs shaking as I burned hotter right where his fingers moved. "Yes!"

He shifted some beneath me as his chest vibrated against my back with a soft chuckle. "Good. Because I'm going to fuck you right here."

There was no time to process his words. His dick plunged deep inside of me.

CHAPTER 13

Zagan

I'D WANTED TO FUCK HER SENSELESS AS SOON AS I SAW her curvy body in that red dress. It took all the patience I had in my bones not to take her right there in that bathroom, but I knew if I did that, Eden would barge in with a demand to join. So I waited. I planned to continue waiting until we were done here, but that was *before*.

Before her ass swayed in that tight red dress to multiple songs.

Before her chest heaved with heavy breaths, her nipples poking through the thin material.

Before her hooded eyes grew sensual and hungry for more than Eden's attention.

I couldn't fucking take it anymore.

It didn't help the straining of my cock when one of our songs came on overhead. The way she always reacted to my singing—physically and sexually—was intoxicating for me. For so long now, all our songs did was remind me of my struggle to write. Yet I went from never wanting to hear another one of our songs again to needing them on constant repeat, all because of the way it made the brown of her eyes shimmer with lust, the way it made her pulse race with the melody, or how it made her body automatically seek out mine.

Now, my dick sank into her warm, wet pussy, and I groaned at the pure ecstacy of it. She felt so good wrapped around my cock, and the sounds she made as I entered her were like my own personal symphony. I could feed from her, listen to her, and feel her all day long and never grow tired of it.

Which was good considering I was stuck with her for the foreseeable future.

Once I was fully inside her, I placed one hand on her hip and let the other continue rubbing and toying around the edge of her bundle of nerves. Despite wanting her, I didn't make a move to thrust, and I didn't actually touch her clit. She was about to take the lead on that.

With my finger teasing her but not fully touching her where she wanted and my dick filling her up but not moving, she began to squirm restlessly. I grunted, because just that subtle movement felt *divine*, and she hadn't even truly started moving yet.

"Zagan." She whimpered my name in a desperate plea.

"You want more?" I asked, gravel filling my voice.

She hesitated a moment, her anxious eyes scanning the room. It was a huge audience, and I waited with baited breath to see which my sparrow wanted more—to let her desires run free or to let her fear win. Finally, she nodded.

I chuckled low at her answer and squeezed her hip. "Better get moving then. You control what happens right now. How deep I go. How my fingers touch your wet cunt. How much passerbyers see of what we're doing. It's all you right now."

She shivered and groaned like a cornered animal afraid and unsure of what to do. I smirked, growing restless for more myself, but I held firm, not giving her more of my fingers or any deepening of my cock.

My sensual song continued to wrap around us, and maybe it was the lyrics guiding her or maybe it was her own desperate need to keep going with what we'd started. Either way, her hips shifted the tiniest fraction, pushing back against me and brushing my fingers through her slick lips.

White hot pleasure shot from my groin and up through my body. She let out a small gasp like she couldn't believe how good that small motion felt. The fingers of my left hand dug into her thick thigh, and the other waited for her to grind against it, hovering just shy of her clit.

Her head swiveled around slowly like she was double-checking who watched. She gripped the table's edge and lifted her hips to rub herself over my finger and sink back down on my shaft. This time, she didn't pause after just one movement. She bucked again, making my fingers drag over her clit and send my dick pushing in and out of her.

I growled deep in my throat, absolutely loving the way it felt to sink in and out of her. She squeezed me tight and grinded her ass into me like she wanted to go faster, wanted to ride me harder, but was holding back. Every move she made was careful. It was obvious she was trying to be discreet with her reactions and body, but that worry didn't stop her from continuing to rise and fall on my cock.

"More," she whispered, her head falling forward on a breathy exhale. She leaned back with another plunge of my shaft, and the motion made her long brown hair cascade down between us like a shining waterfall, one that begged me to run my hands through it. "Zagan, I need more. I-I don't know what I'm doing."

I trailed my tongue up the side of her neck, awfully satisfied with her pleading. "It's because you're holding back."

The song overhead neared some lyrics that were fitting for this moment, so I released her thigh and gripped her throat, pulling her back flush against me to sing in her ear, "'Take what you want from me. Let your pleasure crash down like a raging sea.'"

Lust clouded her eyes as they stared at my mouth, listening to me usher her on. It was like a switch had been flipped, because she shifted against me again to take me deeper, and her eyes closed as her lips parted on a throaty moan. I groaned at the sweet sound and the pure ecstasy engulfing my body.

She leaned forward and placed her forearms on the table to brace herself as she moved her hips in a way that let her ride my dick harder and faster and rub her clit fully against my digits. I squeezed her throat and let my head fall back as she coaxed me closer to the point of no return. The delicious taste of her mounting pleasure filled the back of my mouth and my chest.

Feeding off sex was like light growing inside your gut. It was dark and empty when slowly, at your core, it got brighter and fuller until you were brimming with this warm, buzzing ball of pure energy. Nothing compared to that feeling, and *her* sexual pleasure and satisfaction was *blinding*. In my long ass life, nothing had ever tasted or felt as good.

Her movements became frenzied as she bounced on my cock and stroked herself against my hand. I could tell she was getting close, and her hunger to feel that blissful explosion made her grind her hips harder, clearly no longer caring if someone looked over here and saw her flushed face and shuttered eyes as she bounced up and down.

"That's right," I urged, digging my fingers into the skin of her neck. "Ride me like it's the last cock you'll ever get." *Because it is*, I thought with a sense of self-satisfaction. Just as I couldn't sleep with anyone else because of the bond, she couldn't, either.

Her throat spasmed under my palm in what would've been a scream if I hadn't been cutting it off. Her pussy tightened around me as she came. I grinned at the fullness now in my gut, and wanting to finish things right, I released my tight hold on her throat, grabbed both her hips, and pumped myself in and out of her hard and fast. She gripped the table tightly, meeting me with each thrust, and finally, I, too, reached that electrifying release, spilling myself inside her tight little hole.

"Fuck," I gasped, breathing hard. "I may just stay buried inside you forever."

Her back slumped against my front, and she tipped her chin back to look at me. "It may be kind of hard to walk like that."

I laughed, the sound coming easier than it typically did for me. "Yeah. I'd say so."

I pulled out, and she quickly grabbed her dress to cover herself as she fell into the seat beside mine. I didn't take my eyes off her flustered, fumbling movements, even as I tucked myself away.

Her gaze met mine again, and she watched me like she was searching for something. Finally, she asked, "Does your voice enchant people? You know, like a Siren."

I quirked a brow at her, fighting the mirth that tried to rise up in me. "No. I'm not an enchanter or Siren. Just a demon who happens to be good at singing."

She seemed to process my words with a measured nod. "Interesting. Your voice ... It always does something to me, especially when you sing."

I smirked and rested my cheek on my fist. "Oh? Pray tell."

She shrugged. "It's just the way it sounds. Beautiful and sexy and dark and everything in between. It makes me ..."

Her hesitation only fueled my interest more. I nudged her. "Makes you what?"

Her eyes refused to meet mine, and she fiddled with the hem of her dress. "Want things."

I licked my lips and tilted my head knowingly. "Like the things we just did?"

"That," she said, a pink blush blossoming on her cheeks.

Figured. I chewed on my lip around my piercings and flicked some trash on the table, watching it bounce across the surface and over the edge. Part of me wanted to tumble to the ground with it.

Her answer was typically the response people had to my songs and my singing. It made them horny or made them fantasize about me and all the things I sang about. Which was fine. I loved sex and being what men and women dreamt of having in their bed. But sometimes I wished my voice made them want—

"And more," Iyla added.

Everything inside me stilled, and I raised my eyes back to hers. *More?*

She cleared her throat and met my gaze with a resoluteness that hadn't been there before. "It makes me want to ... I don't know. Jump. Scream. *Fly*. It makes me feel like I could do anything and it be okay. Like I can really *live* and it be okay."

I stared at her, and I wasn't sure if I was breathing anymore. The way she *heard* me, like my voice and songs were more than just fuel for a good time, made my own heart begin to pound—a heart I often forgot existed. A tightness filled my chest. The overwhelming swell of emotion was one I couldn't put a name to. All I knew was I liked how this caged bird heard me in a way others didn't. My fleeting words in a song became a map to herself.

Schooling my face so she couldn't see the effect her statement had on me, I asked, "So you don't feel allowed to live right now?"

She seemed startled by my question, like she hadn't realized saying what she had would admit something she'd been denying this whole time. I sat back and waited as she looked down at her lap and gathered her words.

"Fine. I admit it," Iyla said softly. "I-I do, sometimes ... maybe ... slightly, feel like my life isn't my own." She pinched her fingers to make a small gap and glanced at me. "Only a teeny bit."

"A teeny bit," I repeated with a humorless chuckle. "I see. Well, let me give you some seasoned demonly advice. You can do anything. The only one stopping you is *you*."

She sighed and rubbed her forehead. "It's not that easy. My Mom—"

"Has her own life. This one is yours. Stop trying to live it for her."

Her brow furrowed slightly, and she searched my gaze with a sort of desperation, like she wanted to believe me but struggled to. I'd had a hunch that a parent was what kept Iyla on such a tight leash. I hadn't seen any religious artifacts in her home or signs of any other reasons to keep her constantly on edge. From the small comments she'd made about her mom's rules or from that short but hostile phone call this morning, it became clear that Iyla's mom had a strong hold on her.

I'd been willing to bet everything Iyla did—every step she took, every belief she had about herself, every plan she made for her future—stemmed from her domineering mother.

"Have you ever tried speaking up?" I asked. "Have you ever tried telling her what *you* want?"

She slowly shook her head. "Not since I was little. I got shot down a lot and stopped trying."

"Maybe it's time to give that another go. You're both adults now. Tell her what you want and start living how you see fit. Don't live under her control anymore."

She swallowed hard, and her eyes watered. She opened her mouth, closed it, then whispered, "I don't know who I am if I'm not *her* version of Iyla."

The admission seemed to scare her. It was probably the most honest confession she'd ever made, and we both let the weight of it hang between us. Who was Iyla without a leash? Who was Iyla when she let go and breathed on her own?

I offered her a supportive smile and leaned in until our noses nearly touched. "So let's find out together."

CHAPTER 14

Iyla

I STILL COULDN'T BELIEVE HOW I'D OPENED UP TO ZAGAN. I'd never dared to speak about my feelings on how I lived, yet the person I chose to disclose that to was a *demon*?

My lips and mind had seemed to loosen under Zagan's influence. After having mind-blowing sex right there in a room full of people, something had changed inside of me. I kinda felt like a badass for doing something so daring and taking control of what happened, so afterward, the words and confessions just came easy.

His words of comfort helped, too.

So let's find out together.

The mere idea of even trying to talk to my mom about potentially having a bit more freedom—less random check-ins, deciding what I wore for myself, listening to music again—terrified me. But I didn't have to figure out who I was alone. Zagan offering to be beside me for the journey made it seem less daunting, if not a little exciting and nerve-wracking. Thinking back on his offer caused my heart to beat harder in a way that startled me.

It wasn't like he had a choice. We were bound to each other for the rest of my life, so he *had* to be along for the ride. That was probably the only reason he offered.

Still, his inspiring words had me believing that maybe I *could* talk to Mom. There was nothing wrong with having a conversation about me gaining a bit more wiggle room. I could be my own person with my own ideas and desires.

Now that I was back in my quiet, lonely apartment, though, the confidence I'd felt with him rapidly dwindled. While at the club, a place full of demons in this seemingly other world, life felt separate from this one where my mother existed. I felt safer from her and the reality of my situation, but that sense of strength and security was gone now. I was back in my mother's domain, and now, I questioned if Zagan really knew what he was talking about. I questioned if *I* knew what I'd been saying.

My mom was brilliant, and she just wanted what was best for me. What was wrong with wanting to make her proud?

I wanted Mom to accept me and love who I was as a daughter. So I pushed aside what Zagan and I talked about as I prepped for midterms.

I spent all of Saturday organizing my notes from the semester and going over them. I rewatched any lecture I had a video of and reworked old homework problems. By the time Sunday morning rolled around, my eyes felt full of sand, and when I sat down at my kitchen island to get back to work, my brain felt like putty. It desperately needed a break from philosophy of law, public policy, and government.

My fingers twitched with a need to relieve the stress by doing what I loved. I stared at my hands, which were ready to move over ghost keys, but instead of playing a nonexistent piano on my cold countertop, I curled my fingers inward and took a deep breath.

Coffee. I just needed some coffee.

And Nahla.

I grabbed my phone and called my best friend. It was nine in the morning on a Sunday, so I wasn't sure if she was actually awake, yet.

Still, I needed to hear her voice to distract me from the tightening in my chest as I ignored the need to get lost in Bach or Mozart.

"Perfect timing," her voice suddenly said from the other end of the line.

I nearly dropped the glass coffee pot when I realized she was actually awake. "Wow. You're up," I said disbelievingly, holding the coffee pot under the sink faucet to fill it up. "Why's it perfect timing?"

"Because I'm coming up your apartment elevator right now."

Instantly perking up, I rushed to my door. I peeked my head out just as Nahla appeared at the other end of the hall. Her long hair had been straightened and partly pinned back with a gold clip. She wore a thin gold turtleneck, black pants, and held two cups of coffee from a nearby café.

Awake *and* dressed? Was the world ending?

"I've brought the goods," Nahla announced, holding out one of the cups for me.

"Perfect," I said, taking it and letting her in. "I was just about to make some."

She dropped her purse by the island and collapsed onto the barstool beside mine. I immediately joined her and sipped on the warm brew as I eyed her expectantly. She was being oddly quiet, *and* she was up before noon on a Sunday.

I stared at her while she looked around the apartment, seemingly too afraid to meet my eyes.

"Nahla," I said slowly. My heart was beginning to pound harder as potential reasons for her odd behavior darted through my head.

Was she pregnant?

Was she sick?

Was her sister, Noya, hurt?

Had Noya dropped some secrets, and it was actually *Gemma* who was hurt?

"Is that a new couch?" she asked, pointing at it with a forced edge of normalcy to her tone.

I couldn't tear my eyes from her face. "No. It's the same couch I've always had."

"Really? It looks—"

"Spill it, Nahla," I demanded quickly. "You're freaking me out. What's going on?"

Her mouth clamped shut, and she finally faced me. I held my breath as she took a deep one herself. "I ..."

I couldn't move. Couldn't speak. I was ready to pass out from the anxiety soaring through me right now.

She covered her face with her hands and peeked at me between her parted fingers. "I went on a date."

My eyes doubled in size, and I leaned forward to grab her hands to pull them off her face. "What?" I squeaked, bringing out my inner boiling teapot.

She blushed. Actually *blushed*. I'd never seen Nahla *blush*.

My heart raced for a whole new reason now as the fear slipped away and excitement took its place.

"You went on a date?" I asked in a string of words. "This morning? With who?"

"Do you remember Iseul? The girl we met at the Sinners Do It Better VIP party?"

Iseul. She'd been the quieter of her trio of friends, the one with the black bob. She'd also been the one Nahla had been eating out while getting pummeled from behind by Dante.

I flashed her a knowing smirk. "I remember."

She laughed. "Yeah, well, she and I hit it off. *Obviously*. We exchanged numbers and have been talking ever since. We went to the movies last night and got coffee this morning."

I shoved her in the arm. "How could you not tell me this was happening, you jerk?"

She ducked her head and fiddled with the lid of her coffee cup. "I know. I just wasn't sure, yet. You know me. I don't do dates. I don't do serious. But Iseul … she's different. She … makes me happy. Really happy."

I squealed and threw my arms around Nahla, overjoyed to hear how great this new person in her life made her feel. It also made me think about the new person in *my* life and how I'd not divulged that information to her. But how did I explain it? Zagan and I weren't dating by any means. I wasn't even sure if we were friends. We were more like business partners—each offering the other a service in exchange for something.

But I definitely couldn't say that.

My phone buzzed then. Nahla and I looked at it at the same time, and when I unlocked my phone, I saw a text from an unknown number. *His* number. I'd forgotten to save it as anything.

> ?: Come over.

Nahla grabbed my phone and pulled it closer to her face. "Who is this?" She scrolled to see the previous messages before I could snatch it back. "Why do they have a photo—" Her eyes widened. "'Let's fuck.'" She dropped the phone to the counter and grabbed my arms with a strength wrestlers would be envious of. "Iyla Marie Winters, who the hell is that, and *why* are they asking to fuck?"

I cringed.

Nice timing, Zagan.

"I-I wasn't sure what it was, yet," I said carefully, repeating her own explanation to me. "I still don't, to be honest."

She held up a manicured finger to stop my words. "Are you telling me you lost your fucking V-card, and you didn't *tell* me?"

Guilt pricked at my insides. Even if I didn't know how to explain what happened between Zagan and I that night, I should've told Nahla. We shared everything with each other, yet I'd kept something huge from her.

"I'm sorry," I apologized softly. "I wasn't sure how to say it. Just like how you don't date, *I* don't do … *that*. I think I've been too afraid to say it out loud. Like if I do, I'm somehow admitting my shortcomings to Mom, even if she isn't here to hear me."

Nahla squeezed my hand. "Babe, there is *nothing* wrong with what *you* choose to do with *your* body. If you want to have sex as the adult that you are, you can do that."

My throat clogged with emotion, and I found it too hard to speak. I nodded so she knew I heard her, but I wasn't sure if I believed it. Not when my mom had taught me how wrong it was or how dirty it made me to want or like those things.

"I know it must've taken a lot of courage for you to do it," Nahla continued. "So I won't hold it against you for not telling me. *This time*. But you *better* tell me every detail from here on out. Starting with who this is." She tapped her finger on my locked phone.

I nibbled my lip nervously, because *that* was going to be yet another huge shock for her. I decided the best way to tell her was to just come out and say it, like ripping off a band-aid. "It's Zagan."

She stared at me, completely frozen. Seconds ticked by, and she still hadn't moved. I started to fear I'd broken her when she finally blinked and said, "Come again?"

I nodded like I, too, struggled to understand it. "It's Zagan."

"Zagan," she repeated, sounding each syllable out like the name didn't make sense on her tongue. "As in, Sinners Do It Better?"

I swallowed and bobbed my head once.

Her chin nearly hit the floor. "*What*? You—You're—Holy fucking shit! Are you serious? You're joking. Oh my God. You're dating *Zagan*?"

I quickly shook my head. "No. We're not *dating*. We're—" I sighed with a shrug of my shoulders. "It's complicated. I'm not sure what we are."

Her mouth was still a gaping hole, so I placed a finger under her chin and closed it. "Careful. You'll catch a bug like that."

"I can't believe you're fucking Zagan," she breathed out in a string of words. "Like, you're partners. He's *texting* you."

I grabbed my phone to read his text again. Last time I'd taken too long to respond, he popped in. Not wanting a repeat of that, I quickly typed out a reply.

> I'm studying for midterms today.

"Studying my *ass*," Nahla shouted. "You already *know* everything."

I rolled my eyes. "I don't know *everything*. So dramatic."

"You know everything for these stupid exams," she argued, gesturing to all my notes and books still littering the counter.

My phone buzzed again.

> ?: Bring it with you then. I need that pretty pussy on my cock. Maybe I can fuck you while you study.

Nahla choked on her coffee, completely oblivious to the brew now dripping down her chin and onto her sweater. "Oh, hell yes. You're going."

"Nahla—"

She snatched my phone and typed out a reply for me, letting him know I was going to get ready and be there soon. She beamed at me as she handed me my phone back. "You're going. So get out of those pajamas, and get your ass in gear. I'll be waiting to hear *all* the dirty details later."

AN HOUR LATER, I WAS KNOCKING ON ZAGAN'S FRONT door in a school-themed sweatshirt and shorts with my backpack slung over my shoulders. Nahla's persistence and constant supervision remained right up until I got into my car. She'd been grinning from ear to ear as she watched me leave, and I was fairly sure she was more excited about this hang-out than I was.

Looked like my study buddy for the day was a demon. Yay. I briefly wondered if he was even any good at this stuff.

The door swung open, and a damp-haired Zagan stood there in nothing but black sweatpants, which meant his many tattoos and pierced nipples were on beautiful display for me. His human-looking blue eyes spotted my backpack, and he sighed. "You really did bring your stuff to study."

I gave him an incredulous look as I breezed past him. "Obviously. I told you. I have to study for midterms."

"Right," Zagan said, drawing the word out. "Where do you study best? The couch?" He gestured to the lush, black furnishing. "Or the bed?" His lips tipped up with the last word.

I knew which one *he'd* prefer, but too bad for him, that wasn't happening right now.

"The couch is good," I answered. I sank onto the L-shaped couch and dropped my bag by my feet.

Zagan watched me with an annoyed purse to his lips as I unloaded my books, notes, pencil bag, and laptop onto his coffee table.

I didn't say another word as I heaved my Government textbook onto my lap and leaned back against the cushions.

"Remind me what you're studying to become," Zagan suddenly requested as he stood over me.

I glanced up at him before refocusing on the book. "An attorney."

He made some sound of acknowledgement. "What made you want to be an attorney?"

"It's a good career," I answered, even as the disdain for the words burned my tongue. They were what I'd been fed by my mother. A good career. That was all I needed.

"Really?" he asked disbelievingly. He grabbed my legs, and I gasped in surprise. He held them up as he sat next to me then draped them over his lap, staring at me over my textbook. "What do you love about it?"

My brow furrowed. "What I love ... about becoming an attorney?"

He nodded and held my gaze while I tried to think of an answer. My silence stretched on, though, and eventually, he sneered, "You can't think of anything, can you? Because *you* don't really want that job." He cocked his head and pretended to ponder. "Let me guess. Mommy-dearest wants you to be an attorney."

I couldn't hold back my glare, beyond irritated that he was able to read my silence so easily. "Just because my mom wants me to do it, doesn't mean *I* don't want to."

"Fine," Zagan relented. "So then tell me, Iyla. What drives *you* to do it? What about it gets your heart racing? What about it has called to you for as long as you can remember? What part makes your blood pump with excitement?"

I had an answer for each of those questions. They came to mind immediately—what part made my heart race, what part called to my very soul, what part made my blood pump with a certain hunger. But with a cold dose of reality, I silently acknowledged that my answers didn't pertain to law or the judicial system.

Successfully playing a piece I'd practiced for weeks made my heart race.

Gliding my fingers over black and white keys as melodies filled a vast room called to every fiber of my being.

The sense of pride in my chest and the sound of applause from an outstanding performance made my blood pump with every bit of elation a human could feel.

I couldn't lie to myself. I couldn't lie about what I truly wanted, and apparently, I couldn't lie to him, either. He saw right through me.

So I grumbled, "Stop distracting me. I need to study."

It didn't matter if I hated the degree I was striving for. It didn't matter if I wanted to pluck my brain right out of my skull and chuck it across the room every time I had to sit through another class about policy or civil law. I knew my place. I knew what was demanded of me, and when I stepped out of line, there were consequences.

He mumbled something under his breath—an accusation about me being miserable—before grabbing my pencil pouch. He dug around in there, holding up and studying different pens and markers. I rolled my eyes at his constant, shameless curiosity of my belongings and focused on my textbook again.

As soon as I found where I'd been reading, Zagan's palm landed on my bare thigh and a soft tip started dragging along my skin. I quickly looked over the top of the book and found Zagan drawing carefully on my upper leg with a black pen.

"What the hell do you think you're doing?" I screeched, trying to pull my leg away.

His hold on my thigh tightened to keep my leg where he wanted it. "I'm keeping myself busy while you're reading. Just do your thing. Don't mind me."

"Why don't you work on music or something?" I asked.

His lips pulled down ever so slightly, and the look in his eyes changed, growing darker and troubled. Instead of acknowledging my suggestion, he tapped his pen on my textbook. "Thought you needed to study. Get to it."

Guess I wasn't the only one who had issues. I'd noticed his avoidance of his own music when we'd gone to see Gemma last, and now he was ignoring a chance to go work on his songs. It was my turn to be nosy. "Why don't you like your music?"

He drew back slightly, as if I'd slapped him. "What makes you think I don't?"

I shrugged. "You didn't like hearing it in the car. You mentioned the other day how you were supposed to be writing a new song but were dancing instead. So, what's up?"

He stared at me in the same way I'd probably just been looking at him while he pried into my secrets. I wondered if he was going to be honest, or if he was going to hide from it like I chose to do.

"Study," he finally snapped with another point of his pen at my book. "I can quiz you if you need me to. Maybe we can make a game out of it. You know. Get one wrong and lose an article of clothing. Get one right and get an orgasm. Something like that."

So, hiding like me.

I laughed at his suggestion and not-so-subtle avoidance of my question. Shaking my head, I said, "Not happening. I don't think I can have that many orgasms that close together."

He raised his pierced brow and shot me a wicked grin. "So you *do* know this stuff already. Why the hell are we studying then?"

"Because you can never be too prepared," I answered, readjusting my heavy book to focus on the text.

Zagan got quiet, seemingly letting me get to work. I figured he was just happy to not be talking about whatever was bugging him with his music. I glanced at what he was drawing, which was a line so far. I was glad to see he at least chose a pen and not a sharpie.

Still, I was unsure what his inner artist was about to bring out, so I said, "Please don't draw any penises on me."

His hand stilled against my skin, and his eyes narrowed at me. "I'm not a fucking child."

I let him get back to his drawing, and I watched him long enough to confirm that he *wasn't* drawing body parts. It looked like the start of a rose, so I turned back to my textbook.

I wasn't sure how long I flipped through old sections I'd learned so far this year. I jotted down key points, looked over old notes and exams.

All the while, that rounded point dragged across my skin and those warm fingers pressed into my thigh. He moved my shorts higher to continue his drawing all the way to my hip, and I didn't even try to stop him. I actually found it kinda relaxing—the careful trailing of the pen and Zagan's hand constantly on me, making my body prickle with warmth and awareness.

Eventually, my eyes burned with a need to take a break. I dropped the book next to me, rubbed my eyes, and let out a tired sigh.

"All done?" Zagan asked, the pen still moving over my leg.

"I wish. I'll take a break from reading and notes if you'll quiz me."

I closed my eyes and leaned my head back against the couch cushion. The pressure to do well wound my shoulders tightly. I wanted this dinner with Mom. I wanted to hear her say, "Well done."

"Sure," Zagan said. His hand and the pen finally left my leg. "I finished my drawing, so I can quiz you now. I'm gonna grab a drink first. Want some water or coffee?"

"Coffee," I immediately replied. "Please and thank you."

He slipped out from under my legs, and I listened to his footfalls against the tile drift further away. I kept my head leaned back with my eyes closed until my curiosity to see what he'd drawn got the better of me.

When I looked at my leg, the exhaustion fizzled away as awe took its place. Wanting to get a better look at the image that took up the entirety of my skin from my panty line to my knee, I quickly leapt to my feet and went to the towering mirror that stood across from the stairwell. My mouth dried when I met my reflection.

I must've been studying for a long time, because his drawing was elaborate and *beautiful*. A round cage sat nestled in roses and vines, which looked too real and vibrant to have been made in the time they were. The door to the cage was open, and standing inside, looking at the open door, stood a sparrow.

I swallowed hard, and my eyes watered. It was gorgeous.

And heartbreaking.

Zagan appeared behind me in the mirror. The coffee brewing in the kitchen to our left was the only sound as he looked at his drawing then met my eyes in the reflection. "Do you like it?"

I stared at the drawing, one that could easily be mistaken as a tattoo. It made me feel beautiful, like I myself was a work of art. My lip trembled. "No."

"Because you see yourself in that sparrow?" he challenged. "So much beauty beyond the cage. The sparrow could easily fly away. Be free. But it stays in the cage. Too afraid to even try opening its wings to soar."

"Maybe it's afraid of falling, because it doesn't know how to use its wings," I argued.

"Is it afraid of falling?" He cocked his head and leaned in closer to my back, dropping his voice. "Or is it afraid of *flying*? Of realizing the safety of the cage had always been a lie, something that was actually hurting it instead of protecting it?"

A tear slid down my cheek as I held his unwavering gaze in the mirror. I couldn't answer. I couldn't move. He turned and walked back to the kitchen while I stayed rooted to the spot. I looked back at the sparrow tucked in her cage.

I couldn't be that sparrow.

I *wouldn't* be that sparrow.

I vowed as I stared at my reflection that I'd one day spread my wings and fly.

CHAPTER 16

Zagan

I WAS ANNOYED. *REALLY* ANNOYED. I'D BEEN IRRITATED since the day Iyla came over to study. I watched the way she poured over all this shit that she didn't actually care about until her eyes got red from lack of rest or her shoulders got tight to the point where she constantly had to move and rub them. She was wearing herself out, and for what?

A mother who didn't give a damn about her.

I never claimed to be an expert on parenthood. For starters, I wasn't one, and I didn't have any. Demons were created when there was a need for more temptation to keep the balance in the world, so I didn't know everything when it came to a parent-child relationship. But I'd seen millions of families throughout my time, and Iyla's mom was far from a good one.

So she gave her money for living expenses. Big fucking deal. It wasn't out of love. It was so she could maintain control. If she controlled Iyla's house, school, food, her sister, her beliefs, she controlled Iyla. And *that* was what she wanted. Not a relationship with her daughter. *Control* of her daughter.

Iyla was a good person. Even as a demon, I could see that. So watching her try to be this obedient husk of what she *could* be pissed me off.

Iyla was *my* bond.

I wasn't about to let her break herself to please someone. The only person she needed to please was herself.

And me, of course.

So when she came over the day before her first midterm, I decided enough was enough. I wasn't reading off anymore fucking study guides for her or handing her colored pens and highlighters at her request so she could rewrite old notes.

As soon as she stepped inside, I grabbed her backpack right off her shoulders and hoisted it onto my own. I ignored her protests and stalked up the stairs toward my bedroom. I'd been helping her study this whole week—me, *helping*—but today would be different. If she insisted on doing this bullshit, we were going to do it my way.

"Zagan," she huffed irritably. She made it to my room just as I threw her bag into my closet. With a snap of my finger, I sealed the door so she couldn't open it. No one was getting through that door unless I let them.

She ran to the closet and yanked on the doorknob. When it failed to open, she turned to glare at me. "What the hell?"

"You know the material, Iyla," I said, crossing my arms. My eyes raked over her leggings and t-shirt. Damn. She really did look good in *everything*.

"What if there's something I missed?" she argued, her voice coming out frantic with unfounded worries. "What if I forgot something or—"

"I'm going to quiz you like I have been." That was the unfortunate part about assisting her all this time. Every bit of that mind-numbingly boring material was now ingrained in my own fucking brain. Once a demon learned something, it was always there. Which meant I was now stuck with a shit ton of knowledge I didn't want any part of.

Surprise crossed her pretty face. "Without the study guide?"

"Without the study guide," I parroted dully.

I was done with those papers. I was done with her thinking she wasn't ready or good enough.

Because, goddamnit, she *was*.

But her mom had her too fucked up to ever see that in anything she did.

The notion reignited the anger in my blood. "Get naked," I ordered. I narrowed my eyes and dropped my voice lower. "Now."

Her chest rose sharply as she sucked in a breath. A nice pink flush rose to her cheeks, but she did as she was told. I watched her from across the room as she pulled her top and bra off then stepped out of her pants and underwear. She shifted on her feet once she stood naked, and my dick twitched at the beautiful sight of her standing there, waiting for my next command.

I tipped my head to the black leather chair in the corner. "Go sit."

She kept me in her line of sight as she slowly moved to the chair, no doubt afraid I'd pounce on her. Her naked ass sat back in the seat, and as soon as she was settled, I let my power unfurl.

Black wisps of shadow appeared around the chair, and with a quick mental nudge, the long, thin tendrils wrapped around her wrists and ankles. They yanked her limbs to pin her hands to the arm rests and her ankles to the chair legs, spreading her thighs wide open for my own personal viewing. And damn, was I definitely looking and loving the wet arousal already coating her open lips.

Her chest rose and fell sharply, and her mouth parted on a gasp as she looked at the shadowy bindings. "What is this?"

"Me," I answered. "A bit of my power manifested as shadow. It was quicker than getting real rope to tie you up, and we need to get to work now, don't we?"

Her throat worked on a swallow, and her pink nipples hardened. I smiled as I got on my knees between her parted legs, and her body twitched, most likely eager for what she thought was coming. And she *was* going to get that, but not before she answered my questions and saw for herself that she knew all the material.

"Philosophy is going to be an essay, right?" I asked, tracing a single finger over the shadows on her ankle and slowly up her calf. "Walk me through what you'll say. Utilitarianism versus Kantianism."

"Right now?" she squeaked disbelievingly, glancing at my hand, which continued a slow ascent up her knee and onto her inner thigh.

"Now. We're studying," I said coyly. "Like you wanted."

She bit her lip as my finger brushed against the outside of her pussy, but instead of touching her there, I backtracked and retreated down her thigh. She growled and fought against her restraints, which didn't budge.

"Utilitarianism versus Kantianism," I repeated firmly. My finger made it back to her ankle then immediately started up again.

Her head fell back against the chair, and her eyes fluttered shut. She slowly managed to get words out, reciting the material *I* knew *she* knew. I didn't let up my soft touch on her leg, close to her pussy, and back down. It was torture for her, and the feeling was mutual. I couldn't keep my eyes off her hard nipples or the juices seeping from between her folds. And *fuck*, the sweet smell of her desire was actually making me dizzy.

Goosebumps broke out on her skin, and her hips twitched with clear arousal everytime I got close to her center. The more she talked, the closer I got to touching her where we both really wanted me. I brushed the pad of my finger along the top of her cunt and stopped just as I reached the start of her seam. Her breath quickened, but I kept my finger rooted in place.

Her entire body seemed to shake with anticipation. "Zagan, *please*."

I smiled. "Please what?"

She panted and zeroed in on my unmoving finger. "I said all the key points. I explained everything."

"I know," I said, yet my finger didn't move any lower. I loved seeing how wet that made her—wanting my touch so badly but being denied it. "What's your point?"

Helplessness tightened her brow, and she wiggled in her seat as a fine sheen of sweat beaded over her breasts. "So ... Don't I get rewarded?"

I let out a small chuckle and leaned closer so that my breath fanned across her already sensitive core. She moaned, and her eyes rolled back into her head while her hips bucked futilely against my breathy caress. "We still have four more subjects to go over."

Her eyes snapped back open, and her chest fell and rose faster. "I-I can't wait that long. This is already maddening."

I feigned an apologetic shrug and moved my finger slowly around her glistening folds, making sure to stay on the edge of all the good stuff. "You wanted to study. You wanted to make sure you knew everything, remember? We can't stop after only one subject."

She shook her head, her fingers curling and digging into her palms. Her entire body quivered. "I know it all."

I raised my pierced brow. "You do? Are you sure? You were worried you didn't just a minute ago."

"I do, I do," she argued hurriedly. When she looked at me this time, fiery confidence now hardened her features. "I know the material. I don't need to be quizzed. I'm ready."

One corner of my mouth rose in a smirk, and I finally let my finger drag through her moisture, starting at the bottom and working my way up to her clit. She immediately gasped, and her hips grinded in an attempt to get more from me. The scent of her arousal drew me in like a bee to honey, and I leaned in close to let my tongue join in on the fun.

While my finger swept down to plunge into her tight hole, I curled the tip of my tongue along her bundle of nerves. I groaned at the taste that actually danced along my tastebuds, as well as the one that filled my gut with her essence. She was *perfection*—the sounds she made, the way she shook for me, the way she tasted.

I'd already had her wound up so tightly that it wasn't much longer of flicking my tongue and claiming her with my fingers before she arched her back and absolutely exploded with her release. My name burst from her lips, and my cock begged to get free at the sound.

"That's my girl," I praised hoarsely, pulling my fingers out so I could shove my pants down. I released the shadowy bindings as easily as I'd conjured them.

Once she was free, I grabbed her arms and yanked her toward me where I still knelt on the ground. She fell into the floor between me and the chair, and I gripped her face to squeeze her cheeks between my fingers and nipped her lip teasingly. "Turn around and grip the chair."

She didn't hesitate. She turned and grabbed the edge of the chair, lifting her back end for me. I smiled at that. My sparrow already knew what to do. I fisted her long hair, placed my other hand on her hip, and shoved deep into her cunt.

"Fuck, yes," I groaned, relishing in the warmth of her.

I pulled back before pushing back in, and pleasure shot through me with the motion. I grasped her hair tighter, pulling on it as I thrusted hard and fast. Her breathy moans were music to my ears, and they spurred me to angle my hips to get even deeper.

"Yes!" Iyla gasped. "God, yes!"

"Not my name, baby," I said, fisting her hair harder. I tugged her hip back to meet each of my thrusts. "What *is* my name?"

"Zagan," she moaned.

"Say it again," I growled.

"Zagan."

My pace didn't let up, even as I felt her shatter around me on another orgasm or as I neared that place myself. "That's right. That's the only name you're allowed to cry out when you're getting fucked. Understand?"

"Yes," she bellowed, digging her fingers deeper into the chair.

I pumped hard and fast. My balls tightened as I let my head fall back. My cum filled her tight entrance, and her intense pleasure filled my gut like a fire suddenly catching. I pulled out and released her so she could slump against the chair and catch her breath. I leaned back on my hands and took the moment to soak in the buzzing energy of her pleasure now coating my insides, as well as appreciate the view of my cum slowly dripping out of her hole and down her thigh.

"You really know how to motivate someone," Iyla said as she turned to lean her back against the chair.

I smirked. "What can I say? It's a gift."

She laughed softly and shook her head at me. Her eyes were transfixed on the floor between us, and I could see her mind already leaving this moment to dwell on her upcoming tests.

I nudged her foot with my own. "Stop. You know you're ready. You just admitted it."

"I know, I know." She brought her knees up to her naked chest, hugging her arms around her bent legs. She rested her chin on top of her knees, and after a pregnant pause, she admitted, "My mom wants to take me out for dinner if I do well."

It took everything in me to keep from rolling my eyes. And *why* didn't I want to roll them? I refused to look too deeply into that right now, not when there was her mom to discuss.

"So that's why you're pushing yourself so hard. It's not even for your own sense of pride in succeeding. It's for her."

She looked away sheepishly. "Yes. She never spends time with me. She's always so busy, you know? We only really see each other when we go visit Gemma. So I want these midterms to go perfectly so that I can have this with her."

"Do you not think it's weird that you have to work so hard just to get time with your own mom?"

Her big brown eyes locked on mine then, and she seemed startled by my question, like she'd never thought about it. A daughter shouldn't have to go the extra mile to see her parent. Even *I* knew that. The fact that Iyla seemed surprised by the idea just went to show how far her mom's claws dug into her.

"Well, when you say it like that ..." Her shoulders slumped, and her mouth flattened.

Seeing that troubled flash of hurt cross her features made something twist in my chest. Things had been hot and freeing, but now, the air was tinged with melancholy.

Eager to bring some of that lightness back into the room, I grabbed her arms and pulled. Her naked body fell into me, and I rolled so that she was sprawled beneath me. My hands pinned hers on either side of her head—fingers lined up with fingers and palms pressed into palms. Her legs leaned into my sides as I settled between them, and my cock hardened when it brushed her sweet heat. The heaviness faded from her gaze as a sensual calm overtook them.

"Stop thinking about your mom. Do well because *you* want to," I said, letting my fingers finally intertwine with hers so I could squeeze. "If you do that, you'll do great for two reasons."

"Oh?" she probed. "What reasons would that be?"

"One, you had the world's greatest study partner. You're welcome for that. And two, you're insanely smart. You *know* this stuff. Stop doubting yourself just because your mom does."

Iyla's eyes softened as they searched mine. Finally, she asked, "Are we friends?"

My brows rose in surprise. "Friends?"

She nodded.

The word had always been one of indifference for me. I didn't consider anyone a friend because of just that—I didn't *consider* anyone. I was selfish. I had no room in my self-centered soul to care about others. I didn't even know what it meant to be someone's friend.

I pursed my lips and asked, "What does it mean to be friends?"

She seemed taken aback by my question. "You don't know what being friends means?"

The amount of shock in her voice made me feel a bit self-conscious, like how she surely felt when I'd probed her about her mom. They were easy concepts to us when we asked them but complete mind-fucks for the other person.

"Friends," she said slowly, "are there for each other. You pick each other up when you're down. Help each other when the other needs it. You can have fun and talk and just be yourself with them."

It sounded simple, but I knew it was a complex relationship. Still, when I thought about all the things she described, I realized that *did* fit us. We were definitely there for each other, even if it was because of the bond. But hadn't we offered each other support and fun outside of what our deal required?

"Yeah," I finally answered. "We're friends."

As soon as the words left my mouth, everything about her brightened. A twinkle flooded her eyes, his lips formed the most stunning smile I'd ever seen, and her fingers squeezed mine. I had to look ridiculous, because all I could do was stare at her, frozen and heart beating like a drum. Something clenched in my chest, and if I didn't know better, I'd say it was emotion—*real* emotion—brought on by Iyla and the beauty of her happiness.

But that was crazy.

I must've been crazy.

Because emotions like what bubbled up in my chest when I stared down into her smiling face wasn't possible for someone like me.

CHAPTER 17

Iyla

I'D JUST GOTTEN MY GRADES FOR THE MIDTERMS, AND I was over the moon to learn that I'd aced all of them. It wasn't really the score I cared about, but the reward I got for *getting* that score. A night with my mom. I was excited for this chance to spend time with her.

But also apprehensive.

Zagan's drawing on my leg and his words about having to fight for my mom's time had gotten into my head, which I was pretty sure was his goal.

Just like at the club, I questioned my mother and the control she had over every facet of my life. I was back to thinking that I needed to at least talk to her and see if I could gain a bit more freedom.

I pulled up Zagan's contact on my phone. He'd noticed at one point when I'd been over in the past week for one of our many sex meet-ups that I still hadn't saved his number. He'd immediately changed it to, "Demon Daddy," which I then swiftly changed to, "Mr. Ego."

He was in New York at the moment for some dance classes he was helping with and some shows he was doing with his band. I wasn't sure if he was busy right now, but he'd wanted me to call him when I got my grades. Apparently, he was invested in them since he'd declared himself my study buddy.

The phone rang three times before his voice filled the other end. "Sparrow."

"Mr. Ego," I greeted. "What are you doing? Were you busy?"

It sounded loud on the other end, but he said, "Nah. Just trying to record a new song with everyone."

"Oh, crap. I'm sorry. I didn't mean to—"

"No, you're good." It sounded like a door shut and the other end got quieter as if he'd stepped out of the room. "I'm honestly glad to get away from it for a minute. It's not ... I don't know." He sighed. "It's a mess, but whatever. It doesn't matter. What *does* matter is that you called, and I'm assuming it's not because you missed me and just *needed* to hear my voice."

I smiled at the teasing lilt in his tone. "Aww. You disappointed that's not why I called?"

"Heartbroken," he answered. "So how'd you do? What were your final grades?"

I let the silence hang, leaving him to stew in the uncertainty.

"Iyla," he warned.

"I got A's on all of them."

"Hell yeah!" Zagan cheered, and it sounded like he was smiling. "I knew you would."

Excitement bubbled up inside me like a soda can about to pop. The reaction to his praise was unexpected but not unpleasant. "I appreciate you helping me study. It helped a lot."

"Of course. What are friends for?"

I pressed my lips together to keep my smile contained. Ever since we declared the status of our friendship, he'd been referring to us as that every chance he got, like he was still getting a feel for the word and what it meant.

Even though he'd said he didn't know what it meant to be friends, I actually found him to be a good one. He instilled a certain confidence in me that I'd just never had before. And he let me forget my worries and just have fun, which was priceless in my rigid, strict life.

"Did you tell your mom?" he asked.

I plucked at nonexistent lint on my pants. "Yeah. She said she'll pick me up for dinner at six this Friday."

He made a sound like he was acknowledging something he didn't like. "Are you going to try talking to her during the dinner?"

A heavy weight settled in my gut, suppressing the glee. The two of us had come up with a plan for me to talk to Mom during this meal since I didn't have many opportunities to do it any other time.

"Yeah," I answered reluctantly. "I'm gonna try."

"Good." There was a sudden burst of commotion on the other end of the line, and Zagan cursed under his breath. "Sorry, Iyla. I've gotta go. They need me back in there."

"No worries. I hope the new song comes out good."

"Doubtful," he grumbled before hanging up.

With the loss of his voice, my silent apartment became my sole company. Nahla was in class right now, and Gemma had appointments all day. I slumped in my chair with a lonely sigh.

I wish Zagan was here.

My eyes widened, and I sat up straighter as soon as the thought entered my mind. What was I thinking? Had I really come to crave and miss the demon's presence?

With a small smile, I realized, yeah. I did. I missed my friend.

Friday crept up on me, and now that it was time to go out with Mom, nerves burrowed deep into my skin. I'd hyped myself up to talk and speak my mind about what I wanted—a bit more privacy, the freedom to eat and dress how I wanted, the choice to listen to music again—but now that she was on her way to get me, I was ready to jump ship. I paced my living room in my pleated pants and crisp blouse as I chewed on my thumb nail.

"You can do it," I chanted to myself. "It's just talking. You can talk to your mom."

My lunch from hours earlier threatened to come back up.

I can't do this.

Zagan was still in New York. I had no idea what he was doing right now, but before I could think about what I was doing, I reached for my phone to call him. I needed his deep, sultry voice to calm me down before I paced a hole right through my floorboards.

"Zagan's phone," a chipper male voice answered. It took me a moment to recognize it as Xander.

"Um—"

A shuffle erupted, and I heard Zagan's distant voice demanding his phone back. After a few seconds of major commotion, Zagan finally said, "Iyla? Sorry about that. Xander took my phone."

I closed my eyes and waved my hand dismissively, even though he couldn't see me. I had bigger worries than Xander. "I can't do it, Zagan. I'm freaking out. I—I'm just going to go through dinner how we normally would. In silence."

"Hey, hey. Deep breath. You're psyching yourself out. You're the one who said you wanted to be free, remember? This isn't free, Iyla. It's *fear*."

I worked to calm my breathing like he said, and hearing his voice helped to get my sporadic heartbeat a bit more under control. It didn't stop the anxiety crashing through me, however.

"I—"

My phone chimed in my ear. I pulled it away to look at the notification, and my stomach plummeted when I saw the text from my mom.

"Oh god, she's here," I shrieked in a panic.

"You can do this, Iyla," Zagan encouraged calmly. "You can talk to her."

"I wish you were here," I groaned, holding my head. The air lodged in my throat when I realized what I'd just said, and I slapped my hand over my mouth. "I mean ... I ... you know ... bye."

I hung up and stared at the end call screen. I couldn't believe I'd just said that to him. Our friendship was still new, and I wasn't sure how to feel just yet about how easy and comfortable I felt with him. So to admit that being around him made me feel better was kinda embarrassing.

I pushed that mortification down as I took a deep breath and prepared to walk downstairs to meet my mom. It was amazing how I'd gone from being so excited to spend time with her to making myself a trembling, sweating idiot over it. That was my sign that talking about my future and potential slack in rules wasn't an option.

I made my way downstairs and outside to where Mom's car sat idle by the curb. I climbed in and offered her a smile. "Hey. Thanks for picking me up."

She nodded and pulled away from the curb. "I hope you're hungry. I'm taking you to that new restaurant that just opened downtown."

The place she referred to was a new local high end eatery that had a variety of food. My chest warmed when I realized she was taking me to such a nice place, and it made relaxing in my seat easier. I couldn't remember the last time Mom had done something so thoughtful for me.

"That sounds wonderful. Thanks, Mom."

The car fell quiet with only the sounds of exterior traffic filling the space. I swallowed and twiddled my thumbs in my lap as I searched for something to say. It was typical for our car rides to be quiet, but this was a special day. I wanted things to be different today and maybe even change how we interacted with each other in the future. Her decision to take me somewhere nice only fueled that hope.

"How was work?" I asked.

She glanced at me then focused on the road again. "Busy."

I waited for her to elaborate, but nothing more came. All I got was the one word, but hey, that was one more word than what we'd usually share.

Baby steps.

After twenty minutes, we pulled up to the brick restaurant. I walked alongside my mom in her cream pantsuit. Her hair was pulled back in a perfect French twist with not a single strand out of place.

I'd tried to put on my own dignified outfit to impress her, but I had no idea if it worked. She hadn't complained about what I wore, so I assumed that meant I'd succeeded.

The hostess greeted us, confirmed our reservation, and immediately led us into the packed, dimly lit dining room. Mom and I took our seats at a table off to the side.

"What can I get you two to drink?" the waiter asked.

"Water for the both of us, please," Mom answered for us.

I smiled at the waiter in lieu of a response since she'd made one for me, and as I watched his retreating back, a new party being led into the dining hall caught my attention. It was a good thing Mom was studying her menu, otherwise she would've seen me nearly topple out of my chair as my jaw hit the floor.

Zagan took a seat in a booth behind my mom's chair so that he was to her back but facing me. He immediately caught my wide eyes and winked with a smirk.

I looked at my mom and cleared the urgency from my throat. "I'm going to run to the restroom quickly. I'll be right back."

She briefly glanced up at me before refocusing on the menu. "Hurry, please."

I stood and shot Zagan a pointed look as I passed his booth and swept down the hallway that led to the bathrooms. When I turned around, Zagan was there in his black dress pants and shirt with a wide grin.

"What are you doing here?" I hissed, grabbing the waist of his shirt to pull him further into the hallway. We were well out of view of Mom and the rest of the dining hall, but the fear of her seeing us still horrified me. "How did you get here? I thought you were in New York."

"I was in New York," he said, dropping his voice so only the two of us could hear. His large hand lightly touched the underside of my arm that desperately held onto him. "I can be anywhere I want in the blink of an eye. You know that."

My eyes raked over him. He looked *amazing*, and I'd love more time to appreciate the way the formal clothes hugged his toned form or the way his tattoos peaked out of the sleeves, but now wasn't the time. Didn't stop the sight from making my blood run hotter.

"What are you doing here, though?" I repeated.

"You said you wanted me here."

My heart tripped over itself. I stared up at him as unexpected warmth blossomed in my chest. "You—You stopped what you were doing to be here for me?"

He tilted his head slightly as if he wasn't sure why I had to ask. "Yes."

"Why?" I whispered, squeezing his shirt tighter.

"Because you said you wanted me here," he said again with a soft chuckle. His head dipped lower, making the space between us even smaller for him to whisper, "Why *wouldn't* I come?"

He said it like it was obvious, like it was the only thing that made sense. Maybe it really was that simple for him, but I couldn't wrap my mind around someone dropping everything they were doing just to come support me when I needed it. Yet he'd done that without hesitation. My heart pounded furiously as a sweet buzz wrapped around it.

"Thank you," I said, finally releasing his shirt.

"Don't thank me. I'm doing it for purely selfish reasons. I'm trying to upgrade from friend to best friend."

I covered my mouth with my fingers to stifle my laugh. "Nahla might fight you on that one."

He shrugged. "I think I can take her. Now get back out there. I know you really want this. Even if *she* doesn't deserve *your* time. Just ... be yourself. Don't shy away from who you are and what you want. Okay?"

I licked my suddenly dry lips and nodded. Zagan sent me back out first, and I sat in my seat as calmly as I could.

Mom barely held back a glare as she watched me sit. Her mauve painted lips were pulled down in a frown. "I had to send the waiter back without giving our order because you weren't here."

"Sorry. There was a small line," I fibbed.

The restaurant was busy enough that the lie seemed plausible. Zagan came out of the hallway and went back to his booth, and I wasn't the only one who noticed. Patrons threw star-struck glances his way, no doubt recognizing him from Sinners Do It Better. He ignored all the adoring smiles and whispers, though, focusing on me over Mom's shoulder. He offered me an encouraging smile. The comfort his presence brought made it easier to sit across from my mom.

Be yourself.

What a seemingly easy yet horrifying idea. Still, with the way Zagan encouraged me, being more open and honest with myself and my mother seemed possible. Especially with him right there. It was crazy how brave I felt with the demon close by.

"So, what will you have?" Mom asked me.

I scanned the menu and all its delicious options. I figured this was a good time to practice my speaking-up-for-what-I-wanted skills. "Since it's a special occasion, I thought I might have something a little different. Maybe like the shrimp linguini."

Mom scoffed and sipped on her water. "Don't be ridiculous. You know you gain weight at the drop of a hat, Iyla. Do you want to get fat?"

I blinked, already feeling myself get smaller. "I—"

"Attorneys pride ourselves on how we look. Our appearance and how we hold ourselves in the courtroom is half the battle of winning. No one wants to see you busting at the seams when arguing your case, all because you couldn't say no to pasta."

Sand filled my mouth, and it took me multiple times to swallow down the feeling. My arms subconsciously wrapped around my pudgy middle, and I tried to let her jabs roll right off me. It wasn't like I hadn't heard them before. It was why she controlled what groceries came in and out of my house. She never let me forget my weight.

Without meaning to, I glanced at Zagan over her shoulder. His glass was paused halfway to his mouth, and his eyes lasered into the back of my mom's head. The blue of his eyes churned with the threat of going black, but when his gaze flicked to meet mine, they calmed, like thunderclouds receding. He sat his glass down and dipped his head in silent encouragement. The message was clear.

Stand up for yourself. Tell her you want the food, so you're having *the food.*

The waiter appeared then to take our orders just as a trio of girls approached Zagan's table with a napkin and pen—most likely seeking the star's autograph. I refocused on my own situation and opened my mouth, prepared to order what I wanted, despite my mom's disagreement, but the quiet words that came out were, "I'll take the strawberry salad, please."

"Great choice!" the waiter said. He took Mom's order then whisked away with our menus.

With our order complete and nothing else to do, Mom went to observing the room—because Heaven forbid she actually talk to me.

I took the moment to look at Zagan, trying to gauge if he'd seen my failure amid his fan interaction. My stomach churned when I saw him staring past the three girls—who still hovered around his table—with a tight frown pulling his mouth down. I nibbled my lip as shame flooded me.

It probably made no sense to outsiders looking in. I was an adult. I should be able to speak my mind and to express myself without issue.

But Mom had broken that voice inside me a long time ago.

After years of trying and always failing in her eyes, after years of yearning for her attention only to be met with indifference, after years of having my opinion smothered, I didn't know how to speak to her about anything *real*.

But I wanted to.

I wanted to understand her and have her understand me. I wanted a relationship that we both cherished. Maybe appealing to her own desires in life could be a gateway to helping her understand mine.

Needing a change for us, I sat up a bit straighter in my chair and focused on her. "Mom. I was thinking about you the other day and realized I don't know how you got into law. What made you want to be an attorney?"

She finished off another sip of water and folded her hands on the tabletop. If a stranger were to look at us, they'd definitely see a business meeting instead of a mother-daughter pair out to celebrate.

"I wanted success," she answered. "Authority. Respect. It was a career that offered those things, so naturally, it was what I chose."

I smiled, happy to get more insight into her. "So that was your dream?"

Mom's brow creased in the middle, and her mouth flattened. "Dream?"

"Yeah. Your dream job. It—"

"Iyla."

The quick snap of my name instantly made my blood run cold and had my voice breaking off in my throat.

"I know what you're doing," Mom said as she openly glowered at me. "Stop. You're an adult, not some child. Dreams are for sleeping. This is real life. I don't want to hear any nonsense about dreams or piano. Do you understand me? I've brought you to this nice restaurant to celebrate your success, and *this* is how you want to behave? Bringing up issues we've had before and already settled?"

I shook my head. "I wasn't trying to upset you. I just—"

"That's *enough*. I won't hear another word."

The cracks that always resided inside me, the ones that I'd deluded myself into refilling with hope, split open all over again. I wanted to cry, but I was so used to this that the tears wouldn't come. I should've expected this reaction. I *did* expect this reaction. But Zagan's enthusiasm had been infectious, and I'd somehow latched onto it and convinced myself that it was possible. My mom would hear me, and she'd accept me.

How wrong I'd been.

I swallowed down the hurt and lowered my eyes to the table. "Yes, ma'am."

Mom and I didn't say another word the rest of the evening, and I couldn't find the courage to look at Zagan again.

CHAPTER 18

Zagan

MY BLOOD BOILED PAST THE POINT OF FUMING. I was ready to maul, burn, and fucking *destroy* the world so that Iyla could stand atop the ashes of everyone who tried to keep her caged—her mother being at the bottom of that pile where she belonged.

Do you want to get fat?

Dreams are for sleeping. This is real life.

The world was full of pricks like Mrs. Winters who made life suck for everyone else. People like her were why demons like me existed—to show the chained and discarded that they were more than what kept them bound.

There was nothing wrong with Iyla's curves. Humans were beautiful, no matter their shape, size, or color. It was why demons coveted humans so much. Just existing and having a soul that shined like a beacon in the dark made them exquisite. Shallow assholes like Iyla's mom made people cower from themselves, shaming them for what made them beautiful.

And to tell Iyla that she shouldn't dream? Shouldn't strive for something wonderful that *she* wanted?

Fucking bullshit.

Iyla was allowed to have her own passions, ones that didn't include her mother's wishes. And that clearly had to do with piano. Mrs. Winters had connected the instrument to Iyla's talk about dreams, and even now, I remembered the way Iyla's entire body froze when she saw my piano. It was like it had called out to her on some deep level, but she'd forced herself to ignore that urge.

She'd forced herself to walk away from her dream.

The memory of those words leaving that woman's mouth made my human guise threaten to crumble all over again. Iyla couldn't even look at me after that. She'd kept her eyes down, slowly eating her shit salad while her mother did the same. The only reason I didn't storm to that table and rip that woman apart, casting her into the deepest, foulest pits of Hell, was because I knew she was important to Iyla.

For some fucking reason.

I lingered like vapor in the shadows of Iyla's apartment, waiting for her to appear after leaving the restaurant. The lock unlatching sounded in the quiet room. I watched Iyla slowly walk inside alone and trudge through the dark. She didn't make a move to turn on any lights. She found the first surface she could sit on—the kitchen island chair—and sank onto it like all the energy had been zapped right from her body. Her disappointment and hurt permeated the air, and I felt an overwhelming need to reach out to her and find some way to make this better.

This night was supposed to celebrate her hard-earned success, but it couldn't have been further from that.

I stepped out of the shadow and quietly crossed the room to her side. She didn't lift her head from the countertop, even as her muffled voice said, "I know you're there, Zagan."

The fact that she knew that made me smile a little, but the grin fell away just as quickly. "Tonight didn't go as planned, huh?"

She gave a humorless laugh and lifted her head to prop it on her fist. "That's an understatement."

With a snap of my fingers, the kitchen light came on. Iyla blinked a couple times with the sudden light. Her eyes were glassy and red like she wanted to cry, but no tears came. Something told me she was a professional at keeping her tears at bay.

Which only reignited my temper.

"Your mom is a bitch," I stated flatly.

I knew humans were protective of their kin and got riled up when someone talked poorly about them, but I didn't give a shit. Carrying someone for nine months didn't make someone a mom. That was a title that got earned by how you raised, loved, and supported your kid. I didn't see any of those qualities in Valerie Winters, so even though that was Iyla's "mom," she was undeserving of the name. She was undeserving of *Iyla*. And I wouldn't show the woman an ounce of fucking civility.

Iyla didn't argue with my assessment, which only reaffirmed my stance. She stared at the countertop like even though she was *here*, her mind was still back there in the restaurant, being shit on by the one person who should always love her.

I leaned across the island until my face was right in hers. She looked up at me then, and I offered her a comforting smile. "It's over, Sparrow. She's gone. So come back to me. We need to talk about what you want to do."

"What I want to do?" she repeated.

I nodded. "To celebrate. This night was supposed to celebrate your achievement, remember? But that clearly didn't happen. So we're having a re-do. If it were up to you, what would *you* like to do to celebrate?"

Her eyes searched mine, and I could see the wheels in her head turning. Because, *of course*, she hadn't already thought about what *she'd* like. She had to think about it to figure it out.

Finally, she whispered, "Cake."

I ran my finger thoughtfully over one of my lip rings as I took that information in. "Cake?"

She nodded. "Cake. I'd like to eat some cake with Gemma and Nahla." She paused, then added, "And you."

It was so simple. Cake with those closest to her. And somehow, I'd managed to get myself on that short list. Fuck, if that didn't do something to me …

"Okay," I said. "Why don't you text Nahla? See if she can hang out or something tonight. Tomorrow, you and I will go see Gemma."

Finally, my sparrow smiled—a beautiful, glowing grin that made this mostly dark apartment feel as bright as a full moon. "Sounds good."

I stood to my full height again, ready to leave so she could have a girls night, when something else occurred to me. I placed my hands back on the counter. "By the way …"

She looked up from her phone.

I leaned in until our noses touched. "You eat all the goddamn cake you want."

She laughed, trying to avert her gaze. "Right. Shrimp linguini, too?"

I saw it the moment her mom's jab re-entered her mind, and I refused to let that ruin Iyla's night anymore. I crooked my finger under Iyla's chin to keep her locked on me. "You're beautiful, Iyla." I tilted her head to brush my lips over hers. It was a soft sweep of our lips—softer than I usually did. But it felt right. I pulled back only enough to repeat, "Beautiful."

Her hazy gaze went from my mouth to my eyes. "I'm beautiful," she whispered.

I grinned. "Damn right you are."

I STOOD IN FRONT OF IYLA'S APARTMENT DOOR AND SHOT her a text to warn her I was about to pop in. She didn't like me lurking in the shadows unannounced, so I figured as long as she had a heads-up, it was cool.

With that text sent, I moved in the darkness, passing through walls and stepping into Iyla's place. I found her in her bedroom, pulling on a maroon sweater to go with her leggings. Her long hair fell down her back, and she pinned part of it with a black clip.

I appeared then, leaning against her bedroom door frame. She nearly jumped right out of her boots when she spotted me. I laughed at her startled expression before I could stop it, even as she clutched her chest and tried to calm down.

"You jerk!" she shrieked, smacking my arm. "You scared me!"

"So I saw," I said. I schooled the mirth from my voice. "You ready to go?"

With a quick nod, she grabbed her purse. The two of us made our way downstairs and to her car.

"How was your night with Nahla?" I asked.

"Amazing," she answered, pulling out of her parking space. "We relaxed and watched a movie she'd been dying to see."

I watched the passing trees as we drove to Bloomings. "The face masks were cool."

"They actually were. I—" She stopped, and I looked sideways just in time to see her staring at me with suspicious eyes. "How did you know we were doing face masks?"

The corner of my mouth tipped up, despite myself. "I just wanted to make sure you were having a good time after the shit show you'd had to endure."

Her narrowed gaze bounced from the road to me, and suddenly, her cheeks turned red. "You don't do that often, do you? Like, you don't watch me while I ... shower or anything, right?"

No, but that was a great idea. My hardening dick agreed.

"I don't do that," I answered. *Yet.*

She finished telling me about her night with Nahla, and she asked me about how things went in New York. We had a concert up there, some shows to do interviews for, music to record, and I helped with the dance class. It was a busy week, and I loved most of it.

"It all went well," I finished after walking her though the chaotic schedule.

"Did you finally come around to liking your new song?" she asked.

I lolled my head against the headrest to look over at her. She'd been honest with me about multiple tough subjects, and if we were friends, that had to go both ways. So for the first time in my long life, I opened up a bit.

"No. I still hate it." I swallowed hard. "The beat feels too repetitive. The words are meaningless dogshit. I don't feel anything when I hear or sing it. But the guys said it was good enough."

"But you don't want to be just 'good enough,' I take it?"

"Would you?" I looked at her fingers gripping the steering wheel and decided to push a little on my hunch. "Would you want to play the piano 'good enough?'"

Her lips parted slightly, and she briefly looked at me. Her fingers tightened on the wheel. She was quiet, and I figured she wasn't going to answer since it had to do with a very obvious sore subject. So I was surprised when she whispered, "No. No, I wouldn't."

I nodded, satisfied with both her answer and the confirmation that answer gave me about what *her* goal was in life. "Exactly." I looked out the front windshield as we pulled into Bloomings. "I want my music to be *more*."

"I think you can do it," Iyla declared as she parked. "You'll write something that will make you fall in love with music again. I know you will. You just need the right motivation or inspiration."

I hoped she was right, but I wasn't so sure anymore.

We got out and made our way inside. I sent Iyla ahead of me to Gemma's room while I approached the nurses station. A couple nurses, all of whom I recognized from my previous visits but couldn't put names to, smiled at me as I approached.

"Hello, ladies," I greeted, turning on the charm and leaning on the counter. "Did my delivery arrive and get set up in the sunroom?"

"Yes, sir," one of the darker girls answered, batting her full lashes at me.

"Perfect," I said. "I'm gonna take Iyla and Gemma in first. All the other residents and staff can go in after we leave."

"You're so kind, Zagan!"

"Thank you so much!"

"I can't believe how generous you are!"

I let the compliments roll off my plastered on facade. My actions weren't for them. They were all for Iyla. But whatever they needed to believe to make this easier was fine with me.

I found Iyla and Gemma sitting on the edge of Gemma's bed. Iyla had both arms wrapped around her shoulders with her cheek pressed to the top of Gemma's head as they both looked at a drawing Gemma had been working on.

"This is my dragon," Gemma explained to her sister, pointing at the paper. Her hand moved across the page. "And this one is Zagan's. I still need to know your dragon so I can draw it with ours."

Iyla kissed the top of Gemma's head. "I guess I'll have to start thinking about my dream dragon then. Yours will still be the coolest, though. Rainbow scales and butterfly wings? Heck yes!"

Gemma giggled.

I cleared my throat, and the sisters looked up at me. "Sorry to interrupt, but I have a little something for you."

Iyla raised her brow at me in silent question, but she didn't argue. She helped Gemma get into her wheelchair since she was feeling weak today—a fact that had Iyla noticeably stiffer—and I led them down the halls to the closed doors of the sunroom.

I gripped the door handle, but I didn't open it yet. I met Iyla's curious stare and asked, "Remember what you said you wanted last night?"

She hesitated then dipped her head in a nod.

I opened the door wide for Iyla so she could push an equally bewildered and excited Gemma through. They both gasped when they saw the sunroom, and I also took a second to survey everything. With a nod, I decided I was satisfied with the arrangement.

I'd made two phone calls after leaving Iyla's place last night. One to here, confirming that it was okay to do this and another to a local bakery. Now, I got to see the results of those phone calls.

Ten tables were arranged in the room, and every inch of those tables were occupied with cake in every color of icing and fondant possible. Name cards stood next to each, explaining the flavor of cake, frosting, and filling combination. There were forty-three cakes in total, and it had the room smelling like sugar and spices.

"Holy moly," Gemma squeaked. "Look at all this delicious cake!"

Iyla's wide eyes swept over the dozens of deserts before finding my gaze. "Why—"

"You said you wanted cake." I gestured to the tables. "I wanted to make sure you had every option possible."

Iyla stared at me. Unblinking. Unmoving. I didn't even think she was breathing. Gemma excitedly read off the flavor cards on the table closest to us, but Iyla seemed none the wiser. Her big brown eyes didn't leave mine, and I found myself sinking deeper into those dark depths, watching appreciation and awe flood them. But more than that, a brimming happiness crashed through her gaze like a tidal wave overtaking every other emotion. My own chest got tighter. Seeing her joy was like feeling sunshine for the first time.

She felt like sunshine in my frozen, dark world.

Gemma reached up to tug on Iyla's shirt. "Let's have some!"

Iyla finally looked down at her sister with a hard swallow, the trance between us broken. "Right. Okay. Let's see what all the options are."

Iyla pushed Gemma around the room to see all the different treats. They both oohed and aahed over every single one we passed, and I worried that we'd be here all day while they tried to decide which one to have.

Iyla beamed as she read off another flavor card.

You know, staying here all day might not be so bad.

"There's plenty," I said, gesturing around us. "You aren't limited to one kind. You can try as many as you'd like and *eat* as much as you'd like. Both of you."

"This is the greatest day of my life," Gemma declared.

She immediately requested slices of three different cakes. I cut them for her, ensuring they were small enough so that she didn't fill up on one flavor before getting to eat the other two. With my back to the girls, I pricked my finger and let a drop fall onto the cake. I watched the black blood disappear into the spongy food. I handed her the plate and fork then turned my attention to the eldest Winters.

"Iyla?" I probed softly, waiting for her to tell me what she wanted.

"Can I try the spice cake with cream cheese frosting, please?"

I grinned. "You can have whatever you want, Sparrow."

I went to that table to cut some cake. A hand suddenly gripped the shirt at my lower back, and I looked down as Iyla held onto me and leaned in close to my side. Her shining eyes held mine as she whispered, "Thank you for doing this. It … It means so much to me."

Nothing could keep the smile off my face. Not when she looked at me like I made the world a better place. Me—a *demon*. "You don't have to thank me. You earned this, remember?"

She let out a small laugh and looked around the room with a shake of her head. "I don't think I deserve *this*. It was just midterms."

"Midterms for classes you hate," I reminded her, gaining her attention again. "For a degree you don't want. For a woman who doesn't treat you right. So yeah, you don't deserve *this*. You deserve so much more."

She swallowed hard, and, again, that warmth she kept directing at me swelled to life in her eyes. "Don't say things like that. Otherwise, I'll start to believe you."

I leaned down so we were nose to nose. I was so fucking tempted to kiss her but opted not to because of our young audience. "Good. I'm counting on it."

I handed her the plate with the cake she'd requested. After making a plate for myself, the three of us made our way back to Gemma's room. I gave the ladies at the nurses station the greenlight to let the staff and other patients get what they wanted of the cake, too.

Our little trio made ourselves at home at the table by the window in Gemma's room. Iyla and I sat across from each other with Gemma between us, facing the window. We dug into our cake, and the girls nearly fell out of their seats from how much they loved it. I learned they'd not had cake in years since their mom didn't allow it.

Shocker.

We worked on a one-thousand piece puzzle of a—of course— dragon. I was starting to notice a theme with the little girl.

Nurses and patients popped in every so often to sing me praise for bringing the cake for everyone. I was used to constant attention and random people coming up to chat or request photos. It came with being the lead singer in a popular band, so it was always easy for me to smile and go along with the interactions. Anytime. Anywhere.

But for some reason, both last night at dinner and now, I wanted them to leave me alone. I wanted to hold onto this moment where I sat in this little room with Iyla and her sister. I wanted to sit uninterrupted, watching the way Iyla savored her cake, seeing the way she lit up in pure delight while talking to her sister, and laughing at how she wiggled in her chair when she found a matching puzzle piece. I wanted this moment to stay here for just the three of us.

Which was exactly why I let people continue to barge in.

What the Hell was wrong with me—getting swept up in a human to the point of doing outlandish things just to see her happy ...

I mean, we were *friends*, something I was still new to. Maybe these feelings—also something I was new to—was just part of being a friend to someone. It was no wonder that it freaked me out a little.

"So how have you been this week?" Iyla asked, casting a nervous look at Gemma while she sorted through more pieces.

Gemma shrugged. "It's been weird."

Iyla went ramrod straight and stared at her sister. "Weird? Weird how?"

Gemma didn't seem to notice her sister's alarmed reaction, too focused on shoving more cake onto her fork. "There are days where I don't feel tired at all and want to run around and play. I don't stay cold those days, and I don't get sick. I even heard Dr. Seward telling Mom my tests come back normal on those days. No extra bad cells or something. I don't know."

Iyla's wide eyes found mine, and I knew we were thinking the same thing.

My blood is working.

We just had to keep up the weekly dosage, and soon, Gemma should start improving greatly until she really *was* better.

"That's good to hear," I said to Gemma, handing her a puzzle piece I found in my pile that matched what she was working on.

She smiled conspiratorially at me. "It started when you came, Zagan. Maybe you're the cure to my sickness."

Iyla choked on her water, but I just laughed at the very spot-on statement. "Maybe so. I'll keep coming around then."

"Yay!" Gemma cheered.

We finished our cake, and none of us left even a crumb on our plates. The puzzle soon followed, detailing a dragon soaring over a castle.

"Isn't it beautiful?" Gemma asked, beaming down at the completed puzzle.

Iyla smiled at her younger sister, her eyes never even glancing at the puzzle. "It is."

Gemma looked at me. "Thank you for the cake."

I ruffled her thin, dull hair. "You're welcome. I'm glad you liked it."

"If I get to leave one day, can I go see you in concert?"

"Is that even a question? You *better* come see me." I gently poked her in the side, which earned me a giggle. "I'll even get you VIP passes."

Iyla cleared her throat and stared at me with clenched teeth and a quick shake of her head.

I gave her a disbelieving eye roll and whispered, "Not *that* kind of VIP pass. *Obviously*." What did she take me for? I was a *demon*, not a child predator. I turned back to Gemma. "I'll make sure you get to see backstage and meet the whole band."

She clapped, and her glee seemed infectious for Iyla.

The excitement of the past hour and a half seemed to catch up to Gemma. She yawned and her eyes grew heavy. Iyla helped her into her bed, and she sat next to her until the younger girl fell asleep. Even at my place from across the bed, leaning against the wall, I could see the tears lining Iyla's eyes as she stared at her sleeping sister.

She swallowed, stood to place a kiss on her forehead, and whispered, "I promise I'll make you better."

The weight Iyla carried on her shoulders was huge, and it wasn't fair to her. The burden of trying to impress and obey her mother. The burden she'd taken on to save her dying sister. Those weren't weights she should have to carry, yet she shouldered them with her head held high.

I didn't know whether I was awed by it, pissed off by it, or pitied her for it. Probably all three.

We said our goodbyes to the nurses and staff, and I got a few more thanks on our way out, *including* one from Nurse Patrice.

"The cake was delicious," Patrice said as she bumped into us as we were leaving. I didn't miss the strain in her voice, like praising me caused her actual pain. "Thank you for bringing it."

"It was my pleasure, Patrice." I grinned and shot her a wink just to ruffle her wrinkly feathers.

She huffed and left in a hurry after that.

Iyla laughed and pressed in close to my side to whisper, "I can't believe Patrice was nice to you."

I grabbed the front door and held it open for Iyla to go first. "I know. Maybe she got laid and—"

"Iyla?"

Iyla and I stopped in our tracks. We looked out into the parking lot at the same time, and dread immediately washed away all the warmth from before.

Things were about to go very, *very* wrong.

CHAPTER 19

Iyla

"M om," I gasped with nails suddenly filling my throat.

Her hazel eyes bounced from Zagan to me. "What's the meaning of this? Who is he?"

With alarm quickly flooding my system, I turned to Zagan and whispered, "Can you go wait by the car, please?"

His blue eyes tightened slightly at the edges. He glanced at Mom, who still stood frozen by her car, then back at me. "Sure."

As he walked toward my car, I approached her with caution. My heart thundered, and the world swam a little as nerves shot through me at blinding speed. I was a fly caught in a spider's web— stuck with no way of escape.

"Iyla Marie," Mom snapped. "Who the hell is that man?"

I nearly tripped as I came to a stop in front of her. She never cursed. That was my first warning sign that the carefully crafted bridge between us was crumbling, and I wasn't sure if there was anything I could do to stop it.

"His name is Zagan," I answered. My voice came out small like I'd reverted back into the child she used to reprimand at the drop of a hat. "He's my friend."

"Friend?" She scoffed and shook her head. "Iyla, I've prosecuted *criminals* that look like that man."

My body went rigid, and my skin crawled at the comparison. The tattoos. The piercings. The disheveled waves of black hair on top of his head. Black clothes. She saw these things and immediately judged him off it. She saw his self-expression as some sort of admission of unlawfulness.

And that lit an unexpected fire inside of me.

I was used to her jabs at me. I was used to her breaking me down and smothering my self-expression. But she had no right to judge him.

"He's not a criminal, Mom," I argued with strength pouring into my words. "He's actually a singer in a band, and—"

She rolled her eyes and cut me off. "So he's some poor junkie who takes handouts on the street for a meal? I raised you better than this. How dare you act out like this? How dare you bring that kind of trash here, around these impressionable youth, around your *sister*? Have you lost your mind?"

My annoyance spiked as a burning desire to defend Zagan washed over me. "He's been amazing to Gemma and *all* the patients here. He even went out of his way and brought food for everyone today."

Her nostrils flared, and her voice rose. "You are awfully defendant of him. Friends? I wasn't born yesterday, Iyla. You're not friends. You're his *slut*."

The word was like a slap to the face. Shame, hurt, and guilt followed the sting, rendering me speechless and frozen.

"I have been so good to you your entire life," she plowed on. "I've given you *everything* there was to give, and all I asked for in return was for you to follow my very simple, easy rules. But you couldn't do that, could you? You had to leap at the chance to open your legs for some damn *thug*."

"Stop it," I begged as emotion clogged my throat. My pulse pounded in my ears to the point where I wasn't even sure if my words were coming out loud enough for her to hear them. "Zagan is a *great* guy."

Her lip curled in disdain, and she crossed her arms. "Stop seeing him."

My lip trembled as I stared directly into her eyes. For the first time in my life, I squared my shoulders and said the one thing I'd always been too afraid to. "No."

Her eyes widened, and she reared back like I'd hit her. She'd expected me to lay down, give in, and continue being the obedient daughter I'd always been.

But this was something I couldn't do. Zagan and I were bonded for life with no way out except death. He was always going to be there, no matter what Mom said. He was also proving to be the greatest sign of hope we'd had for Gemma, and I'd never jeopardize that. Today was proof that our plan was working, which meant we couldn't stop now.

Even more than that though, I liked having the demon in my life. Somewhere along the journey of sex and healing, I'd come to enjoy him and his presence. There was a certain confidence he gave me, and when I was with him, air came easier. Laughter came easier. The worries of the world fell away for a bit, and life felt fun, something it never had been before. Our friendship had carved space for itself in my heart, and I refused to sand it down.

Mom dropped her arms back to her sides and stepped closer to me, the vision of a stormcloud closing in. "Last chance, Iyla. Stop. Seeing. Him."

"I. Won't," I said through clenched teeth.

Mom flashed me a sinister grin, and the sight made nausea roll through me. The look could only mean one thing—the bridge had finally collapsed.

"Then consider yourself disowned," Mom said. "Your allowance, your bills, your apartment, your schooling, *everything*. It all stops here."

I felt the color drain from my face, and the ground seemed to shift beneath my feet as I rocked slightly. "Mom—"

"I'll give you the afternoon to get your things—*yours*, not the things my money bought—out of the apartment. You're on your own. Find somewhere new to stay. Since you've decided to whore around, I'm sure you can find plenty of men to pay for what you need. It doesn't concern me anymore. I warned you, Iyla. Actions have consequences. You'll have to live with yours."

My blood pumped hard, and my chest hurt from the marathon my heart ran. The shock and horror coursing through me quickly morphed into something sharp, hot, and bitter as I stared at my mom—the woman who was supposed to love me unconditionally, the woman who was supposed to always protect me, the woman who was supposed to support me in my attempt at life.

"Right," I said tightly, not bothering to contain the rage in my voice anymore. "I have to live with my consequences. Just like you. Right, Mom? Just like how *I* was the consequence for *your* actions. So now you do everything you can to punish *me* for *your* mistake."

The slap across my cheek came so fast, I didn't even have time to see her hand move. The loud crack of her palm against my face echoed in my ears, and lightning erupted behind my eyelids as searing pain flooded my cheek.

I reached up to grip my face just as my mom gasped and screeched, "Let go of me, you heathen!"

Tears swam in my eyes as I looked up to find Zagan standing between my mom and I. One hand stretched out to block me behind him while the other gripped Mom's still raised arm. His knuckles were white from how hard he gripped her wrist, and a cry brushed past her lips.

"Don't you *ever* lay your fucking hands on her," Zagan warned, his voice dangerously low.

Mom's chest fell rapidly as her frantic eyes stared up at Zagan. "This is assault! I'm a powerful prosecutor. I will have your ass in jail before you can even blink!"

Zagan's low chuckle seemed to echo in the space between the three of us like some dark melody plucked right from a nightmare. "Oh, please try. Do your worst, Valerie. I promise you that whatever you try to do to me won't be near as bad as what I'll do to you when I drag your fucking soul to the deepest pits of Hell."

Her face blanched, and her eyes darted between the two of us. "He's mad! You're both lunatics! I'm so ashamed of you, Iyla. To think this is the company you keep."

Ashamed.

The word pierced my heart, striking harder than any other insult she'd ever thrown at me. All I'd ever wanted was to make her proud, to have her smile at me with love and acceptance. That wish fizzled out like a match finally losing fuel and burning away into nothing but smoke.

She yelped as Zagan yanked on her, and he smiled wide like a crazed predator about to get his meal. "Didn't you know? Demons make great company." He got nose to nose with her. His smile fell, and he hissed, "Until you piss us the fuck off."

His fingernails sharpened and turned black while his horns appeared in his hair.

I gasped and grabbed onto his arm, which still pressed into the front of my body to shield me from my mom. I clung to him and shouted at him to stop, but it was too late. His human guise was gone, and my mother's mouth gaped open as she stared at him in horror. Her legs wobbled, and her eyes rolled back into her head as she sagged. Zagan released her arm to let her limp body crumble to the asphalt, and he sneered down at her unconscious body.

"Zagan," I cried in a panic. I tightened my grip on his arm and whipped my head around us, frantically looking for any people who might be around. "Please change back. Someone else is going to see you!"

He inhaled deeply through his nose like he was wound up tight and trying hard to calm down. Finally, his black-and-red eyes, nails, and horns disappeared. His attention never left my mom. "Tell me why I shouldn't kill her right here, right now. Because the only thing stopping me at the moment is the fact that you're standing here and would have to watch."

I swallowed hard. His words were more of a reminder of *what* he was than his actual demonic form. He could easily steal her life and banish her to Hell. For a moment, I actually considered letting him. But I knew that was anger and hurt talking. I couldn't let my mom meet a fate like that, especially not by Zagan. I didn't want to think of Mom's death when I looked at him.

"Zagan, you're already going to be in deep shit since she's seen you *and* you threatened her. We don't need to add *murder* to the list right now."

"Deep shit, my ass. She won't do anything."

He curled his lip at her limp body and crouched. He slapped her face a few times—harder than necessary, but I wasn't about to argue with a fuming demon—until her eyes fluttered open. As soon as she looked up at him, she went to scream, but he quickly shot his hand out to squeeze her cheeks in his grip, squishing her cheeks together and forcing her mouth closed.

"Shut up," Zagan barked. "You've seen me, so now you know to fucking behave. You won't do shit to me, because nothing you do can *touch* me. Nothing you do can touch *Iyla*. You want her gone and ties cut? Fine. I've been waiting for that to happen. But don't think for one second that you've won. Look who's standing," Zagan said, tipping his head in my direction. "And look who's folded on the ground, pissing themselves."

I noticed then the gray material of her pants darkening with urine around her thighs. Some twisted part of me took satisfaction in seeing her rendered to that state.

"You think you've gained some sort of power over Iyla by cutting her off?" Zagan barreled on, his voice eerily calm. "Wrong. Iyla doesn't need you. So keep your damn money, apartment, and control. Because *she's* the one that's done with *you*."

He tossed her head to the side as he released her face, and already, bruises formed where he'd gripped her. His large body towered over her trembling form as he added, "And in case it wasn't obvious, you're going to keep what happened here and what you saw a secret. That threat *criminal* enough for you?"

Zagan slipped his hand in mine and pulled me along with him toward my car. I started to glance over my shoulder, but without even looking at me, Zagan warned, "Don't you dare look back at her."

My gaze trained on the asphalt as I heeded his words. I could practically feel the rage pouring off him in waves, yet I couldn't find it in myself to be afraid of him. If anything, I leaned further into his arm, feeling safer than I had in a long time.

He led me to the passenger seat, and for the first time, he slid into the driver's seat of my car. His grip on the wheel made me worry for the wheel's safety. I half expected it to melt at his touch or break in half. But I didn't say anything, not even when he gunned it out of the parking lot.

At some point, I'd gone numb inside, though I could still feel the biting sting of my mom's hand against my cheek. My head leaned limply against the window as trees sped by at the same blinding speed my heart still went.

Mom really wanted to get rid of me.

It hit me how fragile my relationship had truly been with her. All this time, I'd given one-hundred percent to her in all I did. She'd been watching me fight and claw and struggle to keep up with the furious effort, waiting until that one-hundred slipped even a fraction. If I wasn't giving it my all anymore, she'd finally have her excuse to get rid of me like she'd always wanted to do.

A tear finally slid down my cheek.

Always.

CHAPTER 20

Tyla

I SCANNED THE LIVING ROOM OF MY APARTMENT. MY stomach sank as I realized that it wasn't *mine*. This was going to be the last time I'd walk into this place.

"Where am I gonna go?" I whispered to myself.

I'd sent Zagan to get me some boxes for packing my things. I didn't own much as far as things my mom hadn't purchased, but I did have a few items that needed packed—clothes Nahla had given me, photos, a stuffed dragon Gemma gave me one year, and a couple other gifts from friends and family over the years.

I felt like I was moving through molasses as I pulled out all of *my* belongings. The clothes and furniture that remained were meaningless. I didn't care that I was losing them. It was what the loss represented.

The loss of my mom.

The loss of the girl I'd been my entire life.

What was I supposed to do now?

With Mom no longer expecting anything of me, it should mean new open doors for me, but I still clung to what I'd always known. Faithfulness. Obedience. Maybe if I stayed on track with my schooling and did as I'd always done, she'd welcome me back.

My stomach soured at the thought. Did I really *want* her to welcome me back?

I wasn't sure of anything anymore, and I didn't think *now* was the time to figure it out, not with the uprooting of my life being so fresh. My head would be clouded with too many emotions to think clearly right now.

I sat on the floor with my belongings, waiting for Zagan to get back. After almost two hours of looking over the things I was bringing with me, Zagan appeared in a plume of shadows. He held a stack of broken down cardboard boxes.

"Sorry it took me so long," Zagan apologized, sitting the boxes down. "I had a couple things to take care of while I was out."

That made me look sideways at him. "You didn't go ... finish off my mom, did you?"

He smirked. "It was a tempting idea, but no. The first thing I did was go get you this." He held up a phone. "I'm assuming your mom is going to demand yours, so I got you a new one. Hand me your old one. I'll transfer everything over while you start packing."

It was true. My phone wasn't one I had procured myself, which meant it was one of the many items that had to stay behind. I handed Zagan my old phone, and he held each device in a hand, his blue eyes bouncing back and forth between the two.

I grabbed a box and started folding.

Zagan knelt beside me and my things, momentarily glancing up from the phones with a furrowed brow. "Where's the rest of your stuff?"

I gestured to the small pile of items. "This is it. This is all I have that's mine."

I placed the clothes, trinkets, and photos in the box and sat back on my heels. One box. All of my things fit into *one* box. Emotion clogged my throat as I realized how little I truly had and how much my mom provided.

"Am I a bad person?" I whispered, unable to tear my eyes away from the box. "She did so much for me, and—"

Zagan's hand touched under my chin and lifted it. My gaze locked onto his beautiful blue ones. They were firm, steadfast, and sure as he said, "Don't you dare. Don't you think that shit for even one second, Iyla. If you want to see what a bad person looks like, look at your mom. Hell, look at *me*. What's happening is not a reflection of *you*, okay? This is your mom's loss of control. That's it."

I shook my head, sure he was wrong. "Look at how much she did for me, Zagan. She provided everything for me."

His eyes pinched like they were pleading with mine. "Sparrow, this stuff wasn't a symbol of her love for you. This was your *cage*."

I stopped breathing as his words struck a chord deep inside me. Looking around at the apartment, I took note of the cold space, the stiff furniture, and the impersonal items I never asked for but was given nonetheless. And for what reason? My mother and I didn't have a close bond, so why did she go to such extremes to give me what I needed?

My cage.

I'd welcomed the apartment and the money for my needs as a safe place and as a sign that I had a small place in her heart. But I realized now that Zagan was right. She didn't provide all of my things out of love. She did it so that I had no choice but to rely on her, to obey her, and to stay in this gilded cage of lies and sorrow.

I was tired of the bars holding me back.

I turned back to Zagan and whispered, "Let's go."

He grabbed my hands and helped me to my feet. He tossed my old phone into the room. The device landed somewhere with a loud crack, but Zagan didn't even bat an eye, uncaring of where it landed or how badly it just broke. I wanted to chase it down and carefully examine the damage, but I held myself back. That was still the girl inside of me who feared disappointing her mom.

I had to let that girl go, because she'd already done so much more than disappoint.

Zagan handed me my new phone. I distracted myself from my spiraling thoughts by double-checking my numbers and photos, all while he grabbed my box of belongings before I had the chance to. I bit my lip to fight the grin trying to take over when I noticed he'd changed his contact name back to, "Demon Daddy." I decided to let him win this time and left it.

When we got to the parking lot, I started for my car out of habit, but I drew up short. It wasn't mine anymore. Just as I wondered what we were going to do, I spotted Zagan approaching a matte black Camaro ZL1.

He placed the box in the backseat and gestured for me to go around to the passenger side. "Come on."

I climbed in without argument, and I took a moment to admire the beautiful interior. It smelled like him—spicy, clean, and a little like fire.

Zagan started the black beauty up and left my apartment behind in record time.

I didn't look back as we peeled onto the road. I kept my head facing forward like I was leaving behind my past and facing whatever came next as strongly as I could. And just how strong was that? I didn't know, yet.

The first task to complete was finding somewhere to go. I was now penniless and homeless. Lead filled my insides at the prospect of trying to figure everything out. My entire world had been obliterated into a blank slate, and I somehow had to start all over with nothing.

"I've gotta find out where I'm gonna stay now," I grumbled, raking a hand through my hair and fisting it in frustration. "I—"

"You're staying with me."

I looked over at the demon in surprise. "What?"

He didn't even blink, unfazed by my shock. "My place is plenty big. I already have a room getting set up for you as we speak, which was the other thing that held me up so long. I'm not always home since I travel a lot, so you'll still have your time without me if that's what you're worried about."

It wasn't what I was worried about. I actually liked having him around. It was the idea of seeming like I was using him or taking advantage of him. I quickly shook my head. "I can't stay with you. I don't want to freeload or—"

Zagan laughed. "Are you kidding? It's not a big deal, Iyla. We're literally stuck together for the remainder of your life. Living together just makes our arrangement easier. Stop overthinking it. And money isn't and will never be an issue. In case you haven't noticed, I'm loaded."

I swallowed hard, and after a few seconds, I accepted his reassurance. How could I not when he made such excellent points? With that acceptance, the first sense of relief since everything fell apart swept through me.

I was going to be okay. Zagan was by my side. I didn't have to face whatever came my way alone.

"Thank you," I said softly. "For everything."

He waved off my thanks. Instead, he shifted in his seat and cleared his throat, looking rather unsure as he probed, "Can I ask you something?"

I leaned my head back against the seatrest and turned it toward him. "Of course."

"When you and your mom were arguing, you said you were her consequence. What did you mean?"

I dropped my eyes as tucked-away hurt tore through me. That was a story I never told—to *anyone*—nor did I ever give it the time of day in my head. When I thought about it, my heart ached tenfold, and I still couldn't believe that Mom had ever told me the story or her brutally honest thoughts on the matter. Though, I supposed she did it to teach me a lesson.

Sex was wrong.

Wanting sex made me a whore.

If I opened my legs for someone who wasn't my husband, only bad things would happen.

The acidic burn of hurt filled my throat, but I swallowed it down. I stared at the tattoo on Zagan's arm, and I traced the detailed ink to give myself something else to focus on as the words poured out of me for the first time.

"Mom and Dad didn't love each other for the first part of their marriage."

He glanced over at me. "No?"

I shook my head. "Mom has always been the smartest girl in the room. Dad was the romantic, creative one. They went to the same high school but didn't run in the same circles. At least, not until one night at some senior year celebration when they decided to let loose. It was their first time, apparently. The first time Mom decided to be a little wild. The *only* time she got a little wild. Because that one time was all it took for her to get pregnant. She was seventeen."

I followed the scales of the snake on his arm, getting lost in the pattern as the somber tale continued. "She was from a religious family, so you can imagine their outrage when their unwedded, teenage daughter dropped the news of the unplanned and unwanted pregnancy. They forced her to get married to my dad." I paused, my throat tight. "She didn't want me, but they made her keep me."

My eyes moved to his other arm to trace the vines and cobwebs. "She was supposed to go to Harvard before she got pregnant. She had this entire plan already made for how her life was going to go, but I threw a wrench in those goals. When her first semester at

Harvard started, I was a newborn. Dad gave up his full ride to a performing arts school so that he could stay home and take care of me. He wanted Mom to focus on her career and doing what she wanted since he thought she'd been cheated out of her dreams. He was kind like that. Always thinking of her, even though he knew she didn't want him or his baby."

I cleared my throat of the raw emotion trying to climb up it and said, "Even with a lot of the burden off her plate, Mom realized she couldn't handle both the workload of Harvard and taking care of a baby. So she dropped out of Harvard and went to a community college for her undergrad instead. She didn't get into any of the law programs she wanted, she didn't get a serious doctor for a husband like she wanted, and she didn't get the child she wanted. Or rather, *lack* of a child. All her plans were ... gone. The end goal still came partly true. She's a very successful prosecutor making big money. But it took longer and was harder than she wanted it to be."

I closed my eyes and fought the tremble in my lip as I whispered, "I think she's always resented me for ruining her plans. I made her dream impossible, so now, she doesn't want me to have mine. I ... I feel like it's my fault things were hard for her, so I always obeyed and did exactly what she asked. I wanted to pay her back for ruining her life."

Saying that final truth out loud cut my soul into tiny pieces until I nearly felt empty. It was a bitter fact that I'd kept tucked away in the recesses of my mind, never allowing them time or energy to fill my thoughts. If I didn't acknowledge it, it wasn't true.

But that was just me deluding myself.

I could ignore it as much as I wanted, but that didn't make the reality of how my mom viewed me any less real.

Zagan's hand suddenly slipped into mine. He threaded his fingers between my own, and the warmth of his touch made some of the air come back into my lungs. It grounded me in the here and now, pulling me out of my head.

"I'm sorry your mom doesn't realize how lucky she is to have you," Zagan said, his deep voice wrapping around me like a hug.

I squeezed his hand. His words acted as glue, gathering up those tiny fragments of myself to reassemble.

Lucky.

Zagan saw my worth where she hadn't. He saw how hard I fought for her, how desperately I clung to any sign that she might care about me, or how much I strived to be the daughter she wanted. I tipped my chin up higher as his words finally hit home. She *was* lucky to have me.

And I was done trying to make her see that.

"Where is your dad?" Zagan asked after a moment of silence.

Fresh pricks of pain stabbed my heart like needles in a pin-cushion. "He died when I was sixteen. He was grabbing dinner for everyone, and he got hit by a drunk driver." I looked down at our joined hands and traced a lazy pattern over his tattoo with my free one. "It destroyed all of us, even Mom. She had come to love him by then after years of being married and having Gemma together. She found happiness with him and the new daughter she'd had. The one she'd *planned* for. So when he died and Gemma got sick shortly after, she took a turn for the worse. Got stricter. Quieter."

"No excuse for how she's treated you. You lost a father, too. You watched your sister fall ill, too. All without the support of your mom, I'm sure."

It was true. I didn't have her support. I had to grieve on my own. Nahla was there for me, but it wasn't the same as the comfort of a mother. I guessed Mom was too broken by then to bother trying with me. I wasn't worth the effort, and I realized with a deep breath that I never would be.

CHAPTER 21

Iyla

I FOLLOWED ZAGAN INTO HIS PLACE. HE CARRIED MY BOX up the stairs, and I trailed behind him until he stopped by a closed door near his own room.

"I thought this room could be yours," Zagan explained, nodding his head toward the door.

My chest warmed with his generosity. "Thanks. I really appreciate you letting me stay here." I grabbed the handle to open the door for him. "I might sleep on the couch until I have furn—"

The words died on my tongue, and my fingers slid off the doorknob, falling uselessly to my side. I'd just stepped into a dream. That had to be it, because ... *what?*

The light gray bedroom was the size of my previous kitchen and living room combined. A four-poster black bed with a beautiful dark purple bedspread stood in the center of the white-carpeted room, the headboard pressed against the wall. A black dresser stood to one side by some doors that I assumed was a closet, and a large TV was mounted on the wall across from the bed. In one corner of the room was a set of bookshelves and a large plush reading chair and table. A record player and neighboring shelf stood in the other corner.

Zagan sat my box on the king-size bed, and he gestured at the bookshelf. "I went ahead and bought you some romance books that came highly recommended from the bookstore downtown, but I also made sure you had plenty of shelf space to start building a collection. Same with the record shelf. I didn't get you any records since I wasn't sure what you like as far as music goes." His eyes suddenly glimmered with amusement as he smirked. "Except for a Sinners Do It Better record. I *did* get you one of those to start you off right."

My heart thundered as I looked over my dream room. "How—How did you know that I—I mean, this is my ..." I was at a loss for words.

He raised a dark, pierced brow. "You told me."

I looked at him, dumbfounded. "I did?"

"Yeah. That first day I came over to the apartment. You mentioned this was the stuff you'd like to have in your room."

Something light and warm filled my chest like an unfurling flower. That had been such an off-hand comment I'd made. It meant nothing, or so I thought. Yet he'd remembered it all. He'd *heard* me. And now he'd given me exactly what I'd always envisioned for myself. My hands shook with an overwhelming sense of gratitude and something else, too. Something unfamiliar yet startling strong.

I stared at the demon, too overcome with the blinding rush of emotions to even move. His thoughtfulness meant more to me than he'd ever know, and my chest constricted with the profound affection flooding it.

"Thank you, Zagan," I said. My voice was tight, but I kept talking. "This is ... incredible. *You're* incredible. I-I have no words. Thank you for doing this."

He smiled, only this time, there was no trace of teasing or seduction. It was all warmth, one that came out when your whole being felt the effects of whatever bliss coursed through you. "I was glad to do it."

He came over to where I still stood in the doorway. "I've got a meeting to get to with the group, so go ahead and get settled in. Since you don't have more clothes, I'll see about sending Eden over with some. Just relax, okay?" He tucked some hair behind my ear and stared down at me. "You deserve some time to unwind."

I held his gaze, which searched mine. My heart felt too full after what he'd done, both this morning with all the cake and again now. As I looked up at him—this demon that I'd accidentally gotten stuck with yet come to care about—something deep inside of me urged me to lean into him. To place my hands on his firm chest. To press onto my tiptoes so that I could feel his lips on mine.

But I didn't know where that desire came from, and that scared me. It scared me how badly I wanted to get closer to him.

So instead of doing anything that my body begged, I smiled and whispered, "Thanks."

Zagan left in a plume of shadows. With the abrupt lack of his presence, I finally drifted into the room. The first thing I did was flop back onto the bed. It welcomed me like the softest cloud, and I nearly stayed there because it felt that inviting.

I shot Nahla a text while I laid there, telling her how Mom had kicked me out. With that done, I forced myself to get up. I moved to the gorgeous record player. I eagerly got the Sinners Do It Better vinyl out and placed it on the turntable, starting the record up. The pulsing and sensual song filled the room, and I smiled as Zagan's deep voice sang sweet words and filthy promises.

The next stop on my room tour was the bookshelf. I pulled each of the ten books down, gushing over the covers and reading the synopses. I'd read a couple of Nahla's books over the years, but to have my own books to hug and flip through was surreal. Especially since they were romance books, the genre I'd been most drawn to.

By the time I finished flipping through and looking over the books, the record player finished playing the Sinners Do It Better vinyl. I switched off the player and replaced all the books, knowing that I needed to unpack before I got swept away in their fictional worlds. I turned the TV on and thumbed through the streaming sites. I landed on one that had *The Conjuring* and immediately turned it on to watch while I sorted through my belongings.

As I put away the few remaining things I had, I waited to feel the lingering effects of my new reality. Hurt. Turmoil. Grief. Anger. *Something*.

But all I felt was *happy*. Zagan had taken a horrible situation and actually made it seem exciting and like a new beginning instead of an ending.

I finished putting all of my things away, and with nothing left to do, it hit me how drained I was. Even though I wasn't lingering on the dark turn of the morning, I couldn't deny how stressful it had been, and that wild rollercoaster of emotions was catching up to me. I nestled back against the many pillows on my new bed, hugged the dragon from Gemma, and focused on the movie.

About thirty minutes into the film, Zagan reappeared in my room.

I smiled at him. "Welcome back."

He smirked. "You look cozy."

"Very." I sat up a bit and paused the movie. "How did the meeting go?"

"Funny you asked."

He looked at the vacant air beside him, which thickened with shadows. In the next instant, Coldin appeared next to him in his dark sweats and t-shirt. He was as straight faced as always with eyes that would be solid black, if not for the flames dancing in them. His swooping black horns stood tall in his brown hair, and his clawed black fingers flexed by his sides.

I gasped at the sudden appearance of the demon.

Zagan gestured to Coldin. "He'll be staying with us." Zagan looked at his bandmate. "Go ahead and change."

Coldin wordlessly darkened and shrank until a long, thick black snake sat on the ground where he'd just been standing. His forked tongue flicked out into the air as he slithered around my room.

"Holy shit," I whispered, watching his tail disappear beneath my dresser. I guessed he'd been searching for a dark place to hang out.

"Yeah," Zagan said with a small laugh. "All the guys are getting places here in Tennessee since I'll be staying here often now. That's what the meeting was about. Us relocating here instead of New York. We'll still have things to do up there, but we can record music here just fine with the studio I have."

He nodded in the direction Coldin had disappeared and explained, "Coldin is a ... well ... *different* kind of demon, and he isn't allowed to just roam free. He has to stay with one of us, and when he isn't doing a job—band stuff or his more particular assignments—he has to stay as a snake. So you shouldn't ever see much of him. He'll just be doing whatever it is snakes do."

I swallowed hard, still staring at the spot where he'd disappeared beneath my dresser. I glanced warily at Zagan. "What kind of demon is he, and what's his *particular* job?"

Zagan scratched the corner of his mouth, his lip ring flashing in the light. "You don't wanna know." He looked at the TV and came around the bed to flop down next to me. "What are you watching?"

"*The Conjuring*," I answered, my eyes inadvertently tracing the hard lines of his body. I was astutely aware of him and every move he made as he settled against the pillows beside me.

"Oh, that horror movie based on a true story, right?"

"Yep," I said, hitting play again, since he clearly wanted to watch it with me.

We both fell quiet, intent on watching the dramatic and suspenseful scenes unfold on the screen. The demon haunting the family made her first appearance, and my attention stayed glued to the chaotic moment.

"You know ..." Zagan said slowly. I reluctantly peeled my eyes away from the screen, only to find him focused on the movie. "I know that demon."

My jaw dropped before I could stop it, and my gaze darted between the TV and him. I squeezed the stuffed dragon in my arms tighter. "What? Really?"

He looked at me, his face the perfect mask of seriousness. I held my breath as I waited for him to answer. Suddenly, he gave me a shit-eating grin. "No, not really."

I released the breath I'd been holding on a laugh and gently punched him in the arm. "You asshat!"

He chuckled and looked at the TV again. "In all honesty though, I hate how humans portray demons in movies. We don't all smell like rotting meat and death. I mean, do *I* smell like that?"

I already knew the answer, but I made a show of sniffing him, which earned me a fleeting glare. "Nah. You smell good. Though, I feel like that's part of *your* particular job description. It would be kind of hard to get laid if you smelled like shit."

"Exactly. They're generalizing us. Only the flashy, attention seeking demons stink up the place. They have a thing for dramatics and think they're better than the rest of us demons because they can possess people. As if we can't be violent or cause destruction since we *don't* possess people."

I raked my eyes over him. "Can you be destructive like that?"

He turned to me, and his arm brushed mine. It sent a jolt right down to my fingers and toes.

"Of course," he answered, oblivious to what his brief contact did to me. "Incubi and Succubi can still beat some ass when we want to. You almost got to see that first hand today. It takes a lot to rile us up, but if we *do* get to that place, everyone knows to watch the fuck out."

And he'd gotten to that place today. Over *me*. The thought made my cheeks hot, and I bit my lip to keep from grinning. For some reason, having him get pissed off on my behalf made me feel fuzzy inside.

It also turned me on, which was freaking odd. Was it normal to be turned on over something like that?

"You got pretty heated today," I teased him in an effort to alleviate the feeling inside my chest.

His eyes never left my own. "Of course I did. You're mine, and no one fucking touches what's mine."

I stopped breathing. I licked my suddenly dry lips, and his blue eyes flicked down to my mouth as I whispered, "Yours?"

Something swelled to life between us. The air grew charged, like a livewire sparking with the threat of exploding into flames. I didn't know who moved or if we both did, but our faces drew closer, the distance between us getting smaller. We were two magnets being drawn to the other, unable to deny the pull.

"Knock, knock," a sing-songy voice suddenly cheered from the doorway.

I reared back and looked at the dragon in my lap as my entire face heated with embarrassment.

Eden appeared in the room with her arms loaded down in shopping bags. Her golden eyes spotted us on the bed, and she covered her mouth with her fingers as she gasped, "Oops! Did I interrupt you two? Feel free to continue. I don't mind watching."

I ducked my head even lower. I couldn't believe she'd just walked in on ... well, I wasn't sure *what* she'd walked in on.

"Eden," Zagan grumbled, and I didn't miss the trace of annoyance in his tone. "Glad you made it. Are those all the clothes?"

Eden raised her arms, jostling the shopping bags. "Sure are. I brought loads of goodies for our darling Iyla."

I turned the movie down as Eden brought the bags over to deposit on the bed. Her strawberry blonde locks were pulled back in a braid, and she sported a tight strapless green dress that stopped just shy of her knees.

She started pulling garments out of the bags and chattering away about the articles. Jeans, dresses of every kind, blouses, loungewear. It seemed never-ending, and—

My eyes widened as she held up something black and lacey. "What is *that*?"

Zagan chuckled, the sound all lust and no humor. "I like that one."

I glanced at him and found his lustful eyes trailing over my still seated form. I gave him an incredulous look. "Of course you do. I'd basically be *naked* in it."

"You're gorgeous," Eden said, tossing me the lingerie. "And like I always say. If you have it, flaunt it, babe."

"Couldn't have said it better myself," Zagan agreed.

My phone vibrated while Eden continued showing off more of what she'd brought me. I had her hold and stepped out into the hall to answer Nahla's call.

"Hey—"

"Your Mom kicked you out?" Nahla's shrill voice demanded from the other end.

I sighed and gave her the cliffnotes version of what happened. She listened intently, only cursing under her breath every so often. When I finished telling her what happened, the anger in her voice was unmistakable.

"I can't believe her! That gaslighting, controlling bitch! Honestly, you're so much better off without her, Iyla. Seriously. It's probably good that this happened. I know it doesn't feel that way right now, but—"

"Actually," I said slowly, "I'm doing okay. I was pretty hurt over the whole thing at first. And pissed off. But Zagan ..."

I wasn't sure how to finish or how to explain how he'd somehow made everything *better*. The situation that could've been far worse, with pain that went much deeper, felt like a mere flesh wound inside me instead. And it was because of him.

"Are you staying with him?" Nahla asked, and there was no missing the curiosity in her voice.

"Yeah. He gave me my own room here. It's literally everything I've ever wanted."

"So you guys are finally dating?" she asked excitedly.

My stomach flipped at the word. *Dating*. I quickly ignored that feeling and answered, "No. We're just ... friends."

"Right," she snorted disbelievingly. "*Friends*. Do you and your *friend* want to go out tonight? I feel like you need it. Me, Iseul, and Addie were just trying to plan something to do."

The idea of going out with Zagan and my friend did sound like a good way to end off the day. After the shitty morning and the uncertainty of my future looming overhead, their company was exactly the medicine I needed.

I peeked my head into my room. Zagan stood by the bed now, holding up the underwear Eden had brought me while she hung clothes up in my closet.

"Hey," I called to both of them. "Do you guys want to go out tonight? Nahla is asking."

Eden's eyes lit up like a Christmas tree. "Hell yes!"

Zagan dropped the panties. "Sure."

I relayed the message to Nahla who then requested to come over with Iseul and Addie to get ready. Zagan agreed, and Eden practically came out of her dress from how hard she bounced excitedly on her heels.

An hour later, Nahla, Iseul, and Addie were walking through the front door with eyes nearly bugging out of their head as they took in the magnitude of the home.

"I can't believe you live here," Nahla whispered as she held tightly onto my arm.

I laughed and pulled her after me. "My room is this way."

"Can't we have a tour first?" Nahla begged, trying to steal a glance of everything we passed.

"Don't be rude, babe," Iseul chuckled, shoving Nahla gently along.

"I'm gonna pass out," Addie said breathlessly. "I can't believe I'm in *Zagan's* house."

I figured this was surreal for the trio, considering they'd been long time fans of Sinners Do It Better. Most fans never got to meet their idols, let alone go to their house.

Eden and Zagan waited in my room. Zagan now lounged back in my new reading chair, and Eden sat on the edge of my bed. She leapt to her feet as soon as she saw us, smiling wide at everyone.

"Keep cool, keep cool," Nahla chanted under her breath as the three girls looked at Zagan across the room. She cleared her throat and said, "Hey, Zagan. Thanks for letting us come over."

Zagan smirked at Nahla's words, but his eyes were fixed on me. "No problem. Any friend of Iyla's is a friend of mine."

"Oh my God, that's so hot," Nahla hissed in my ear.

I fought off the blush trying to take over my cheeks as I introduced Eden to the girls and vice versa.

"No way!" Eden said, staring open-mouthed at Addie. "Are you Addie Parkland, the designer?"

Addie's smile widened with pride. "I am."

"Holy shit! I love your clothes!"

The two of them immediately burst into conversation about clothes and designs. I shared a stunned look with Nahla and Iseul.

Iseul rolled her eyes with a sigh and whispered, "They'll probably be here forever if we don't stop them. I've seen this same scene more times than I care to admit."

"Eden," I said gently, placing a hand on her arm. "Get ready now. Talk fashion later."

"Oops," Eden giggled. "Sorry." She leaned in to whisper to Addie, "I'll get your number, and we'll talk later."

"Now that that's settled," Nahla said, starting toward my closet, "let's find—Ahh!" Her scream triggered shrieks of horror from everyone else, except Zagan. She pointed a finger at the floor. "Sn—Snake!"

Coldin slithered across the carpet. He looked like he'd been minding his own business, but now that he'd gotten a reaction out of Nahla, he slithered closer.

Addie gasped, the scream we'd all shared from pure reactiveness completely forgotten. "He's beautiful." Her pretty blue eyes found mine. "Is he a pet?"

"Umm ..." I glanced at Zagan, not sure how to respond.

Zagan rubbed a finger under his mouth, which twitched with the threat of a smile. He watched his bandmate approach Addie's feet. "Yeah, he's a pet."

It took everything inside of me to keep my eyes from widening at Zagan's lie.

Addie fidgeted like she was trying to contain herself and asked, "Can I hold him?"

Zagan shrugged. "Go for it. Can't promise he won't bite."

Addie waved off the warning and picked up the large black snake. He wrapped around her arm, and she ran a finger over his scaly back.

Nahla flashed me a desperate look and said, "Let's get ready now that I've officially shit myself." She turned to Addie, and her nose scrunched in disgust. "I can't believe you like snakes."

Addie held him closer, smiling down at him. "Why? Don't you think he's gorgeous?"

Coldin's tongue flicked out, touching Addie's cheek. I flashed

Zagan a wary look, which he ignored. I really hoped the demon wasn't about to eat my new friend.

Zagan left the room while the four of us girls—and Coldin—got ready. I wanted to kick the serpent out since some of us were changing, but that would've been a pretty odd request since, to them, he was just a pet snake. Plus, he seemed mighty content, slithering up Addie's arm and over the tops of her pillowy breasts. Pretty sure he was trying to nestle in her cleavage.

The girls oohed and awed over all the clothes Eden had shown up with, some of which were actually clothes Addie designed and made. Me, Nahla, and Iseul chose something from among the garments with Addie and Eden's help. By the time we were outfitted with hair and make-up, the sun had set.

I looked in the mirror over my dresser one last time to see the silver one-shoulder long-sleeved shirt and tight black pants and heels. My brown hair had been straightened, and Addie had applied some natural but beautiful make-up to my face. With the dangling diamond earrings and necklace to finish it off, I actually felt ... pretty—something I was unaccustomed to feeling, thanks to the rules that had always governed what I was allowed to do when presenting myself.

Eden opened my bedroom door and called out to let Zagan know he was good to come back in. She sat on the edge of the bed by Addie, who had changed into a miniskirt and leotard top. Her blonde-and-pink hair fell down her back with sections pinned back on either side of her face. She still held Coldin in one hand while stroking his scales with the other.

"What club should we go to?" Nahla asked as she swiped the last of her lipgloss on. Her warm complexion stood out beautifully in her wine-red dress.

"I know a great one," Eden said with a vibrancy that never seemed to dim.

"No, Eden," Zagan said, appearing in the doorway. He gave the bubbly demon a deadpan stare. "We aren't going to that one."

A lightbulb went off in my head after seeing the pointed look he gave her. She'd wanted to go to the demon club, but the only human in the room who knew about demons was me.

Eden crossed her arms and puffed her cheeks in annoyance. "Party pooper."

"I know a place," Addie offered. "It has great security, which I assume we'll want given our celebrity friend over there." She gestured at Zagan.

The four girls started talking about the suggestion, but the conversation was lost on me when I met a pair of blue eyes. Zagan's attention was firmly locked on me, and his eyes made a slow sweep of my form where I leaned against the dresser. With every inch of skin his gaze touched, I got hotter and *wetter*. How could his mere attention alone feel like his hand actually running over my throat, between my breasts, over my pussy, down my legs, and back up? By the time his eyes locked on mine again, my heart thundered, and my clothes felt too tight.

It didn't help that he looked like a snack himself in his silk long-sleeved shirt. It had a loose neckline that opened up halfway down his abdomen, exposing the dagger tattoo in the center of his defined pecs and the edges of his moth and spider tattoos. A loose silver chain draped around his throat, and his hands were shoved into the black-and-silver pinstripe pants. Part of his hair had been slicked back so that only a couple strands fell across his forehead.

"Can you ladies give Iyla and I a moment?" Zagan asked, cutting off whatever they'd been saying.

The girls got quiet and immediately shared knowing whispers. Mine and Zagan's eyes never strayed from each other, even as the girls left and threw catcalls our way. The door shut, solidifying this electrically charged moment happening between us. My chest rose and fell harder as my demon slowly moved across the space until he stood directly in front of me.

He tilted his head, and his eyes glossed over with smoldering heat that had my toes curling in my shoes. "Are you trying to go out, or are you trying to make me fuck you until you can't walk?"

My breath came out sharp and fast, but I didn't look away. I *couldn't* look away. "I take it that means you like my outfit?"

The corner of his mouth tipped up. "Yeah, Sparrow. That word works for what you're making me feel right now." His eyes dropped to where I pressed my thighs together in an effort to stave off the furious heat between them. "What are *you* feeling right now?"

"A lot of things," I answered.

"Is my pussy dripping for me?"

His pussy. God, why did that make me flush hotter?

I didn't answer. My tongue was stuck, suddenly useless in my mouth. At my silence, Zagan reached forward and drug his finger over the sliver of skin visible between my top and bottoms. Goosebumps broke out on my skin, and a flutter of desire swarmed my gut. His fingers dipped into the hem of my pants, and with a gentle tug, he pulled my pants and underwear down. I couldn't stop my quick breathing as my fingers curled around the edge of the dresser behind me. Zagan helped me step out of the garments, and I widened my legs slightly, eager for his touch to find me between my folds.

His blue eyes briefly stared at my pussy before locking on my hungry gaze. He smiled and held my pink panties up on a single finger. I could see my arousal coating them, and my knees buckled when he ran his tongue over the wet fabric. Every fiber of my being wished those panties were *me*.

"I'll keep these as my appetizer for the evening," Zagan said, his voice rough with his own need. "And I'll let you walk around like that. *Wired.* Absolutely *hungry* for me and what I can do to you."

He stood, pulling my pants back up with him. I stared up at him, dumbfounded that he was actually stopping. I was on *fire*, but he made no move to give me release. He shoved my panties into his pocket, winked, and opened the door to gesture for me to go first.

It took everything to keep my chin from hitting the floor.

Asshat.

CHAPTER 22

Zagan

I YLA WAS HORNY AS FUCK. NOT ONLY HAD HER PANTIES been soaked, but when I reached out with my senses, her arousal hit me like a freight train. Even now as we climbed into a booth at the club, she kept shifting in her seat next to me, biting her lip, and glancing at me with those fiery eyes.

And goddamn, it took everything inside of me to not take her away where I could fuck her all night long. It had been a few days since we'd had sex, and that time had been a quickie since I was working and had to rush to get back to that. So I was just as eager to get her in bed as she was.

But I also liked tormenting her. There was something undeniably satisfying about watching my sparrow squirm under the intensity of how much she wanted me.

We'd just gotten settled in the round booth on the upstairs balcony of the nightclub Addie had suggested. The lounge was for VIP guests, and with one look at both Addie and I, we were admitted without issue, along with the rest of our group. They didn't even ID any of us after realizing what celebrities they had in their midst, which worked in Iyla's favor, considering she was still only twenty.

Nahla ordered a round of shots to start the night off, and when they arrived, we each grabbed one and raised our glass in the air.

"To Iyla and her newfound freedom!" Nahla cheered. "And to her first shot *ever*!"

There was a chorus of agreements that rang out before we all threw our shots back. Iyla's face immediately screwed up in disgust as she swallowed the burning liquor. I laughed and offered her another drink to chase it. She greedily drank the beer, but the aversion didn't clear from her face.

"Gosh. People like that stuff?" she asked, staring skeptically at the shot glasses.

"Hell yeah," Addie said. "Tequila makes everything better."

Iyla stared at her like she'd lost her mind.

"I'll go grab you a better drink," I said, leaning in close to Iyla so she could hear me over the loud music.

Eden was right on my heels, following me to the upstairs bar. I leaned on my forearms and gave my order for Iyla's drink. Eden ordered herself a jack and coke, and the two of us watched the bartenders get to work.

"You know, I never thought I'd see the day," Eden said playfully.

I looked sideways at her where she rested her chin in her manicured hand. She batted her big green eyes at me like she knew something I didn't.

"What do you mean?" I asked her.

"The day our little Incubus went soft. It's cute."

I quirked my pierced brow at her and turned so that I faced her with only one arm resting on the bar. "Excuse me? Soft?"

She nodded and tipped her chin back at our table. "For Iyla."

For some reason, my stomach bottomed out at the suggestion, and I scoffed. "Please. You're delusional. I've not gone soft."

She laughed and rolled her eyes. "Right. *I'm* the delusional one. You're the one in denial, but don't worry. I won't tell the other demons that you care about a human."

The uneasiness in my gut amplified, and now, any trace of humor left me. I stared at Eden, brow furrowed, and heart beating harder. "What are you talking about?"

She turned to mirror my pose, facing me with one arm leaned on the bar. "Come on, Z. I've known you for over a millennium. You've never treated humans the way you treat Iyla. It's not a *bad* thing. I think it's good that you have feelings for her."

My heart had never pounded as hard as it did now, and for a second, I worried I was going into cardiac arrest. Until reason reminded me that demons couldn't do that. "Feelings?"

I looked back at our table where Iyla watched her friends talk and throw back drinks. Her brown eyes pinched at the sides in a bright smile, and she threw her head back in a laugh at something Addie said. The beating in my chest stopped. The air in my lungs stilled. Time suspended until all that remained was Iyla and her gorgeous laughter. The delighted sound blanketed me in warmth, like a song written just for me.

I quickly remembered myself and turned back to Eden with a cough. "You're wrong. She and I are friends because of our bond. That's why I treat her the way I do."

The bartender slid us our drinks, and Eden grabbed hers without looking away from me. She gave me a knowing smirk. "Really? Because I don't look at my friends the way you look at her." She shrugged. "Just some food for thought."

She spun on her heel and left me standing there with my heart in my throat. Feelings? For Iyla? That was impossible. Demons couldn't feel anything for people. At least, *most* of us couldn't. Sure, there were a few instances where demons had fallen in love with people, but that was a rarity. And *I* wasn't one of them. Iyla was just a human with whom I got along. That was all.

I made it back to the table with Eden's stupid words still trying to till up my thoughts. Iyla's big eyes found mine, and a smile was still plastered onto her perfect lips. I handed her the drink I'd gotten her and watched her taste it.

"Better?" I asked.

She took a few tentative sips and finally nodded. "Much better. Thank you."

Nahla threw back a shot then grabbed her girlfriend's hand. "Dance with me, baby."

She and Iseul rushed to the dance floor below. Addie and Eden weren't far behind, and they easily found partners to dance with once on the floor. Iyla and I slid out of the booth to watch from the balcony above. I rested my arms on the railing, and when I noticed how Iyla shifted restlessly next to me, I made sure my arm brushed against her. She shivered, and I fought a smile at the reaction. She was still teetering on the edge of trying to keep her head *here* and not on the desire to get railed. My straining cock begged for the latter, but it could wait. I didn't need all these human eyes watching me fuck someone in public. *That* would be a shitstorm for the band's PR team.

"What do you think Coldin's doing?" Iyla asked like she was fishing for something to distract her from whatever she was really thinking about.

I shrugged, watching the bodies below. "Probably finding a dark corner somewhere in the house to hang out in. That's all he really does as a snake."

"Why didn't you let him come here with us?"

I hesitated and raised a brow. "I didn't even think about it, to be honest. I don't really give much thought to him or anyone else."

"That's not true."

I looked over to find her staring at me. The lust in her eyes had been replaced with a sudden seriousness. "You're very thoughtful," she argued. "Look at all you've done for me."

Eden's words tried to push their way to the forefront of my head, but I quickly shoved them back.

"You're different," I said.

A crease formed between her brows. "Why?"

I frowned. I didn't know how to answer that. Eden seemed to think *she* knew the answer, but she was wrong. She had to be. So then, I was left asking myself: why was Iyla different? It didn't make sense to me, either.

"Because I'm your bond?" she probed.

I chewed thoughtfully on the inside part of my lip ring, but no matter how I considered it, that answer didn't feel right. "No. That's not why."

"Because I'm your friend?"

That sounded closer to what I was feeling, but I still didn't know. I'd been bonded to humans before, but I never felt the need to do shit for them. I fucked, I left. Rinse, repeat.

Iyla was more than a person I was stuck with. I *wanted* to do things for her. I *wanted* to see the sparkle light up her eyes or to see the way her lips lifted after being held down for so long or to see the way her chest rose sharply when overcome with some sort of emotion. She was more than a deal for me. She was ...

"Yeah," I finally answered with a nod. "Because we're friends."

That had to be it.

She smiled at me, and the sight made it harder to breathe. I quickly looked back at the dance floor to clear my head of the confusion her questions and Eden's thoughts had caused. The music gripped me, and I focused on that until my limbs itched to get down there.

I angled my body toward hers and gestured to the floor below. "Want to dance?"

She looked down, and when her eyes met mine again, they shined with a newfound sense of excitement. "Yes."

I grabbed her hand and pulled her downstairs to the dance floor just as PLVTINUM's "Come My Way" came on over the speakers. The high energy beat fueled my body as I moved in time with the tempo, and I swiftly pulled her against me. I pressed one hand firmly into her lower back, and we started moving to the music.

She laughed, seemingly enjoying the lure of the music and the quick-paced dancing. Her movements got less rigid, and she swiveled her hips and pressed into me as I guided her along with me. The music reached the exciting chorus, and I spun her out at arm's length then twirled her back into me so that her back was pressed to my chest. I gripped her hips and gyrated against her to the song. Spinning her out and back into me so that she faced me again, I saw the euphoria plastered to her lips, and *damn*.

Nothing compared.

Her smile was sunshine breaking through the darkest storm clouds. The sight and what it did—not to my cock, but *inside* me— had me pulling her closer so that we were chest to chest, nose to nose, grinding and swaying as our breath mingled and hearts raced together.

The music carried into another sultry song, but the sound got lost on me. My world zeroed in on the girl wrapped in my arms. Our foreheads pressed together, and I kept my hands firmly on her waist while hers gripped my biceps. We swayed to our own beat, lost in our own song, and it was unlike anything I'd ever felt before. The sense of peace, of wholeness, of …

My chest tightened. What was it? What was this fluttering warm feeling that consumed me when I was around her? Not knowing, especially after Eden spouted off her nonsense, was going to drive me crazy.

Her fingers dug into my biceps, and her chin tilted so that her lips were a breath away from mine. "Zagan."

My cock thickened and pressed into her at the way she said my name like a plea to her god. She wanted me. She *needed* me. And what kind of savior would I be if I didn't answer her prayer?

I closed the rest of the space between us. My lips swept over hers, and she immediately opened up to let my tongue slide in.

The blood rushed straight to my dick as the kiss deepened, and I gripped her tighter around the waist. I needed her fucking skin on mine. I needed to have my hands all over her. I needed to shove myself deep inside of her.

I pulled back only enough to growl against her lips, "Come with me."

I grabbed Iyla's hand and found a hallway to disappear down. I found a vacant bathroom, shoved her inside, and pulled her against me again. Shadows immediately folded around both of us. She gasped and gripped me tighter. When the darkness cleared, we were back at my house, standing in the middle of her bedroom.

I held onto her as she swayed unsteady on her feet. She clutched her head like she was dizzy, which made sense. We'd just walked through the shadows to get where I wanted to go. That, no doubt, had to be discombobulating for a human.

"Did you just transport us back here?" she asked as she finally got her bearings.

"I thought you'd prefer this over fucking in a bathroom stall."

Her cheeks got red, and her eyes locked on mine. "Is that what we're doing?"

"Yeah, baby. That's what we're doing."

I swept my hands into her hair and pulled her into me. My mouth dropped to hers, and she let out a breathy sigh as my tongue swept into her parted lips. Kissing her was unlike any high, unlike any buzz, unlike any *sin*. The sparks her lips and tongue made inside my gut were intoxicating, and I pushed deeper, craving even more of it from her.

My hands moved from her hair, down her back, and stopped at the hem of her shirt. I quickly pulled it off, but my lips were right back on her. I couldn't stay away for too long, not when her kiss was like sweet lightning in my chest.

I pushed her back toward the bed and ran my hands up her bare stomach to reach underneath her bra. My palms squeezed her perfect tits, and she groaned a sweet little sound as I tweaked her budded nipples.

"I like it when you touch me," she said breathlessly.

"Oh yeah?" I nipped her lip and took her bra off. My mouth salivated at the sight of her breasts, the nipples pink and hard with desire. The diamond necklace she wore rested at the top of her cleavage, and I took pity on the gemstone. That elegant gem could never hope to compare to her.

"You're so good at everything," she said. Her hands found my open shirt, and her nails scraped into my skin as I pinched and pulled at her breasts. "I won't mind having you as my only partner for the rest of my life."

I chuckled and kissed the skin on her neck. "Good, because I'm all you'll ever get."

She leaned back as I pressed her down, and she fell back onto the bed. I watched her scoot backward, her eyes locked on me like she was ravaging me with her gaze alone. Those big browns didn't leave me as I stripped off my shirt and let it join hers on the floor.

"So when you feed off me," she started slowly, watching my fingers undo my pants, "do you get full based on my satisfaction?"

I raised an eyebrow at her curiosity, and for some reason, I liked her asking questions. I liked her wanting to know more about me.

"Basically," I answered. "The more you like it, the better I eat."

I immediately saw the wheels turning in her head, and my own intrigue skyrocketed. What filthy little thoughts now floated around my sparrow's head? I hadn't done anything very kinky or crazy with her yet since she was still getting a feel for what she liked, but the spark of curiosity in her eyes made me wonder if she was ready to start venturing into darker waters with me.

"We can only sleep with each other because of the bond." It was a statement, not a question.

I stepped out of my pants so that only my black briefs kept my raging hard-on away. "Correct."

"What if my kink was group sex or something? It's not, but I was just curious about how all of this worked. Like, would you starve to death because the other person wasn't completely satisfied?"

My blood heated, and there was no stopping the smirk that pulled at my lips.

This was going to be fun.

CHAPTER 23

Iyla

MY HEART FELT LIKE IT WAS RUNNING AWAY FROM me. I was completely wound up and eager for him to touch me and fuck me. But I was also curious about him—more specifically, the demonic part of him. He fascinated me in every sense of the word.

"What would I do if my bond liked more than one partner?" he asked.

I swallowed hard. The grin he wore and the gleam in his eye had turned alluring and seductive, like he was just waiting for me to say the word, and when I did, he was going to devastate me in the best way possible. Mustering up my courage, I nodded.

Zagan's amusement never faded, even as the air seemed to vibrate around him. Shadows rolled off his body and gathered in the air next to him. My breath stuttered, and my core clenched with newfound desire as the black smoky substance grew and solidified until I stared at two identical Zagan's.

"Holy shit," I said under my breath.

Seeing the real Zagan basically naked in all his tattooed, pierced, and ripped glory was already enough to have me hot and wet. To now have two times the eye candy was sending my heart into overdrive.

"If they like group activities ..." my Zagan said as he approached me while his double slowly circled the bed. "I'd just have to make more of me."

My gaze bounced between the two Zagan's that stalked toward me like predators on the hunt. I shifted to my knees to get in a better position to keep an eye on both of them. The burning heat between my thighs intensified, and my mind raced with ideas of what was about to happen. I'd merely been asking about multiple partners to understand Zagan's position and limitations better, but the idea of being showered in attention by *two* of him ... My skin prickled with fresh waves of desire.

The clone got on the bed behind me, and I watched his movements like a starved man seeing food for the first time. My Zagan suddenly gripped my chin and forced me to look at him.

"Eyes on me," he growled.

I released a shaky breath and smirked. "My eyes *were* on you."

A sharp slap on my ass had me yelping, but Zagan kept a firm grip on my chin to keep me from whipping around. Hands grabbed my hips and yanked them back, and Zagan kept his hold on my chin so that I was forced to get on my hands and knees in order to hold myself up.

My heart pounded as my pants and panties were pulled down by the hands at my back. Desire so potent, it hurt, curled tightly in my core, and it only got worse when the air hit my wet folds. One hand that had been on my thigh reached between my legs to slick a finger along my seam, rubbing back and forth against my clit. My eyes nearly closed, and my body jolted from the ferocity of the pleasure that hit me. Whimpering, I wiggled against the fingers massaging me right where I wanted.

Zagan's blue eyes swirled with darkness, and his fingertips elongated until they poked into the skin of my cheeks. His horns appeared in the tousels of his hair, and he gave me a fanged smile as his free hand shoved the band of his briefs down.

I sucked in a sharp breath as his hard cock sprang free right at eye level. The body behind me pried my legs further apart so that he sat between them, his fingers still rubbing on my clit in a tauntingly slow pace. My eyes nearly rolled back into my head when I felt him grind his still confined erection against my dripping pussy.

"You're gonna be a good girl and suck my cock while I fuck you from behind," Zagan commanded, low and husky.

I tried to nod, eager to finally *feel* him, but his grip was too tight for me to move. Instead, I raised my eyes from the head of his dick to meet his black-and-red gaze. "Yes. I'll be a good girl."

He squeezed my cheeks harder, and understanding what he wanted, I opened my mouth wide. In the same instant that his dick plunged into my mouth, the hard cock at my back shoved into my pussy in one deep, hard thrust. I gasped around a mouthful of Zagan's shaft, and my core tightened around the length filling me up.

"Suck me nice and slow, baby," Zagan cooed above me, gripping my hair in one hand while still holding my chin with the other. "Show me how much you love my cock."

My nerves were high, as I'd never done this before. I had no idea what I was doing, but I was hungry enough for him that I threw worry to the wind. I ran my tongue over the head and sucked, but blinding pleasure made me lose sense of the task as the demon behind me shoved in and out at a tempo that touched toe-curling places inside me. I clawed at the comforter beneath me, trying to suck on Zagan's huge dick while getting railed by the other one.

Wickedly delightful pinpricks of sensation swept across my skin and settled between my thighs where the second Zagan still swept his finger over my sensitive bud of nerves. The hot pressure built with each shove into my pussy, each swipe of his fingers, and each bob of my head as I swallowed more and more of Zagan's length. Trying to fit all of him inside my mouth was impossible, but that didn't stop him from meeting me every time I was shoved forward by his counterpart's thrusts.

"Good fucking girl," Zagan praised above me as his hand tightened in my hair. "Just like that."

I moaned around another deep mouthful. It was too much. The silky smooth cock shoving into my throat. The feeling of being blissfully filled between my legs. The sparks of pleasure burning brighter against my clit. The combination of everything had the heat curling in my center pulsating even harder and faster until my release crashed through me. My eyes rolled back into my head, and I would've toppled over if not for the sets of hands holding me up on both ends.

"You're not done yet," Zagan growled as he continued to pump into me from both ends.

I tried to breathe around his dick, but it was hard to get a good breath around it. It didn't help that the other Zagan was still driving into my pussy with hungry thrusts. I gagged and fought to inhale through my nose while still maintaining the pull of his dick with my tongue and mouth.

His head fell back, and his clawed fingers squeezed me harder until pricks of pain broke out on my cheeks. Something warm and wet rolled down my skin from his fingers, but I ignored the pain as dizzying waves of bliss hit me all over again.

I moaned harshly against his cock, and he grunted as he spilled into my mouth.

His slitted eyes immediately locked onto my lips as he pulled his dick out. "Swallow," he ordered.

His command made my nerves return. Swallowing his cum felt intimate and sensual, but then again, so did everything else we just did. My teary gaze never left his. I pressed my lips together and swallowed the salty cum. When it was gone, I opened my mouth wide to show him I'd completed the task.

He grinned. "Good girl." He snapped his fingers, and the body at my back disappeared in a plume of shadows that rushed back to Zagan.

I swayed on my jelly-like hands without the demons holding me up from behind and front. Zagan grabbed my weak arms and pulled them until I was forced to raise up on my knees. In the next instant, he lifted me off the bed and wrapped my legs around his waist, his still-hard dick poking into my ass.

I wove my arms around his neck to hold on, and the pulsing in my core picked back up as my naked body pressed to his. He squeezed my ass and ran his tongue along the spots on my cheeks where the needle-like pain lingered. I tilted my head back and let my eyes close, relishing the feeling of his tongue all on my chin and neck. The small pricks of pain disappeared with the pass of his tongue, and if I had to guess, I'd say he'd healed them.

He walked us across the hall to the bathroom, and with one hand holding me up, he reached the other into the glass shower and turned it on. His attention to my throat had momentarily stopped while he got the shower ready, and my skin tingled with the lingering sensation of his lips. The feeling made me think about the black collar-like shadow that stayed hidden there, and I ran my fingers lightly over his own neck where his mark lived beneath his skin.

"Have you been bonded a lot?" I asked, still staring at his neck.

He stepped under the warm water and set me down on my feet, though he stayed pressed against me so that the water overhead rained down on both of us.

"It's happened a bit, yes," he answered, swiping some of his wet hair back. "When it was less acceptable for people to be free with their bodies and what they did with them. The majority of bonds resulted from cults or individuals tricking us. They'd trap us with the bond, forcing us to do their bidding through this."

He swiped his clawed thumb over his neck in a quick pattern, and the black ink swelled to the surface of his neck. My own skin heated in the same place, and I figured if I looked at my reflection right now, I'd see the marking there, too.

"You have to obey your bond?" I asked since that was news to me.

He gave me a teasing smirk. "Getting ideas, Sparrow?"

I rolled my eyes and tried to feign indifference even as heat swept up my cheeks. "I don't want to be the one giving commands."

Lust lowered his eyelids, and his gaze appraised me from head to toe. "Damn right you don't."

He slapped my ass hard, and I jumped against him, feeling his hard length press against me.

I cleared my throat and jabbed a finger into his firm chest, right over the spider tattoo. "I'm serious, though. You have to obey whoever you're bonded to?"

The heat in his black-and-red eyes faded a bit as he seemed to take my question seriously. "Yeah, I do. There's a certain incantation that, when used in conjunction with a command from my bond, I have to listen. This," he tapped the dark mark on his neck, "makes us. Demonic magic and seals are no fucking joke."

His eyes locked onto the mark on my own neck. "The seal is also what hinders and protects you. It's what keeps us both from sleeping with others. It would electrocute the shit out of anyone who tried. It's also what keeps me from killing you. If I come at you with malicious intent, it won't let me get anywhere near you."

"Wow," I mumbled, touching the band around his neck again. "Definitely no joke."

It sucked that such a thing existed—something that could trap demons like Zagan into contracts they didn't want. Even now, he was stuck with me, because I'd decided to pretend I knew about sex firsthand.

Guilt pricked at the edges of my mind. I'd done to him what selfish others had done before. I didn't *know* hiding the fact that I was a virgin would lead to this, but shame hit me all the same.

"What's that look for?" Zagan asked, tipping my chin up with a clawed finger.

"I'm sorry," I apologized, my voice coming out softer than I meant it to. "I wasn't trying to trap you or force you into being stuck with me."

His black-and-red eyes widened, and he stopped breathing. "You—You feel bad? For *me*?"

I nodded.

He gave a disbelieving chuckle. "Iyla, I'm a *demon*. I'm the last creature on earth you should feel bad for."

I frowned. "So what if you're a demon? More than that, you're *Zagan*."

Yes, he was a demon. But he was also surprisingly thoughtful, fiercely supportive, and kind to someone he didn't have to be. I'd thrown his world one hell of a curveball, keeping him from indulging in a new body each day, making him move to Tennessee, and forcing him to supply my sister with his blood. Yet he did it all—and *more*—with a smile.

"You're a really good friend," I said, letting my hands slide down his chest where they stayed.

His demonic eyes never left mine as the warm water continued to rain down on us. I didn't know what he was looking for or what was going through his mind, but without a word, he walked me backward to press me against the tile, hiked my leg up and over his side, and sank his hard length into me.

He fucked me hard and rough like he was trying to find the answers to all his questions inside my body. I wasn't sure if he found them, because we didn't stop making the other cum until I passed out in my new bed.

CHAPTER 24

Iyla

Something moved over my foot. My eyes snapped open, and a scream lodged in my throat as I yanked my foot up to my chest and threw my blankets off me. Coldin slithered over the mattress, unfazed by my reaction.

I gripped the front of my t-shirt and tried to calm my erratic heartbeat. "Coldin," I snapped. "You can't *do* that! You scared the shit out of me! You shouldn't ... *slither* across people while they're sleeping."

His forked tongue flicked out in response, and he continued his trek along my sheets until he disappeared back under my blanket.

Not wanting to share my bed with the unwelcome guest, I got up and went across the hall to the bathroom. My entire body was hella sore from a night of unrelenting and mind-blowing sex. The lingering satisfaction of each release still burrowed in my limbs, and when I walked, I *really* felt the aftermath of it.

Zagan and I went multiple rounds last night, and guilt over not returning to our friends tried to nuzzle its way into my chest. I shot each one a message, explaining mine and Zagan's sudden departure, which earned me the excitement I was starting to expect when talking to my friends about my sexual endeavors.

I went back to my room after relieving myself and doing my morning routine to fish some yoga pants out of my dresser to slip on with the shirt I wore—something Zagan must've put me in during the night since I hadn't fallen asleep in it. It was a band t-shirt with his face front and center. I smiled to myself.

Of course, he chose this one.

My first night in my new room was memorable, to say the least. I wondered if it would feel awkward, like when you stayed at a hotel or a friend's house. That unsettledness never came, though. I felt more at home snuggled up in those sheets than I did in the bed at my apartment. I wasn't sure if it was because of Zagan's smell on the blankets or if it was because I knew I was no longer under Mom's thumb. Either way, I'd slept better in my new room than I had slept in a long time.

I crept into the hall and down the stairs when I heard music coming from the lowest level. Figuring Zagan was down there dancing or something, I continued to that floor. I was surprised to find him, not in the dance room, but in his writing and recording studio.

Zagan leaned back on the couch in his human form. He wore black silk lounge pants and a matching robe, which was open so that I could see his tattooed torso and pierced nipples in all their mouth-watering glory. His pierced brow was furrowed as he stared at some music sheets in his hand.

I cleared my throat and crept slowly into the room. "Hey."

He looked up at me then, and there was no missing the defeat in his eyes. "Hey."

"Whatcha up to?" I probed, sitting adjacent to him on the couch.

He sighed and held the papers up. "Working on a new song."

The disdain in his voice was pungent, and it was punctuated by the way he glowered at the sheet music. I knew he'd been struggling to write a song he enjoyed, and despite not liking the latest song they'd just recorded, he let the group use it to appease their demands.

We were our own worst critics, so, eager to relieve some of that self-loathing clouding his features, I asked, "Can I hear what you have so far?"

He looked reluctant, maybe even a little embarrassed, but he grabbed the guitar next to him and began to sing. I listened, fully swept away with the melody and the beautiful sound of his voice. I held my breath as he sang, too afraid to even move out of fear that I'd somehow miss a sound.

He stopped abruptly and looked at me. "That's all I have so far."

I immediately grinned. "I like it!" I glanced at the music sheets spread out on the table as the lyrics replayed in my mind. "It has a nice sound, and the lyrics are fun. Very on brand for you guys."

"But ..." he encouraged, staring at me like he knew the word was right there on the tip of my tongue.

I bit my lip. I wanted to help him, not make his frustration worse. Maybe being honest was the help he needed, though. "But ... it *does* sound pretty similar to the music you already have out. You know. Sex. Pleasure. Sin."

He sighed and sat the guitar aside to rake both hands through his already tousled black hair. "I know. That's my issue. I just can't seem to get inspired or write something different these days."

This was important to him. Music was Zagan's passion, and struggling with it was weighing him down greatly. He needed a solution. He needed some inspiration. He needed a *break*.

"Maybe you need to step away from it a bit," I offered slowly. "Forcing yourself to come up with something isn't going to help. It needs to be natural, and for that to happen, breaks are occasionally needed. Try listening to or playing a different type of music for a bit. You've been honing in on this one style for so long, which can make you stagnant. Change things up. Play a different instrument or something."

He seemed to weigh my suggestion before nodding. "Yeah. Yeah, you're right. I might try that."

Offering him a suggestion he found helpful made pride swell up inside me. I beamed at him. "Good. Now then, I was gonna make some coffee. You want some?"

The demon perked up. "That sounds great."

He followed me down the hall and up the stairs to the main floor. I waltzed into the open kitchen to make the hot brew while he continued on into the house.

"How was your first night in your new room?" he called from one of the neighboring rooms.

"Good," I yelled over my shoulder so that he could hear me from wherever he was. "That bed is amazing. I really appreciate you getting it for me. I appreciate the whole *room*."

"As I said before. There's no need to thank me," came his far-away response.

I hit brew on the coffee pot just as a new sound began to filter into the room. My entire body locked up, and I took in a sharp breath. Goosebumps prickled over my skin, and my heart beat faster as my ears tuned into the slow, beautiful sound of the piano. I turned on autopilot and stared at the stretch of wall separating the ballroom from the kitchen and living room, and as if pulled by the piece, I trudged closer to the doorway. I stopped just shy of the entrance and pressed my back to the wall, listening to the haunting and somber movement of the piece. My eyes slipped shut, and Zagan's melancholy spirit practically touched me in a ghostly whisper with each note.

I stood there, enraptured and in awe for the entire first movement. When the coda finished and he didn't continue into the next movement, I peeled my eyes open and took what felt like my first breath in the past six minutes.

I finally rounded the doorway and found Zagan at the piano bench, hands now on his thighs, looking like a fallen god.

"Beethoven. 'Moonlight Sonata.' First movement," I said, but I wasn't sure who I was really saying it to. Probably myself. It was a reminder to the girl who'd been buried inside me. She still knew these pieces as well as she knew her own reflection, even after all this time.

Zagan looked up at me and gave me a small smile. "You know it?"

I nodded once, but I couldn't move anything else. I was frozen, staring at the sleek piano. The instrument was my deepest temptation manifested. I could still feel the dark movement of the sonata gripping my chest.

Zagan ran his fingers over the black and white keys. "It *is* a pretty well-known piece."

I cleared my throat and gestured to the instrument. "You played it beautifully. Can—Can you keep going?"

His eyes trailed over my form in the doorway, the gaze like a tentative caress. I didn't think he was going to meet my request when finally, he hovered both hands over the keys and began the second movement. This was the shortest of the three movements in the piece, but it was the start of what would lead into the fiery third movement.

I lingered in the doorway like a ghost haunting the room, listening with eyes closed, as Zagan commanded the music like a master.

When it finished, and he made no move to keep going to the finale, I opened my eyes to find him watching me.

"You play," he stated, staring at me with unwavering certainty.

I blinked and tried to clear the haze of the piece from my mind. "What?"

He pointed at me. "You were mirroring the keys on your leg."

I looked down, and sure enough, my fingertips were still posed in the ending notes of the movement. I hadn't even realized, but now, my throat squeezed with emotion trying to climb up it. I curled my fingers into fists against my legs.

I didn't answer him. I couldn't. Instead, I finally closed the space between us and gingerly sat beside him on the bench. With the black and white keys *right there* in front of me, close enough for me to reach out and touch, the ache in my chest intensified like a seismic wave rolling through a city.

"Keep going," I whispered, my eyes never leaving the keys. "Please."

I could see him watching me from the corner of my eye, but with less hesitation than before, his tattooed hands hovered over the keys. The fierce final movement began. There was no faltering or stumbling as he moved with the skill of a seasoned pianist.

I closed my eyes, brow furrowed and lips parted, as I focused on the intense movement. The music carved into me with its fire and strength, infusing me with its power for this moment in time.

Until suddenly, it stopped, not even three minutes in. I was getting *sick* of him stopping. I turned my glare on him, and, once again, I found him watching me.

"What?" I demanded.

"Why do you close your eyes while you listen?"

"Oh." The annoyance inside me slipped away, and a softness replaced it. "It's something my dad always did. He ... He played the piano. It was what he wanted to do with his life, what he got a full-ride to university for. Anyway, he would have me close my eyes while he played or while we listened to one of our records, because it was one less sense to take away from the music. With your eyes closed, all you can focus on is the sound of the instrument telling you their story through the notes and melodies. You can *feel* the song better that way."

Zagan stared at me thoughtfully, his eyes softening. "Your dad sounds nice."

Tears burned the backs of my eyes, but I blinked them away. "Yeah. He was."

Silence fell over us, and Zagan didn't make an effort to break it. It was like he wanted me to have a moment to exist in my dad's memory. It was something I didn't do often—think about him. Like music, I kept him tucked away in my mind, hidden in a box for safety where nothing Mom said or did could tarnish the man he was in life.

A musician, who played with the beautiful touch resembling composers of old.

A husband, who did everything from simple to grand gestures just to make his wife smile.

A father, who loved his daughters more than life itself.

He was warm, selfless, and he was *mine*—my hero, my best friend. My dad.

"I miss him," I whispered, a tear finally rolling down my cheek.

Zagan reached over to gently wipe the tear with his thumb. His hand lingered, and I leaned my cheek into it, letting his touch soothe the ache now searing a hole into my chest. His strong palm acted like a beacon of light as I navigated the turbulent sea of years old grief, and with it, the pain slowly rolled back into the cracks of my heart like the receding tide. I sniffled as I looked down at my lap.

Zagan nudged me lightly, and in seemingly an effort to distract me, said, "Your turn. Play something for me."

My gaze bounced between him and the piano and back again. The mere suggestion had my heart pounding and my nerves scattering. I quickly waved my hands dismissively. "No, no. I don't know how to play."

His eyes narrowed with skepticism. "Liar. You were just doing the fingering for the piece."

I wanted to hang my head like a child who'd just been discovered breaking the rules. There was no denying that I knew how to play, not when he'd *seen* me.

"Fine," I gritted out, not meeting his gaze. "I *won't* play."

"Why not?" Zagan questioned as he turned toward me fully. "I know piano means something to you. So why won't you play?"

"Because!" I snapped, my eyes finally searing into his. He didn't back down at my outburst, which only spurred on the rush of an answer. "Because playing will make me want it too badly, and that's something I can't want."

His jaw worked, and his shoulders pulled back in defiance. "Says who? Your mom? She doesn't control you, Iyla. Not anymore."

I heard him. I knew what he was saying, but I couldn't be sure I believed him. Sure, I lived in this new place with new things that existed outside of Valerie Winters, but I'd never be free of her. She'd always be there.

Her voice in the back of my mind, scolding me when I tried to eat something fattening.

Her sharp eyes watching my every move and how I behaved around boys.

Her disappointed scowl staring back at me as I tried to embrace myself and what I wanted.

The thunder cloud of her memory would always loom above me, ready to strike me with lightning and rain down feelings of inadequacy, discomfort, and self-doubt.

Could I live with that? Could I live with feeling like a failure of a daughter, all because I wanted to live my way and reach for my dreams?

I wasn't sure if I was strong enough to shoulder those feelings.

And that scared me enough to hesitate, even when freedom was fingertips away.

I *should* feel confident in who I was and what I wanted, but that confidence had been stolen long ago. Even without a direct tie to Mom, I still felt chained to her, and I wasn't sure how to break free of that.

The strong smell of freshly brewed coffee filtered into the ballroom, and I latched onto the scent as my excuse to leave.

"I think the coffee's ready," I mumbled. Without another word or backward glance, I got up and left Zagan and his words behind.

245

CHAPTER 25

Zagan

I YLA WAS PISSED. OR UPSET. OR BOTH.

Ever since she'd left me sitting alone at the piano, she'd been quiet, and her gaze was distant like only her body remained here while her mind was far away. And I knew *exactly* where it was. I could whisk her away to my place, but I couldn't take away the lingering mental damage her mother had inflicted.

I didn't expect her to understand or accept her new freedom a day after being disowned. There was no way she'd see this as a good thing when the hurt was so raw. But to see the way she lit up like an explosion of fireworks when she listened to me play made me want to always keep that look in her gaze. I wanted her to do what she loved so that the light in her eyes never dimmed.

Piano did that for her.

It also made me want to keep playing. I, myself, had forgotten what it was like to successfully play such a well-respected piece, and having an enraptured Iyla as my audience was a major serotonin boost. It reminded me what it felt like to love music again, something that I'd been struggling with lately.

So after a silent coffee break where I watched her over the rim of my mug while she stared off into space, I made my way back to the piano and played whatever came to mind.

My heart raced as my fingers moved, falling back into the memory of old pieces. There was no stopping. I bounced from piece to piece, composer to composer, style to style, all at random. There was no time to think, no time to stress over the crumpled up music sheets downstairs or the lack of inspiration for my own songs. I just *played*, and fuck, did it feel great, like reuniting with a long-lost love.

"That doesn't sound like a new song."

My fingers froze mid "Goldberg Variations," and the calming sound faded. I looked up at the sound of Dante's voice. He stood in the doorway with the rest of the band, including a human-looking Coldin.

"Nope," Perseus said, drifting closer. His hair was pulled back in a bun at the back of his head, and his muscles strained beneath the maroon crew neck sweater he wore as he leaned on the piano. "Sounded like Bach."

I flashed the golden-haired guitarist a teasing smirk. "Wow. You actually know something other than our songs? Color me shocked."

He sneered at me, unamused by my jab. He couldn't argue, though. I'd never known him to listen to anything other than our albums.

"Thought you were working on another song today?" Xander asked as he came over with the rest of the group. Strands of his black hair fell into his eyes as his ringed fingers tapped a few keys in no particular fashion, sending out an unpleasant pierce into the air. "Doesn't look like you're being very productive."

I glared at Xander's fingers touching the keys and immediately closed the lid. He quickly pulled his fingers back, narrowly avoiding having the digits smashed. He snarled at me, but I ignored the empty threat.

"I'm taking a break from working on music," I admitted, getting up from the bench.

The guys followed me out of the room. I glanced at the living room for Iyla but found it empty. She must've been in her room, probably still stressing over what to do now that her lifelong plans had been altered.

"Taking a break?" Dante asked incredulously.

I hopped onto the kitchen counter by the coffee pot and poured me some as Dante stared at me like I'd lost my mind. "We just released 'Moonlight Magic,'" I argued. "We don't need another song right now."

"You're right," Perseus said, leaning his tattooed arm on the island while he flicked his dangling dagger ear piercing with his free hand. "We need a whole *album*."

Tension bracketed my mouth, and my shoulders coiled tightly. The relief and ease I'd had while going through memorized classical pieces on the piano faded like thunder clouds rolling in on a previously clear day.

I'd felt something again—a spark of what used to exist inside me—while playing the piano, but the moment these guys showed up with their reminders of the need for more, that spark fizzled into nothing. I *wanted* to love our music. I *wanted* to be passionate about what we did. But I couldn't fucking do that like this.

"Zagan," Dante said carefully. His large frame leaned back against the island across from me. He crossed his arms, making the green t-shirt stretch over his dark skin, and he stared at me with an imploring gaze. "What's going on? You've never struggled like this before."

I puffed out a tired breath and looked down into my mug. "I just hate what I'm writing these days, man. Nothing feels right. Nothing sounds right." I looked back up to meet each of their gazes. "I just need some time to find my spark again."

The guys stared at me, each with a varying expression. Dante seemed almost sympathetic with his soft frown. Xander looked baffled with his raised brow and open mouth. Persues appeared to process my plea with pursed lips, and Coldin ... well, he stared at the ceiling, probably not even listening to anything we were saying. His head was tilted back, stretching out his tattooed neck. The skull depicted on his skin had a better chance of tuning into our conversation than he did.

"We can put a pause on releases," Dante finally offered. "We can stick to doing video appearances and concerts for now. If anyone asks about upcoming titles, we'll just let them know we're on a break as far as that goes. If there isn't pressure, do you think that will help?"

I thought about it. I wasn't sure if that would fix my problem, but it was *something*. So I nodded. "Yeah. Maybe without that, I can refocus and get back to where I need to be."

"You didn't have to keep trying if it wasn't working, Z," Perseus said, giving me a supportive look. "We thought you were just being a perfectionist when you complained about hating the songs, not actually asking for a break. You should've said what you needed sooner."

"Yeah," Xander chimed in, grabbing himself a mug and pouring the last of the coffee for himself.

I nearly flicked the shaved half of his head. Iyla could've wanted that.

"We can do whatever the fuck we want," Xander continued once he had his drink. "If we don't want to release an album right now, we don't have to. *We* control our group, not some label or higher-ups. People can just deal with it."

I gave a small laugh. Sometimes I forgot that I didn't have to do this. It was a career I *chose* to do, because I loved it. I really did. I just needed to remember *why* I loved it. Xander's reminder that this was our band to do with what we wanted made some of the stress lift from my shoulders.

"I hope to get back into the swing of things soon," I announced, raking a hand through my hair. "I'll let you guys know when I'm ready again."

Dante stood up to his full height again and plastered on a devious grin. "That's what I like to hear. Now that we've settled that, how about we go out tonight? I'm ready to have some fun after moving all my shit here from New York."

Perseus and Xander hollered their agreement.

Normally, I would've jumped at a chance to go out for a night of debauchery, but …

I glanced at the stairs leading up to the third floor. Iyla had been distant since our talk, and I wasn't sure how interested she'd be in going out. On the other hand, I wasn't sure how comfortable she was here yet since she'd just moved in yesterday. Being in this mansion all on her own might not be fun for her.

"Are you sick?" Perseus demanded, staring at me with concern. "Why are you hesitating?"

"He and the wife are having a spat," Coldin answered, his deep monotone voice piping up for the first time.

I glared at the demon dressed in all black, who still stared at the ceiling from where he leaned against the fridge. "We aren't having a spat."

Xander fought a laugh as he nudged Perseus, nearly sloshing the coffee out of his mug. "I love how his first instinct was to deny *that* part."

My stomach bottomed out, and my mouth dried as I realized he was right. *What the fuck?* Why had *that* been the part that bothered me the most instead of the jab about Iyla and I being in a relationship? Maybe I really was sick. Maybe demons could get ill now, and I was experiencing the first ever demon disease.

Dante moved across the space between us so that he stood right in front of me. His dark eyes searched mine as his brows creased. "You—You don't *like* that human … do you?"

I recoiled instantly, but my heart beat harder. Dante was too close. His words were too jarring. Eden's taunting from the other night joined in with his question, and suddenly, I felt boxed in. I placed my arm on Dante's broad chest to move him away and hopped off the counter. I opened my mouth to deny his accusation, but my throat closed up, stopping the words from coming.

"Holy shit!" Perseus gasped, his eyes widening. We stared at each other like the realization hit us at the same time. "He does! He—He likes a human!"

Xander threw his head back in a boom of laughter and came up to me to throw his arm around my shoulder. "You've got it wrong, Pers. Zagan would *never*. None of us would." His mirth-filled eyes met mine, and silence descended as the teasing slowly faded from his gaze, replaced by open-mouthed shock. "Oh my Hell. You really do."

My breath came too quick, and I couldn't seem to slow it down. Everything in my mind was firing too quickly for me to think properly.

Xander pulled his arm off my shoulder and took a couple steps back. "You—"

"He doesn't like a goddamn human," Dante suddenly snapped. All eyes went to him as he strode over to me, stopping so that we were eye to eye. He poked my chest hard and gritted out, "You *don't* like some human girl. You're just confused or some shit. We" he gestured to everyone here, "*can't* have feelings like that. So get your head out of your ass and back on your shoulders where it belongs. You're a *demon*. Not a weak, emotion-guided human."

He stepped back enough to finish, "We're going out tonight. Seven. Meet at Hell's Gate."

He didn't wait for a response. He disappeared in a plume of shadows, and with a rather awkward glance thrown my way, Xander and Perseus followed.

I stood there with sand still filling my mouth and my heart sprinting. Dante was right. I'd been feeling off for a while with all the issues I was having with my music, so it was probably those mess of emotions contributing to the strange flutter I got around Iyla. Eden and Xander were mistaken.

Iyla was just another human to me.

Something inside me twisted painfully at the thought. The unsettled flurry now stampeding through me was evidence enough that Iyla *wasn't* just another human, just another body to feed off of, just another bond. So what did that mean?

I looked sideways at Coldin, who hadn't moved or changed back into a snake. "What do you think?"

His green eyes finally left the ceiling to meet mine. He shrugged. "What does it matter what I think? What do *you* think?"

My eyes narrowed. "You're the one who started this by joking that she was my wife."

His expression remained as stoic as ever. "So that should tell you what I think."

Without another word, his body morphed and shrank until only a black snake remained. He slithered along the floor, heading for the kitchen cabinets.

"I should donate you to the fucking zoo," I hissed under my breath.

With a heavy sigh, I left the kitchen and made my way upstairs. Iyla's door was open, and I stopped at the edge of the doorway. She sat criss-crossed on the floor, staring at her closed textbooks that she'd spread out in front of her. Just the sight of her in my band t-shirt sent my heart soaring, and I knew right then there was something seriously wrong with me.

My sparrow had fucked me up somehow, but I didn't understand what it was or what it meant.

All I knew was, I couldn't breath past the swelling heat in my chest.

The first time I'd played an instrument was over a millennium ago, and I still remembered how it felt. It was the piano of all things, and when I moved my fingers over the keys and heard the twinkling and booming sounds, it was like opening my eyes for the first time.

Where there'd been nothing but darkness and emptiness before, there was suddenly blinding light, a kaleidoscope of colors that I'd never even dreamt could be real, and beauty unlike any other. Beauty in the world that I hadn't realized existed outside of the darkness. Beauty in music and the way it could convey entire emotions and stories without uttering a single word. Playing music—and, eventually, writing my very own—was like finally understanding what it meant to be alive.

That same feeling hit me now as I watched Iyla's slender hand tuck some hair behind her ear.

The blinding euphoria corrupted my mind as she chewed her lip and scanned the various textbooks. The overwhelming sense of warmth barreled through me as her chestnut eyes rose to lock on mine, stealing all the air and any sense of reason from inside me.

This little human was music, was beauty, was life.

She was *my* sin, *my* temptation.

She was ... *everything*.

"Are you okay?" she asked slowly, her eyes raking over me like she was searching for some sign as to why I stood silently in her doorway.

I cleared my throat and tried to keep my voice level and calm so as to not give away the absolute chaos happening inside me right now. "I'm good, yeah." I went over to where she sat and sank to the floor across from her. "What are you doing?"

Her shoulders sagged a fraction as she looked back at the textbooks. "I brought these with me, but I realized, like almost everything else, that I didn't pay for these. I tried calling Mom to see what to do about all my school stuff since she demanded every-thing back, but she won't answer me."

She hugged her knees to her chest, her eyes never leaving the books. "I don't know what to do anymore. I have class tomorrow, but do I even go? Do I keep trying for this degree that was meant more for Mom than it was me? Part of me thinks I can still fix things with her if I keep trying, but I-I just don't know." Her eyes squeezed shut, and she held her head in her hands. "I don't know what to do, Zagan."

I knew what she should do. She should give that woman the middle finger and tell her to kiss her ass. But my reaction wasn't Iyla. She didn't need a suggestion from a selfish demon. She needed one from a friend.

"Iyla." Her name left my lips gently, like the sound itself was made of glass and saying it too hard would make it shatter.

She looked up at me, despair and desperation clouding her eyes. Just seeing the desolate expression made my chest constrict with the need to bring some light back to her, to make her troubles disappear.

"Forget your mom," I began. "Forget the expectations you've always had placed on you. Forget the money and the schooling. Hell, forget what I've said, too. What would *you* like to do if you were given the chance to do anything? Don't think about how or the logistics of getting there. Just tell me. What is your dre—"

"To play piano," she whispered, cutting me off. Her teary eyes held mine, and they seemed almost pleading as she admitted, "I want to play piano."

I smiled at her honesty and gave her an encouraging nod. "Okay. What do you want to do with that? Teach piano? Be in a band? Work at hotels? Work with an orchestra?"

"I want to perform," she answered immediately, like the answer had always been tucked away inside her, begging to be let free, and now that it was out, there was no stopping the rush of truth. "I want to be a pianist, traveling and performing classical pieces all over the world with different orchestras."

I grabbed her hands and pulled her across the sea of textbooks to settle in my lap. She straddled me and wrapped her arms around my neck while I placed mine on her lower back.

Her eyes bore into mine as I answered, "Then that's what you'll do. I'll make damn sure of it. You're not living for anyone else from this moment on. Going forward, you're going to reach for *your* goal. You're going to be a pianist."

Her brows plunged, and she shook her head. "But I don't know how to get there. I've already spent three years studying—"

I lightly pressed a finger to her lips. "Excuses. Those are excuses to cover up the fact that you're scared. And I get it. Figuring out how to get where you want to go can be scary. Starting over can be scary. But if anyone can do it, you can." I squeezed her tighter to me and added with a teasing grin, "You won't have to do it alone. I'll be there with you, and having a demon at your disposal will definitely make things easier. I *can* literally do just about anything."

She laughed, and the sound went straight to my heart like an arrow striking true. Her fingers mindlessly played with the hair at the back of my head as she smiled at me. "You are a demon, aren't you? I forget sometimes."

Her words reminded me of what she'd said the night before. I was more than a spawn of Hell. To her, I was *Zagan*. I wasn't a sex demon, only good for one thing. I wasn't some creature that existed solely to inspire sin in the world. I was *more* in her eyes, and I'd never realized how much I needed to be that until she came into my life and showed me.

"Thank you," I said softly, looking deep into her eyes. I wanted her to see how much she'd helped me just by being herself.

She raised a brow and tilted her head slightly. "For what? I'm pretty sure *I'm* the one who should be thanking you after everything you've done for me."

I shook my head at the suggestion. Swallowing hard, I said, "Thank you for seeing me."

Surprise lit her eyes for a moment before a small smile replaced it. "Thank *you* for hearing me."

Iyla

TERRIFIED WAS AN UNDERSTATEMENT. I WAS LITERALLY starting all over, and Zagan was right. Starting from scratch wasn't going to be easy. Despite feeling absolutely horrified at the idea, I had to admit that I was a little excited at the prospect, too. For the first time ever, my dreams felt possible. Far away, sure. But possible. I was allowed to think about it at the very least, and that was more than I'd ever been allowed before.

How was I going to get there?

That was what I was trying to figure out as I sat down across from my advisor come Monday morning.

"It's good to see you," Mrs. Yates said as she repositioned in her brown leather chair. Her gray hair hung around her face in a sharp bob, and her black glasses hung around her slender neck on their beaded necklace. She placed her folded hands on the top of her desk, the air of complete professionalism radiating off her. "I looked over your grades on your way over here. They are looking as fabulous as always. You're really excelling."

Her praise made the nerves in my stomach run rampant. I forced a smile and said, "Thank you, ma'am. That means a lot."

She waved a wrinkly hand at me and asked, "So what were you needing to meet about?"

I swallowed the sand in my throat. "I recently got to thinking about my future, and I ... well, I wanted to see what steps I needed to take to change my major."

She raised her slender black brows. "Change your major?" She plucked the glasses dangling over her chest and put them on as she grabbed some papers. "Political science is the best major for someone who's looking to become an attorney. Are you wanting to just add a minor, or—"

"Music," I breathed out, making her freeze in her search for a pen. "I want to be transferred to the music department."

Mrs. Yates stared at me over the rim of her glasses. She'd gone as still as a paused movie, stalling in place so that her gaze bore into mine. Finally, she repeated, "Music?"

I nodded and shifted nervously in my seat. "I know it sounds crazy. We're nearing the end of the first semester of my junior year, and I've already taken so many pre-law courses. But I—I really want to do this. I want to play piano professionally."

Mrs. Yates slowly leaned back in her chair, her blue eyes tracing my face like she couldn't believe I was actually sitting here and saying all of this. "Can I ask where this is coming from? You've never shown an interest in the music department before. You've never even glanced at the music electives."

"Actually," I started, my hands fumbling with the material of my pants in an effort to keep my shaking fingers busy, "it's something I've always wanted to do. I just never thought I could until now. It took a long time, but I finally feel ready to reach for it. For my dream."

And it was all thanks to a demon who refused to let me continue hiding away in my cage.

Mrs. Yates watched me skeptically, and the confusion previously marring her features slowly morphed. Her nose turned up slightly, and the faintest condescending smile pulled at her lips in an expression I knew all too well from interactions with Mom and her colleagues. It was a look they reserved for people they deemed beneath them.

"And do you know *how* to play piano?" she questioned, that haughty tone just barely shining through her professional one.

I ignored it and nodded. "I do."

It had been years since I'd played, and I'd never actually *studied* music and all that went into it. I'd have a lot of work cut out for me, and it was going to feel near impossible. But the prospect of doing that for the rest of my life—learning new pieces, performing for audiences here and far—made the resolve in my gut harden. For the first time, I was sure of myself. This was what I wanted, and this was what I was meant to do. Not study cases to argue in a stiff suit in the courtroom.

I wasn't a lawyer.

I wasn't my mother.

I was a pianist.

Mrs. Yates slowly took her glasses off and held them tightly as she rested her chin on her knuckles. "I love that you have this calling to play the piano," she said, her tone all forced politeness. "That's a great hobby to pick up. I'm sure you could find a course or private lessons to do on the side. You don't need to change your entire major and career choice for that. You're such a gifted individual, Iyla. Smart with a successful mother in the same field. Throwing that away would be ..." she paused and waved her glasses as she searched for the words. Finally, she finished with, "A pity."

The churning in my gut grew. Only now, there was bitterness mingling with the anxiety. Bitterness at her dismissal of what I wanted, and bitterness over her judgmental attitude.

It took me a few moments to find my voice. "With all due respect, Mrs. Yates, this isn't a hobby. Playing piano *is* a career, and it's what I want to do with *my* life. My mother is successful, but her success doesn't determine what mine should look like. I want to do this." I took a deep breath and added, "Please."

She stared at me, looking like she was contemplating dismissing me and pretending this exchange never happened. Her chair swiveled slightly from side to side as if it, too, were debating what to say or do. Did she fight me on this to try and keep me on the path that had been laid out for me, or did she let me carve my own?

"You understand that changing now means more work for you, right? You won't be able to graduate next year. There's also no guarantee of a good, well-paying job in the career field you're seeking. Have you truly taken the time to consider this?"

"I have," I answered. "I understand, and I'm willing to put in the work and deal with the potential risks."

Her lips thinned in disagreement. I knew she'd hoped I'd reconsider, but that wasn't happening.

Finally, she leaned forward to grab some papers. "Alright. If anyone could start over this close to the end, it's you. I meant what I said. You are very talented and smart. I'll reach out to one of the advisors in the music department and get you switched over for the start of spring semester."

Excitement as bright as the rising sun and as bubbly as a fresh soda rose up inside of me. I beamed at Mrs. Yates as I thanked her and left the office. I knew that was merely the first in a long list of looming struggles, but with that one completed, the rest felt less daunting. It felt like this was really possible. My dream was on the horizon, just beyond these upcoming grueling battles.

I could do it. I knew that now.

And it was all thanks to Zagan.

I SAT NEXT TO GEMMA ON THE GARDEN BENCH, SOAKING up the warmth of the evening sunshine. Her complexion was clear of any gray undertones, warm with a pretty pink flush against cream-colored cheeks. Her eyes held a warmth like polished brass instead of muted murky waters. Even her frame seemed taller and stronger as she sat up straight on the bench, people-watching as she ate her red jello and gossiped about the drama at Bloomings.

"So that's why they broke up," Gemma finished, nodding at two patients that were currently on opposite ends of the garden—one doing a puzzle at a table and the other being wheeled through the shrubbery by a nurse.

"Wow," I said, forcing some shock into my tone. "I can't believe Tony did that. Sharing his crayons with another girl is definitely not cool."

"*Exactly*," Gemma said incredulously. Her voice held so much passion and life that it nearly choked me. She was really improving. "Poor Martzia cried for hours when she found out he'd done that. He even gave the turquoise one to Raylee, which he *knew* was Martzia's favorite color."

I tried not to laugh at the scandalous drama that was the seven year olds lives.

"The audacity," I gasped with a shake of my head. I finished off my own cup of jello and set it aside. "I don't have anything as juicy as that to share, but I do have a little bit of exciting news."

Gemma faced me fully then, her jello forgotten and her eyes locked on mine with the utmost curiosity. "What?"

I pressed my lips firmly together and watched her lean closer as she waited on pins and needles for me to speak. After letting the tortuous silence stretch on for a few seconds, I announced, "I'm going to play piano again."

Her eyes doubled in size with nothing but glee. "Oh my gosh! Really?"

I nodded, unable to fight my own grin. "I talked to my school about it today. I'm officially changing my major so that I can be a pianist instead of a lawyer."

"I always loved hearing you play. And Dad. You were both so good at it." Gemma's eyes took on a dreamy look as though she were traveling back in time to old, blissful memories of Dad standing next to me while I practiced Beethoven or Chopin, Gemma watching from the carpet on the floor with a wide smile.

She'd been young when he passed—only seven. I loathed the fact that she didn't get more time with him, yet she and I clung to the memories we did have. Knowing she still remembered the sound of his playing made my throat burn with emotion.

Worry quickly clouded the expression as her eyebrows dipped. "Does Mom know?"

Dread deflated the excitement flooding my chest. I shook my head. "No."

Gemma stared at me. "You've always done what Mom says, though."

I chewed my lip and ran my fingers through Gemma's brown hair, letting the soft strands slide through my fingertips. Feeling how much healthier it was, no longer brittle and thin, helped me find the confidence to say, "I know. But sometimes, what Mom says and wants is wrong. As crazy as it sounds, moms and dads aren't always right. I'm only just learning that. So even though Mom wants me to be what she is, I need to be who *I* am. Does that make sense?"

Gemma smiled softly and nodded. "I'm glad. It always made me sad when Mom was mean to you about the things you liked and wanted, but ... I thought maybe that was just how it was supposed to be."

I frowned, and the weight on my chest grew heavier. I realized then that Gemma must've watched me and Mom all these years and thought that treatment was normal—being put down and told that your dreams were wrong was okay.

Regret as potent as a mouthful of pennies filled my mouth. "Kids should listen to their parents. *Most* of the time. Parents should guide you and teach you so that you can be a better person than they were, and a lot of the time, they're motivated to do that by their love for you. But sometimes, the things they do and say are wrong. It can be hard to tell when that's the case, which is why you have to trust that voice inside you. When it comes time to decide whether you'll listen or make your own choice, I hope you'll choose what you want, Gemma. You shouldn't obey at the expense of your own happiness. I'm so sorry that I haven't been a better example of that for you."

Gemma's eyes widened, and she grabbed my hands. "Are you kidding? You're the bestest sister in the whole world. I love you and want to be just like you when I grow up."

Emotion clogged my throat. I squeezed her hands, not afraid of bruising her for once, and smiled. "I love you, Gemma. So, so much."

Gemma grabbed her jello cup again and worked to scoop a bite. "Just remember, when you're famous and playing the piano everywhere, I was your biggest fan first. So get me lots of free tickets to see you play, okay?"

Laughing, I twirled some of her hair around my finger and watched her eat. "It's a deal."

CHAPTER 27

Iyla

WHEN FRIDAY ROLLED AROUND, ZAGAN WAS EAGER to let loose, and for once, I was excited about that prospect, too. Since the meeting with my advisor, I'd spent the past week attending my classes to finish out the semester while also planning for my music courses with my new advisor. I'd gathered all the material I'd need to start re-learning the piano, and each step that brought me closer to that dream made the next step easier.

Except for one.

I hadn't actually begun playing again. I'd made it to the doorway of Zagan's ballroom, but as soon as my gaze locked onto the piano, my heart began to pound and the cold claws of my mom's demands wrapped around me, forcing me to turn around. I'd fight past her hold one day.

That day just wasn't *today*.

Zagan had also been busy this past week. I'd had the mansion all to myself while he and Coldin met the other members of the band in New York. They had some filming to do for a couple programs, and they sat down to announce their hiatus to their fans. I'd watched the livestream where they'd talked about it, and the chat had *flooded* with an outpouring of love, support, and sadness.

People were already counting down the days until they returned from their break.

It had been a bit lonely in the big house without Zagan there, so I'd had Nahla, Iseul, Addie, and Eden come over a few times. Now with Friday night here, we were taking the chance to let off some steam by meeting the rest of Sinners Do It Better at Hell's Gate.

Was I excited to have some fun? Yes.

Was I eager to get back to the morbid and dark decor of the place? Not particularly.

I ran my hands down the length of my knee-high red dress. Two thin straps held the dress up on each shoulder, and the material hugged every curve and dipped low to show off an ample amount of cleavage. I'd thrown my hair up into a high ponytail and applied just a dusting of makeup.

While looking like this in the past would've made me feel guilty—like dressing up meant I was doing something wrong—I felt good in my own skin today. It was a new feeling, but I liked it. I hoped this same sort of confidence followed me as I started my journey toward my new life.

The other members of Sinners Do It Better and Eden were already gathered at a spacious table near the dance floor, throwing back shots and smoking something that had a pink haze of smoke lingering in the air.

Dante was the first to spot us. He narrowed his eyes when he saw me, but they quickly slid to Zagan and lost their hostility. "Looks like our boy made it."

"And he brought wifey," Xander hollered, his gold eyes trailing down my body.

Eden giggled and slapped Xander on the arm.

My eyes widened at the name, and I looked sideways at Zagan. "'Wifey?'" I whispered, my voice coming out almost like a squeak.

Zagan rolled his eyes and scowled at Xander. "Ignore him. It's a joke they came up with because we live together."

I nodded slowly, but the heat didn't leave my cheeks. They were teasing Zagan about me being his wife? The mere thought had my heart stampeding for some odd reason. It wasn't like I really was or was even close to anything like that. He and I were just friends.

Friends who had sex.

And now lived together.

I chewed the inside of my lip to keep the embarrassment from completely overtaking my face. My gaze, seeking somewhere to go, found Dante's. His red-and-black eyes were trained on me once more, and they were cold, narrowed slits. The look made my skin crawl, and I stepped just a hair closer into Zagan.

"D-Did I do something wrong?" I whispered to Zagan, turning my body away from the table to appear like I was taking in the club. "Dante seems mad at me or something."

Zagan waved a dismissive clawed hand and kept the other firmly on my back. "You didn't do anything. Like I said, the guys have been making stupid jokes lately, and they put him in a bad mood."

I could understand being grouchy, but it felt like that grouchiness was directed at me, as if *I* were the one who'd made the teasing remarks that pissed him off. Still, I accepted Zagan's answer, and we turned back to the table.

"Iyla," Eden chirped. She gestured at the empty seat across from her and Perseus. "Come sit here."

Happy to have the bright-eyed demon here, I went over to the free seat and sank down. Zagan took the chair at the head of the table between Coldin and Dante. I glanced warily at Perseus directly across from me and Xander on my left. Dante, who sat to my right, ignored me as he started talking to Zagan about some book he was reading, but even so, I could feel the tension rolling off him in my direction. It didn't take a genius to know that he didn't seem to want me here, but I wasn't sure what I'd done to offend him.

"So, Iyla," Xander began with amusement glittering in his gold demon eyes. His tall-and-thin horns jutted up into the air from both the shaved and dark-haired sides of his head.

I'd learned in my time with the demons that you could tell the many different kinds apart by their horns and eyes. Incubi and Succubi, like Zagan, Perseus, and Dante, had black eyes with a red vertical slit in the center, as well as rather short black horns. Mischief demons, like Xander and Eden, had gold eyes with gazelle-style black horns. And then there was Coldin's kind of demon, one I still didn't know much about. They had thick, curved black horns like a ram, and their eyes were solid black with orange flames dancing in the center. Even now, seeing his eyes unnerved me a bit.

"You're living with our leader now," Xander finished.

I shifted in my seat under the obvious appraisal of his gaze. "Looks like it. My living situation ... got messed up, and he was kind enough to let me stay with him."

Eden rested her chin in her hands and listened to me with a smile plastered on.

Perseus scoffed before chugging some of the amber drink in his glass. "'Kind.' Right." Perseus leaned forward on his forearms and met my gaze. "If we do something, it's for selfish reasons. It's not out of *kindness*."

Eden's smile fell, and she quickly slapped his arm and glowered at him. The two started bickering in hushed voices, too low for me to make out. I didn't bother trying to listen. I was too caught up in my own irritation.

Perseus was wrong—maybe not in the general sense, but definitely when it came to Zagan. Zagan had done countless things for me. He helped me study, dropped what he was doing to be there for me, brought me heaps of cake, spent his free time with me and Gemma, and let me live with him. Even if some of his motivations stemmed from other reasons, Zagan did them because he was a good friend. The fact that Perseus didn't understand that made me wonder how well his bandmates really knew him or if they just saw another demon when they looked at him.

I glanced over at Zagan now. He ran a clawed, black finger around the rim of his glass as he listened to Dante talk. The sight of him made warmth unfurl in my chest, and that feeling washed over me from head to toe.

Everyone at this table saw his horns, his eyes, and everything that made him a demon. When I looked at him, I saw what made him *Zagan*. I saw someone who managed to always turn a bad situation into a brighter one. I saw a man passionate about his work but also struggling to find that spark. I saw a person who cared and supported me when he didn't have to. I saw a friend.

Friend.

The word had a snake-like grip coiling around my ribcage and squeezing.

Eden, in her pink bra and black leather shorts, stood then. She held her hand out for me and called, "Come on, Iyla! Let's go dance."

I let the giddy demon pull me onto the dance floor, and with little convincing, the two of us began to sway our hips and move to the music. Every set of eyes watched Eden with a sensual hunger, and I didn't blame them. The way she moved was hot, and I could only hope that I looked even half as good as she did while dancing beside her.

"That's it!" Eden cheered me on. "Keep dancing like that and—" Her eyes narrowed as they zeroed in on our table, and her erotic movements slowed to a mindless sway. "Shit."

I slowed, too, nearly stopping altogether as I turned to see what had caught her attention. I sucked in a sharp breath when I saw the scantily-clad red-head sitting in Zagan's lap, her blood-red nail trailing down his neck while the other pressed to his chest. Her gleaming violet eyes held his as she shared words with him, and her black horns curled behind her head. Zagan's face was unreadable as he listened to whatever she said, and he sat still against her roaming hands.

It wasn't the first time I'd seen someone in his lap like that. My first night here, Eden had literally been straddling him *topless*. But it hadn't fazed me then. I didn't *know* Zagan back then. I didn't …

This time was different. My stomach soured to the point of near nausea as the well-endowed woman smiled seductively at Zagan and leaned down to run her tongue over his ear.

I quickly whipped my head back around and choked out, "Who is that?"

Eden continued glaring in that direction. "That's Babette. She's a Bargainer demon and the owner of Hell's Gate. She's also been obsessed with Zagan since the dawn of time."

There was clearly a part of me that took pleasure in torturing myself, because I looked back. Babette now stood by Zagan's chair, and she leaned down, her breasts nearly spilling from her green dress, and whispered something in his ear. She stood back to her full, slender height. Zagan's eyes stayed trained on the table as she sauntered away, leaving demons drooling in her wake.

Nagging voices inside me wondered what she'd said to him. Had she asked him to slip away with her for their own little fun? Did he only decline because he had no choice, chained to me like a dog that craved freedom? The chaotic questions fired off inside my mind, and the knots in my stomach only got worse with each one.

Zagan's head started to swivel in my direction, so I quickly looked away with a sharp inhale. I couldn't let him see me watching. It wasn't my business, bond or no bond.

"If you're trying to hide your feelings, you're not doing a good job," Eden said, leaning in close to be heard over the music. "It's written all over your face. If you really want to act like you didn't see or didn't care, *dance*. Show everyone just how okay you are with your body."

She backed away, raising her arms above her head as her body began to move in a rhythmic, hypnotic dance. I swallowed down the unease inside me and tried to do what she said. I'd never considered myself sexy or a very skilled dancer, but right now, I was giving both things my all.

I swiveled my hips and ran my hands up my body and into my ponytail, letting the music and sudden whistles of approval fuel my slow and erotic movements.

I'm not fazed by the woman flirting with Zagan.

I closed my eyes and made a figure-eight with my hips.

I don't care if he wishes he weren't stuck with me.

I ran my hands back down my body and let the music thrum through my limbs.

I'm fine.

"Back that pretty ass up," a raspy voice whispered in my ear.

I gasped and spun around to find a Mischief demon smiling salaciously at me. His dirty-blond hair stood up around his tall black horns, and sweat shined on his bare torso. He danced closer and reached for my hands to pull me into him.

"What's a tasty human like you doing out here all alone?" he chuckled, his golden eyes raking over me.

My heart thundered, and unease prickled my skin. It was times like this that I remembered who I was and what exactly filled this room. I was prey, and I stood face-to-face with a predator. Though, this one only seemed interested in dancing as he pressed into my front and grinded to the beat.

I glanced at our table to see what Zagan made of the demon trying to dance with me. But he wasn't watching. He'd turned in his seat to stare after the Bargainer demon, who kept throwing teasing smiles over her shoulder at him. It was an invitation to follow her up the stairs.

My stomach soured, and I quickly turned back to the demon in front of me. It didn't matter if Zagan was interested in Babette.

I didn't care one bit that he wanted to go after her. In fact, I didn't care *so* much that I held my head higher and flashed a coy smile at my new partner.

"What does it look like I'm doing here?" I finally fired back. I swayed my hips and grabbed the belt loops of his pants to pull him flush against me.

His grin widened, and he licked his lips, almost like he was hungry and eager to taste me. He pressed in and held my waist as the two of us moved to the pulsing music. Dancing with this stranger wasn't like dancing with Zagan. There was no rush of excitement or desire for more. No flip in my stomach, no pulse racing under my skin, no itch to get even closer and breathe him in until I was drunk on his smell.

But he was here, and Zagan wasn't.

A fact I was reminded of when I looked up and saw gold eyes and a lopsided grin without piercings. The tattoo-free hands skimming across my body to grope my butt and brush across my breast didn't encite sweet electricity, but rather, annoyance. I was irritated that this stranger thought he could touch me like that, and I was even more aggravated with myself for comparing everything about this demon to *my* demon.

Not wanting to stare at this stranger, I turned in his arms to dance on him with my backside, and there was no missing the feel of his erection against my butt—something that *really* didn't send sparks flying inside me like it would've with Zagan.

There was a gasp from right behind me and a split second where the body at my back disappeared. Just as quickly as it vanished, a new firm torso pressed into my back, and two large hands gripped the skin of my bare thighs. Spice and warm cedar wrapped around me, and I knew without looking over my shoulder who now held me.

"What the fuck do you think you're doing, letting another demon touch what's mine?" Zagan demanded in a low, husky voice.

A shiver ran up my spine with his hard body pressing into my backside and his lips hovering over my ear. My heart was back in my throat as his hands moved from the sides of my bare thighs to the front of them, brushing over the short hem of my dress.

"You didn't seem to mind," I said, my voice coming out shaky with that lingering tension still pooled in my gut.

Seeing Babette seek him out had clearly jarred me more than I cared to admit.

"Tell that to the ashes of the demon who'd just been touching you," he chuckled darkly.

My eyes widened, and I looked down, seeing a heavy dusting of ash beneath our feet. Shock shot through me at a blinding speed when I realized Zagan had killed him, but more than that came a hot, intense swell of desire. It was such a strange reaction to a really fucked-up thing, yet there was no denying how turned on I was.

All because Zagan had killed a demon out of jealousy.

Over *me*.

It spurred my body to resume my hypnotic dance moves, swaying my hips and rolling my body against Zagan's.

He groaned and pressed his hard cock against my backside. "You're fucking killing me, Sparrow. I'm supposed to be the temptation, not you."

Zagan's lip rings teased the skin on my earlobe. He nipped me lightly and dug his claws into my thighs, just hard enough to elicit a small sting that quickly mingled with the hungry awareness pulsing between my legs.

"Yet here you are, calling to me like the sweetest, sexiest sin," he purred.

"Is that right?" I asked breathlessly.

I bit my lip and leaned my head back onto his chest. I didn't stop dancing, and he didn't try to make me. He moved with me, grinding against me and moving with the swivel of my hips to the pounding music. Every inch of me was blissfully aware of every inch of him.

It also served as a reminder that these same places had just been touched by Babette, and that twist of nausea flooded back, spurring my tongue to move on its own accord. "Who was your friend?"

I hated this sickening coil in my gut. I'd never felt like this, and I didn't know how to make the feeling go away.

Zagan trailed one hand up my body and over my breast until he gripped my neck. He tilted it back until I had to look at him over my shoulder. A smirk tugged on his pierced lips. "Is that jealousy I hear?"

Was that what that bitter churning was? Jealousy?

"No," I answered quickly—*too* quickly.

He chuckled and brought his mouth closer to mine. It whispered against my lips as he purred, "I only have interest in one body, Sparrow."

My heart stuttered. His words filled my veins with fire, warming me from the inside out. Until reality doused it in water.

Of course, he only had interest in me. I was his bond. He didn't have a choice. Otherwise, he probably would've followed that gorgeous red-head to fool around.

"Because I'm your bond?" I asked finally, voicing the burning thoughts in my head, though my voice came out meeker than I'd intended.

His black-and-red eyes searched mine. "What if I said yes?"

Something sharp, like tiny crystals of frost, encrusted my insides, but I ignored it. Feigning indifference, I shrugged.

His hold on my neck tightened, and he forced my head down so that I had to stare at the scattering remains beneath my feet. His whisper teased my ear. "And what if I said no?"

I froze, no longer hearing the music or the voices of people around us. All that remained was Zagan and me.

He trailed one hand under the hem of my skirt. His fingers brushed against my bare wet core while the other ran down my throat to grip my breast through the thin red dress. "What if I said it's because I love the way you taste?"

My eyes fluttered closed, and I reached my arms behind me to grip his bent head as his fingers rubbed along the seam of my folds and his palm squeezed my breast.

In the back of my mind, I knew where we were. I know there were hundreds of demons and eyes all around us, but I couldn't find it in myself to give a damn. The bitterness that had enveloped me when I saw him with Babette eased with each second his hands were on me. Maybe being claimed so publicly like this was exactly what I needed right now to make the unfamiliar sting go away completely.

"What if I said it's because I love the way your pussy squeezes my cock?"

I inhaled sharply as pleasure zipped up my spine and made my legs quake. His finger slicked between my folds and rubbed on my clit, and I gasped, the sound lost in the loud music. A breeze hit my pussy, making me astutely aware that my dress had ridden up enough for people to see every detail. While I liked having him touch me in the middle of the bustling club, I wasn't brave enough to let people see my naked parts.

Seeming to sense my hesitation, Zagan released my breast and removed his hand from under my dress. He grabbed my arm and spun me around so that my chest pressed to his torso. He smiled down at me and wound my arms around his neck. Without warning, he hoisted me into his arms and wrapped my legs around his waist, pressing my bare and aching clit right against the bulge in his pants.

He brushed his lips across my jawline, teasing me with their soft caress. The graze of his lip rings made me grind against him, hungry for all of him. "What if I said it's because you're beautiful, and taking my eyes off you is impossible?"

Emotion tightened my throat in a vice-like grip as he punctuated his words by meeting my gaze again. I searched his face for some sign that he was teasing but found none.

I'd never given much thought to whether I was beautiful or not. All I cared about was looking clean and classy like Mom had raised me to be. Zagan calling me beautiful was pure sunshine raining down on me. I soaked up the complement and all the warmth it created inside me.

I tightened my hold around his neck. "What if I said that would make me happy?"

The corner of his mouth rose. "That's all I want, Sparrow."

His lips found mine, and a sweet heat swelled inside me as his tongue teased my own. My grip pulled him closer, and I angled my head to deepen the kiss. The hands holding me up shifted so that he held me with one hand and undid his pants with the other.

He nibbled my lip before sweeping his tongue back inside my mouth. At the same moment, his dick plunged inside of me with a delicious burn. I moaned into his parted lips, and he swallowed the sound with another hungry kiss as he gripped my butt to pull out then shove back in.

People continued dancing around us, completely unfazed as Zagan held me to him and fucked me right there on the dance floor. I wasn't sure if it was because this kind of thing was normal here, but I didn't care at the moment.

My every thought was zeroed in on the demon that kissed me with the hunger of a starving man. Pleasure hit me hard and deep with each plunge of his cock, and I felt myself clamp around him. He managed to touch dizzying places inside me that were downright sinful, and I leaned my head back as I chased that blinding heat.

"So fucking good," Zagan moaned against my throat. His tongue ran from my collar bone, up my neck, and to the tip of my chin. His sharp canines grazed my skin, making it pebble with heedy desire. "You're so fucking good, Iyla."

"More, Zagan," I gasped, leaning down to press my lips to his. "Please!"

His grip on my ass tightened, and he met my request with hard, almost desperate thrusts. My eyes rolled back into my head, and my entire body began to shake. Waves of electric bliss shot through me and ended right where his dick pushed in and out. One of his hands suddenly reached between us, and with the skill of a sex master, he immediately found my clit and pinched.

A scream that was all pleasure tore from my lips as my orgasm burst free, turning my cobra-like grip into limp noodles. Stars burst behind my eyelids, and for a second, I lost all sense of where I was.

When I got a hold of my bearings again, I was still firmly in Zagan's arms, my legs wrapped around him and my head pressed to his shoulder. I breathed hard, and my heart practically ran a marathon. Zagan's cock slipped free of me then, and I whimpered at the sudden loss. With a quick movement, he got himself tucked away, and he slowly set me back on my feet.

I wobbled on my jelly-like legs, but he kept his arms around me to hold me up. Something wet dripped down my inner thighs, and I had no idea which of us that was from.

I started to pull away and looked up at him. "I think I need to go clean up."

"Hell no," he said, running his hands around my frame to rest on my hips. "You're gonna stay out here and dance with me while my cum runs down those pretty legs. I want anyone who didn't see me fuck you to see the evidence of it and know you're mine. Maybe then they'll know not to fucking touch you again."

Something inside me warmed at the fierce possessiveness in his voice, and even though the wet, sticky cum felt weird being left to drip down my legs, having his attention fixed on it made it worth it. So I did as I was told. I wrapped my arms around his neck and resumed the sensual dancing that we'd paused in order to fuck. All the earlier jealousy I'd felt had completely dissolved. All that remained now was the heedy, fluttering I always got when Zagan looked at me. I still wasn't sure what it meant or what I really felt, but that was fine. I didn't need to know. Having him here was enough.

CHAPTER 28

Zagan

I LEANED MY HEAD ON THE DOORFRAME, CAREFUL TO STAY quiet as I peered into Iyla's room. Her hands rested under her cheek, and her lips were slightly parted as she slept soundly. We'd stayed out late into the night, and I'd kept her busy dancing and fucking. By the time we were done, I'd had to carry an exhausted Iyla to the shower and then to bed. She was still asleep, and I wasn't about to wake her.

This week had been eye-opening. My world had turned upside down with the realization of what Iyla meant to me, and when I looked at her now, I still reeled from the truth of it.

She probably had no idea how I felt—hell, *I* barely knew—and I wasn't sure how or if I should say it. I mean, would she want a demon's affection? She was everything good in the world, and I was the embodiment of sin. For the first time in my long-ass existence, I worried about tainting her with my darkness. But I also wanted to share it with her. I wanted to give all I had to her and do everything I could to make her happy.

If she wanted a piano, I'd get her an entire music hall. If she wanted to travel the world, I'd give her wings to fly. If she wanted a star, I'd soar up to the sky and gather her the whole goddamn galaxy. Anything, if only to see her smile.

The familiar itch in the back of my mind started up, and I straightened, my heart suddenly beating hard. I quickly turned on my heel and raced down both flights of stairs to the recording studio. I couldn't take in a full breath as my shaky fingers grabbed the blank music sheet and pencil. I ran back up the stairs and made my way to the grand piano, placed the paper and pencil on the music desk, and reached my trembling hands out as the notes and words suddenly poured out of me.

My eyes closed as the slow, romantic melody and lyrics spilled from inside of me like a geyser that finally erupted. I couldn't even stop to write down the notes and the words. I couldn't stop singing or playing, not until the song ended and my breathing evened out.

"Holy shit," I mumbled in the quiet of the ballroom.

The sweet hum of inspiration still lingered in my chest, burning brightly like the sun. It had been so long since I'd felt its presence inside me, and feeling it now as I thought of Iyla made adrenaline rush through my bloodstream.

She was what I'd been missing.

She was what I'd needed to find myself again.

The song was rough around the edges. It needed work and fine-tuning, but it was a start to what I knew I could do. The buzz of life that I'd missed so much but felt now was proof of that.

I'd just finished jotting down the first chord on the music sheet when my phone vibrated in my back pocket. I pulled it out of my jeans and tried to contain my annoyed huff when I saw Leo's name on the display.

"Yeah?" I answered, rubbing my forehead. I'd just gotten into things, and already, I felt the song slipping away from me again.

"I'm outside your house," Leo announced, his voice all business. "Let me in."

My irritation spiked, and I hung up without another word. Getting up, I went to the front door and opened it to find the big bald man in his business-casual shirt and slacks.

"Zagan," Leo boomed. "Good to see you." The hulking man swept past me and stood in the center of the room, surveying the expansive living room and kitchen. "I haven't seen your place yet. Looks good."

I shut the front door and leaned against it as I leveled my blank stare on my manager. "I'm sure you aren't here to see what my house looks like. So what? You here to gripe about us going on hiatus?"

Leo raised his brows and placed his hands on his hips. "Hiatus?" He chuckled and shook his head. "I wish that's what this was about. I can deal with you guys taking a break from releases and concerts. What I can't deal with is the fans' outrage over this new rumor going around."

My brow furrowed. "Rumor? What rumor?"

The guys and I weren't privy to most gossip that circulated about Sinners Do It Better. We didn't give two shits about what humans had to say or what they whispered about us, so tuning in to talk about the band wasn't something we did. We all had social media platforms, because that was the only way to promote yourself these days, but even that was out of our hands. Leo ran our accounts. I didn't even know what my socials looked like.

Was it smart letting a rapist control our accounts? Sure.

The one time he thought he could revert back to his human ways and be a pervy sleeze with our faces, he learned the hard way how wrong he'd been. He'd been strapped to a bed where Coldin then peeled each layer of skin off his dick, shoving the bloody, flappy pieces into his throat to choke on. And that was just Coldin's first stage of torture. I didn't know what else the demon did as punishment. I didn't want to lose my dinner by asking. To make things even better, Leo was forced to stay awake the entire time, thanks to a little demon magic, and no matter what he endured, he couldn't die.

Leo sighed at my lack of awareness and pulled out his phone. After tapping away a bit, he held it up for me to see some article with a photo of me and Iyla leaving Bloomings and another of the two of us dancing at the club Addie took us to. I skimmed the article, digesting the anger in the writer's voice as they accused me of dating in secret and not being available for my fans. They linked my "relationship" to the reason for the lack of new music and our recently announced hiatus.

Even after years of being in the music industry, it blew my mind when people got like this. Humans had a tendency to make claims on things and people they idolized, despite there being no foundation for it. I didn't know this author or even ninety-eight-percent of my fans, yet they felt some sort of ownership of me, because I was their prized idol. If they couldn't have me all to themselves, no one could. I'd seen the same scenario play out countless times where a musician or some other celebrity started a relationship and people attacked that significant other for trying to keep the celebrity to themselves.

It was bad rep for the person coming into the relationship, the celebrity, and their success rate. Announcements of a supposed relationship were typically followed by a decrease in viewership and sales.

Meeting Leo's gaze again, I shrugged. "So?"

Leo gave me an incredulous look. "*So*? So we need to play clean-up. Now. You've been seen multiple times with this girl, and fans are getting pissy about it. Is it true? Are you dating?"

I walked past him to head for the kitchen, sparing a fleeting glance for the stairwell that led to Iyla's room. I hoped she was still fast asleep and not listening to this bullshit. The relentless bastard was right on my heels.

"It's no one's business if I'm dating." I grabbed a water from the fridge and turned back to Leo whose knuckles had gone white as he gripped his phone. "Let them think what they want."

"And let your career tank? Let your friends' careers tank?" Leo ran a tired hand over his face and shook his head. "This *is* your fan's business, Zagan. You are a public figure, demon or not. Your fans have a vested interest in all of you guys, so when things like dating spring up, the fans feel like they have a right to know, reasonable or not."

My patience with this conversation was growing dangerously thin. I didn't stop working on that song that I actually *felt* something for to be nagged at about some unfounded—well, not *totally* unfounded—rumor that wasn't even anyone's business. I didn't give a fuck if I was a "public figure." It gave no one a right to me and my personal life.

I walked over to Leo and jabbed him in the chest, harder than necessary. "If you're that worried about it, you clean it up. This is your punishment for *your* sins, remember? Doing as we fucking tell you. So do your job and squash the rumor to calm the Sinners down."

Leo's eyes narrowed while his lips curved in an icy smile. "I figured that's what you'd say. So I already did. You and the rest of the boys get your suits ready. We'll be doing a charity event this Friday at Bloomings."

"WHAT A FUCKING JOKE," DANTE GROANED. HE LEANED back next to me, readjusting the lapels on his maroon tux. "I can't believe we have to put on a show for these cameras all because you got caught with your human."

I ignored Dante's dozenth complaint of the week.

"I don't even get what the big deal is," Perseus said. He sat across the limo from Dante, Coldin, and I. His navy tux jacket was open, exposing the crisp white shirt beneath. "It's a known fact that we mess around. Why does it matter if Z got spotted with Iyla?"

"Because she's a threat to the fans," Xander chuckled.

The asshole had found the whole situation amusing ever since Leo broke the news of the rumor and clean-up plan to us. Xander didn't see tonight as an annoying inconvenience like Dante did. He saw it as a chance to poke fun at me and the fan's insane outlook on us.

"People aren't allowed to claim us, remember?" Xander added, flicking a piece of non-existent lint off his forest-green tux. "We belong to our fans as their distant lover. They see Zagan being with Iyla as him cheating on them."

"I'll never understand humans," Perseus grumbled and stared out the window.

"We don't have to understand them to enjoy them," Xander grinned, licking his lips suggestively.

"None of that tonight," I warned Xander. "This is a charity event for Bloomings. It's just a bunch of sick or injured kids and adolescents. Not your thing."

"Won't the nurses and doctors be there? Family members of the kids?" Xander asked with a single raised brow.

I rolled my eyes, realizing the demon was going to find someone to leave with, even if that wasn't what we were here for. I wasn't going to waste my breath trying to convince him to keep it in his pants tonight.

Leo's "brilliant" plan to do away with the rumors of me dating were to explain the mystery girl in the photos as a fan who'd reached out with a heart-wrenching story of her sick sister. Together, she and I were putting together this event for the patients and their families, and the reason we'd gone to the club was to check out different DJs for the event—at least, that was the story Leo gave the press. The members of Sinners Do It Better would come, pose for some choice photos, and make a hefty donation to Bloomings.

The only thing that kept me from being irritated with the whole charade was the fact that this place was important to Iyla, and our donation would actually help them. So if it made Iyla happy to host this event, it wasn't an inconvenience.

Anticipation broke out inside me like a crashing wave. I hadn't really seen Iyla today, only popping my head into her room to tell her bye as I left to meet Leo and the band for final preparations for today. I couldn't wait to see what dress she and Addie had picked out for tonight, though she could show up in a fucking potato sack, and it wouldn't matter. She'd still be the most gorgeous girl in the room.

The limo pulled around to the front doors of Bloomings. There were three cameramen already there, practically chomping at the bit to get the best shots of the night. We got out of the limo with our plastered-on charm—except for Coldin, who always appeared bored. We brushed past the photographers in a chorus of flashing lights and waltzed into the building.

Dr. Seward and the nurses met us at the doors with bright smiles, their scrubs and doctor's coat traded in for evening dress wear.

"Thank you so much for coming," Dr. Seward greeted, shaking each of our hands. "We're so thankful for your donation and your putting this all together."

Flashes captured the handshake and grins exchanged by the doctor and myself.

"Please," I said politely. "It's the least we could do. You guys are doing some great work here, helping and treating those who need that constant health care attention. We're proud to contribute anything we can."

"I have a feeling you'll be contributing much *happiness* tonight," Dr. Seward said with a hearty chuckle. "All the residents are over the moon to have you guys here." He leaned in like he wanted to share a secret and whispered, "The little ones have no idea who you guys are. They just know someone famous is here."

I grinned. "Glad to hear it."

He swept his arm wide, and the nurses parted like the Red Sea as Dr. Seward said, "This way. We're holding the celebration in the sunroom."

Over the moon was right.

From the moment we entered the extremely packed sunroom, we were all bombarded with squeals of delight, requests for photos and signatures, and shy hugs. Everyone, family members and patients alike, were dressed up for the evening, and the sunroom had been turned into a scene right out of some low-budget movie about high school prom.

Tables lined the edge of the room with refreshments, monitored by my favorite—Patrice. Her pointy nose was turned up at us, though I saw the hint of a smile when she saw how happy the residents were. Red-and-black balloons had been blown up and clung to the ceiling as the helium forced them to fly. Little cheap multi-colored strobe lights sat in each corner of the dimly lit room, and tables had been brought in for all the people to sit around, arranged perfectly around the center of the room, which had been left open as a dance floor.

The photographers from outside had shuffled into the room and were capturing plenty of shots of all five band members interacting with the crowd. As I put on a show of smiling and engaging in small-talk, I tried looking around the room in search of Iyla. I didn't spot her anywhere, and the impatient anticipation to see her doubled.

"Looking for someone?" Dante whispered, giving me a knowing smirk that looked more like a sneer.

"No," I lied. "Just taking it all in."

Dante clapped my shoulder. "Right." He looked around the room. "Hopefully we can take these photos and get out of here."

Two older teen girls—one walking with crutches and another with a portable oxygen tank—came up to Dante, their eyes glittering as they stared at him, shyly asking for his autograph. He plastered on a grin and turned his back to me to offer his attention to his fans, and I took the chance to slip away from him.

My get-away was interrupted as three girls from the group I'd met my first day here came over with their families trailing behind. I smiled brightly as they called my name.

"Don't you all look lovely tonight," I praised.

All the girls wore make-up, flowing dresses, and had their hair done. A man, presumably Arianna's dad, pushed her wheelchair today, and her yellow dress practically spilled over the seat in a mess of fabric. Kaylpto, who typically had an ashy undertone to her otherwise beautiful brown skin, looked bright and much healthier than the last time I'd seen her. She still clung to her walker, but she no longer had an IV as she walked around. Even Marla looked far better. She'd pinned her dark hair up, leaving every inch of her burned flesh exposed for people to see. She'd even worn a short-sleeved mauve dress that showed off her scarred arm.

"Look at you," I said to Marla. "Very pretty."

She beamed at me. "Thank you."

The girls introduced their family members to me, and I made a show of listening and caring about who these people were. Really, every part of me coiled tightly, like a predator lying in wait for their prey to appear.

After introductions were made and a pop song came on over the speakers to pull the girls toward the dance floor, Marla's mom stepped away from her daughter and approached me.

"I just wanted to say thank you," the round woman said to me. Tears filled her eyes, and she watched her daughter as she turned Arianna's wheelchair in their own little dance. "Marla has really struggled ever since the accident. She's—She's hated the way she looks, but her confidence has grown leaps and bounds ever since she spoke to you. I can't tell you how grateful I am to you for helping my daughter see that she's not less than just because of her scars."

I gave the woman a comforting pat on the arm. "No thanks necessary. I'm glad Marla's been doing well."

She nodded and wiped under her eyes. "She has been. Dr. Seward thinks she'll be able to come home soon. Her burns aren't causing her nearly as much pain as they used to, and she hasn't had anymore self-harm thoughts. We're over the moon that she's made this much progress, and we know a lot of it is because of what you told her."

I wasn't sure my words held as much power as Marla's mom believed, but if it meant that much to her, who was I to argue? I smiled, accepted her thanks, and continued my rounds about the room.

"Zagan!"

I turned at the excited sound of my name coming from what could only be Gemma. Despite being called to by her, I didn't even see the youngest Winters daughter. Every part of me locked onto the vision standing in the doorway beside her. Iyla's long hair had been curled, and it hung around her in a silky curtain. A dusting of make-up had been applied, accentuating her big brown eyes and plump lips. Her gold gown with a plunging neckline hugged her torso while the skirt moved about her legs with grace and ease.

In that moment, I became lost in her. Lost in the way sunshine filled the room when she smiled at me. Lost in the shining constellations of her eyes as they held mine. Lost in the flush of her cheeks and the inhale of her breath as she walked toward me with her sister. She was a vision of all that was good and beautiful in the world come to life, and in that moment, I found my salvation in her.

"Hey," she said when she and Gemma reached me. "You look very handsome."

It took me two times to swallow the grit from my voice, and I cleared the rest from my throat. "Thank you. You—"

"Zagan," Leo interrupted, coming to stand beside us. He forced a smile as he glanced at Iyla. "Since she's here, let's get some photos of you three and another one with the doctor and nurses." Leo looked around Iyla and Gemma then leaned in to ask her, "Are your parents here? It would be good to have them in the photo, too."

"Oh," Iyla said, her eyes dropping sheepishly. "No. Our dad passed away, and Mom ... She's not here. I'm not sure if she'll be coming."

Of course she isn't.

I tried to keep the loathing of her mom off my face as I followed Iyla and Gemma to the windows where Leo positioned us for the cameras.

I looked down at Iyla as the three of us got positioned—me and Iyla standing on either side of Gemma—and my heart beat against my chest like a drum. I'd never felt anything like what I did when I looked at her. Hell, I didn't even know I *could* feel this surge of affection when looking at another person. A demon like me, who thrived in the dark and twisted, craved for her light and goodness. It was new and kinda fucking scary, but it was also thrilling. She was stunning at every turn, every angle, and I wanted to keep my eyes on her all night.

Flashes lit up the corner of my vision, and I suddenly remembered we had an audience. My eyes desperately wanted to stay locked on Iyla's profile, but I forced them away to smile for the cameras. Dr. Seward and a handful of nurses joined us for some other photos and then the rest of the band joined, too.

It felt like an hour of nothing but forced smiles and shuffling of poses when someone finally turned up the music and people disbanded into smaller groups at tables and on the dance floor.

Iyla followed Gemma to the refreshment table, and my eyes trailed after her. I started to follow when Perseus stepped in front of me.

"Don't," he ordered flatly. "Don't make this entire night be for nothing. If you go chasing after her all evening, people are going to see what you're trying to hide."

I narrowed my eyes at the golden-haired demon. "And what am I trying to hide?"

He chuckled and shook his head. "Your infatuation with that human."

I dropped my head to fight off my laugh. "You're one to talk, considering your latest obsession."

Perseus's green eyes darkened, and his jaw worked. "That's different. Mine is a game. It's not real. *Yours* is."

I glanced over his shoulder at Iyla, who laughed at something Gemma said. My chest tightened with a pressure so unfamiliar to me that it rendered me speechless. I wanted to argue with Perseus, but he was right about one thing. As long as the cameras were still here, they could snap plenty of photos to paint the rumors as true. So with great effort, I turned my back on Iyla and joined Sinners Do It Better on the other side of the room—if not for the sake of avoiding more rumors, for the sake of proving Perseus wrong about what was happening to me.

CHAPTER 29

Iyla

MY CHEEKS WERE SO HOT, I FEARED TOUCHING them would burn my fingertips. But what did I expect when Zagan stared at me like his world started and ended with me? He stood on the opposite side of the room now, but that did little to calm my racing heart. It didn't help that he looked like seduction in his all black tux with his black hair combed back. Wetness gathered at my core just looking at him.

"Is this lemonade?" Gemma asked Patrice at the drink table.

The woman who wore a dark, matronly dress tonight nodded. "It is. Would you two like some?"

"Yes, please!"

Sienna appeared at Gemma's side then. Her lime green gown looked gorgeous against her deep brown skin, and for once, she didn't wear a cap or toboggan over her bald head but an elastic headband with a white flower attached.

"Sienna," I beamed. "You look like a princess!"

She giggled and looked down at her dress. "Thank you. Daddy said the same thing." Her gaze found Gemma's again. "Come dance with me."

Gemma looked up at me as if to silently ask permission. Smiling, I nodded toward the dance floor. "Go on. I'll get your lemonade."

She took Sienna's hand and left in a flutter of purple silk. The two girls joined other kids and teens who danced to the loud pop music. The party had seemed to invigorate everyone, giving those who usually appeared weary, a boost of energy. Those in wheelchairs laughed and danced with their arms. Teens who were weak held onto a friend or family member, otherwise oblivious to their ailments. Even Gemma, who'd been on the up and up with Zagan's weekly doses, swayed and bounced gently from foot to foot as she danced with Sienna.

There were still IV poles among the crowd, face masks on certain people, and signs of reasons why everyone was *really* here, but for tonight, it seemed no one saw those things. How could you when so much life and light poured into the space?

I accepted the lemonades from Patrice and moved to the side, watching my sister dance with a wide smile on her face. A couple months ago, I never thought I'd see her like this. Boisterous. Dancing. *Living.*

Yet here she was, twirling around and laughing.

My gaze drifted to the corner where Zagan currently smiled down at Marla, who wore her burns proudly tonight. He grabbed her blistered hand and twirled her around, making her face light up in glee.

My heart soared into my throat, and I couldn't fight the budding emotion filling my chest.

He'd done this. He'd brought this warmth into an otherwise dreary place. He'd given a chance at life back to my sister, and I ...

"Having fun?"

I turned my head, startled from my thoughts by the sound of Noya's voice. She wore a pink closed abaya and matching hijab, and she smiled at me.

Catching my breath, I returned the look. "I am. You?"

She nodded and turned to the sea of patients and their families. "It's nice seeing everyone like this, isn't it? They deserve to have nights like this when they can. I'm glad you met Zagan and brought him here. Otherwise, this probably wouldn't have happened."

At the mention of his name, my eyes inadvertently sought him out. He was now surrounded by the teen girls and boys who took turns dancing with him. That hot, ticklish sensation filled my chest again.

"I'm happy for you," Noya suddenly admitted.

I looked at her, the confusion clearly painted on my face.

She laughed at my expression. "You've been best friends with my sister for a long time. I know you, and I can see how much you've changed since he came into your life. You seem ... lighter. Happier. You've always looked so shut down or like you were afraid of happiness. But you don't seem scared anymore."

A sharp pierce joined the already sporadic feelings inside me. I had to blink a few times and take a deep breath to keep from crying right there. My whole life, I'd lived on autopilot, and it just got worse after Dad died. I did as I was told like an obedient, pre-programmed robot. Just like Zagan brought life into this room, he'd brought it to me. Where once being free would've scared me, I now embraced it.

Noya was right.

I wasn't afraid of myself anymore.

"He's a really amazing guy," I whispered.

The music playing overhead suddenly slowed and turned into a soft melodic rhythm, and people broke apart to slow dance with a parent, sibling, or friend.

"I can tell." Noya paused and pursed her lips thoughtfully. "I hope I find someone someday who looks at me the way he looks at you."

My heart stuttered, and I bit my lip. "The way he looks at me?"

While I'd noticed the lingering looks from the demon, there had been a part of me that thought I was reading too much into it.

But Noya had seen something, too. The knowledge made the air thin in my lungs.

"You haven't noticed?" Noya asked with wide eyes. She laughed softly and gave me a pointed look. "It's the same way *you* look at *him*."

I stared at her, too dumbfounded to do more than uselessly open and close my mouth. My cheeks warmed. Had someone turned up the heat in the room?

A throat cleared.

Noya and I turned to find Zagan, flanked by lots of giggling patients.

The demon smiled at me and offered me his hand. "Would you like to dance?"

What Noya and I had been discussing was still on the forefront of my mind, and now, I had an audience of teens, eagerly watching as Zagan held his hand out for me. I practically moved solely by instinct, taking hold of his outstretched hand. The moment my skin touched his, though, a sense of rightness flooded my system, like my hand had been made to fit in his. The nerves and confusion over my sporadic feelings slowly seeped away as I followed my demon to the dance floor.

He swung me around in a grand flourish, and I was laughing when he finally pulled me in, clutching my hand and holding the small of my back with the other. I squeezed his hand and rested my free one on his shoulder, offering him my own smile.

"The cameras finally left," Zagan murmured softly, his voice for me alone. "I figured it would be safe to ask you to dance now."

"You wanted to ask me to dance?" I teased with a raised brow.

He shrugged and feigned indifference. "I was being forced into it. Did you know? Teen girls are relentless when they want something. They've been breathing down my neck all evening about asking you."

I glanced at the teens, who sure enough, sat at nearby tables, watching us with their chins in their hands and stars in their eyes. Laughing under my breath, I looked back at Zagan. "They definitely seem invested."

Zagan stepped back and raised his arm as he spun me around with ease then pulled me back into his strong arms again. When my hand found his shoulder and his found my waist, his eyes had softened at the edges. "You look beautiful, by the way. Absolutely stunning."

There was no fighting my grin. "Thank you. Addie helped me with everything." I let my gaze drink in his fitted black tux and the crisp black shirt beneath it. My insides warmed with flames of desire, and I had to swallow hard before saying, "You look very nice, too. I like you in this outfit."

He quirked a pierced brow. "What about *out* of it?"

I laughed but quickly tried to stifle the sound so as not to gain even more attention than what we already had. "I definitely like you that way, too." I bit my lip as guilt tried to weave its way through me. "Also, I wanted to apologize. I know you were forced to do this party tonight. Because of me and ... and those rumors."

Zagan had told me about the articles circulating once he found out from Leo. I didn't know what to think or how to feel about them at first. The fact that people thought we were dating made me feel kinda good, which was immediately followed by feeling silly. Because really—Zagan and me? Sure, I was his bond that he fucked, but our arrangement was solely something forced onto him.

If there wasn't demonic magic tying us together, he'd get rid of me in an instant. And if an opportunity presented itself where I could die in an accident, he'd stand by and watch. It was nothing against *me*. It just *was*. He'd been forced to keep me around by magical demands, and that was the only reason we stood here. No matter what our friendship meant to him, his freedom meant more.

"Don't apologize," Zagan replied. "I don't mind it."

It was my turn to quirk a brow at him. "But it's an inconvenience, which we both know you hate."

"This party might be for Bloomings benefit, but I'm here for you. And nothing about you is an inconvenience."

I pressed my lips tightly together and stared up at him. His blue eyes never left mine. They were unwavering and as steadfast as his words. He meant what he said, and that … that confused me. I'd been nothing but an inconvenience since we'd met. He thought he was venturing down one path, and I constantly threw walls up on it, forcing him to turn around and venture elsewhere. Everything about us was "inconvenient." Everything about us was lack of choices.

So why had I never felt freer?

"Iyla."

I snapped out of my thoughts to look down at Gemma. Gone was the ecstatic little girl, and in her place stood a distressed, fidgeting child. Her frantic eyes moved to the doorway, and I followed them, already figuring who I'd see.

Mom didn't cross the threshold of the sunroom. It was like she thought doing so would be acknowledging Zagan's gift, and she'd never do that. It was why she'd ignored the invite to tonight's event, sending the RSVP card back to Bloomings with no response. She wanted no part in anything concerning me or Zagan.

Mom's fuming eyes were locked on me, and the girl of old reared up inside me, trying to make me cower in the face of the woman.

I cleared my throat and placed a hand on Gemma's shoulder. I gave her a reassuring smile that she no doubt saw right through. "I'm gonna go talk to her. You stay here and keep dancing."

My eyes briefly found Zagan's, and the disdain simmering there couldn't be clearer. But he didn't stop me as I crossed the room to where my mother waited. He knew I needed to face my demon, and for once, that wasn't him.

When I neared the doorway, Mom spun on her heel and stormed down the hallway, already assuming I would follow. Because, of course I would. I always had, and part of me worried that I always would to some degree.

She waited in Gemma's room, and I found her standing at the window, staring into the night. She hadn't bothered turning on the light, nor had I. Only the moonlight streaming through the window lit our battleground.

"What were you thinking?" she hissed before sucking in a sharp breath. Just speaking to me seemed to agitate her.

"About what, Mom?" I asked flatly.

She whipped around and pointed a slender finger at me. "Don't you dare call me that! You aren't my daughter. You are not the girl I raised. Disobedient. Dishonest. *Delusional.*" She heaved a laugh and ran a hand over her hair, which had loose pieces falling from her usually pristine bun. "I mean, should I be surprised given the company you keep?"

I tried to take a calming breath, but each of her words were a fresh cut on my heart, stealing my ability to take in a full gulp of air. "You don't know him. You don't understand what he's done for—"

"What he's done?" she snapped. "What that—that ... *thing* has done? Let me think. He assaulted me, which you didn't give a damn about. He's corrupted my eldest into someone I don't recognize, and that same imbecile is bringing him around children. *Kids*, Iyla! He's—He's ... *evil*! He could be a predator. Do you understand *nothing*? You are ruining your sister. And for what? Because you don't know how to keep your legs closed? Because you see one attractive man and become blind to your morals? I've never seen someone more selfish."

My blood boiled, getting hotter and uglier with each of her accusations, the last bringing me to a boiling point. "Why is being with Zagan selfish?" I demanded. "Why is trying to be happy *selfish*?"

"Please," she scoffed. "Have you truly deluded yourself into thinking this is happiness? Ruining your life, my life, your *sister's* life? How could you do this to her? She is *dying*, Iyla, and you come strutting in here, showing off some monster, trying to darken her mind with impurities. You make her feel less than, acting like you have everything while she sits here alone, sick and dying."

My lip trembled, and I bit it in an effort to keep it hidden. I couldn't let her see that she was getting to me—that she was *hurting* me. Because that would only give her fuel to keep going.

All her words from over the years came back to me, hitting me with the force of a freight train.

Desire is wrong, and giving into that makes you no better than trash you find on the streets.

Piano isn't a real career, and I won't have you dragging our family's name through the mud just so you can tap away on some keys. Real success comes from a real *job.*

The world is full of lazy, ungrateful, and sinful people, Iyla. You don't want to be one of them, *do you?*

You need to set a good example for your sister. Do as you're told and she'll thrive, too.

The sharp words funneled through my mind in a whirlwind, slicing me with each sweep, knocking me down smaller and smaller. But the worst of them all was the idea that reaching for my own dreams was hurting Gemma.

Was I showing off? Was I making her feel bad when I brought Zagan here, making her think I had things she'd never get to experience?

"I love Gemma," I whispered, tears brimming my eyes too quickly for me to fight off.

"Do you?" Mom demanded. "Because from where I'm standing, all you care about is yourself. All you care about is sleeping around and trying to hurt this family with your acting out. Do you know how stressed Gemma is because of you? Because she knows you're doing wrong and is *worried* for you?"

I shook my head slowly as if doing so would keep the words from reaching me.

"You're killing your sister faster," she snarled.

The world was falling out from under me. I wobbled on my legs and had to grip the foot of Gemma's bed to keep from crumbling to the floor. Mom was wrong. She had to be wrong. Words wouldn't come to my lips, and my brain misfired as it worked to fight against the idea that I had been hurting Gemma all this time.

Shoes tapped against the tiled floor, walking calmly into the dim room. I couldn't even turn to see who it was. I was stunned, rendered immobile.

A dark figure appeared beside me, facing my mother with hands shoved in his pockets and his posture the perfect picture of ease.

"You," Mom growled, but for all her effort to sound fierce, I saw her shift backward.

"I know you're probably struggling," Zagan's deep voice rang out calmly. "You're afraid of losing Gemma. But you should really think about what you're saying before you lose *both* daughters."

She scoffed and came to stand directly in front of me. The eyes that had only ever been cold and hard toward me never left mine. "She's already lost to me."

She swept past us, leaving Zagan and I alone in the dark room. My insides went numb. My body ran cold. The tears rolling down my cheeks didn't even bother me as I stared into the empty space where my mom had been.

"Iyla …" Zagan's soft voice cut through the fog.

I couldn't bear to hear him right now. I couldn't face him. The numbness ebbed with a sudden need to get away.

"I-I need to go," I croaked. "Can you tell Gemma I had to leave and that I love her?"

I didn't wait for an answer. I spun on my heel and barreled for the exit without looking back.

I GRABBED THE GLASS NECK OF THE BOTTLE AND TOOK AN-other deep swig. It burned on the way down, but I welcomed it. I welcomed the pain. I welcomed the fog of the alcohol.

My feet dangled off the wooden pier that stretched out into the dark waters behind Zagan's home. I'd lost my shoes somewhere on my quest to get through the house and out here, and I kicked my now bare feet back and forth, watching the two limbs peek out from the hem of my gold dress with each pass.

Selfish.

I was selfish, and it was killing my sister.

I squeezed my puffy eyes shut and took another drink.

Footsteps approached behind me, and I stared blankly beside me as Zagan sat down. He'd discarded his tux jacket, now in only his black slacks and button-up. He dropped his legs off the pier and rested his forearms on the tops of his thighs to look at me with a furrowed brow.

"Have you drank all of that?" he asked, nodding toward the bottle of bourbon.

I looked at the glass bottle and nodded, my heavy head bounc-ing with the motion. Giggling, I said, "I'm glad I found this. I came home, and wow! There it was on the counter. So I took it to drink, because I'm selfish. That's me! Selfish Iyla, coming through!"

I took another swig and hung my head to stare into the water. My murky reflection stared back up at me, flickering with the water's movement and glinting moonlight overhead. "I've neglected what I've been taught. I've taken for granted all that Mom has done for me and given me. I've put my own agenda and life before Gemma's, making her feel bad about her own situation."

"Do you hear yourself?" Zagan demanded. "Do you know how far from the truth that bullshit is? You *aren't* selfish. Everything you've done your whole fucking life has been for other people."

I sniffled and tilted my chin high into the air. "I know."

Zagan drew back slightly and stared at me in confusion. "You know?"

"I realized on my drive here how wrong Mom was. Gemma doesn't see us that way, and I'm literally trying to save her, not kill her."

"Then why are you—"

"Because," I growled, turning my tear-filled eyes on him. "Because I've *always* been the version Mom wanted, yet she *still* sees me as selfish? As a daughter that's lost to her?" I threw my head back in a humorless laugh.

"I think that's enough bourbon for one night," Zagan said carefully. He tried to grab the bottle, but I snatched it away and rose unsteadily to my feet.

"It's idiotic," I screamed, watching him get to his feet in front of me. "I've given my all for her. I've loved her through all the heartbreak and hurt, yet I make one decision for myself and am thrown away?" I clutched my forehead and shook it. "Everything was fine before. She and I were fine. She *loved* me."

The hurt morphed into anger as I glared up at him, fresh, angry tears falling. "Why? Why did I do it? Why did I go to that stupid concert and accept those dumb VIP passes? I was a good daughter. I tried my best for her."

"Iyla ..."

He tried reaching out to me, but I shoved at his chest with as much strength as a drunk human could muster. He didn't even move an inch as I beat my empty fist against his chest. "I gave up every wish I've ever had for her, yet the one night I decide to do something *I* want, to be selfish for one goddamn night in my life, I wind up getting stuck with a fucking *demon* who ruins *everything*!"

Zagan's eyes widened. Even in my intoxicated state, there was no missing the hurt that flickered in his gaze the moment the words left my lips. Yet the buzz of the bourbon kept me from caring. The buzz made the clenching of his jaw and his looking away from me mean nothing. Because that was all that was left inside me.

Nothing.

"You're drunk," Zagan said flatly, his head still turned away. "I think we should talk about all of this tomorrow."

My eyes didn't follow him as he headed back toward the house. I stared at the wooden pier beneath my feet, numb to it all.

Numb to my mom's lack of love.

Numb to Zagan's hurt.

Numb to my pain.

A chill swept over my bare arms, and I was reminded that I came out to the water in nothing but my sleeveless dress. My insides were warm with the booze, but the sting of the November cold was enough to make me want to take my drinking pity party inside.

I turned on my wobbly legs, and the world spun with me. The deck edge went out from under me, and my arms wheeled as I fought to grapple with something. There was nothing.

I tumbled back into the dark, frigid waters. My cloudy mind panicked at the sudden cold waters dragging me under, and the immediate shock knocked some sense back into me. I fought to reach the surface as my throat closed up, but it felt like the surface wasn't getting any closer. My throat burned with the need for air, but no matter how hard I kicked my legs and clawed my hands, the surface remained far away.

Terror seized me as pinpricks of pain and the need to breathe grew to a near-bursting height. I fought harder, yet I still found myself submerged in the dark depths. My mouth pressed together as the fire in my chest reached its breaking point.

This was it.

I was going to die.

Hands suddenly grabbed my upper arms and yanked me in the opposite way I'd been frantically swimming.

The moment my head broke the surface, I sucked in huge gulps of air and choked as tears streamed down my cheeks. I was slung over a broad shoulder, and the warm body at my torso carried me away from the water until we reached the grassy backyard.

Zagan set me back on my feet and grabbed my upper arms tightly as his wild eyes searched my soaking wet body. "Are you okay?"

Shivers shook my entire frame. I'd almost died. The shock kept my wide eyes locked on him, his own dark hair clinging to his forehead as rivulets of water ran down his face and body. "F-Fine."

He released me then, and his blue eyes swirled dark. I blinked, and in that short second, the human Zagan had given way to the demon. His clawed hands snatched the bottle of bourbon from my hand, which I hadn't realized I'd held through that entire ordeal. He chucked it at the house, smashing the drink in a spray of liquor and glass.

"You're cut off!" He turned his fuming black-and-red slitted eyes on me as he raked his hands through his wet, dark hair. "What the fuck were you thinking? You could've died! Do you understand that? I get you're—"

"You saved me," I said, breathlessly. My heart continued to race, but it was no longer from the adrenaline of nearly drowning. "I could've died."

He sneered at me, exposing his fang-like canines. "I know. I just fucking said that."

I stared at him. The cold air hit my wet body and clothes, but the feeling couldn't be further from my mind. "It—It would've been an accident."

He placed his hands on his hips like he was fighting to not rip me apart where I stood. His nostrils flared as he snapped, "Glad to know it wasn't on fucking purpose."

"Zagan," I said softly, taking a step forward. My throat tightened all over again, and the bourbon left me as quickly as it had hindered me. "Why would you save me? It would've been an *accident*. You— You would've been free."

I saw it the moment he realized what I was getting at. His shoulders stiffened, and he seemed to stall out. No breathing. No blinking. He just stared at me. Slowly, he turned his head away, staring off at nothing. "Forget it, Iyla."

My brows slammed down, and I took another step in his direction, my wet dress clinging to my legs. "No. I won't forget it. Why did you save me? Why—"

"Shut up!" He roared, shoving both hands into his hair to grip his head like he was trying to silence it and me. His chest rose and fell sharply with heavy breaths, and he paced a few feet away.

"Zag—"

"Goddammit," he growled, his slitted eyes finding mine as his hands dropped to his sides. He rushed forward in a blur of darkness, and his clawed hands gripped the sides of my face as his lips crashed into mine. A warm flutter broke out inside me as he kissed me hard, almost desperate in the sweep of his lips and tongue.

A groan sounded in the back of his throat as I fisted the front of his wet shirt, just as hungry for him as he seemed to be for me. His body pressed into mine, forcing me back, and a dizzying rush hit me.

I opened my eyes just in time to see a plume of black shadows erupt around us. When it cleared, we no longer stood in the yard but in my bedroom.

"Fucking crazy," Zagan growled as he nipped at my lip with his fangs then swept his tongue against my own.

"What is?" I asked breathlessly. My heart raced, and my entire body burned like a glowing ember.

His palms coasted over my shoulders, down my arms, and onto my torso where he grabbed the dress and yanked it over my head. All I had on beneath it was a nude thong, so as soon as the cool air met my hot flesh, my skin pebbled and my nipples hardened. I squirmed, feeling wet heat coat my core.

"What's crazy?" I questioned again, watching his slitted eyes drink in my mostly naked body.

"Everything, Sparrow," he whispered as he leaned down to suck on my neck and bite at my throat. "Everything about us is fucking crazy."

He shoved me so that I fell onto the bed, landing on my back. He smirked as he crooked a clawed finger under the side of my panties so that he held them off my body. The nude material darkened and grayed until it fell apart into ash. My eyes widened.

He hooked his arms around my thighs and hoisted my bottom half up so that I practically hung upside down with only the tops of my shoulders and head remaining on the bed. His warm breath hit my wet, pulsing pussy before his mouth closed over my clit.

My legs trembled where they rested on his shoulders, and I gasped as sweet pleasure shot down my spine, rushing through me like the blood rushing to my head. Dizzying waves hit me one after the other while his tongue circled and flicked along my clit. His forearms were wrapped around my waist to hold me up, and I gripped them tightly, trying to hold onto something since I was upside down and the world was becoming increasingly fuzzier. The blood racing to my head had it feeling heavy and full, and the darts of pleasure choking me didn't help.

"Zagan," I gasped, my attention zeroing in on where the tip of his tongue circled my bundle of nerves then moved lower.

My fingernails dug into his forearms as his tongue plunged into my hole, and my eyes rolled back at the sheer pleasure that ricocheted through my limbs with the curling of his tongue. Just as something blinding and fierce built between my legs, he pulled out from my entrance and trailed his attention back up the seam of my lips to flick my clit. The sudden brush to the burning spot made my entire body shake in his arms, yet he continued to hold me without struggle.

"I love having my face buried in your sweet pussy," Zagan purred, letting his lips and tongue coast over my clit as he did.

His warm breath and feather-light friction against my aching core sent a fresh wave of dizziness and hunger soaring through my body. My hips bucked all on their own, desperate to have him keep going.

"Zagan," I pleaded breathlessly. My grip tightened on his arms, and I futilely tried to raise my head to alleviate some of the pressure settling in my head.

Zagan wasn't as keen to help me. He chuckled, low and dark. "Does my sparrow want to cum?"

"Yes! Please!" I answered.

I *needed* relief—from the fiery pulsing between my legs and from the heaviness in my skull.

His tongue swirled around my entrance then dragged at an agonizingly slow pace up toward my bundle of nerves, but he didn't touch it when he reached it. He teased the area all around it, drawing out more squirms and furious pants from me. He chuckled against my skin, amused with my frustrated desperation.

"Do you think you deserve to cum?" he questioned, flicking my clit once with the faintest brush of his tongue. "Do you think your stupid behavior outside warrants a reward?"

My brain wasn't functioning with my current position, but I had enough clarity left to hone in on his words. I'd definitely been over-the-top outside, but more than that, I realized with a heavy weight of remorse what I'd said to him in my drunken haze. I remembered the hurt so clearly clouding his eyes.

"I'm sorry," I whispered, sagging against his body, no longer straining to hold myself up.

He made a sound of acknowledgment and sucked my clit into his mouth. My lips fell open, and my body tightened again as a rush of fiery bliss shot through me.

"Lucky for you," Zagan murmured against my skin, "I can't resist the taste of your pleasure."

His expert tongue devoured my parted folds with quick, hard flicks and sucks so that my body couldn't stop quaking in his hold. Within no time at all, he brought me to that edge and pushed me right off it so that my back arched against his torso and my scream tore through the room.

I was still trying to catch my breath and let the blood settle back in my body when he laid me flat on the bed once more. He watched me catch my breath and shift to sit on my knees while unbuttoning his shirt to discard.

I stared at him as the air came back to me, and I licked my dry lips before saying, "I didn't mean it."

He pulled his shirt off and got to work unfastening his pants, though his eyes never left mine. "Didn't mean what? Drinking yourself stupid? Falling into dark waters while impaired?"

I looked away as shame turned my cheeks hot. "Well, all of that."

I met his eyes again right as he finished ridding himself of his wet clothes. He knelt on the mattress in front of me and pulled me onto his lap so that I straddled his hard cock.

"I wasn't referring to that, though," I went on just as the tip of his dick pushed inside me. I sucked my lip between my teeth, and my eyes fluttered at the sweet stretch.

His heavy gaze held mine as firmly as his hands held my hips to guide me further onto his shaft. "What *were* you referring to then?"

"What I said out there," I answered in a breathy rush. "I didn't mean any of it. I don't—I don't regret meeting you." I swallowed hard and noticed he'd paused the guidance of his dick inside me. "I'm glad I wound up stuck with you."

The admission was close to a confession, and the honesty in my words had my heart racing. Was admitting that I wanted to be with him like admitting something even deeper than that? I wasn't sure, and while the prospect of declaring these turbulent feelings inside of me frightened me to no end, I couldn't deny their truth. I couldn't deny that ... I was glad for what happened between Zagan and I.

He searched my face before he shrugged and looked away. "Odd thing to be thankful for. I *am* a demon, remember? Most people wouldn't be thankful to have us as company. I don't blame you for wishing things were different."

I placed my hand on his jaw and turned his head back toward mine. "You are so much more than just a demon, Zagan. I don't give a damn what you are. I'm grateful to have *you* in my life. I'm so sorry I said otherwise. If I could go back to that night when we got bound and change things, I wouldn't. I'd make the same decision to end up right here with you."

We stared at each other for a long time, both of us seeming to hold our breath with my words hanging between us. Again, I wasn't sure what I was truly confessing, but it felt right saying them. If I knew then what I knew now, I'd still choose the same thing—because I'd choose Zagan.

Zagan's arms wrapped around me, and he leaned me back so that I laid out on the comforter with him nestled between my legs, his dick still firmly inside me. My hand never left his cheek, and our eyes never wavered.

"Why?" he finally asked. His voice came out strained, and his eyes were searching.

I wasn't sure how to answer that. The answer seemed so simple, like it was obvious and staring us both in the face, but the words to explain it were stuck on my tongue, refusing to come out.

"Why did *you* save me?" I whispered.

He opened his mouth like he was going to answer, but like me, the words wouldn't seem to come. Regardless, a sort of understanding seemed to grow in the small space between our naked bodies. One that grew stronger as I brought my other hand up to cup his jaw with both hands. One that pulsed as his eyes softened while looking down at me. One that became all-consuming as he kissed me, not with a fierce hunger but with something slower and sweeter.

His lips claimed mine with a sensual and slow caress as he gently thrust inside me. We'd never had sex like this. Slow. Tender. Yet I almost liked this more than the harder and wilder sex. This felt *real*. It made what was happening between us—the physical and emotional—feel real.

ZAGAN SLEPT SOUNDLY AS I CREPT OUT OF THE ROOM, tying my black silk robe around my otherwise naked body. I expected to feel the aftermath of my drinking the night before, but all I felt was revived. I moved quietly down the hall and stairs to make my way to the ballroom. Morning sunlight filled the vast space, streaming onto the black piano like a sign from the heavens. I stopped only a moment to swallow down the last of my fears before slowly approaching the piano bench.

Last night had been a wake-up call, one that I'd needed to finally break free the rest of the way. I'd made major strides in claiming ownership of my life, but I'd yet to take the biggest and most difficult step—sitting down to play the piano. Mom's hold had remained steadfast over that one thing, but after how she'd tried to hurt me with her spiteful words last night, only for Zagan to pull me up from the dark, that hold had finally cracked. When Zagan came to me and reminded me that I'd made the right decision, it crumbled the rest of the way. I'd chosen the correct path, and I refused to let my old demon hold me back.

Instead, I'd embrace my new one.

I stared down at the black-and-white keys and drank in the silence. All was still in the room. All was quiet. With a deep breath, I rested my fingers on the cold ivory-and-ebony keys, closed my eyes, and let memory take hold.

The first slow notes of "Nuvole Bianche" broke the silence. My fingers shook like they'd been waiting for this moment as long as I had. The first few measures came out rushed from lack of practice and out of eagerness to finally be playing again. I quickly found my rhythm, though, my fingers gliding and the music soaring into the air and through the room with the swelling passion I'd been silently harboring all this time.

Moisture gathered in my shut eyes, but I hardly noticed as the piece poured out of me like a desperate, burning scream that had been building up in my lungs for years. It finally burst out of me, only instead of a roar tumbling from my lips, it came in the form of my bent fingers plucking the piano keys. Never had an outpouring of emotion felt this powerful or this freeing. Never had I felt more at home.

The piece slowed into its gentle ending, and even when silence descended over the room, I didn't take my fingers off the keys or open my eyes. My lips trembled, and tears streamed down my cheeks.

Arms circled me just as cedar and spice filled my nose. Sucking in a sharp breath, I turned on the stool and wrapped my arms around Zagan, crying into the crook of his neck. I held onto him like a woman who was falling into darkness with only him holding her up.

"That was beautiful," he whispered against my hair.

I choked on tears and squeezed him harder. "I've missed it so much. How could I have done that? How could I have sacrificed a part of myself for so long?"

"You did what you thought you had to." He pulled back to look at me, and he cupped my cheeks, wiping the tears that rolled down them. "But that's not the case anymore. You're free, Iyla. So play for me, Sparrow. Play so the whole world knows you won't be fucking stopped anymore."

I didn't stop crying. I couldn't. But I turned back to the piano, and with Zagan right beside me, I let everything go and released it in the form of music.

My grief for lost time.

My anger at having been caged.

My hope for a future I intended to claim.

And my love.

For my friends—both old and new. For music and piano. For Gemma and her improving health.

For my demon.

CHAPTER 31

Zagan

"So," I probed slowly, twirling a strand of Iyla's hair around my finger.

She lifted her head off my bare chest to look up at me. We were stretched out on the couch with some drama-filled dance show playing, but neither of us had been paying much attention.

As soon as I'd found her on the couch in one of my band t-shirts, I'd stripped her of everything, bent her over the couch, and fucked her until she couldn't stand anymore. We moved to lay on the couch for round two, and now, she was pudding in my arms as she rested on top of me.

My sparrow kept me well-fed these days.

"So what?" she asked, her hand resting on my chest. I loved the way she would idly trace my tattoos when we were like this, and she did that now, also taking the opportunity to flick my nipple piercing as she passed by.

I'll have to punish her for that later.

Restraining myself from jumping into round three, I pursed my lips conspiratorially and revealed, "Your sister told me a bit of news at the party the other night."

Iyla's slender finger paused where it had been working on my dagger tattoo, and her big brown eyes locked on mine. "What did she say?" she asked hesitantly.

I smirked. "December third."

Iyla's eyes doubled in size before narrowing in a glare. "She's a traitor."

Laughing, I ordered, "Clear that weekend. You'll be mine for the entire duration, which means this will be the best birthday you've ever had."

Her skepticism remained as she mumbled, "Somehow, that only scares me more."

THERE WERE TEN MINUTES LEFT OF THE FLIGHT. IYLA WAS in the back room of the band's private jet, getting ready with all the things I'd bought her specifically for this trip. I still hadn't told her what we were doing. Hell, she didn't even know where we were actually going right now, and I planned to keep it that way for as long as possible.

Life had been a bitch to Iyla, and the accumulation of it all nearly knocked her over the edge. Just remembering the bullshit her mom had said, seeing the tears fill her sweet eyes, and feeling the pain she'd tried to drown in alcohol—then *actually* drowning—pissed me off all over again. I'd seen every type of human over the years, and Iyla was unlike all of them. She didn't deserve the shit-hand she was dealt, and I was determined to give her everything she *did* deserve.

Starting with her birthday.

I shifted in my seat and rested my forehead on my fingers as I worked on my new song. Ever since that day I'd felt the spark of in-spiration again, I'd spent every spare second I had working on new music. I couldn't seem to write or work on them fast enough with how quickly they were coming to me. When I felt myself coming up on a brick wall, I'd stop and go talk to Iyla or watch her play the piano or take her dancing in our home studio.

Yeah. *Our.*

I wasn't sure when I'd started thinking of my house as *ours*, but nothing had ever sounded more right.

I closed my eyes, letting my pencil still on the sheet of paper, and sang through the lyrics I was working on to make sure I liked the sound. It was slower and a bit more on the romantic side compared to our older songs, but the melody and words reached down to touch something inside of me that had never been tapped into before. And I fucking *loved* it. I felt like myself again.

As the words died off my lips, an angelic voice came from behind me. "That was beautiful. As always. No one sings like you do."

I looked over my shoulder to see Iyla shutting the back cabinet door. She turned to face me, and my throat closed up with no sign of ever opening again.

I was well-acquainted with beauty since my line of work—the demonic and human kind—attracted that. Yet no exotic beauty, no seductress dressed to the nines, no person had ever come close to my sparrow.

The dark navy one-shoulder dress hugged her curves and just barely brushed the ground as she walked in her silver high-heels. The glittering crystals adorning every surface of the gown caught the light, making it look like she wore the star-filled night sky for a dress. Her curled dark hair had been pulled to one side and pinned with a diamond clip, which matched the dangling diamond earrings and necklace resting at the top of her breasts.

And when she smiled at me ... she shined brighter than any of the jewels she wore.

I stood, breathless and heart racing. I couldn't stop drinking her in, and my voice came out rough as I said, "You are very gorgeous, Iyla Marie Winters."

I didn't think it was possible, but her smile widened. She looked down at the dress and ran her newly painted nails over the gown. "I still can't believe you got me all of this. It seems way too expensive."

The clothes, jewelry, and shoes were a mere drop in the bucket for me, but I didn't say that. Instead, I opted for, "You deserve something nice and extravagant. Think of it as me investing in potential outfits you'll wear when you're traveling the world and playing as a pianist."

Her cheeks pinkened, and she looked at the dress again. "It would look pretty on the stage, wouldn't it?"

Not as pretty as the girl wearing it.

The intercom clicked on, and the pilot's voice piped up to instruct us to sit and buckle as we prepared for landing. The two of us got in our seats, which faced each other across a table. She buckled. I didn't. I leaned back, watching her gleaming eyes stare out of the window, no doubt trying to figure out where we were going. With a devious smirk, I glanced out the window and conjured a blur of clouds that blocked her view. I couldn't let her figure it out so soon.

When we landed, I helped Iyla off the jet and shuffled her into the limo that waited at the airport.

"Would you tell me where we're going and what we're doing already?" Iyla asked with an exasperated sigh.

I straightened my tux jacket as we settled into the cozy seating area and leaned back to get comfortable. It was just over an hour drive to our destination, and while I could've gotten us there in the blink of an eye, I decided to get there the human way. It meant I got to watch Iyla squirm with the anticipation of the unknown, and that amusement was worth any long drive.

Iyla studied every sign we passed and quickly gathered that we were in New York, but she wasn't sure what we were here for. She threw out guesses—shopping, going to a place I liked from my time living here, a Broadway show—but I shot down each of them. Even if she got it right, I'd probably lie and tell her she was wrong just to keep her guessing.

Finally, the limo drove through the streets of New York City, and Iyla looked as mesmerized by the tall buildings and bright lights as a kid seeing a Christmas tree lit up for the first time. The sight warmed my chest, and I had the urge to reach over and tug her into my arms. Seeing as how we were pulling up to the Lincoln Center, I decided that would have to wait until later.

When we got out of the limo, Iyla beamed at the lit-up buildings with the bubbling fountain between them. "The Lincoln Center?" she asked slowly. She turned toward me, understanding quickly dawning in her eyes. "Are we here to see the philharmonic?"

I grinned and wove my fingers with hers. "They're performing Mozart's, 'Ch'io mi scordi di te,' his 'Piano Concerto No. 25,' and Mahler's, 'Symphony No. 4.'"

Her lips parted, and her glossy eyes searched mine with a mixture of shock and awe. I just smiled at her and pulled her up the steps and past the fountain for David Geffen Hall. I'd gotten us centermost seats on the second tier balcony, and Iyla practically vibrated in her seat as she stared down at the stage below. Her eyes were constantly moving, watching the crowd find their own seats and taking in the grand lighting and set-up of the stage.

"I can't believe we're here," she whispered, her lips coming so close to touching my skin. Her hand squeezed mine, which she'd not let go of since I took hers outside.

I chuckled. "Just wait until they start playing. You're going to love it."

Sure enough, by the time the lights dimmed and the musicians got in their starting positions, Iyla's eyes had become permanently glued to the magic happening on stage. The music swelled to life, and the singer's voice carried loud and strong through the theater as "Ch'io mi scordi di te" started the night for us.

I knew I should've been watching the performers below, but my head stayed tilted just enough so that I could keep Iyla's face in my constant periphery. Her eyes glimmered with adoration, and every time the pianist moved through particular notes, her breath would hitch and she'd give a soft nod as though to silently say, "Well done."

Before I knew it, the first performance was over, and we were already moving on to Mozart's, "Piano Concerto No. 25." Iyla was even more drawn into this one, practically on the edge of her seat as she listened.

By the time we made it to Mahler's, "Symphony No. 4," I'd basically missed the first half of the show, too busy watching one of my own. I finally faced the stage below and watched with quiet appreciation as the musicians commanded their instruments with expert grace and skill. The sound flooding the room was soft and enchanting. I glanced at Iyla again to see what she made of this piece, and I found her with her chin tilted slightly into the air, eyes closed, and a soft smile on her lips.

The first time she'd heard me play the piano, she'd listened with her eyes shut. She'd said it let her feel the music better, and my chest tightened with a need to know what she felt. I wanted to experience the piece through her ears. So I faced forward and closed my eyes, letting every part of my senses focus on the music.

The small jolts of the melody in the floor beneath my feet and in my chair.

The light sound of strings and winds twirling with each other to create this brief thunder of unease that finally gave way into serenity as the final movement brought us to a close.

The theater fell silent, and then a sudden eruption of applause poured out from the mezzanine and gallery. I opened my eyes as patrons stood, clapping for the bowing conductor and philharmonic. Iyla and I stood, too, clapping for a beautiful performance. Our gazes met, and we shared a warm smile as the high from experiencing the production lingered.

"That was ..." Iyla beamed, shaking her head as she tried to find the words. She laughed and looked up at me. "Everything! I mean, really. I have no words."

There was a chill in the night air as we left the building, so I pulled off my tux jacket to drape it around her shoulders. She bit her lip and gave me a small thanks as she pulled the jacket tighter around her shoulders.

"The night isn't over, yet," I said, placing my hand on the small of her back. "We're not too far from where we're headed. Are you okay walking there, or do I need to call for a cab?"

She shook her head and leaned into my side. "I want to walk! I've never been to New York before. I want to see what it's like."

Her enthusiasm was infectious, and as I walked her down the streets of the city, pointing out different things and telling her stories from my time here, the city I'd known since its very beginning seemed brighter than it ever had before. But I wasn't surprised. Iyla made everything better.

Iyla's cheeks and the tip of her nose were red by the time we reached the Plaza Hotel. I let her take in the elegance of the lobby as I checked in with the receptionist, who was already excited to see me since I was *the* Zagan, but smiled even wider at me once he learned I was the guest who'd booked the grand penthouse suite.

I got stopped twice more by fans before Iyla and I finally managed to reach our suite.

"Oh my gosh," Iyla breathed out in a rush of awe. She slowly walked around the luxurious first floor of the suite, and it seemed she couldn't take in everything fast enough, just as I couldn't keep up with her ever-changing amazement.

I grabbed her hand to pull her up the stairs, which led to the second floor of the suite. "Are you hungry? I had dinner prepared and set up for us."

She nodded, and with that, I brought her to the private balcony. The doors were already open, the curtains blowing gently in the chilly night air. Outdoor heaters had been set up near the table, which had been outfitted with candles and roses. The steak and lobster dinner and bottle of wine waited on us.

It was far more romantic than anything I'd ever done, but then again, I'd never had Iyla in my life. While something like this would've made me cringe in the past, I now found myself eager to see her reaction to it all. I wanted to see the light fill her eyes or the color swarm her skin as the happiness overflowed from within her.

Something had been stirring inside of me for awhile now, and while I couldn't put words to it, I could *show* her what I was feeling. I could profess these raging emotions through gestures like this, if only to make her understand that there was more happening.

There was more than a bond that kept us here.

There was more than a deal to save her sister tying us to one another.

I just didn't know what to call it or what it all meant.

"You did all this?" Iyla asked, her voice so low, I wasn't sure I would've heard it had I not been a demon.

"I've never put together a surprise for someone, let alone one for their birthday," I admitted, scratching sheepishly at my chin. "I hope everything's been okay."

She turned to look at me with unshed tears glistening in her eyes. "Are you kidding? It's been ... amazing. No one's ever done something like this for me. Any of it. The clothes. The concert. This." She waved her hand at the patio and gave a small laugh and disbelieving shake of her head. She squeezed my hand. "Thank you, Zagan. Not just for tonight, but for ... everything."

I wasn't sure what to do with such profound gratitude. People didn't typically thank me for things, other than an orgasm I gave them. When they did, it was never like this—whole-heartedly, the emotion practically pouring out of them to hit me in a wave of warmth. I didn't feel like I deserved it. To me, doing this for her was the bare minimum. Doing this was just the tip of the iceberg as far as everything I wanted to shower her in.

This was just the start of our song.

IYLA STOOD AT THE WINDOW IN ONE OF THE BEDROOMS, staring out at the nightlife of the city beyond. A soft, care-free smile painted her full lips. She'd shed my jacket after we came inside. I unbuttoned the cuffs of my shirt to roll up the sleeves, watching her eyes glitter with a glee that made my own chest swell with that now constant yet still unfamiliar emotion.

I shoved my hands in my pockets and stood there for endless minutes, content to watch her watch the world. It was amazing how things changed like this. Me being satisfied with one person? Me enjoying the mere sight of their contentment and not focusing on my own?

How the right people changed us for the better.

I approached Iyla from behind and stopped at her back, meeting her eyes in the reflection of the window.

She smiled at my reflection and said, "I bet the city is beautiful when it snows."

"Would you like it to snow?"

Her eyes widened. "C-Can you make it snow?"

For you, anything.

I kept the immediate response to myself, and instead, looked past our reflections to the open air outside. With a single thought and a ripple of magic, fat, fluffy snowflakes began falling from the sky. Would I have been able to do such a major display of power like changing the weather for any other person? No. But our bond changed everything. The possibilities of what we could do heightened to ensure we met most demands of whoever we were bound to, and I'd never before been happier that was the case.

Too bad it wasn't that easy to alter the health of someone other than our bonds. I knew that—saving Gemma—would've been the gift she truly wanted most.

Iyla gasped and leaned closer to the window to watch the snow gracefully fall to the earth below. I placed my hands on her arms and stepped further into her. I leaned my head down so that my lips brushed her ear, and I nearly came undone when she shivered against me.

"Happy birthday, Sparrow," I whispered.

Her palms pressed into my thighs, and her head leaned back against my chest. I pulled her hair securely over one shoulder and pressed my lips to the column of her throat then moved lower to her shoulder. The scent of her arousal permeated the air around us, prickling my skin like static, and I inhaled deeply, my demonic features practically itching to come out at the intoxicating aroma of her desire.

I licked the skin of her neck where her pulse fluttered, and her ass pressed against my aching dick. I reached behind her to unzip the dress and watched it fall off her cream-colored skin to pool at her feet. My dirty little sparrow had forgone any underwear, so the moment the garment was off, she stood naked and beautiful.

"Zagan, the window," she squealed.

She tried backing away from it, but I caged her in, pressing my front to her bare back and placing my hands on the window on either side of her.

"You're not going anywhere," I said. I took my hand off the glass to reach for her full tit and squeezed it before pinching and rolling the nipple in my fingertips.

She bit her lip, and her eyelids fluttered as she pressed further against me. "What if someone looks up here?" she asked breathlessly. "What if they see?"

"Then they should thank you for blessing them with the sweet sight of you," I answered, continuing to palm her breast with one hand while I gripped the front of her thigh with the other. My hand trailed up the smooth flesh until I met the crease where her leg met her pussy, and I dragged my finger softly across the skin there, teasing where she had grown deliciously wet.

"Now," I murmured against the shell of her ear, "be a good girl and lean over for me."

Her breath hitched, and I saw the color rise to her cheeks in the reflection. She immediately obeyed, leaning the top half of her body forward until her face practically pressed into the glass. Her breath created clouds of fog on the window. She spread her thighs slightly, and I grabbed her leg to force one knee to rest on the windowsill, opening up her pretty cunt for me. The lips glistened with her hungry desire, and the beast inside me practically paced with the impatient need to taste her, fuck her, and *claim* her.

I smirked as my eyes stayed trained on her dripping core, and my dick pressed against my slacks with the threat of ripping clean through the material if I didn't free him soon. So I didn't bother with all my clothes. I undid my pants enough to free my hard cock, slid it through her moisture, and sank into her with one hard thrust.

She let out the sexiest fucking sigh and arched her back. Already, the taste of her pleasure filled the back of my mouth, and it only intensified when I leaned forward to grip her breast with one hand and touch her clit with the other. My sparrow loved having her pussy played with while I pounded into her, which was what I did. I pulled my hips back and slammed them forward again, fucking her with relentless thrusts. Her hands pressed into the window and curled against the foggy glass as her chin tilted back so she could moan for me.

"That's right, baby," I praised, pinching and rolling her nipple and flicking her clit in time with the movement of my hips. "Yell for me. Scream. Tell me how much you love it when I fuck this pussy."

"I love it!" she cried as her own hips shifted to meet each of my thrusts. "God, I love it!"

I let go of her tit and reached up to fist her hair tightly. She whimpered as I pulled on it, stretching her neck as far as it could go. "Say the words. Say what it is you love."

Her breath heaved around another moan as my dick touched sweet places inside her. Finally, she screamed, "I love it when you fuck me with your cock!"

I smiled. "That's fucking right."

She tightened around my shaft, and her body shook as her orgasm crashed through her. My own skin burned with the mounting pleasure, rushing through me to settle where my dick pushed in and out of her hard and fast. I continued rubbing her clit, despite her squirming against my touch to her now-sensitive bud. I pulled her hair harder as my release got closer and closer until finally, I spilled myself inside her tight hole.

I was hot and full—full of her pleasure and full of my own satisfaction.

But I was also just getting started.

CHAPTER 32

Iyla

I'D NEVER HAD SUCH AN AMAZING WEEK. ZAGAN'S SUR-
prise birthday trip was followed by finals and the end of the
semester, which meant, come spring semester, I'd officially be
working toward my dream. Gemma was on the rise health-wise
thanks to Zagan's consistent small doses of blood, and I was finally
playing the piano again. For once, I felt good about life.

Even now, my smile wouldn't disappear, despite stumbling over
some notes as I practiced Bach's, "Prelude No. 1." There was a certain lightness filling my chest that had never been there before, and
as I finished out the piece without any more mistakes, I realized it
was hope.

Hope for my sister.

Hope for my dreams.

Hope for what the future had in store for me and the demon
who'd changed me.

"You've gotten better."

I looked at the entryway to the ballroom where Zagan leaned
against the doorframe. I drank in the sight of him in his dark jeans
and long-sleeved gray shirt, and my mouth naturally watered at the
attractive sight of his tattooed hands and pierced flesh.

"Thank you," I beamed. I closed the lid and stood from the piano bench. "Did you finish working on the song?"

He'd been finalizing the details of a song he'd been working on for the past couple of weeks, and I took his presence now to mean that he'd finally completed it.

He offered me a smile of his own and answered, "I did. I thought I could play it for you once we got back from visiting Gemma."

I practically bounced the rest of the way to him, equally excited to see my sister and hear Zagan's new song afterward. I'd been swamped after getting back from New York, then focusing on finals, so I hadn't seen Gemma since the party. Now, I couldn't seem to get to Bloomings fast enough, grabbing Zagan and pulling him after me toward his car.

The moment we stepped inside Bloomings, something felt off. A sixth sense flared to life and picked up on something I couldn't yet see. Unease pricked at my insides like frost slowly encasing them. The bustle of activity carried a bit more urgency, and the whispers were like nails grating on a chalkboard. I spotted Noya coming out of Gemma's room, and the moment our eyes met, I just knew.

There was a split second when I froze where I stood, just holding Noya's sympathetic eyes. Then terror collided into me like a meteor crashing into earth, and I ran down the hallway, deaf to Noya and Zagan's voices. My heart beat furiously until I stood in Gemma's room. The pounding in my temples stopped as quickly as it had started so that all I could hear was the slow beep of her heart rate monitor. My breath cut off in my throat.

I stood just inside the doorway and stared at my sister, who looked nothing like the last time I'd seen her. Gone was the peachy warm flush to her skin, the shine to her auburn hair, and the utter bliss in her smile. Her eyes were shut, and her dark eyelashes stood out against her gray skin, which appeared sunken beneath her eyes and on her cheeks. Her brown hair was spread out on her pillow, thin and muted in color. Her gown had slipped down, giving me a view of her sharp collar bones protruding through her skin like her body had suddenly shriveled up. A nasal cannula sat across her face, giving her extra oxygen through her nose, and an IV drip currently poured something into her through the IV in her hand.

"G-Gemma?" I croaked.

This couldn't be real. I was in a nightmare. It was the only explanation, because this ... She ...

I took a step toward her, but the moment I moved, my knees gave out. Zagan grabbed me at the same moment, falling to the floor with me. My wide, tear-filled eyes met his, and I gripped his arm with every bit of strength I had left and whispered, "What happened? Why ..."

I'd never seen the look of utter disbelief and fear on Zagan's face, yet he wore the expression now as he swallowed. "It ... my blood ..."

He didn't have to finish. I knew what he was trying to say.

His blood hadn't worked.

And now, her illness was catching up to her.

I clawed at Zagan's arms like a mad woman trying to grapple at ropes as she dangled off a cliff. "I killed her. I killed my sister."

"No," he said with a firm shake of his head. "She's not dead, yet. She could still pull through this, Iyla."

"How?" I whispered. The tears finally spilled over.

He looked from me to Gemma lying still in her bed then back to me. I saw the helplessness in his gaze even before he answered, "I don't know."

This couldn't be happening. Not my baby sister. Not when she'd just started getting better.

"Iyla."

I turned to the doorway where Noya appeared. The grief she was trying to hide but failing to do so made my own ramp up. She wrung her hands in front of her as she said, "Dr. Seward called your mom. She should be here anytime now. We don't know what happened. Gemma has been doing so well when all of a sudden ..."

Zagan had warned me. He'd told me his blood was no guarantee and that it could even kill her. I'd chosen to try it anyway. I'd heard the risk and threw it away, too focused on potentially saving her. Instead, I'd signed her death certificate.

Mom appeared beside Noya at that exact moment, shoving her aside as she barreled into the room. Her hair was as pristine as always, her make-up in perfect condition, and her pantsuit crisp. She wasn't the picture of a fearful mother but of a business woman on a mission, which didn't zero in on Gemma but, rather, on me.

Mom's nostrils flared, and her chest heaved as she pointed a finger right at me. "Get them out. Get her out *now*!"

Staff crowded the doorway at Mom's furious shrieks with Dr. Seward pushing his way to the front.

"Mrs. Winters," Dr. Seward started hesitantly, his eyes bouncing between her and me. "I know you're upset, but ..."

Zagan helped me to my feet, and his hold was the only thing keeping me standing.

"I want her out!" Mom screeched. Her eyes never left me even as she barked at Dr. Seward, "Remove Iyla from the approved guest list. She is not to be allowed back in this building."

"Mom," I cried pathetically, shaking my head in disbelief.

The nurses and Dr. Seward stood speechless and passed helpless glances between mother and daughter. No one liked her, yet *she* was the guardian. Who would they listen to in this moment? The raging mother, or the loving sister?

Finally, Dr. Seward looked at me, his frown apologetic. "Iyla. I'm sorry. You—You're going to have to leave."

My heart fractured, and the world swam as my breath seemed to run away from me. This was all my imagination. Gemma wasn't dying. I wasn't being removed from Bloomings. Mom wasn't glaring at me with more hatred than a singular person should be capable of.

"Come on," Zagan soothed in my ear, but I barely heard him.

I couldn't seem to hear or think past the whooshing in my ears. It wasn't until we were back in the parking lot with the December wind kissing my wet cheeks that reality caught up to me with a vengeance.

"Gemma!" I wheezed, turning in Zagan's arms to try to rush back inside.

Zagan held onto me with strength beyond this world just as Mom barreled out the front doors. Her heels clacked against the concrete as she stomped toward me with a crazed look in her eye like she was ready to hit me. At the last minute, it seemed to register who stood beside me, and she stopped short, breathing hard and glaring at me.

"Please let me see her," I begged between sobs. "You can't do this."

"I'm her mother. I can do as I damn well please," she snapped, and in that brief hiss, I saw it—the flash of something truly nasty in her eye. Zagan must've seen it, too, because his arms tightened around my chest where he held me.

I didn't have the strength to understand what it was, though. All I could do was plead, "Let me see her. Please. I-I need to see her."

Before it's too late.

The thought only served to bring more tears to my eyes. I could still remember the glow Gemma had the last time I saw her, yet now ...

"You make me sick," Mom growled, raking a hand over her pristine curls. "Such a worthless child. It's ridiculous! Gemma shouldn't be the one in there. It should be you in that bed!"

The ache clouding my mind opened partly enough for me to take note of my mother's words. There were no tears on her face, and instead of being inside with Gemma, she'd followed me out here to spew more biting words. That flash in her gaze came back, and now I understood what it was.

Glee.

She took pleasure in hurting me. She found joy in cutting me down.

Gemma was the last piece connecting the two of us as I carved a path for myself, and with her gone, there wouldn't be any chances for Mom to get her hits in. Instead of taking this time with her youngest, she was using the time left to get her final punches in, to inflict the most damage she could. She was doing the last thing she could to hurt me the most—denying me my chance to see my sister and say my goodbyes.

Her hatred for me was more than her love for Gemma.

I realized then that this woman didn't care. Even if she grieved, it wouldn't be for *Gemma*. It would be for the loss of the child she'd chosen. It would be for only having the one child she'd always resented left. If one had to die, it should've been the one she'd never wanted.

"Do you even love her, Mom?" I demanded. "If you did, you wouldn't be doing this. You wouldn't be using this time to follow me out here just to hurt me. You'd be in that room with Gemma *and* me, because that's what *she'd* want."

"How dare—"

My lips trembled as I stepped away from Zagan to close every inch of space between me and her. I held her gaze with every ounce of conviction inside me as I whispered, "I wish it was me in that bed. I *wish* I could trade places with her, Mom. But I can't. So instead of standing here, trying to kill me off with your words, let me see her. You might hate me, but she ... she doesn't. She would want me there."

Her lip curled as she got in my face to hiss, "Go to fucking Hell, Iyla."

She turned on her heel and stormed back inside. The crater in my chest opened wide, pulling me into the waiting darkness. My head hung, and sobs choked me until pinpricks of fog darted across my head like thunder clouds rolling in.

"Fuck that," Zagan growled. He gripped my hand and pulled me to his car. "You're seeing Gemma, even if we have to wait all goddamn night."

He sat me in the passenger seat and went around the car to his side.

Everything spiraled inside me. The sight of Gemma lying nearly lifeless in her bed. Mom and our venomous exchange. Tears clouded my vision as her words replayed in my head.

It should be you in that bed.

I looked up at the ceiling of the car, crying helplessly. I didn't want Gemma to die. She was my world, and she had yet to truly live her life. There had to be something I could do to save her. I couldn't let this happen.

Zagan wove his fingers with mine and brushed his thumb over my skin in an effort to soothe me. As I stared at his inked hand, I realized who I had next to me. Or rather, *what*.

I turned in my seat to lock my desperate eyes on his. "You're a demon. And you're my bond."

His brows plunged in confusion. "I know."

I gripped his hand tightly and brought it close to my chest. My voice broke as I pleaded, "Then help me. We can still save her."

He slowly shook his head. "We tried. My blood—"

"Me," I interrupted, my voice rising. "You can switch our places. Give her my life, and let me trade places with her."

The blood drained from his face, and his pierced lips parted as he fell speechless. My heart raced with the new answer staring right at me, and I tried to make him see in the way I gripped him tightly that I needed this.

His eyes were still wide in shock as he shook his head once. "No."

Tears rushed out of me anew and spilled down my cheeks. "Please, Zagan. Please! I can't let her die!"

His jaw worked, and his eyes hardened. "I can't."

I glared at him. "You can't, or you *won't*?"

He didn't answer. He turned away from me and focused his attention outside the window. My head hung in defeat, and I sagged in my seat. This was the only answer I had, but if I couldn't get Zagan to cooperate, what was another solution? I didn't have one, and that reality broke me all over again. I was at a loss for a way out of this. I was alone in my search for a way to save my sister.

An hour passed with Zagan practically vibrating with some wound up energy next to me and my own panic and grief tormenting me. Mom was only there for a freaking hour—apparently that was enough time to spend with her seriously ill child.

As soon as her car pulled out of the parking lot, Zagan turned to me. The hard anger that had been simmering in his eyes after my plea vanished, and they softened once more. "Let's go."

He held his hand out for me, and the moment I took it, shadows erupted around us. It felt like I was floating away in the cold, dark, endless void with only Zagan's firm hold on my hand keeping me from getting lost. Slowly, Gemma's room came into view, until it was like I was looking through a haze of smoke from the corner of her room.

She slept soundless and motionless, alone once more in the dim room. No lights were on, and only the overcast sky offered light through the window. The room seemed to reflect how desolate I felt seeing my baby sister like this.

"The coast is clear," Zagan murmured. In an instant, the haze cleared, and the staticky charge touching my skin faded. "I've put a veil over the room for now. If anyone tries to come in, they'll forget why they wanted in here and leave. You should be fine to spend as much time with her as you want."

I squeezed his hand, grateful that he was doing this, even if he wouldn't do the one thing I asked of him. My throat had closed up again, only getting worse as I slowly approached Gemma's bed. I stared down at her ghostly, frail body, and I nearly broke. I wanted to turn back time to when she was laughing and having fun with me and her friends. I wanted to rip all the medical gadgets off her and plead with the world to let me take her place.

But instead, I carefully sat beside her on the bed then leaned back so that I laid beside her. I rested my head beside hers on the pillow and gently took her hand in mine. My lips trembled when I felt how cold and how frail it had gotten. I feared it might crumble right there in my hold.

Her eyes slowly fluttered open. My heart lurched, and her bleary eyes took a few minutes to focus on me beside her. I was grateful I wasn't a sobbing mess right now. I didn't want her to see and know what we all worried was coming.

"Hey, you," I said softly, plastering on as much of a smile as I could. I wasn't even sure if I succeeded.

She blinked, and her muted hazel eyes were slow to open again. "Iyla." Her chapped lips barely opened as she uttered my name, and her voice was more of a rasp than the sweet, jovial sound it usually was. "I was … worried I wouldn't … get to see you."

She spoke slowly, like just the mere act of forming words sucked all the energy out of her.

I had to swallow multiple times before I managed to croak, "I'm always gonna be here. *Always*. I'd never not come to you."

Her exhausted eyes closed again, and it felt like minutes went by before they reopened. Her small fingers wrapped tighter around my hand, but I noticed how weak even that was. I tried to keep the misery off my face, but I knew glimpses of it slipped through the mask I wore.

"Will," Gemma asked quietly, her eyes finally locking on mine, "dying hurt?"

My eyebrows slammed down, and I shook my head adamantly against the pillow even as a tear slid down my cheek. "You aren't going to die. You—"

"Please," Gemma begged. The first sign of strength entered her voice and came out with that one word. "I know ... it's coming. I don't want to ... be reassured. I just want the truth."

I stared into her eyes—the eyes of an eleven year old who seemed to have aged a lifetime since I last saw her. The eyes of a little girl who had to grow up in pain and sickness. The eyes of a girl who'd never get to see everything life had to offer. The eyes of a gift to this world.

I couldn't fight my tears anymore. I shifted closer to her and tucked her head under my chin while wrapping my arms around her. I kept my grip loose to protect her weak form, yet still held on with all the love I had in me. I closed my eyes as tears fell from my cheeks and into her hair.

I didn't want to give her honesty. I wanted to lie and say she'd pull through this, because more than anything, that's what I wanted. But it wasn't what she *needed* from me.

My throat burned with emotion as I finally whispered, "No. No, I don't—I don't think it will hurt. I think ... it will be like falling asleep."

Her small frame seemed to relax slightly in my arms, and that only made the fierce ache in my chest twist sharper. What a fucked up world we lived in that she found comfort in the prospect of dying.

"Do you think ... the place we go when we die ... will be scary?" Gemma asked softly against my chest.

"Not where you're going," Zagan suddenly answered.

I looked to where he stood at the foot of the bed. He briefly met my eyes, and when I saw the urgency swirling with the pain in his gaze, I realized he was answering as much for me as he was Gemma. He wanted—*needed*—us to know that Gemma would be going somewhere good. He was trying to offer some semblance of reassurance to the both of us.

I felt Gemma's attempt at a smile against my chest and heard the faint trace of it when she said, "Maybe I'll get ... to see Dad there."

I sucked in a shaky wet breath and had to tilt my head back to force the tears to fall away. "I bet you will. I bet he's already there, waiting with one of his big, warm hugs."

"I'll make sure ... to hug him for you, too," Gemma said, releasing my hand to wrap her arm around me.

My nose scrunched at the fresh onslaught of tears. I wanted to pull Gemma in tight and hug her hard, but I was too afraid of breaking her. So I kept my arms loose around her frame and just pressed my face further into the top of her head, biting my lip to keep from crying out until something metallic filled my mouth. The two of us didn't move for some time. She clung to me with her weak arms, and I shook with silent tears that fell into her hair.

Gemma eventually pulled her arm away and leaned back so that she could look up at me. Her cracked lips lifted into a faint grin. "I wish I could hear you play piano one last time."

My mind went back to that day I'd told her I was going to play again. She'd been so excited for me, and I knew that if she could, she would've come to every show. She'd always loved listening to me and Dad play, and now ... now she'd never get to again.

Zagan cleared his throat, drawing both of our attention. He looked between us and offered a small smile. "I can help with that. Gem, can you close your eyes for me?"

My heart constricted with the nickname he'd given her, and I couldn't help but think about Gemma and how she'd never find *her* Zagan, the person who faced the storms with her and came out on the other side a better person because of it.

Gemma's eyes closed.

Zagan looked at the open space in the corner of her room, and with a wave of his hand, a small vertical piano appeared. He gave me a small nod then looked at Gemma. "You can open them now."

Gemma's eyes slowly blinked, and an excited glimmer briefly lit them with life again when she saw the piano now in her room. "How—"

"I had a feeling you'd like to hear your sister play, so I had it arranged to wheel this in here," Zagan lied with all the confidence in the world.

Satisfied with the answer, Gemma turned to look at me again. "Can you play it for me?"

It wasn't even a question. There was nothing I wouldn't do for her. I just wished I could do more. I wished I had tried harder or been here for her more. I wasn't sure if not giving her Zagan's blood would've made a difference. She'd already been on a decline with no answers on how to stop her body from slowly attacking itself.

Did giving her Zagan's blood kill her faster? Had it actually kept her here longer than if we hadn't tried? Did giving her the blood give her enough life and energy to enjoy these past few weeks to the fullest? I didn't have the answers to the questions plaguing me, and I probably never would.

One thing I did have, though, was this moment with her. I had time to grant her this last wish.

So with a small nod, I answered, "Okay."

CHAPTER 33

Zagan

IYLA'S BARELY CONTAINED PAIN PIERCED ME DEEPER THAN any arrow ever could. The dark anguish of her heart practically strangled me where I stood, watching her sit on the small stool of the piano I'd conjured. Tears continued their relentless journey down her face as she stared at the piano keys, too lost to the grief to move.

She desperately wanted to take away the death moving in on her sister, and likewise, I wanted to take this pain from her. But not at the cost of killing her. She'd asked the impossible of me, because while she couldn't lose her sister, *I* couldn't lose *her*. Not like that.

So instead, I stood uselessly to the side.

Iyla finally looked up at her sister. "What would you like to hear?"

Gemma rested among the many blankets and gave Iyla a dreamy sort of grin. "I want to hear that song Dad always played and sang to us and Mom. That Justin Bieber song that Tommee Proffitt made a version of."

Iyla's eyes briefly shut like the mere suggestion was already too much. But with a nod, she looked down at the keys, brought her fingers up to them, took a small breath, and started to play. I recognized the song Gemma had requested as "Anyone" as the first notes twinkled into the air, and my heart lurched when Iyla's sweet voice began to sing. I held my breath, enraptured by her with every sweep of her fingers and every word she sang.

She always told me that when I sang, it did something to her. She said my voice was *beautiful*, a description I'd never been given. Now I knew how wrong she was, because she ... *she* was beautiful. For a moment, I thought I'd lost touch with reality and somehow stumbled into Heaven to hear an angel singing.

But it was just her.

Just my sparrow.

Her voice cracked on the lyrics about a loved one moving on. Tears stole her voice, and her body hunched forward in an effort to keep singing and playing through the hurt. With her quickly losing the ability to keep going, I moved toward her and began to sing, too. She looked up at me through swollen eyes as I picked up where she couldn't, though her fingers never stopped their playing.

I sat beside her on the bench and wrapped my arm around the small of her back as the chorus started. She took a deep breath and started singing again, our voices mixing and blending in a harmony unlike any other. Demon and angel—voices filling the room in a song about love and about needing more time.

And as Iyla sang and played for her sister, my own eyes never left Iyla. They were glued to her profile as I sang with her and without her when the tears prevented it. I sang, realizing that every line was for her. Every word was for her.

Even if she didn't know it.

The song finished, and the room would've been silent if not for Iyla's hiccups and the beeping of Gemma's machine. We both looked at Gemma, whose eyes had drifted closed at some point. She laid motionless.

I saw the instant fear swarm Iyla's eyes, but I quickly placed my hand on her back and reassured, "She's just sleeping."

Relief washed over her, and it seemed only after I'd pointed it out that Gemma's minute rise and fall of her chest became clear. Iyla ran her fingers over her wet cheeks and stared hopelessly at her sister. "Do you think it will happen today?" Her voice caught on the last word, and the sound damn near ruined me.

"No," I answered, and I meant it. I didn't actually know, but I'd *make* it true. "It won't happen today."

She closed her eyes and took a deep breath. "Then we should let her rest. We can come back tomorrow. Maybe we can bring her that new dragon book that just released. You know, the one the two of you talked about?"

Tomorrow.

I cursed inwardly. If only things had turned out differently.

I cleared my throat of the tightness there and nodded. "Yeah. Yeah, we can do that."

She got up and slowly went back to the bed. I waved my hand at the piano, making it disappear. When I looked back at Iyla, she had her lips pressed to Gemma's forehead and her hands clutching Gemma's slender fingers.

"I love you," Iyla whispered against Gemma's temple. "So, *so* much."

I wanted to take Iyla's pain away. I wanted her endless stream of tears to vanish. I wanted to give her what she wanted and save her sister for her.

I could never truly understand what she was feeling. I didn't have siblings, and I viewed death as a necessary part of life for humans. I'd seen thousands of deaths over the millenia I'd been here, and none of them had fazed me. I'd even go so far as to say that I'd always found it annoying when humans made such a big deal over a very natural thing that they knew had to happen.

This was different.

Seeing Iyla cling to her sister. Hearing the sobs still spew from her lips as we drove home. Practically tasting the heartache in the air around her.

Nothing else seemed to matter. The only thing that did was taking Iyla's anguish away, no matter what it took or what it meant.

The moment we stepped through the front door of our house, Iyla ran a shaky hand through her hair and looked at me. "There's got to be something I can do. I-I can't let this happen. It's all my fault that she's like this."

"Iyla, slow down," I soothed, holding my hands out to her. "You didn't cause this."

"I did," she sobbed. "The blood. It was my idea. I—"

There was no convincing her otherwise when she was so distraught, so I snapped my fingers. In the same instant, her eyes rolled back into her head, and her body went limp. I caught her in my arms and stared down at her sleeping face.

"Just rest," I whispered to her. "I'll make this right. You won't lose your sister."

I carried her up the stairs to her bedroom and tucked her in. She would be out for a while, so after shutting her door behind me, I trudged downstairs to my music studio. I dropped onto the couch and stared at the finished song I'd left there that morning— the song I'd written for her.

Every line and every note was crafted with Iyla in mind, and it had easily been my best song yet. But what did I expect when writing a song for the girl who made my existence mean something?

I leaned my head against the back of the couch and stared blankly at the ceiling as I called out, "Dante."

I waited in silence as the call traveled to wherever Dante was. It was roughly a minute before the demon appeared in a plume of shadows.

"This better be important," Dante grumbled, holding a naked hardback book in his hand. He shook it at me and hissed, "I was just about to find out who the killer is."

I smirked, despite knowing the rather bleak conversation we were about to have. "Sorry to interrupt."

He flopped down on the couch cushion adjacent to mine and dropped the book next to him. He stared at me for a second like he was trying to solve his own mystery of why I'd randomly called him here through shadow speak. We didn't really call out to each other like that anymore, not since phones were invented. We only did it when it was about something urgent, which no doubt left him puzzled now.

"What's up?" Dante asked with only a hint of caution to his voice.

"Starting today, I'll need you to take Coldin with you."

Alarm furrowed his brow. "Why? He stays with the leader of the group, which is you. I don't know if I want the responsibility of making sure he stays under control."

I didn't answer right away. I pressed my lips together as I mulled over what I wanted to say. Talking, especially about *feelings*, was fucking weird for us. Not only did we not really have a variety of them, but we didn't get deep like that. Just the thought of opening up to others made my skin scrawl.

So, I finally decided on, "You know, I don't think I've ever done anything for the sake of someone else. Even when I did things that others perceived as kindness or as selflessness, I always had my own motives. I always saw it as benefiting me, one way or another."

Dante frowned, clearly confused by my sudden change in topic. "Glad to hear it."

I chuckled and looked down at my tattooed hands, running my thumb along the design. "Iyla changed that. I've grown to ... *like* doing things. Not for me, but for her. And not even for my own satisfaction but because I actually want to see her happy."

"Are you trying to make me puke?" Dante asked with a roll of his eyes. "I can't believe you called me here just to spew your delusional nonsense."

I sucked one of my lip piercings into my mouth, toying with the ring in an effort to brace myself for my next words. "Iyla's sister is dying. My blood didn't work."

Dante shrugged his large shoulders. "Big deal. Humans die every day. What do we care?"

"It's Iyla's sister."

He raised an indifferent brow. "So?"

"It's breaking Iyla. She can't lose her sister." I met and held Dante's gaze as my voice hardened. "I *won't* let her lose Gemma."

I'd been wracking my brain for some way to save Gemma ever since I saw the devastation it caused Iyla. Plus, I had to admit, the little girl had grown on me. We *did* bond over dragons. I'd considered trying more blood to save her but worried that would only make things worse. Then I realized the solution was obvious.

A Bargainer demon, one who made trades and deals. Their abilities were limitless, so long as they received a payment for their deals.

Gemma's life saved in exchange for something else.

It sounded simple in theory.

But what most didn't realize when going into a deal with a Bargainer demon was that they never asked for things easily given, even from their own kind—hell, *especially* from their own kind. It didn't matter the cost, though. Not if it meant saving Iyla's sister.

Now I understood why humans threw caution to the wind and made deals with demons.

Dante seemed to piece together what I was suggesting, and his dark eyes narrowed into thin slits. "Are you fucking insane? You know what she's going to demand in exchange."

I nodded. "I do, which is why I'll go to her. She'll ask for something I can easily give, whereas I don't know what others would require. I won't risk them demanding something impossible, not with so little time left."

Dante leaned forward to brace his forearms on his legs, and desperation creased his brow tighter. "Easily given? Dude! You've lost it! Why would you do that? How could you even consider doing something so stupid for some human girl?"

"Because I love her."

I'd never said the words out loud, and I didn't even know I was going to say it until they were out there. Honestly, I'd never even let myself think them. Yet the moment they were given life, I realized nothing had ever been more true. That warm, bubbling emotion that had been swirling around inside me all this time made so much sense now.

Love.

I loved my sparrow.

Dante stared at me, completely speechless for once. His lips were open, but no words came out. He didn't even blink. Just when I feared I'd officially broken him, he snarled, "We're demons. We *can't* love."

"Says who?" I shot back, suddenly determined to defend what I knew to be true. "Look, all I know is that Iyla makes me better. She makes *existing* better. When she smiles, the sun shines down on me. When she walks into a room, I can breathe in a way I never could before. With her, I feel ... at home. If what I feel for her isn't love, I don't think such a thing exists."

He shook his head slowly. "So you're really going to do it? You're going to throw away everything?"

Despite the gravity of what I was about to do, I actually smiled. "For her? I'd do anything."

"I don't understand you," Dante huffed disbelievingly.

I clapped him on the shoulder. "Maybe you will someday."

CHAPTER 34

Iyla

RINGING FILLED MY EARS. I GROANED AND ROLLED OVER in bed, fumbling on my nightstand for my phone. *Huh. Bed. How did I get here?*

I didn't remember going to bed or falling asleep. I didn't even know what time it was. One look at my phone had me shooting upright, though. It was the next morning, and Noya's name flashed on my phone. The pit in my stomach instantly opened up, and I placed a shaking hand over my mouth to keep the bile from rising up my throat. If she was calling me, that could only mean ...

"Hello?" I answered. My heartbeat pounded furiously in my ears, and I worried I wouldn't be able to hear her.

"Iyla!" Noya's frantic whisper filled the other end of the phone. "I'm not supposed to be calling you. I could definitely get fired for this, but you *need* to get down here. Gemma—She's—"

"What?" I croaked. I bunched the comforter so tightly in my hand that my knuckles turned white. "She's what?"

"She's ... *alive.*"

My heart stopped, and my mind emptied. I was sure I'd misunderstood.

"Just get down here," Noya repeated. "You'll see what I mean."

There wasn't a moment's hesitation. I sprang from my bed and fumbled to pull on my shoes. I was still in my leggings and sweatshirt from the day before, but I didn't give a damn. I didn't stop to brush my hair or do any basic morning care. I called for Zagan as I ran through the house, but when he didn't immediately appear, I just kept going and ran for his car.

I couldn't seem to catch my breath as I drove, and my hands shook against the steering wheel. I called Zagan as I drove, but when he didn't answer, I left him a message, letting him know what Noya said. Though, I still didn't understand what she was trying to say. Was she offering me hope in knowing that, for now, Gemma lived? Or was she stressing something else to me? I didn't know, and that confusion had me pressing harder on the gas pedal.

I got to Bloomings in record time, and it was only from muscle memory that I had enough sense to put the car in park and turn it off before barreling for the doors. In the back of my mind, I remembered that Mom had dismissed me from the approved guest list, but I couldn't be bothered with that right now. Not when something was happening with Gemma.

I ran through the halls, looking every which way for Noya, and I finally spotted her coming down the hall from the sunroom.

Her brown eyes brightened when she saw me, and her pace quickened to meet me. "You're here! She's in the sunroom. Your—"

I didn't stop to listen. I couldn't. I ran with my heart in my throat and dread in my veins. What could be happening?

Even when I saw Mom and Dr. Seward standing just outside the partly closed sunroom doors, I kept going. When they both swiveled their heads at my fast approach, I shot past them, only stopping at the cracked door. I worked to catch my breath, but the moment I peered beyond the door, I froze instead.

Gemma laughed as she spun in a wide circle in the center of the room, throwing her stuffed dragon into the air and leaping around to catch it. The gray of her complexion had all but vanished, giving way to skin that looked like it spent everyday being kissed by the sun. Her hair, which hung flat and lifeless just yesterday, looked like freshly melted chocolate and bounced with volume as she spun. Even her wiry frame had filled out overnight with definition in muscles and power that hadn't been there in years.

My hands shook as they covered my trembling lips. Once again, I was sure I was dreaming.

"Iyla."

I looked back at Dr. Seward and Mom at the sound of the doctor's whisper. He passed a hesitant and nervous look at Mom, no doubt recalling her outburst from yesterday.

Mom stared at me with some cold, bitter expression. She looked past me through the cracked door where Gemma seemed none the wiser to our presence as she did a cartwheel—a fucking *cartwheel*. When Mom turned back to me, her face had gone blank. She nodded to Dr. Seward and grumbled, "It's fine. Keep going. How did this happen?"

I took Mom's indifference as a sign that I was okay to drift closer and hear the doctor's response, which was exactly what I did. I stared at Dr. Seward and hung on his every word as he passed a bewildered look between Mom and I.

"As I was saying," Dr. Seward explained, "she was on a fast decline this past week, with yesterday spelling out the worst. We were preparing for that when this morning, she woke up, and—" He stopped and looked through the doors behind us in awe. "I-I don't like to use the 'M' word, because there's *always* a medical explanation, but right now, all I can say is it's ... a miracle."

Dr. Seward immediately launched into reassuring Mom that he was going to be doing plenty of tests and keeping Gemma under careful observation for the time being, but I'd tuned him out, my eyes trained on Gemma through the door again.

Miracle? No.

This wasn't a miracle.

This was Zagan. I knew it was. I didn't know how he'd done it, but it didn't matter.

My demon had saved my sister's life.

I broke away from Mom and the doctor to drift into the sun-room. Gemma saw me, and my shattered heart began to reassemble when I saw the brightness in her eyes and smile. She ran toward me, and I fell to my knees with my arms open wide, letting her crash into me. I clenched my jaw in an effort to keep from crying, and for the first time in so, so long, I *hugged* her. I squeezed and pulled her into me as hard as I could, clutching onto her with every bit of fear, hope, grief, relief, and love that I had in me.

"I can't believe you're okay," I sniffled against her hair. I squeezed again.

She pulled back to look at me, and her smile never faltered as she wiped my tears away. "Isn't it amazing? It's like magic, Iyla! I've never felt so strong and good before!"

I bit my lip, trying not to let my growing glee slip out as thankful sobs. "It is like magic, huh?"

She took my hands. "I hope now that I'm all better, you can be happier, too. I know you've had a hard time because of my being sick. So be happy now, okay? With piano and with Zagan."

At the mention of his name, something hot and intense filled my chest. It bubbled inside me like carbonation rising up in a soda bottle. It was light, fierce, and all-consuming, and the urge to release the building emotion became impossible to ignore.

I took one long hard look at Gemma, memorizing her lively features. I thought she was lost. I thought yesterday would be it. But she'd been saved, and those features I thought were gone were ones I could see everyday now. She wasn't going anywhere.

With a smile, I pressed a kiss to her forehead. "I need to go find Zagan, but I'll be back, okay?"

She nodded. "Bring him with you when you come back! I want him to see all I can do now!"

With a promise to return with him in tow, I quickly got to my feet and raced back out the door. My mind spun with thoughts of him, and my smile grew wider with each one. I couldn't deny what I was feeling anymore. His saving Gemma made it all too clear, and it was time I told him.

The door to Bloomings shut behind me, and as I stepped off the sidewalk, it opened behind me again. "Iyla!"

I stopped midstep. The cloud I floated on nearly blew away, but not even the sound of Mom's voice could destroy what had built inside me. I slowly turned and looked at her.

She searched me with a sort of caution and fidgeted where she stood by the door. "I wanted to speak to you."

She'd said plenty the last time we spoke. I didn't know what she could possibly add to hurt me at this point. Still, I didn't say anything. I just stared at her and waited for whatever nonsense she had to say.

Clearing her throat, she looked down at her feet. I'd never seen my mom this out-of-sorts, this conflicted. She hugged her arms around herself and flicked nervous glances my way. I gathered pretty quickly that she was debating offering me a sort of olive branch. Yet ... she said nothing. The words may have been on the tip of her tongue, but she couldn't say them.

So I spoke.

"I'm going to play piano," I declared as my smile found its way back onto my lips. I didn't shy away from her gaze, duck my head, and my voice didn't waver.

Her slender brows rose. "What?"

"I'm going to play piano," I repeated, even stronger this time. "I'm not going into law anymore."

"Iy—"

"And I'm dating Zagan," I said. It was technically a lie, but it might as well have been the truth. Maybe it *would* be the truth once I got home.

Her eyes, which had been almost regretful, regained some of their usual sharpness. She opened her mouth to say something, but I cut her off before she could.

"I'm going to be happy, Mom. I'm going to do the things and reach for the things that make *me* happy. I'm no longer letting you take them away. I'm free." I paused to take a deep breath. I smiled at her, and for once, no hurt hid behind it. "I hope you can find your real happiness, too."

I turned on my heel and continued to Zagan's car. Facing Mom like that, confident and sure of myself, added to the high I was already feeling. It was only after I'd left with those parting words that I realized I was okay. I was truly free of her and the pain she'd caused me. She couldn't hold me down anymore.

When I got back to Zagan's, I practically skipped across the threshold of the front door. "Zagan!" I called as I shut the door behind me.

The plinking of the piano filled the house, so with my grin still firmly set, I walked into the ballroom. Zagan's eyes were focused on the piano when I found him seated there. He didn't even seem to hear or notice me as he played some random set of keys.

When I drew closer, I repeated, "Zagan."

His fingers stopped their mindless plucking, and he looked up at me. A softness filled his eyes. "Hey. Sorry. I didn't hear you come in. You went to see Gemma? How was she?"

I had to fight hard to contain my exuberance. I stepped closer and beamed, "She's better. *Completely* better. It was you, wasn't it? You … You healed her."

He bit the corner of his lip near his piercing and looked away for a second. Swallowing hard, his blue human eyes found mine, and he nodded toward the piano. "You know, I finished writing that song yesterday. Can I play it for you now?"

The euphoria filling me fractured just a hair. Something in his tone gave me pause. He sounded almost wistful and melancholic, which wasn't the response I'd expected. Not to mention, he hadn't actually answered me. Still holding onto that happiness from earlier with a vice-like grip, I slowly nodded.

"I ... I actually wrote this one for you."

The confession drew me closer until I reached him. I sat down on the piano bench just as he began to play. The melody filling the room was soft and romantic. Even without the lyrics, emotion as potent as freshly opened champagne swelled inside my chest. It was like Zagan had filtered love right into the song, weaving it among the notes. Then he began to sing, and I found myself no longer looking at the piano but at him.

There was heart like I'd never heard behind his voice and in his words. Confessions of searching and coming up empty, of belonging to the darkness and not realizing he could have the light. The song piqued with a beautiful chorus as he sang about finding himself through what he never knew existed—love.

It was full of longing, full of want, and full of love, and he sang it with a certain desperation, like he was putting every bit of feeling into the song out of fear that he'd never get the chance to say them otherwise.

The urgency in his voice set off some primal instinct inside me, so when the song finished, all I could do was stare at him with tears in my eyes. I couldn't focus on how beautiful the lyrics were or how the piece touched me where he'd made his home inside me. I couldn't do anything, because I just knew.

Something was wrong.

When his eyes slowly lifted to mine, my stomach dropped with dread. Resignation. It pulled the edges of his lips down even as he tried to smile.

"What's going on?" My own voice came out as barely a whisper.

He took my hands in his and squeezed. "Everything here is yours. The house. The car. This piano. I've made sure everything, even my money, goes to you. You won't ever have to want for anything. And now your sister is safe. Everything is going to be okay now."

I could barely hear past my pounding heart. I pulled my hands back and stood on shaking legs. I stared down at him and demanded, "What's going on, Zagan? Why—Why are you talking like you're leaving?"

His jaw worked, but he didn't look away from me this time. His throat bobbed on a hard swallow before he answered, "I couldn't let you lose your sister."

I opened my mouth to ask him what the hell that had to do with anything when a sultry voice chuckled, "Yes. You're welcome for that, by the way."

I whipped around to find Babette, the red-headed Bargainer demon who owned Hell's Gate. She was dressed in nothing but a bra-styled top and leather pants, and she stood in the center of the ballroom. The mischievous grin she wore made ice fill my insides, and her hip popped out as she surveyed me with unimpressed violet eyes.

"What are you doing here?" I questioned.

Zagan growled and rose from the piano. He came to stand beside me and glared at the newly arrived demon. "Babette, can you give us a few minutes?"

My frantic gaze darted between the two of them, and I demanded, "What's going on?"

"It's so sweet, really," Babette cooed like she was talking down to a child. "Zagan knew he couldn't heal your sister, so he came to me."

"Babette!" Zagan roared.

She ignored him. "We struck a little bargain. I healed your sister from her current illness, any future one, and made her stronger than ever before. Again, you're welcome."

I stopped breathing. My eyes watered as alarm settled in my stomach like a cinder block in the ocean. I slowly turned to look at Zagan and whispered, "What did you offer in exchange?"

Zagan's eyes tightened, and he started to reach for me. "Iyla, I—"

Before he could touch me, the space where he'd been emptied. He vanished right before my eyes, and I turned toward Babette right as Zagan reappeared beside her. She flashed me a wicked grin and draped her manicured hand over his shoulder. "He offered himself."

A plume of shadows burst in the air around him, and when it cleared, heavy black chains linked his wrists together with a leash that ended in Babette's hands. The blood drained from my face, and Babette laughed at my horror before waving her fingers at me in farewell. "Bye, human."

"No!" I screamed, running toward them as fast as my legs could carry me.

Zagan's blue eyes stayed locked on mine. They were pinched with something—longing, pain, grief—I didn't know. My own feelings were too lost to panic as I reached for my demon. He gave me the smallest smile and opened his mouth like he was about to say something just as I reached for his bound hands.

I fell through suddenly open air and crashed to my hands and knees against the marble. I whipped my head around, but there was nothing there. No Babette. No Zagan.

He was gone.

CHAPTER 35

Iyla

FIRST CAME DENIAL. THIS WAS ZAGAN. HE WAS A *DEMON*. Nothing could fucking hold him down. Any minute, he'd reappear with a chuckle, explaining that he had a plan to escape all along. It wasn't like Babette could get what she wanted out of him. He could only have sex with me, and the second she realized that, she'd return him to me.

After an hour passed, the grief swept in. He'd done this, traded himself in as a sort of prisoner, all to save Gemma. He'd given himself up for *me*.

All the time we'd spent together, all the memories we'd made, all the experiences we'd given each other. They flashed in my mind, and I cried as I revisited each one, wishing I'd been brave enough to tell him how I felt back then. I pressed my forehead to the cold marble floor of the ballroom and broke for the love I'd just realized and lost. I'd never get to see his mischievous smile, hear his enchanting voice, feel his body against mine as we danced or fooled around.

He was gone.

Another hour passed, and that was when all the agony inside me engulfed in raging flames. From those ashes rose fury. I beat my hand against the marble and screamed out my acrimony. It wasn't fucking fair. He'd made this choice to sacrifice himself without telling me or giving *me* the choice to bargain with Babette. And why? To protect me?

Then he played that song for me, knowing he was about to be taken away.

Coward.

He should've said the words to my face, but we'd both been too afraid. I refused to let it end this way.

Zagan was *my* bond.

Zagan was *my* demon.

And I wasn't going to lose him.

Getting to my feet, I stormed out of the ballroom. "Coldin! Coldin, are you here? Please, Coldin. If you're here, come out."

"He's not."

I gasped. I'd just started up the stairs, but I turned now at the sound of Dante's voice.

Dante stood in front of me with his muscular arms crossed and a scowl firmly in place. The red ball cap he wore nearly hid the expression, but there was no missing that amount of disdain. "I already took him back to my place since Zagan decided to be a fucking idiot and turn into a servant to that woman. All for *you*." He spat the last word like he'd never said something so foul.

I ignored the hate he so clearly directed my way. He wasn't the demon I necessarily wanted help from, but he'd have to do. "We need to bring Zagan back."

He scoffed. "No. The dumbass knew what bargaining with Babette would mean. He made his bed. Now he has to lie in it."

"Please!" I begged, grabbing onto his arm. I squeezed it tightly and refused to back down, even when he bared his teeth at me. "Please, Dante. I-I have to save him. Help me."

His dark gaze searched mine, and for awhile, we had this intense staredown where neither of us budged. I refused to be moved or swayed. I refused to give up on Zagan.

Finally, Dante's eyes narrowed. "You want him back so badly? Fine. You go get him."

Hope soared to life inside me like a kite catching wind. "Okay! Yes. I'll go. Just tell me how I get to him and how I break his contract with Babette."

He shook my hand off, and since I wanted to stay on his good side right now, I let go. He straightened his black hoodie and shifted nonchalantly on his feet. "Babette loves to play games, so it's simple. Challenge her to a game, one you know you can win. Winner gets Zagan."

He was right. That did sound simple—too simple. But it didn't matter that alarm bells were ringing in my head. Risks be damned. I couldn't let Zagan do this. I couldn't let him become her little toy or servant or whatever the hell she had in mind for him. I couldn't *lose* him.

"How do I get to her?" I asked.

"Easy. You summon her."

I DUSTED THE CHALK FROM MY HANDS AND STOOD BACK up to survey the summoning circle I'd just drawn in the center of Zagan's foyer. The large circle surrounded a smaller one, which contained a pentagram. Between the two circles were "words," though it couldn't look further from words to me. Each point on the star also had an ancient symbol, one I could never hope to understand.

I looked at Dante where he leaned against the wall to oversee the drawing of my summoning circle. "Is this good?"

He pushed off the wall and walked around the circle. His eyes studied the white drawing on the floor, and he gave an approving nod as he stopped next to me. "Good enough."

"What do I do now?"

"Now," he grabbed my hand and held it in front of my eyes, "you cut your palm and let the blood drop in the center of the pentagram. You'll say, 'I summon thee. Bargainer. Babette.'"

I raised a brow. "No fancy words or demonic language?"

He gave a humorless chuckle. "If we made that a rule, idiot humans couldn't summon us, now could they? The summoning circle is hard enough as is. How else are we going to find prey to trick and steal souls from?"

I inched backward just a hair. At the mention of stealing souls, images of the humans strung up around Hell's Gate or the ones battered and contorted to make furniture flashed in my mind's eye. Could that be my fate if I failed?

I quickly shoved the thought and gruesome visuals away. If I dwelled on that, I worried it would make me lose focus on what mattered—getting Zagan back. I squared my shoulders and grabbed a knife from the kitchen. My heart pounded when I returned to my place by the circle, and I held my hand out over the pentagram and gripped the knife handle harder.

"Remember," Dante said just as I brought the tip of the blade to my palm. I paused and looked at him as he finished, "Summon her, challenge her to a game, and *win*. If you don't, Zagan's sacrifice will have been for fucking nothing."

I nodded and swallowed hard. "I will."

With that, the demon vanished into the shadows around us, leaving me alone with a blade pressed into my quivering outstretched hand. I took a deep breath and pictured what mattered.

Zagan's eyes pinched in a hearty laugh that he shared with Gemma.

Zagan with his brow furrowed and body hunched forward as he focused on writing a song.

Zagan as he looked up through his dark lashes to meet my gaze and shoot me a charming, tender smile.

It was because of him, because of his hold over my heart, that slicing the cold, sharp knife across my palm became easier. I bit my lip and fought against the tears as red hot blood poured from the wound and fell in fat droplets to the design below.

"I summon thee. Bargainer. Babette."

The blood began to move, slithering along the floor until it found the closest lines of chalk. Like a sponge, the chalk soaked up the blood until suddenly the entire star began to glow red. I held my breath, and for the first time since I'd made the decision to do this, real fear trickled in.

A head of luscious red hair with black curled horns rose up from the glowing star, rising higher to reveal a face, shoulders, a curvy body wearing a black bra and leather pants. Part of me wanted to scream and run out of pure horror. But this wasn't the first demon I'd faced, and she'd taken mine from me. So I pulled my shoulders back and steeled myself for whatever challenge I was about to face.

The moment her whole body was through the demonic summoning portal, she chuckled and swept her judging gaze over me. "Well, this is interesting. It's been awhile since I was summoned like this."

"I want Zagan back," I declared as calmly as I could.

She threw her head back and laughed. "Sorry. I own him now. He signed the contract. He has to pay the price—eternity with me in my world."

Nerves fluttered around my gut like moths taking desperate flight from a pursuing hawk. I had to grip the handle of the knife in order to ground myself and not lose my courage as I demanded, "I challenge you to a game, then. Winner gets Zagan, regardless of the contract he signed."

She raised a brow and tapped a red-lacquered nail to her full lips. Her eyes narrowed in a devious smirk, and with only a few seconds of consideration, she purred, "I accept."

She snapped her fingers, and I gasped as my whole body seemed to tug into the space of the pentagram. Everything turned into a blur of moving shades of red until I suddenly jolted back to awareness and landed on my feet. I had to hold my arms out to steady myself and regain my balance, and that was when I noticed that we'd transported.

Zagan's foyer had disappeared, and I now stood in the center of what looked like an office. A dark and elaborate wooden desk and padded chair stood before me. Shelves lined the wall beyond it, which held nothing but bound golden scrolls.

Babette appeared from behind me then, and she crossed the room with a sway in her hips. She perched on the edge of her desk and flipped her hair over her shoulder, smirking at me as if she found me lacking. She saw no threat in me.

"So," Babette began, "winner gets Zagan?"

I nodded. "The contract that healed my sister remains, but Zagan is free if I win. That's the only thing that changes."

There was no missing the laugh under her breath. She thought I and my request was a joke, which only fueled my need to win even more. I was sick and tired of people looking down on me, because I *was* worth something, just the way I was. Zagan had helped me to see that.

My chest ached.

Zagan.

I *had* to save him.

"Fine," she answered with a shrug. "You won't win so that's not a problem. You'll actually be doing me a favor. The moron got himself bound to you, a little detail he'd failed to mention when I forged a contract with him. I can't even fuck him like I want. Doing this kills two birds with one stone. You'll die, giving me your soul to add to my collection, and Zagan's bond will break with your death." Her smile turned sultry and venomous as she cupped her breasts and moaned, "I can't wait to finally taste and feel him."

I gritted my teeth against the rising outrage inside me. I knew she was baiting me, so instead of giving in, I slowly said, "For the game—"

"Ahh!" She held up a finger to stop me. "*You* challenged *me*, and as our rules go in this world, the one who gets challenged gets to pick the game."

My blood ran cold. Dante hadn't said anything about *that* little rule. I briefly wanted to strangle him for keeping that information from me. But even if I'd known that before I'd gotten here, it wouldn't have changed anything. I couldn't lose my demon.

I *wouldn't* lose him.

"What's the game?" I asked.

She studied me with her vivid purple eyes. I wasn't sure what she searched for. Maybe a potential weakness that she could exploit to ensure I lost. Maybe she was judging me some more, wondering how a human like me got Zagan when she clearly couldn't. All I knew was the longer she watched me, the more my resolve hardened.

This game wasn't for me or about me. This was to save the man who had become my best friend, my light, my rock, my entire world. I'd fight for him until there was no fight left in me.

"I'm curious," Babette said. She pushed away from the desk and crossed her arms as she began a slow stride around me. "Why are you even trying? Don't get me wrong. I'm thrilled this is happening, but why give up your soul for him? For a *demon*?"

She faced me now and waited with a puzzled purse of her lips.

I didn't even need to think about my answer. It had been there in front of me all along, but I'd realized it too late.

"Because I love him," I answered.

She scoffed and rolled her eyes. "Love doesn't exist." She shrugged and turned to saunter back toward her desk. "But if you want to delude yourself into thinking that love can exist between you and a demon, who am I to argue? You'll be dead soon enough, anyway."

I ignored her taunt and said with a clenched jaw, "Still waiting on that game."

"Eager for Hell, I see. Alright." She snickered and tilted her chin up. "Since I can't keep Zagan on a leash to service me the way I want right now, he's downstairs, working in my club. You know. *Tending* to guests. You have one hour to find him. If you don't … well, you already know the consequences."

All I had to do was find Zagan? I'd been to Hell's Gate multiple times, and it wasn't *so* big that I couldn't search for and find someone. Still, I paused, because that sounded too easy. I waited for her to throw some curveball at me, but no twist came.

She held up a finger and repeated with a smile, "One hour. Find him or you're both mine."

She snapped her fingers, and the world spiraled and whirled around me like before. I landed on my feet with a jolt in a sea of gyrating bodies. Pounding electro music, flashing red lights, and strong perfumes overloaded my senses. It took a second of me assessing myself and my surroundings to realize I was in the middle of Hell's Gate's dance floor.

I didn't waste any time once I had my bearings. My heart raced with nervous determination as I scanned the dancing crowd and shoved through packed bodies of demons. I couldn't seem to take in the faces fast enough, searching for even a glimpse of tousled raven hair or a flash of black-and-red eyes or light reflecting off silver piercings.

I shoved through more bodies, and that was when the first sharp slice of pain slashed across my shoulder blade. I cried out at the blinding cut and fell to my knees, reaching back to feel for what caused it. My fingers fumbled over where I'd been hit, and a fierce sting shot through my body at my careful touch, making me jump. When I pulled my hand back around, blood coated my fingers.

"What the hell?" I whimpered.

I looked around me, and while demons laughed at my distress or shot me puzzled glances, I saw no sign of who or what could've sliced open the skin on my shoulder.

With shaking legs, I got back to my feet and shuffled across the rest of the dance floor until I was able to grab onto a standing table. Just as I reached it, another searing cut slit me open near the previous one. I gritted my teeth and held onto the table as tears clouded my vision. I blinked the fat droplets away and looked around the bustling room for a sign of what was happening to me.

My frantic gaze spotted a span of windows near the top of the building that looked like an office overseeing the club below. Babette stood at the window and watched me with a smirk firmly in place. She held up her finger and moved it back and forth, and her mouth moved in the unmistakable words of, 'tick-tock, tick-tock.'

Ice filled my veins.

The slashes were my timer.

For every minute that passed, a new slice would form on my back as a painful reminder that time was running out. Fifty-eight minutes left now. Fifty-eight minutes until the fate of my future was sealed. Fifty-eight minutes left to determine Zagan's life.

I cast one final glare at Babette then pushed away from the table to search for my demon.

CHAPTER 36

MY SEARCH WAS DESPERATE, AND I YELLED ZAGAN'S name as I wove through tables, the bar area, the restrooms, and back through the dance floor again. I braced myself for each cut to my skin, now knowing they were coming, but that didn't help the searing burn.

A hot, sharp invisible blade constantly cut deep into my back, and no matter how hard I fought to ignore it, the pain was greater than anything I'd ever felt. I was slowly being shredded while running through the club, and I was quickly losing my already feeble grip on the situation.

Ten hits in, and tears kept my vision too blurry to see through while my breathing got erratic enough to make my head swim.

Twenty agonizing slits in, and I stumbled around like a girl who had far exceeded her drinking limit.

Thirty cuts in, and I fell against a railing near the dance floor. Warm, sticky blood coated my back, and the pain no longer subsided between each minute. The burn was always there now, continuously draining the energy from me. I breathed hard as I tried to stand up straight, but my legs gave out before I made it to my feet. A wave of nausea hit me at the same time, and I slumped against the bars of the railing. I had to fight hard against the urge to spill the contents of my stomach all over the floor.

"Iyla?"

Hope roared to life inside me at the familiar sound of Eden's voice. I looked up just as the golden-eyed demon got to me.

"Holy Hell!" she cried when she saw the state I was in. Worry parted her lips as she grabbed my arms and helped me to my feet. "What happened? Why—"

"Have you seen Zagan?" I interrupted her.

"Zagan? No. Why? What is happening? How—"

"I'll explain later," I said just as another minute lost split my back open.

Eden's face fell in horror as she held onto me, watching helplessly until my cry of pain faded into a mere whimper.

Taking steady breaths against the onslaught of fire at my back, I gripped Eden's arms tightly and stared straight into her eyes, imploring her to understand. "I need to find Zagan. Please! I have to find him in the next twenty-nine minutes. Help me. He's—He's somewhere in Hell's Gate."

Her eyes widened, which I didn't think was possible with how large they already were. "Hell's Gate? Iyla, this is just one *room* of Hell's Gate. There are ... *hundreds* of spaces just like this one, connected by doors that demons travel through. If he's somewhere in Hell's Gate, that means he could be ... anywhere."

I stopped breathing. I'd thought the cuts to my back had been the catch to make Babette's game harder, but I realized now that *this* was the real one. I'd only ever been to this part of Hell's Gate. I didn't even know there were more rooms, because those "doors" weren't visible to my human eye. I would've spent the full hour in this one massive club, unaware that Zagan wasn't even in this one.

My face scrunched up in bitter fury as I turned my gaze back to the office that overlooked the club. Babette still lingered there, now holding a glass of wine. She saw me glaring, and even from here, her chuckle was obvious. If that wasn't enough, she winked and blew me a kiss.

I threw my head back on an agonized wail as another slash joined the rest. More blood seeped out of my back and soaked into my shirt, and Eden's eyes glossed over with tears as she held onto me.

The pain was all-consuming, and it made my vision swim. I inhaled deeply and gripped Eden with weak fingers as the room tilted and spun briefly. I worried this would be it. I'd pass out and lose the rest of my time, sentencing myself to an eternity of suffering and Zagan to a life as a sex slave. But I didn't faint. I *refused* to succumb.

"Do you have a way to contact him?" I asked weakly. "You know, through demon ways?"

She seemed flustered as she stammered, "Y-Yeah. We can shadow speak." She closed her eyes, and her voice hardened, "Zagan."

We didn't let go of one another as we waited, but nothing happened. I whipped my head around in search of Zagan, but I never saw a glimmer of those detailed tattoos, glint of piercings, or flicker of black-and-red eyes.

"It's not working," Eden announced with a helpless cry cracking her voice. "Something must be blocking him from hearing me. What in the world is happening?"

My head hung, and I braced myself for an incoming blow that was probably seconds away. "He made a bargain with Babette. I'm trying to get him back."

Her gold eyes widened. "What a fucking moron! No wonder he can't hear me. She probably blocked his shadow speak for everyone, except her. I bet she took his phone, too."

Things were quickly spiraling, and my options to get a hold of him were getting dangerously thin. Still, I couldn't give up. Not on him.

I met Eden's stare through bleary eyes and asked, "Is there an intercom system or anything that connects this room to the others?"

Eden looked around, seemingly at a loss. Her attention landed on the stage, and she suddenly perked up with hope. "The stage is set up to broadcast the music to all the rooms."

The stage stood at the head of the dance floor. Instruments were set up there, but no one currently played them, instead letting some mix play over the speakers. Still, renewed hope swelled to life inside me. If we could turn off the pre-recorded music, I could find a microphone and tell Zagan where I was.

Turning back to Eden, I quickly said, "Help me to the stage."

She slung my arm around her shoulder and helped me walk through the throng of people. Three more ticks to the skin on my back slowed us down, but we finally made it to the stage. I was exhausted, on fire, nauseous, and fighting against the black spots clouding my vision. But I'd made it.

Twenty-five minutes left.

"See if you can find a microphone," I mumbled to Eden, too weak to raise my voice more than a casual tone.

We stumbled together around the stage, but there wasn't a mic set up. There were some drums, a single guitar, and a piano, but no microphone with any of them. Defeat tried to creep in as two more slashes cut into me during our search, but I fought against it. I couldn't give up on him. I just *couldn't*.

I wavered on my feet and leaned into Eden's side. My eyes fluttered with the threat of closing for good. "Eden," I groaned. "Need to sit. For a minute."

She nodded and helped me sit at the piano bench. My head lolled as I rested my arms on the closed keylid.

Eden stood beside me, trying not to look at my blood-soaked back, and she nibbled her lip anxiously. "Maybe there's a storage space somewhere around here with the mics."

Maybe there was, but how long would it take to find it? In the time it took to find a microphone and set it up to blast through all the rooms, we might've run out of time. I only had twenty-three minutes left—maybe less with how quickly I was fading. I didn't even have the energy to walk anymore.

I stared groggily at the piano beneath my elbows. Was I going to die here, leaning on what was nearly my dream come true? Was there nothing else I could do? I racked my foggy brain for something—*anything*—as I stared at the piano.

My eyes widened. With a sudden moment of clarity, I looked up at Eden. "So these instruments play all over the club? Even in the other rooms?"

"Yeah, thanks to the way Babette has the place set up. This is the main hub of Hell's Gate, so it's the only one with the stage. The rest are able to hear it, though."

I braced myself as another slice broke my skin. I leaned forward, my head hanging as I breathed through the pain. The glossy surface of the keylid had my drained reflection staring back at me.

The reflection of a girl who'd changed and grown in the past few months.

The reflection of a girl who'd broken free of her cage and found herself because a demon saw her for who she really was and what she was worth.

And that demon needed me now.

Another slit marked my back. My face scrunched in pain, but I saw more than the agony in my reflection now. I saw resilience, and I saw lingering hope.

"Eden," I breathed out. "Can you turn the music off so the piano can play over the speakers?"

She stared at me like she was trying to understand what I had planned, but she nodded and started to walk away. "Sure."

"And," I said, making her stop to look back at me, "when you're done, try to find Zagan in the other rooms again. Tell him where I am in case this doesn't work."

She gave a final nod and darted off to complete her tasks. I'd have to thank her later, because there *would* be a later to talk to her. I was sure of it.

I faced the piano again, raising the keylid to expose the black-and-white keys. I couldn't go over a speaker to tell Zagan where I was since there weren't any mics to project my voice, and I couldn't keep running around to find him since my legs weren't working.

But the thing about me and Zagan ... we didn't need words. Not when we had music.

The pop song overhead nearly drowned out the sound of the piano as I practiced keys to get familiar with the song. I'd never played it, and I'd only heard it once. So while Eden worked to shut off the current music, I played around with the keys to make sure I got the notes right.

Two more cuts to my skin tried to stop me, but I held onto my determination.

Nineteen minutes left.

The music overhead suddenly stopped mid-song. Only the voices of the crowd filled the room now. With my heat soaring, I gingerly played a C on the piano. The sound flared to life, not just from the instrument on stage but through the whole room over a speaker. The crowd turned to look at me, clearly confused about the abrupt change in their party music. I gave a small, breathy laugh as true hope filtered back into me, almost making me forget the pain at my back.

Zagan, I thought with a deep breath. *Please hear me.*

I hovered my fingers over the keys, and I blocked out everything else. I blocked out the room of annoyed demons. I blocked out the pain coursing through my body. I blocked out the fear of failure. When that was silent, all that remained was Zagan.

My hands moved, bringing Zagan's song to life. There were so many pieces I could've chosen to play, but only one would speak our secret language. Only one would get the message across to him—the song he'd written for me. It was a challenge since I'd only heard him play it in its entirety the one time today. But even with a couple of stumbles, the song was distinct. The melody was precise. The message was clear.

My love for Zagan.

It was what made all of this worth it. Chasing him to Hell in order to bring him home was the only answer for me. He'd left everything behind for me—money, a home, the means to a career. I would've had a comfortable life, and I'd have my sister to live it with. But a life without Zagan wasn't one I wanted.

So I played, telling him I was here. All he had to do was come find me.

I finished the song with three new marks to remind me of the lack of time. There was still no sign of Zagan, and the crowd had seemingly thinned, maybe choosing to leave in pursuit of some-where with different music, but some remained and watched me expectantly. With sixteen minutes left, I started all over.

I worked through Zagan's song, pouring the same amount of emotion into it that he had. I thought of everything he'd done for me—studying with me, showing up for me, listening to me. I thought of how he looked with Gemma, the two of them gushing over dragons. I thought of the stolen glances between us, the slow kisses, and his hands on my body. I thought of how he taught me to step out of my cage and fly. I thought of the party at Bloomings and the trip to New York. I thought of the sacrifice he'd made for me.

Tears filled my eyes, and this time, it had nothing to do with the physical torment.

I cried for the future I desperately wanted for my demon.

I cried, because I'd been too afraid to admit what I felt.

I cried, because my fingers were growing weak with the fifty-seventh slash now carving into my back, bringing me closer to the end of our story.

I'd finished another play through of the song, and I nearly fell backward off the stool as blood pooled on the bench and the floor beneath it. My lips had dried, and my hands shook as dark spots webbed across my eyes. Still, I restarted the song, playing slowly. The song no longer sounded smooth, lilting, and beautiful but choppy and jumbled. Extra notes crowded the correct ones as my hands slipped or lost strength and fell onto neighboring keys.

Another cut, and I lost control of my arms. They slipped off the piano and hung limply at my sides. I fell forward, slumping against the instrument. An eruption of random notes sounded overhead as my body fell against the keys. My energy had been zapped, and no amount of fighting seemed to be bringing it back.

It was over.

"Zagan," I whispered into the air.

Tears slowly rolled down my cheeks. My eyes slipped closed with the fifty-ninth slash, and I prepared myself for the darkness I'd soon face. I sent a silent apology to Zagan for failing him.

"Iyla!"

By some miracle, my eyes peeled open to catch sight of a wild-eyed demon leaping onto the stage and running toward me. He was shirtless with only tight black pants on. Thick metal chainless cuffs wrapped around his wrists. Horns jutting up from raven hair and black-and-red slitted eyes drew closer. Even with my life seconds away from draining from my body, I managed to crack a small smile at the dark-haired demon.

"Zagan."

I wasn't sure if the name left my lips or if I'd merely said it in my head. All I knew was one second I was slumped over the piano as nothing more than a limp doll, and the next, I was being pulled into familiar arms—arms that felt like home.

My head fell against his shoulder, and I breathed in the warm scent of spice and fire. "Mmm. Found you."

The club disappeared, and my vision filled with Babette's office.

Zagan and I were on the ground, my limp body pulled into his lap. His arms tightened around me when Babette towered over us.

The glare she fixed on me could've frozen Hell. "This doesn't mean love is real."

I met her glare with one of my own. Or at least, I tried. I wasn't sure if my face cooperated. "I won. A deal is a deal. Give me Zagan back, and make sure my sister stays healthy."

"Deal?" Zagan snapped. His alarmed black-and-red slitted eyes looked me over. "You made a deal with Babette?"

Babette snarled. "Fine. Take your stupid bond back." She snapped her fingers, and the cuffs squeezing Zagan's wrists evaporated in a plume of shadows, leaving only raw red skin behind. "Now get out of my club."

"With pleasure," Zagan growled through gritted teeth.

With another swirling of shadows and a burst of cold air, I found myself back in the foyer of Zagan's place near the summoning circle I'd made. As soon as we were there, Zagan looked down at me, still barely hanging onto life in his lap.

"Fuck, Iyla!"

He gently laid me on my side, facing away from him. He lifted my shirt and let out a string of curses that I was too drained to pay attention to. His fingers pressed into the shredded skin of my back, and the pain flared to life before fading. Like water soaking into a sponge, the bone-deep ache seemed to draw away from the edges of my back and crawled toward the center where Zagan's hand rested. When the pain faded, not only was the burn gone, but energy flooded back into my system, too.

I sat up with a gasp and turned on my butt to meet Zagan's eyes. The moment our gazes locked, all the earlier feelings of impetuosity, determination, and need crashed into me.

Tears flooded my eyes, and I climbed onto his lap to straddle him and cup his cheeks. "I found you. I found you, you big, stupid, selfless demon!"

I gripped the back of his neck and pulled his head toward mine until our lips met. His arms circled me and held me with a tightness that seemed just as desperate as my own hold. We'd both feared that moment in the ballroom would be our last together, so now, we clung to each other and kissed with all the unspoken words raging inside us.

Zagan pulled back, just as breathless as me. He gave an incredulous shake of his head, and his thumbs brushed under my eyes to clear the wetness there. "What were you thinking? Why did you go there? Why would you do that?"

I laughed at his ridiculous question and tangled my fingers in the hair at the back of his head. "Do you really need to ask? You can't think of any reason why I would've chased after you and made a deal with a demon for your return?"

Understanding softened his eyes, and he gently stroked my cheek. I leaned into his touch, unable to help myself. Relief unlike any other spiraled around inside me, mingling with a warm, fuzzy lightness.

"We can't trust Babette to actually uphold the contract that healed Gemma since she didn't get to keep me," Zagan said. He looked to the empty space near us and barked, "Coldin."

I looked around the room to see if the demon was here, but I saw nothing. Facing Zagan again, I explained, "Coldin's not here. Dante—"

Zagan held up a finger. I closed my mouth and waited like he seemed to be doing. The space he stared at was empty when a blink later, Coldin appeared, as straight-faced as ever.

Ahh. That must be shadow speak.

I grimaced, realizing how helpful that would've been if Babette hadn't blocked his ability while in her possession. It didn't matter now, though. I had my demon back.

"Coldin," Zagan said firmly. "I need you to do something. Babette has a contract I made with her. I need you to get it and bring it back." Zagan paused, and his eyes darkened a fraction. "Kill her while you're there."

My stomach dropped with the last order, but then something even more terrifying happened.

Coldin *smiled*.

"Fucking finally," Coldin sneered, his features thinning and darkening.

He vanished, gone too quickly for me to see what he'd started to morph into.

I turned back to Zagan with my heart still racing over their exchange and seeing Coldin's malicious grin. Swallowing hard, I asked, "Don't you think killing her is too harsh?"

Zagan's eyes thinned, and his lip curled in disdain. "Fuck no. Death is the only option for anyone who thinks they can lay their goddamn hands on you."

A shiver traveled down my spine, and for some crazy reason, it wasn't a bad feeling. I wasn't sure if it was because of my own venom toward her for what she did to Zagan, or if it was because of what she had planned to do with the both of us had I failed. But hearing Zagan's growl of possessiveness come out did something to me in places only he'd ever touched.

I trailed my fingertips lightly over his bare tattooed chest. "I'm glad you found me when you did. I nearly lost you."

His brow plunged as something profound and tender overtook him. "I wanted to say it before ..." He swallowed hard and pulled one of his lip rings into his mouth as he fought for words. Finally, he smiled and finished, "I love you, Sparrow."

A flood of emotion hit me straight in the chest and poured over the rest of me. Zagan was freedom. His confession was air to help me soar higher. His love was my endless sky to dive, leap, and fly through.

I couldn't get my own words out fast enough. "I love you, too, Zagan."

His eyes widened in astonishment, like he hadn't expected me to feel the same way. "You do?" Something akin to hurt flashed across his gaze, and his shoulders tightened. "But I'm darkness. I'm sin. I'm—"

I pressed another kiss to his mouth to silence him. He kissed me back with a sweep of his lips and pass of his tongue. When I felt his shoulders relax beneath my arms, I pulled back only enough to whisper, "Zagan. You're *Zagan*, and I *love* who you are. The light and the dark. The kind and the twisted. The man and the demon."

He beamed against my mouth, his lip rings brushing against me. He didn't say anything. Instead, he kissed me hard, and I opened wide for his tongue to tangle with mine. His claws grabbed at the front of my shirt, and with a quick tug on the material, it shredded down the middle. He pulled the remnants off with one hand and my bra with the other. My flesh pebbled as the air kissed my skin, and Zagan's mouth left mine to pay special attention to my hardened nipples.

I gasped and leaned back while holding his head to encourage what he was doing with his tongue. "Zagan!"

"I thought I'd never get the chance to have you like this again." He bit down on my breast while pinching the nipple on the other, and my eyes rolled back in my head. He released me, and his hooded gaze locked on mine. "On your back. Now."

My breath caught as I did as I was told, jolting slightly at the cold floor against my bare back. With a fierce tug, he yanked my leggings and underwear off. His attention devoured every inch of my naked body, making my stomach flutter. Like seeing me was a privilege. And damn, if that didn't turn me on more.

He seemed to sense when that wave of arousal pulsed in me, landing like a hot cinder at my center. His gaze zeroed in on the spot at the same moment that strands of shadows appeared around him. They darted forward and pinned my arms and raised knees in place. I gasped when more wispy tendrils wrapped around my thighs and opened my legs wider for Zagan's viewing.

He licked his lips, and he was slow to undo the pants he wore, which only built the fire inside of me. I wanted him. I *needed* him. I needed his skin on mine to prove this was real. He was truly back beside me.

"Does that pussy drip for me?" Zagan demanded in that deep, husky voice.

A cold tendril of shadow slithered up my leg. I couldn't help but focus on it moving toward my center as I answered, "Yes. It drips for you."

The airy, almost whisper of a sensation, covered my wet, spread lips, and I let out a breathy groan at the wild sensation. It was a touch, yet it was one so light and cool that it made me quake and squirm for something harder and more tangible.

"What a horny little sparrow," Zagan taunted, watching me buck against the open air.

The tendril flicked up and down against my clit with a feather-light touch, and I held my breath, trying to focus all my attention on that feeling. I wanted it to touch me harder and faster, but it stayed slow and achingly soft. To make matters worse, the whisps holding me down kept me from moving against the sensation like I wanted. It was torment of the greatest kind.

Zagan, now naked in all his tattooed and pierced glory, gripped his hard cock and gave it a measured stroke to match the tentative sweep of the shadow against my core. He kept his gaze level on me as he pumped his cock, and my breathing got shallower as I watched him pleasure himself to the sight of me.

Another tendril appeared near my face. It slithered over both of my shoulders, down my breasts, and stayed there where it tickled and taunted my nipples. My mouth gaped with a cry for Zagan to really touch me, but before the words came, the same airy shadow shoved into my mouth, cutting off my words.

"What's that?" Zagan smirked. "I can't hear you."

I wanted to growl at him, but the shadow filling my mouth prevented me from getting anything out. I moaned around the blockage, and my body shook with so much hunger and want as the strands swirling around and over my nipples mingled with the fluttering against my clit. A new, thicker tendril prodded at my entrance, and my eyes widened and locked on Zagan's as the shadow plunged deep inside me.

Zagan groaned, and his face shuttered with desire as wetness gathered between my folds, so much so that I felt it drip down my seam. He continued stroking his cock, watching me come undone beneath his black-and-red gaze. The tickling whisper against my budded nipples, the flickering graze over my clit, and the faint fullness pushing in and out of me all mixed together with the delicious sight of Zagan's veiny, tattooed hand stroking the length of his dick until all I could do was cry out around the shadow in my mouth as pleasure exploded through me.

Zagan smiled, and the shadows left me like a cloud on a passing breeze. I inhaled deeply and went limp, but it wasn't for long. Zagan dragged two fingers up the seam of my pussy. There was no missing the sharpness of his claws, yet the biting edge just made me hungry all over again. He gathered the evidence of my climax, and stuck the clawed digits into his mouth, licking his fingers clean.

"Better than any fucking drink out there," he purred, his fang-like canines glinting with his wide grin. "Wanna taste?"

He leaned down and kissed me deeply, letting me taste myself on his tongue, and he shoved his hard cock in me at the same time.

"Beautiful," he praised and licked my lip before nipping it. "You're so beautiful."

His hips moved with expert precision, and his dick reached places inside me that drove me absolutely wild. He squeezed my breast with one hand and gripped my throat with the other while his hard length worked me toward the edge again.

"Got the contract."

I gasped in surprise at the sound of Coldin's voice, looking from under Zagan's arm at the newly-arrived demon. He looked human with his green eyes and horn-free head of brown hair, but blood covered his hands, face, and clothes. There was a certain gleam in his eye that wasn't usually there, too, but I was too preoccupied with my own demon to figure out what it was.

"Leave it on the couch," Zagan ordered him, though he never took his eyes off me while he fucked me senseless.

I bit my lip to try to keep my sounds muted, but Zagan was relentless in how he touched me. He didn't let up, even as Coldin crossed right next to us to drop the rolled-up parchment on the couch.

Nor did Zagan stop when Coldin looked down at us and said flatly, "Since you're back, I'll stay here again. You have better hiding places than Dante."

"Sure," Zagan answered as his tongue licked a path up my neck and onto my ear. He bit down at the same time that he thrust, and I released my lip as a moan forced its way past my lips.

Coldin seemed unfazed as he shifted, turning from man to snake in a second. When the black reptile slithered down the stairs, Zagan grabbed my chin and forced my attention back to him. "Eyes on me, Sparrow. Don't make me punish you."

The threat did something to me. It heated my body to the point of boiling, and with only a few more deep thrusts inside me, I came hard.

"I love it when you cum for me," Zagan announced. "Almost as much as I love you."

I smiled and held onto him tightly, soaking in the sight of his expression when he spilled himself inside me. It was fierce, it was passionate, and it was *hot*. "Right back at you."

He hovered above me and continued to stare down at me. Neither of us moved, despite reaching our peaks and finishing.

Instead, we kept the other locked in our arms, and I wasn't sure when we'd be ready to let the other go. Probably never.

"I never thanked you," I whispered, trailing my nails gently up and down his back. "You know, for what you did. I *hate* the deal you made because of what it cost you, but I ... I just can't thank you enough for doing that." Emotion climbed my throat, and I had to swallow it down before I could finish, "Thank you for saving my sister."

He leaned down to press his forehead to mine. "I told you I would, Sparrow. I don't care what it is or what the risks are. I'll give you anything, do anything, to make sure you're happy."

"Being with you. *That's* what makes me happy. So don't leave me like that again. Deal?"

He pulled back to look down at me, and he cocked his head as a teasing grin lit up his face. "You trying to make a deal with a demon, Iyla?"

I laughed. "Only if that demon is you."

He kissed me, the caress slow and sweet. "Always me."

Zagan

F UCK YEAH! WHAT AN AWESOME SHOW," XANDER cheered, slapping hands and patting the backs of everyone.

I chugged a bottle of water and hid away my demon features. "I love the responses to the new songs. That excitement never gets old."

I looked up at the clock to see that it read 7:30. Me and the rest of Sinners Do It Better stood around the backstage changing room after finishing our first comeback concert. The hiatus had been a short one but necessary. With Iyla by my side and the pressure off, I'd written— and loved—ten new songs, the most popular of which was "Sparrow," the song I'd written for Iyla.

"Y'all ready to head out?" I asked.

The guys nodded and began changing. I turned to the full-body mirror, and with a wave of my hand, the sweat from the concert vanished as if I'd showered it off. My leather pants and button-up shirt were replaced by my black-tailored suit. I slicked my hair back and spritzed on some cologne before checking my appearance one final time.

"Whatcha think?" Perseus asked when I turned around to evaluate the guys. "Concert ready?"

Perseus had pulled his golden curls into a bun at the base of his neck and traded in his leather for a suit. Xander now wore a dark purple suit that reminded me too much of Babette's eyes, but I let it slide since it was a special day. Even Dante, who'd initially grumbled about tonight's afterparty, wore a faint smile that nearly looked as dashing as his suit. Coldin's brown hair had been left as tousled as always, but he'd at least put on a black button-up and dress pants.

I smiled at my friend's efforts.

I wasn't sure when I'd started thinking of the guys as friends, but I did. It was one of the many things Iyla had helped me see— demons could feel, and having friends was good.

"Looks great," I complimented. "Let's go."

I stepped forward in the same instant that I conjured shadows. When I stepped through them, I came out in the bathroom stall at the theater where Iyla was performing with a philharmonic orchestra. She was still in school for her music degree, but after a recommendation from one of her professors, she'd gotten invited to play piano with the Nashville Philharmonic Orchestra. She'd been practicing non-stop for the job, and now the time to really shine as a pianist was here. But it was like I told her—this was just the beginning of her career.

Not only was this the beginning for her career, but we were also in the beginning of our public relationship. It was still new to the public eye, and while our fans had been annoyed by the announce-ment of my dating at first, Iyla and I were now an official couple that the masses cheered on. Fans threatened us multiple times not to break up, demanding we last forever.

That wasn't going to be an issue, of course.

The guys appeared in the stalls neighboring mine, and once we were all here, we left the bathroom and waited in the front hall as patrons shuffled in. I watched the humans file into the theater until finally, the guests I'd been waiting on arrived.

"Zagan!"

I turned just as Gemma leaped into my arms, and the momentum of her rushing hug had me spinning her around as we laughed. I set her on her feet just as Nahla, Noya, Iseul, Addie, and Eden caught up with the lively eleven year old. The little girl had already moved on to greeting the rest of Sinners Do It Better, who hung out next to me, no doubt crowd watching for potential partners to take home later.

"I really need to get in shape," Nahla heaved, trying to catch her breath.

Noya chuckled and patted her sister on the back. "Don't take it personally. That's just Gemma being Gemma."

That was an understatement. Not only was Gemma no longer sick in the slightest, but she had enough energy and life to power a city. She was doing so well that she'd been released from Bloomings and lived with her mom again.

But while Gemma had healed, the relationship between Iyla and Mrs. Winters had not. But that was fine with Iyla. She'd made peace with it.

"We better get in there and find our seats," I announced since everyone had arrived.

Gemma took my hand, and we walked up the stairs to the private viewing gallery that I'd secured for all of us. The excitement amongst everyone was nearly palpable while we waited for the show to begin, and when it did, everything else stopped existing for me.

All that remained was my girl, seated at the piano, playing with the poise and grace of a fucking goddess. She wore a sparkling sleeveless black gown, and she'd purposely worn one with a slit on the right leg so that the fabric fell apart to expose her new tattoo.

When she'd declared she wanted to get her first tattoo, I wasn't sure what she had in mind. I'd been speechless when she emerged with a nearly identical tattoo of the drawing I'd done on her thigh all those months ago—a cage nestled in roses and vines. Only instead of a sparrow tucked inside to stare out the open door, the cage sat empty, the sparrow inked flying away.

This was her first concert, her first *real* leap at the dream she'd always pretended not to have. It was her big flight of freedom, so she wanted her tattoo on display—even if the only ones who understood the significance of it were the two of us.

Pride, admiration, and love held me captive throughout her entire performance, and when the show concluded with the crowd jumping to their feet in a standing ovation, she stood to bow with the rest of the company.

She raised her head, and like magnets, her eyes found mine in the balcony. She beamed at me, and I smiled right back. I'd never known that love could exist, much less for someone like me, but I was damn lucky and thankful to have been proven wrong by her.

My bond.

My sparrow.

ACKNOWLEDGEMENTS

Firstly, I want to thank all of the amazing people who helped make this gorgeous book! Ludwig Designs, for the STUNNING cover. Enchanted Ink Publishing team, for the AMAZING interior. I consider myself so dang lucky to work with talented people like all of you. Thank you for helping bring my book to life!

I want to thank all of my beta readers! Alayna, Ashley, Dreama, Haley, Jals, Lora, and Taylor. You guys are the best team EVER!! Thank you for all the early feedback. It really helped me polish my story into the version you have today. I hope you guys love the finished product!

To my sister—thanks for always being my cheerleader. Even though this one is about demons, your hype is always top notch. Thank you for believing in me.

To my husband—thank you for supporting my dream. I know it's not easy watching me struggle and fight to be an author, so I appreciate you sticking beside me and helping me. It means so much to me, and I'm so thankful to have you as my rock.

Finally, thank you to each and every reader who read this book. Thank you to every reader who took a chance on me. I truly hope you enjoyed Iyla's and Zagan's story. It was a tough one, but I truly hope it resonates with those who have struggled the way Iyla did. I hope you look forward to the next story from me, and the one after that, and so on!

SYLVER MICHAELA

Sylver is an avid book reader, coffee drinker, true crime junkie, and animal lover. When she isn't hard at work on her next romance novel, she can be found loving on her fur babies, watching the latest Korean or Chinese drama, or reading.

HTTPS://SYLVERMICHAELA.WIXSITE.COM/
MAGICALPRINCESS.COM

INSTAGRAM: @SYLVER_MICHAELA